More Praise for
PACIFIC NIGHTMARE

"A frightening and highly plausible scenario on the way in which the Far East could become the center of a devastating third world war. The account is so authentic that at times one lapses into an unthinking belief it has actually happened."
—*Oxford Times*

"Absorbing and always, thanks to Winchester's intelligence and firsthand knowledge, quite believable."
—*Kirkus Reviews*

PACIFIC NIGHTMARE

HOW JAPAN STARTS WORLD WAR III

A FUTURE HISTORY

Simon Winchester

IVY BOOKS • NEW YORK

Ivy Books
Published by Ballantine Books
Copyright © 1992 by Simon Winchester
Maps & charts copyright © 1992 by Cézanne Wong

Queries regarding rights and permissions should be addressed to Carol Publishing Group, 600 Madison Avenue, New York, N.Y. 10022

Library of Congress Catalog Card Number: 92-16509

ISBN 0-8041-1239-8

This edition published by arrangement with Birch Lane Press, a division of Carol Publishing Group

Manufactured in the United States of America

First Ballantine Books Edition: January 1994

THIS book is for
MISS HELEN RODGERS STEVENSON
OF BROOKLYN AND GENEVA

CONTENTS

THE MAJOR CHARACTERS

THE AMERICANS

President Benson *The successor to George Bush: elected on a strongly anti-Japanese platform.*

Hugh Rackham Charlesworth III *Assistant Secretary of State for East Asian and Pacific Affairs. Founder of the highly influential HK7 committee.*

THE BRITISH

Richard Adaire *Private Secretary to Sir John Courtenay.*

George Clovis *Hong Kong Island Regional Commander of police and supplementary forces.*

Sir John Courtenay *Last Governor of Hong Kong.*

James Gahan *Consul for South China at the time of the rebellion.*

Dr. John Gurdon *Psychological warfare specialist. Responsible for establishing covert links with the Triad groups.*

General Sir William Harbinson *Commander, British Forces, Hong Kong.*

James Hogge *Secretary of State for Foreign and Commonwealth Affairs.*

Lord Inverdonald *Minister of State for Foreign and Commonwealth Affairs.*

Richard James *Reuters correspondent in Peking.*

Sir Jeremy Longford *Ambassador to Washington.*

Sir Peter MacDuff *Ambassador to Peking.*

Captain Richard Margerison *Intelligence agent. Encouraged and supplied the southern dissident movement before the rebellion.*

Captain James Wilkinson *Intelligence officer with the Gurkha Rifles.*

Peter Williamson *Consul-General, Xianggang.*

THE CHINESE

CIVILIAN

Chen Shuqing *Fujian Military District Commissar.*

Duan Keda *Father of Duan Kun and a founding member of the Republican Party.*

Duan Kun *Student leader shot by police in Xiamen.*

Peter Heung Way Yeung *Solicitor's clerk. "Super 489," overall leader of the Hong Kong Triads and pro-Republican terrorist.*

Li Peng *Premier, head of the State Council (the Chinese Cabinet).*

Mao Ren-chin *Chief Executive of Xianggang SAR after 1997.*

Yang Shankun *President of the PRC.*

Yi Juan Ling *Ex-governor of Guangdong Province. Leader and co-founder of the Republican Party.*

Madame Zhang Xiaodi *Senior spokesman for Sino-European Bilateral Matters at the Foreign Ministry. Later executed for her part in leaking information about Mao Ren-chin's appointment and the possibility of PLA revolt to the press.*

Zhu Senlin *Governor of Guangdong Province.*

MILITARY

Major-General Chen Cong Da *C-in-C 63rd Group Army. Republican.*

Major-General Hu Dai-fang *CO 111th Infantry Division. Captured Xinggiang. Republican.*

Major-General Lan *CO 123rd Infantry Division. Republican.*

Brigadier Li Guang *Commander of a tank brigade in the 14th Tank Division. Leader of the disastrous attack on Quemoy. Communist.*

Lieutenant-Colonel Li Guo-hong *CO 46th Battalion, 123rd Infantry Division. The first PLA officer to declare for the people. Republican.*

Major-General Lu Chuanzhi *CO 37th Infantry Division. Defender of Xinggiang. Surrendered to General Hu. Communist.*

Lieutenant-General Tang Zhou Hou *GOC in-C Guangzhou MR. Republican.*

Lieutenant-General Wu *GOC Guangdong MD. Republican.*

Lieutenant-General Yang *CO 15th Group Army. Communist.*

Major-General Yang Xuchu *CO 73rd Infantry Division. Republican.*

LIST OF MAPS

THE FAR EAST
Political Boundaries June 1997

THE FAR EAST
Political and Military Situation November 1999

FOREWORD

From the endless steppes of Kazakhstan to the fogbound cliffs of the Kamchatka peninsula, the entire immensity that the rest of the world once called the Far East, and which it now prefers to call the West Pacific, is today in turmoil and in flames. Those who take the long view will say it has always been so, and that what is happening today is no more than the latest in an endless procession of irruptions of violence that tell us much about the nature of the Oriental mind.

From the feudal battles of China's warring states of the fourth century BC to the spread of the Mongol empire under Genghis Khan, from the Boxer Rebellion to the Korean War, from the Taiping Rebellions to the bizarreries of the Cultural Revolution, there seems invariably to have been some all-consuming fight going on somewhere in and around China and her satellites, spreading itself with a perverse magnificence over the politicians' and the geographers' maps and thereby changing what is written on them, often for ever.

This latest outbreak of war and insurrection, with the Greek chorus of torture and banditry and execution and rapine sounding all the while, started with the event that some modern historians like to refer to as the East's Sarajevo— the long-awaited, carefully planned and yet ultimately shocking handover of the British Crown Colony of Hong Kong to its rightful owners, the People's Republic of China.

The Chinese behaved, as no British official had ever publicly supposed they might, with a wanton disregard for the agreement that the two parties had earlier signed over the colony's future—and the news of their behaviour became known some few days before the handover itself. The revelation triggered a wave of violence in Hong Kong—which led in turn to violence within China herself, and then, as the whole world is now only too well aware, to the outbreak of full-scale civil war.

That war has raged mercilessly for the past three years, and its pace and ferocity show no signs of easing. In fact, a pattern appears to have been set: border conflict and rebellions are eating away at China's peripheries, full-scale war is gnawing at her vitals, and the leadership in Peking is too frightened and too numbed by the events, and too shaken by its own internal schisms, to know just what to do. In the wake of the mercifully brief outbreak of war in Korea, China is now wholly surrounded by non-Communist countries; and indeed, she remains the only unelected Communist regime anywhere on the face of the globe. The dual imperatives of logic and force of history suggest that the Chinese Communist hierarchy, the Chinese Communist system, cannot be much longer for this world.

But the debilitated state of the Chinese body politic attracted, as was inevitable, the scavengers. In particular the Japanese—the most dangerous of all potential protagonists—became involved. Japan's decision to send troops into China brought, at length, a ferocious response from the United States, and reminded the world how easy it is for great powers to become embroiled in regional matters, for provincial affairs suddenly to become transformed into a global crisis.

This brief outline account of the events that we now know to have followed on from the handover of Hong Kong is, I believe, the first such account to appear. Professional historians may well say that this book—and any book produced at such proximity to the fighting—cannot benefit from the luxury offered by a longer perspective.

This is a criticism I anticipate, and am bound to accept. But that is not the point of this book.

I am hoping instead to throw some light, for the benefit principally of readers in the West who are not so closely engaged with the complexities of the East as once they were, on a difficult topic that television viewers and newspaper readers may prefer to ignore. This war, they will say, is far away, it involves people of whom we know little and about whom we care less.

This is an understandable view, but one which I, as one who has chosen to live in lengthy and voluntary exile from my home country, think is profoundly regrettable. That we have at our disposal the means to examine in detail the lives of creatures on distant planets, and yet care to know so little about men and women who live—and now who die—upon our own, is, to me, a sad consequence of our present-day materialism, comfort and *richesse*. We read less and less about the people of the far-away; and I hope I will not sound hectoring if I say once more that I find this a great pity. We inhabit a most extraordinary world: the vast war that is raging on its far side—its dark side, if you like—is the most extraordinary of events. We should know it better—we should know its causes, its principals, its participants and now, as it threatens to spill out to infect us more directly, its prognosis, too.

There are few disinterested documents on so fresh a conflict, other than the files of newspapers and texts of Short Wave Broadcasts, still faithfully monitored by the BBC. China News Analysis, a Jesuit research group now based in Kyoto, publishes regular lengthy analyses of the twists and turns in the battling; and I have been lucky enough to have been given access to a number of confidential British Foreign Office files relating to the last days of Hong Kong and the first of the new Special Administrative Region. I have cited the *Report of the All-Party Parliamentary Inquiry into the Circumstances Surrounding the Final Handover of Hong Kong and Related Developments in South China* (Cmnd 5611, October 1997, HMSO, London) as a document that offered a valuable insight into British handling of the situation. Similar reports have been produced by the United States and Japanese governments.

Much of the help for this account came from diplomats who prefer not to be named. The former—and indeed the last—Governor of Hong Kong, Sir John Courtenay, was unfailingly helpful, and gave me access to his private diaries; as did the Commander, British Forces, General Sir William Harbinson. I have been fortunate enough to have had several interviews with Mr. James Hogge, the former Secretary of State for Foreign Affairs, and his Minister of State at the time, Lord Inverdonald. Sir Peter MacDuff, still at the time of writing Ambassador in Peking, was also interesting on many aspects of British policy and the official Chinese response to it.

Within China itself I am happy to be able to acknowledge the help of Miss Zhou Kwan and Mr. Cui Ping-dan, who assisted me on my single visit to see General Tang's headquarters in Canton City. Since the Battle of Wuhan was in full flood at the time, the General was away from his base; but I was able to speak with a number of assistants to Governor Yi, and to the father of the slain Xiamen University student, Mr. Duan. All spent much time with me, and gave me many insights into the events of mid-July in Canton and Xiamen.

I am grateful to Mr. Xing of the Ürümqi Railway Workers' Recreation Club; to former PLA Lieutenant Ma of Heihe, in Heilongjiang Province, who drove me to meet a group of Oroqen rebels near Mohe; and to Miss Lee Hyong-ju of Seoul, who acted as guide and helpmeet on my visits to Panmunjom and, later, to Pyongyang. That she was permitted to visit the former North Korean capital at the same time was, for her, a reward of unbelievable worth. I am grateful on her behalf to those who made it possible. Ambassador Bengt Jacobsen will recognise the assistance he gave to me: not least, the ample supplies of Glenmorangie over which he spent many an evening watching the fires of Pyongyang burn themselves out.

My assistance in Japan comes principally from the writer Nagai Hiromi, whose recent book *Japanese Bully-Boys* investigated the connections between the *yakuza*—the so-called "Japanese Mafia"—and the right wing of the ruling LDP, and remains a classic analysis of the new reactionary mood that appears to be sweeping through Japan's young people. Others within the *yakuza* organisations prefer not to be named.

I was able to write most of this book in the relative peace and quiet of Kyoto, staying in a small farm north of the city which was loaned to me by my good friend Sakai Yoko during her absence in Europe: my thanks to her for providing the creature comforts that proved so necessary as an antidote to the wretched narrative I had to tell. I then took the manuscript to my temporary home here in Bali, well away from the conflict, and I did the final editing here. Any errors that remain are not, of course, the responsibility of any of those above, named or anonymous, who gave me their time, their help, their coffee or their affection: any such errors must be laid, of course, at my door.

My wife Catherine, who has been as dismayed as I have by all the traumas of the last two years, remains optimistic that, before long, we will be able to return to Hong Kong, where we first met ten years ago and where I first hoped to be able to write this book. Although the new Republican Hong Kong government appears stable enough, the military situation in the city—with Communist Chinese air raids still an occasional occurrence—has dictated otherwise. But my wife's incurable optimism has been justified on so many occasions before that I am tempted to believe her even now.

SBAW—Sanur, Bali
March, 2000.

AUTHOR'S NOTE

The Chinese language being what it is—and allowing for the innumerable possible transliterations into English script—there may be some confusion in the perception of some of the proper names, particularly Chinese family names, that I have used in this account. This arises from the reality that a man who is named Mr. Ng in Canton is named Mr. Wu in Peking: the Chinese character that represents his name is pronounced in two totally different ways depending on whether it is read by someone from Canton or Peking, a speaker of Cantonese or of the mainland mandarin, *putonghua*. Similarly, a speaker of Fukkienese would call the man something else again, as would a speaker of Shanghainese, or Hakka, or Hainanese, or . . .

To minimise this problem for the reader I have given each person in this account the name by which he knows himself or herself—so if Mr. Wong is from Canton, then he is called in the book what he calls himself in Cantonese; and if Madame Zhang is from Peking, then she is named in the book by the name she calls herself in the Chinese capital. The given names make for a further complication; but in that most Western readers will pay little heed to them, I have simply presented them in the book as they were presented to me.

I have retained—principally because of their more pleasing sound—the Wade-Giles transliteration of the names Peking and Canton, and I have changed Hong Kong to the *pinyin** version, Xianggang, on those few occasions where it seemed appropriate. But all other Chinese place names are as approved by the Government of the People's Republic of China.

A substantial amount of directly quoted dialogue appears in the narrative. Readers will understand that in most cases it is a reconstruction from third party and other sources. Naturally I am aware of the dangers of using such materials, but stress that I have generally used such dialogue where it seems to add materially to an evocation of a particular event. Similarly, translations from the various Chinese languages and dialects have been the work of specialists in those particular tongues, and there may occasionally be some variance between the English written word and the original Chinese intention. But on the whole both the dialogue and the translations present, I am persuaded to believe, a wholly fair account of the events I have described.

Readers are additionally cautioned that the names used in this narrative are, with certain rather obvious exceptions—Kim Il Sung, Mao Tse-tung among them—wholly fictitious, and bear no resemblance to any individual, living or dead. He is not him, nor is she her, nor they them. The events described are also entirely hypothetical; these things are not necessarily those things. But none the less it is my earnest hope that readers will discern a fair degree of verisimilitude between all of this and all of whatever that may come to be.

---

*Pinyin is the phonetic transliteration of Chinese, now widely adopted in mainland China, which uses Roman letters rather than phonetic symbols.

CHAPTER ONE

Typhoon Warning

WHITEMAN AFB, MISSOURI

Wednesday, 24 November 1999

It was the eve of the last Thanksgiving of the century, and a bitterly cold northerly wind was sweeping down through the Midwest from central Canada, bringing with it the first bad storm of the winter. The forecasts were universally grim, and traffic advisories and snow and freeze warnings had been posted from the international frontier as far south as Little Rock, Arkansas, and the Red River, on the border between Oklahoma and Texas.

Snow started to fall a little before 8 P.M. in western Missouri. At first it was just a thin snow that looked like a yellow mist as it swirled and eddied in the light of the sodium vapour arclamps on the triple perimeter fence that circled Whiteman Air Base. Before long it had turned into a full blizzard. Air Force sentries, their faces hidden by fur collars pulled right up to the dulled steel of their helmets, stamped up and down, snorting steam into the night. Their rifles glinted in the gleam of the lights. On a normal night there would be no more than two of them, with another couple on the gate, and a patrolling team in a Cherokee truck. But tonight there were dozens of rifles, dozens of sentries. If anyone cared to look, Whiteman Air Base—once home to the 351st Strategic Missile Wing, and now America's most secret strategic bomber base—would, on this particular night, look uncannily and ominously different.

But probably no one would care to look over at the three strange aircraft and their sinister huddles of attendants. In this bleak and featureless corner of western Missouri there were few enough passers-by at this time of night anyway. And in this weather, and on the eve of the holiday, hardly a soul was stirring. This lack of interest was a matter of some comfort to every one of the small, tightly secured group of people—from President Benson downwards—who had reason to be acutely concerned about the maintenance of secrecy on this critical night.

The airport over at Kansas City, sixty miles to the west, was still busy, with dozens of late-night jets bringing last-minute holidaymakers in from New York and Chicago and the coastal cities. A few trucks hummed by on Route Fifty, and a freight train clanked and grumbled its way along the old Missouri Pacific tracks from Sedalia and Jefferson City. But otherwise, in just about all of the rest of Johnson County, from Hughesville in the north to Quick City in the south, people were tucked up in their farms and their trailers, staying warm, watching the TV or the flickering of the fire, listening to the howl of the gathering storm and giving thanks—half in preparation for the next day's feast—that they didn't have to be out in it.

Behind the triple cyclone fences, however, the men of the 414th Bombardment Wing, United States Air Force, were busier than they had ever been in their unit's history. Three of the low, sleek Northrop B-2 Stealth bombers assigned, uniquely, to the Whiteman wing had been loaded with fuel. Normally they were filled with enough for a training mission, somewhere over the Mojave desert. But tonight each of them were filled to the brim with eighty tons of aviation spirit, enough to power the four General Electric F-118 turbo-fans for nearly nine hours of cruising, allowing the three planes to fly to their full range of more than 5,000 miles from base.

More extraordinary still, shortly after nightfall a nuclear weapons technical crew had arrived at the B-2 hangar from the underground ordnance bunker sited behind the earth mounds at the eastern corner of the base. The crew had arrived in a convoy of three heavily armoured vehicles, each of which was driven directly beneath the fuselage (if a B-2 can be said to have a fuselage: its tiny radar cross-section made it look like a flying wing, no more) of each of the planes. They worked silently, behind hessian screens, for more than two hours, departing once they had completed the intricacies of their work. They left the bombers loaded—as the crews assigned to fly them quickly discovered—as no US Air Force plane had been loaded for the previous eight years.

Shortly after 10 P.M., Central Standard Time—0400 Zulu, Universal Coordinated Time, or GMT—each B-2 bomber was taxiing down the runway between the frozen stubble of Whiteman Air Base, carrying eighty tons of fuel, and two live and primed atomic bombs. More specifically, each plane carried two mark B-61 nuclear fission weapons— each one eight feet long, shaped like a torpedo, with a rounded nose and small guide fins on the tail. Each atom bomb was packed with high explosive and enough precision-machined uranium 235 to create a nuclear explosion that would be equivalent to the detonation of nearly 50,000 tons of TNT.

The three bombers left Whiteman AFB at one-minute intervals, with the lead plane clocked out at 0405 Zulu, 25 November 1999. They swept almost silently up through the Missouri blizzard and climbed steadily to their cruising altitude, nine miles above the eastern edge of the Great Plains. At this moment the six Air Force commissioned officers to whose lot this mission fell, two assigned to pilot each aircraft, had no information about their ultimate destination, nor about the nature of their task. They knew only a very few details.

They knew they were headed on the first leg of their mission—a 4,000-mile, seven-hour flight to Hickam Air Base, Hawaii, where they would land and refuel. They knew they would remain at Hickam for no more than three hours, after which they would take off with another set of new, sealed orders. Depending on a possible third set of fresh orders that would be transmitted through a highly secure airborne satellite data link from the National Command Authorities (President Benson in the White House and the Secretary of Defense at the Pentagon, via the Joint Chiefs and the SAC commander at Offutt Air Force Base in Nebraska) they knew that a single one of the three aircraft would then proceed to execute the mission. All three aircraft would then rendezvous after the attack and would be refuelled by aerial tankers before returning to Hickam Field, after which the crews would rest and then bring the aircraft back to the headquarters of the 414th BW at Whiteman.

And they knew that the new top-secret attack orders would be transmitted once only at precisely 2200 Zulu on 25 November. If no orders had arrived on the data link by 2201 Zulu, the attack mission would be considered aborted, and all three planes would return immediately to the designated refuelling rendezvous point "R-3" before returning to Hickam and then to Whiteman. Total radio silence had to be maintained at all times, aside from the five minutes immediately prior to the first landing at Hawaii.

The westbound flight was uneventful. The planes flew high, a mile or so apart, their black and unreflective shapes rendering them nearly invisible to each other, as well as to all the radar devices below and which they were designed to evade. The ice and snow storms eased above the southern Rockies, and by the time the planes had reached Lake Mead the sky was bright and clear, the immense body of water below turned into molten silver by the light of a low full moon. They passed above the Los Angeles basin at around 1:30 A.M., Pacific time: the lights of Hollywood and Pasadena and Burbank were like a clutch of brilliant jewels, and curling freeways like loops of gold chain.

Three and a half further hours spent hurtling southwest over the Pacific and the lead plane spotted Mauna Kea on the Big Island of Hawaii; Major Bill Pringle, the lead pilot, radioed a single message down to Hawaii Oceanic and then to Hickam Control before coming in low around South

Cape to Diamond Head, overshooting Hickam and making a smooth and silent approach from the west. He touched down at 1:16 A.M. Hawaii Standard Time, 1116 Zulu, the others a minute or two behind. It was pitch dark, and comfortably warm. Soft trade winds wafted across the runway, with the plangent sounds of late night guitar music, and cicadas carried on the breeze. "H" hour was now ten hours and forty-four minutes away.

The planes were refuelled at a remote western corner of the field, well away from the freeway bridges. There was no one in sight, and the only signs of life came from one of the warships riding at anchor in the roads, where a party seemed to be in full swing. Sentries had taken up positions around the three aircraft. An unmarked USAF truck brought in a second technical team to check the bombs, and one of their officers entered a series of numerical codes into the firing devices. Finally, moments before the scheduled take-off time a second truck appeared, with two officers and more sentries. They were from the office of CINCPAC, the Commander in Chief, Pacific, whose headquarters were in Camp H. M. Smith on a hill overlooking Pearl Harbor. They demanded positive identification from all six of the B-52 crew members, and then handed over sealed envelopes of orders which were to be read, they said, once the aircraft were airborne. They saluted and left. The three aircraft taxied back on to the main runway and soared up into the black Pacific sky on schedule, at 4 A.M. local time, 1400 Zulu. "H" hour was now eight hours away.

Thirty minutes later, once the three machines had reached their cruise altitude, Major Pringle and his two other colleagues alongside opened the stiff manila order envelopes. Inside each was a single sheet of flimsy paper, with a number of lines of machine-readable type which read, in full:

ZCZC CINCSAC OABNE/OPCDRS 33 SQN 414 SBW HABHI 251330Z NOV 99 MSGRDS+++USING GPS PROCEED AT MACH 0.80 AT FL450 TO POSITION GAMMA COORDINATES 30.00.00N 150.00.00E

AFTER WHICH DESCEND TO FL 350 AND PRO-
CEED AT FULL SPEED AND IN SECURE STATE
THREE TO POSITION DELTA COORDINATES
34.00.00N 140.00.00E EXPECT FURTHER ORDERS
2200 ZULU EX NCA VIA DATALINK CODENAME
OPERATION TYPHOON WARNING STOP REFUEL
POSITION "R" PRIOR DESIGNATIONS STOP
ENDS+++

The commanders calculated swiftly. It was now 3,100
miles to Position Gamma. At the designated speed, and
given the high-altitude weather, it would take the small
squadron six hours and eighteen minutes to arrive. Since it
was now 1440 Zulu the planes should all reach this first position at 2058 hours. The second position, Position Delta,
was a further 620 miles on—one hour and two minutes at
full speed, and in Secure State Three, with all RAM baffles,
ECM screens and signal monitoring arrays switched on, and
with jamming devices readied. It should thus be possible to
be at Position Delta, and probably undetected, at precisely
2200 Zulu—the time at which the final set of orders from
the President should come in over the datalink.

It would be idle to think that these orders—if they
came—would demand any other course of action than that
which was blindingly and horrifyingly obvious. Operation
Typhoon Warning, the name by which these orders would
now be identified, would almost certainly require one of the
three strategic bombers to drop and detonate at least one
of its nuclear weapons. It would be the first time that an
atomic device had been used in anger since August 1945.
Each of the fission weapons in the bomb bays of the B-2s
was four times as powerful as the bombs that devastated
Hiroshima and Nagasaki. Many scores of thousands of people could be less than seven and a half hours away from a
horrible death.

But where were they likely to be? It was the question up-
permost in the minds of the six men as they punched their
course orders into the INS, and as their planes began to
hurtle northwestwards, away from the glow of the Ameri-

can dawn, and towards the deep Pacific night. Just where, each man wondered as he unscrolled his computerised global positioning system map, where exactly on the face of the earth were these two positions?

Position Gamma, it turned out, was in the middle of the ocean, 400 miles northwest of the tiny atoll of Marcus Island, which for the last thirty years—since the Americans handed it back—had supported a small Japanese weather station and a squid-harvesting plant.

Position Delta, 34° 00′ N 140 00′ E, however, was by no means in mid-ocean. It was on the very verge of the Japanese mainland. Ten miles to the west was the island of Miyakejima. Fifty miles north were the beaches and the pearl divers of the Boso-hanto peninsula. And eighty miles away from Position Delta—ten minutes' flying time—was Tokyo itself.

The realisation dawned suddenly on all six men. Though they would have no way of knowing for certain for another seven hours and an odd few minutes, it seemed well within the bounds of probability that the target for nuclear attack under Operation Typhoon Warning was near, or even directly over, the city of Tokyo.

The scores of thousands who would die would be residents of the capital of the most powerful economic state on the planet—the leaders of whom were currently locked in a seemingly intractable dispute, an irresolvable crisis with the United States.

The dispute, which now seemed about to spin out of control and to culminate in the most terrifying of tragedies, had its origins just two and a half years before in a place that was far from, and formally unrelated to, both of the nations that were now locked so ruinously together. Its origins can be traced, in fact, to the summer of 1997, and to what was then the last British Imperial possession in the Far East—the Crown Colony of Hong Kong. It was then about to be handed back, after 150 years of foreign rule, to its rightful owners, the Chinese.

But the ponderous mechanics by which this transfer was undertaken, and the unanticipated realities of the takeover, were to produce an escalating crisis that has kept the Far East in turmoil almost ever since, and which seemed to these young American pilots, so far from home on this still dark Thanksgiving morning, to be readying itself for the most appalling and unspeakable climax.

CHAPTER TWO

Distant Thunder

THE BRITISH EMBASSY, WASHINGTON, DC
Tuesday, 11 June 1996

The first expression of Washington's serious interest in the coming crisis in Asia—though at this early stage perhaps serious curiosity would be the more accurate phrase—came as the result of a very brief chance encounter between two guests at the most celebrated diplomatic event of 1996, the annual Official Birthday Party in honour of Queen Elizabeth II. The meeting, so short as to be almost perfunctory, involved on the one side an Assistant Secretary of State and, on the other, a middle-ranking British soldier with a noticeably new suntan. On the June day that they met it is fair to say there was not even the faintest apprehension of trouble from this quarter of the world. The only apprehension that anyone recalls from the day of this meeting was that of the coming summertime heat.

This hint that yet another of the Potomac Valley's notoriously debilitating summers had settled itself on the American capital caused the half-dozen British Foreign Office functionaries charged with organising the 1996 "QBP" to curse as profusely as they perspired. For it was an unusually large and splendid party they had planned this year, and they were in no mood to see it spoiled, by storm, or humidity, or the insufferable swampy heat.

Two thousand, two hundred and twenty-eight gilt-edged,

heavily illuminated and embossed invitation cards had gone out, three weeks before, to the great and the good of Bethesda, Chevy Chase, Cabin John and Alexandria, and to the better addresses in the District of Columbia, most of them found to the west of Rock Creek Park. A variety of factors suggested that perhaps most of those who had been invited would turn up. After all, it was the seventieth anniversary of the building of the embassy itself, *and* the seventieth birthday of Her Majesty: the party would provide a moment for everyone to toast the further survival both of the monarchy and the present monarch, and to recall the astuteness of the Treasury negotiators who in 1926 persuaded the Government of the District of Columbia to hand over this most commodious piece of land on Massachusetts Avenue for the sum of ten dollars (which, subsequent Ambassadors were wont to remark, was admittedly worth a *great deal more* in those days).

There were other reasons. The friendship between the White House and Downing Street had never been stronger, it seemed, and George Bush, in these closing months of his eight-year Presidency, had come to seem a near-avuncular figure to the succession of Prime Ministers who had been thrown up by the minority governments of the post-Thatcher years. (This feature of modern political life was now making Britain almost as curious and fascinating a phenomenon as Italy had been in the Eighties. Not a few of the American journalists who had been invited would come, the Embassy assumed, because of the extraordinary turmoil which Whitehall had suffered during the last two years— turmoil which had been warmly welcomed by all of those who found the peaceful world dreadfully dull.)

Then again, it had also been hinted that there was a very slight possibility of a visit to Washington—and thus the Embassy—from the Princess (who had been sailing with friends off Bequia, in the Grenadines, and was expected to fly home after a brief stop in some American city). The merest suggestion that she might appear had been enough to give half of Georgetown the most acute attack of nerves, and to treble the business of the local couturiers, dressmakers and seamstresses. In addition, the extraordinary good looks of the young—and still single—new British Ambassador counted for a lot. Sir Jeremy Longford had, it was generally agreed, quite a bit of pulling power.

Yes, concluded the perspiring Second Secretaries and advisers on Protocol and *placement*, all told it was highly likely that most of those who had been asked to come would do so. The Treasury would no doubt grumble again about the ensuing bill: but then the accountants' miserable idea of twenty years before, of staging a mere *vin d'honneur* for only 200 guests, had long gone the way of so many other examples of Cold War–inspired parsimony. One of the more comforting consequences of the so-called Peace Dividend was that British diplomatic parties, all around the world, were now back to being recognised as the best on the circuit. And this one in Washington, to celebrate the dual seventieth birthdays, was due to be one of the grandest of all.

In the event, the Royal Marine security officers later reported a heroic turnout. One thousand, eight hundred and ninety invitations had been presented at the Embassy's Observatory Gate, and a further ninety guests had been welcomed at the door of the Lutyens-designed Residency itself, a mark of special favour for their age, importance, and often both. The substantial acreage of rose-rimmed lawns was thus awash with an immense and multicoloured scrum of people and hats—some of the most remarkable of hats this particular year—tucking merrily into hundreds of pounds of the sweetest of small Norfolk strawberries piled with billows of whipped Devon cream, sipping icy flutes of Krug (though some misguided patriots opted for a rather chalky-tasting Sussex Chardonnay), and chattering over the selections from *The King and I*, *Cats* and the latest London musical, *The Speckled Band*, that were played for them by a visiting Police Band from the Colony of Hong Kong.

The Secretary of State was there, if briefly. So were some fourteen senior figures from Foggy Bottom who were either Assistant Secretaries, Heads of Departments or else enjoyed some especially intimate relationship with Her

Majesty's Government. Hugh Rackham Charlesworth III was one such. He was officially listed as Assistant Secretary of State for East Asian and Pacific Affairs (Japan to New Zealand, Singapore to Tonga). But he was rather more than that: he had been at Keble (as a Rhodes Scholar, and an oarsman) along with Jeremy Longford; and it was thought there was a fighting chance that Charlesworth's sister Anne-Marie might one day become Lady Longford (despite the complications of nomenclature that would then arise for the Countess of the same title).

It was not, however, his perfunctory exchange with Jeremy—*Sir* Jeremy, he said correctly, and with a courtly bow and an amused grin, as he reached the head of the receiving line—that made that June encounter so historically memorable. It was instead a conversation that occurred towards the end of the party that came to assume seminal importance. It was fairly brief, and it took place when Hugh Charlesworth was strolling back towards the Residency steps, and was gazing towards the stolid bronze back of the Churchill statue beyond, wondering if he could now leave without causing offence.

His eye lighted on a fellow of his age, a man whom he had noticed earlier, largely because of his fiercely dark suntan and the startling cut of his pale linen suit. When Charlesworth saw him for this second time he was being given a light by the conductor of the police band. He drew deeply on a small cigar—probably a Burmese cheroot, Charlesworth thought. The policeman then waved at him cheerily, and got back on with the business of conducting a rather thin version of *I'm Just a Gal Who Can't Say No.*

Charlesworth introduced himself. The stranger, it turned out, was a British soldier, a captain in the Gurkha Rifles, currently on leave and attached to St. Anthony's College, Oxford. His name was Wilkinson. He spoke Cantonese, he explained—and Police Senior Inspector Tsui, the band conductor, was an old friend. Indeed he had called on Tsui's son in Hong Kong only one week before, when he returned to the colony after a long journey in the Kumon Hills of Northern Burma, and near by. He had flown to the States for his sister's wedding—she was a Secretary in the Embassy's Private Office. Jeremy Longford had invited him to the party. He knew very few people in Washington: his specialty was China—he had read Chinese at Cambridge, and had been on a short posting in Hong Kong three years before to work with the Gurkhas as an intelligence officer, with a particular interest in the handover of the colony to Chinese rule.

"Little more than a year away, isn't it?" remarked Charlesworth.

"A year and"—Wilkinson looked down at his watch, and counted with his fingers—"and twenty days. And everyone rather nervous, as I expect you know."

Charlesworth had taken a keen interest in the last year's reporting by the American Consulate at Hong Kong. Things were going none too well, he admitted. There had been demonstrations and some spectacular rioting the previous summer. The gyrations of the local stock and property market had caused more than usual alarm. The flow of emigrants had become remarkable—and indeed there was a memorandum sitting on his desk at that very moment from the Immigration and Naturalisation Service, requesting some advice and forecasts on the likely volume of applicants for immigration to the United States. "An atmosphere approaching panic" was a phrase he had noted.

The American Chamber of Commerce in the colony had reported its own concern over the continuing drain of competent people, a tapering-off of foreign investment (except from Japan, which was still increasing its investment, though more slowly and prudently than a decade before), and a 2 or 3 percent decline in the number of American corporate offices in the territory. Most of the latter had moved down to Singapore, though the temptations of Kuala Lumpur and Djakarta had increased since the signing of the Middle East Treaty, and the consequent lessening of tension between America and the more conservative half of the Islamic world.

Relations between the major industrial powers and China, which—with the exception of the eternally prosperous provinces in the south, near Hong Kong—was currently enduring yet another phase of inexplicable barbarism, were very poor: a further reason for everyone to be concerned and dejected about the outlook for Hong Kong, caught in the middle. "Troubling" was the word most commonly used to describe the colony's prospects. "But not terminal," added many of the analysts who were familiar with the resilience and energy of the place. "Down, but not out."

The two men strolled towards the Residency steps, the music fading as they moved away from the little band. The late afternoon air was thick and hot, and Charlesworth suddenly wished he was in creased white linen, and not his regulation Brooks Brothers grey. He had long regretted that he had had little truly foreign experience—not the kind that Wilkinson appeared to have, anyway. His career was based mostly on meetings in embassy offices and on reading mimeographed reports and studying matters of protocol. The man who was strolling beside him seemed by contrast to be making his life a progress through jungles and villages, and into parts of foreign cities that it would be imprudent for a foreign diplomat to visit. He might well hear more—much more—than his colleagues on the conventional circuit. He decided to ask.

"Any ideas about what the Chinese'll do to the place?" It was a casual question, the kind of thing he asked every businessman and foreign envoy and journalist who passed through his office. Most of them replied gloomily. There were guarantees—cast-iron guarantees, the British insisted to everyone else's sceptical amusement—that the system that had made Hong Kong so successful would be permitted to continue for at least half a century more. "Come on!" they all scoffed. "The Chinese won't be able to keep their hands off the place."

"Odd that you should ask," Wilkinson replied. "Well— not odd that you should ask—but odd that I'd meet someone here who was interested.

"Yes, I do have an idea or two. It's all very dismal, as you'd probably expect me to say. But I've kept my ears open during the past couple of months. This trip—I wasn't only in the Kumon Hills, actually. I have some friends from Peking who I meet from time to time over in Yunnan Province. They're people I go climbing with. They've got quite interesting jobs. We talk about things. And one of them did say something on this journey that I have to confess I found rather strange."

Charlesworth paused, fascinated. The buzz of conversation around him seemed to quieten, and the faces that he recognised from time to time blurred into the crowd. They were under a mulberry tree, and there was no one around to overhear.

"You probably know all about the agreement," Wilkinson continued, "concerning who exactly is actually going to run Hong Kong, once the British Governor steps down. It'll be a Chinese, of course. But I'm sure you are aware that the powers that be in Peking were always terribly careful to say that this person, whoever it was, would be from Hong Kong—perhaps even someone who was chosen by the local people. Certainly it would be someone the locals would approve of.

"But from what I hear, that's not going to happen at all. The people in—well, to be frank I'm not sure what ministry they're in, let's just say *some people in Peking*—are getting really rather steamed up about what's happening in South China. They think the place is getting away with itself, becoming too prosperous and falling under all this foreign influence. I'm sure you've read all about it. There are endless pieces in the *Review* and so forth.

"They've put some pretty hard-line people in at the top in the provinces, as you'll have noticed. But they think—rightly, I suppose—that the real trouble comes from Hong Kong. They see it as a sort of illness, if you like. And they want the illness to end—they want to cut it off at the source so that the infection, if that is what it is, stops spreading. The best way of doing that is to make absolutely sure that Hong Kong, once it is under their control, is totally ideologically reliable. So what my friends tell me is that they're planning to put one of their real Stalinists in as the new boss. They're going to tear up that part of the agreement—

not, I suppose, that anyone thought they'd abide by it in the first place. Remember all that nonsense about 'whatever else the Chinese do, at least they stick to their agreements'? How could anyone believe that?

"Anyway, for what it's worth, that's what I'm told. I mentioned it to one or two people in London before I came here. But I don't think they thought much of it. They're not terribly open to that kind of thing back in the Foreign Office. One chap called Cooper took an interest—you might have a chat with him, if you're interested. But the others— they seem to assume I go climbing with the wrong sort of people."

Charlesworth grinned, and thanked Wilkinson for the tip, and promised to keep in touch; and then the pair made their separate ways towards the exit. Longford was waiting, looking with some exasperation over the shoulder of Diane Forgiss, the somewhat overdressed social editor of the *Standard*. He spotted Charlesworth and with relief cried:

"Hugh—how good to see you! Come over here. There's something I want to say to you," and edged him over to the marquee.

"Christ that woman's a bore. Got to pay my dues, they say. Full page in the Style section, or whatever it is. My press chap seems to think it's a good idea, give us more visibility, after all the damage my predecessor is supposed to have done on the social scene. Thank God you rescued me."

"But was there something?" asked Charlesworth, who had a six o'clock with the Indonesian Ambassador, and ought not to be late. "I'm sorry to be so abrupt."

"Not at all, Hugh. Yes, there was one thing. Did you meet a fellow called Wilkinson? I had a mind that I saw the two of you talking. Well, I gather from a person in Policy Planning in London that he's really rather good. He's attached to St. Antony's, as you may know. So his credentials—and his connections—are obviously pretty impressive. And I gather that he may have some interesting views on what the Chinese are up to. Not that I'd know. I can't stand them. No interest at all. But I rather liked Hong

Kong, at least for a day or two. Quite a nice bunch of people there, people who work in Swires,* all very civilised.

"Jimmy Wilkinson seems to think it is all going to go wrong, and that our people aren't taking it seriously enough. He talked to me about it the other day, and I thought he should pop along here and see if he could interest anyone. His view is that the appointment of the chief executive has all sorts of implications, that will go a lot further than Hong Kong itself. He thinks it'll set off—or that it could set off—all manner of problems.

"Something about his manner I rather like. I'd heard a bit about him from one of our Defence Liaison people. He's quite a character: hard but wise if you know what I mean.

"Anyway—you've got to go. I'm seeing your sister tomorrow night. We'll catch up after that. But my advice to you for now is—even if we are pooh-poohing Wilkinson's ideas, you might think about it a bit more carefully. You don't have the blinkers, or the baggage. Think about what he said. Keep it at the back of your mind."

At this time of the evening the traffic on Rock Creek Parkway was northbound only, taking the commuters back to the Maryland suburbs. Charlesworth thus had to drive down 22nd Street, and got stuck in a jam near M Street. He was frustrated, and he was fuming by the time he arrived and discovered that Mr. Thayeb was already in the Ambassadors' Waiting Room, and had been there for ten minutes.

But the delay had convinced him of the need to take Longford's advice seriously—and to make a note to thank him for passing Wilkinson on to him. He, too, had liked the young soldier. He had no way of deciding whether what he had said was true or not; but he was certain that if it was true, then it had profound implications not just for Hong Kong, but for China, and even for China's neighbours. Precisely what these implications were needed to be established. A group ought to be established to monitor the

*John Swire & Co. Ltd., one of the biggest trading firms in Hong Kong, owned by a British family of the same name.

situation, and to report up, perhaps regularly, for the Department.

The EAPAC Hong Kong Transition Working Group—or the Charlesworth "HK 7" Committee as it soon became known—was formally convened two weeks later, meeting for its first session in the Assistant Secretary's private office. There were seven members: two from the People's Republic of China Bureau, one from the Taiwan Coordination Staff, one from the Office of Japanese Affairs, one from the Office of Korean Affairs, a representative from the Central Intelligence Agency and another specialist on Hong Kong and colonial affairs attached to the Bureau of European Affairs. It had a part-time secretarial staff of one, and a telephone number. It was to meet monthly, and to prepare regular study papers on "the likely impact on the East Asian region of the retrocession of the British Crown Colony of Hong Kong on 30 June 1997, with particular reference to matters of United States political, commercial and national security interests." It would report to the Assistant Secretary, who would in turn file the reports with the Office of the Secretary of State.

The Committee's monthly meetings, viewed with the benefit of hindsight, provided a thread of continuity to American policy towards the Far East in the late Nineties that would prove invaluable both to the outgoing Bush administration and to that of President Benson, who won his surprise electoral victory that November largely on the basis of a wave of Far Eastern—or, more specifically, anti-Japanese—interest.

When the regional troubles that Charlesworth's group accurately predicted in the summer of 1996 came to a head, and then in turn precipitated the global crisis of the autumn of 1999, the HK7 meetings became ever more important to the inner circle of Presidential advisers. Hugh Charlesworth is regarded by contemporary historians as the principal architect of US policy towards China, Japan and Korea—perhaps not wholly surprisingly, given his official Assistant Secretaryship. But it is an impressive aspect of the affair, none the less, that senior White House officials, NSC chairmen and the chairmen of the Joint Chiefs of Staff have deferred so often and so uncomplainingly in this matter to the authority and knowledge of a single individual.

The Assistant Secretary himself has simply replied to the publicity he has received as a consequence by saying that "good committee work" seems to have underlain the decision-making process—a reply that appears to have guaranteed him a secure position in the US bureaucracy for some time to come.

CHAPTER THREE

Recessional

GOVERNMENT HOUSE, HONG KONG

Saturday, 28 June 1997

EARLY MORNING

The Foreign Office telegram number 97/54658/GHK, sent over the name of James Hogge, Secretary of State for Foreign and Commonwealth Affairs, was timed at 1845 Zulu, and was dated 27 June 1997. It was heavily coded, was classified Top Secret and marked Flash. It was addressed for "The Personal Attention of His Excellency the Governor of Hong Kong," and was copied to Her Britannic Majesty's Ambassadors in Peking, Washington and to the United Nations, and also, with a number of addenda, to the Commander, British Forces, Hong Kong.

The classification of a British diplomatic telegram as Flash carries the implicit instruction that all intended recipients are to be alerted immediately to its arrival, whatever the time of day or night; and so in Government House Hong Kong, where the time of its initial receipt was logged as 0300 local—when it was pitch dark, on the hot and soundlessly stormy Saturday morning of 28 June—the duty cipher clerk at the Communications Centre telephoned up to Richard Adaire, Private Secretary to the Governor.

Adaire, whose post in the Hong Kong government allowed him handsome official quarters in a block of flats on

Mount Nicholson Gap Road, had for the past six weeks of the Diplomatic Emergency been living in Government House itself, in a poky *pied-à-terre* beneath the eaves of what had long been called the Japanese Tower. He was lying half awake, listening to the subsiding rumble of the night-time riots, when the clerk's call came through. "I'll be down in a second. Tony," he said quietly; and by two minutes past three he was indeed down in the basement Centre, watching as the clerk worked at his IBM terminal to strain some sense from the cryptographic soup that had poured down the line from London.

He was good at his job, and it took him just three minutes to produce a copy of the message that was clean enough to read and to present to His Excellency. Leaving aside all the salutational flummery and the distribution lists, the text, Adaire noted, was very brief. But however spare the prose, the implications were profound. The message, the first formally recorded apprehension of a tide of events that would soon wash across world history with as much power as either of the century's two earlier conflicts, was marked by a lack of both elegance and persiflage:

HMG CONFIRMS STATE COUNCILLOR MAO REN CHIN APPOINTED CEXG STOP PRC AUTHORITIES AGREEING TO WITHHOLD STATEMENT UNTIL 1559 ZULU MONDAY 30 JUNE STOP CIVIL ORDER IMPLICATIONS INDICATE CLEAR NEED FOR CONTINUING DISCRETION STOP CONTINGENT PRECAUTIONS NECESSARY STOP TWO BATTALIONS CURRENTLY BSB THOUGH FCO REGARDS UTILISATION DECIDEDLY IMPRUDENT FURTHER DETAILS IN ANNEXES FOR CBF STOP+++HOGGE

Adaire read the message, shook his head and whistled in disbelief. "Make sure you copy it and all the annexes to Tamar," was all he said at first. He picked up the telephone and punched 211. It was answered immediately. Sir John Courtenay, who was in any case a light sleeper, was half expecting a message from London, and had probably lain awake as well.

"Flash telegram, sir—I'll bring it up right away," said Adaire, fighting to keep his voice calm. He paused. The Governor asked him for a *précis*. "Basically it says that Mao's been appointed, just as they thought. I'm having the text copied to the General. I've got the summary with me now, and Tony says he'll have the lot by half-past three. I'll come right up."

Sir John was in the dressing-room when Adaire arrived, perspiring slightly. He took the flimsy paper from the scarlet folder marked Top Secret and read through it, frowning occasionally. He walked down the stairs to his study and sat at his desk, rubbing his eyes. He picked up the right hand of the three telephones on his desk, which gave him a direct connection to General Sir William Harbinson, the Commander, British Forces.

"Morning, Willy," he said. "You won't have seen the cable yet, but Adaire here says you'll get it in a minute or two. Once you've read it all, come right up here, will you? I'm afraid it looks like trouble. *Big* trouble. You'd better bring Tomsett, too. Let's say an informal meeting at zero four hundred hours. My study."

He hung up, took off his spectacles and rubbed his eyes once again. Adaire thought that for a moment the Governor looked particularly old—though it was probably no more than weariness, and the wretched hour of night.

They caught each other's gaze. Then Sir John shook his head, slowly. "What bloody, bloody fools these Chinks can be. You'd never imagine they'd make such madness. A rod for their own backs—that's what this is. Why? Can anybody tell me why?"

12TH FLOOR, HMS *TAMAR*, HONG KONG

EARLY MORNING

The three Operations Requirements Departments at the Ministry of Defence had clearly had a hand in the prepara-

tion of the annexes to FCO Flash Telegram 97/54658/GHK
which Squadron Leader Bates, the Military Assistant,
handed to General Harbinson at 0332 on the Saturday
morning. They were voluminous, and detailed, and they
talked extensively about the diversion and possible deployment of men, ships, jets, transport planes and helicopters.
The General, who like the Governor was half awake when
Bates telephoned for permission to bring him the telegram,
put them to one side to read in the car on the way up to
Government House; his attention was held by his skimming
of the single sheet of flimsy that held the main message.

If the news that Mao Ren-chin was to be installed as
China's first Chief Executive of the Special Administrative
Region of Xianggang did not exactly surprise Harbinson—
who was a wily ex-Gurkha who had served some tours in
the colony and thus had some foreknowledge of Peking's
ways—it most certainly did appal him. Like Sir John he
whistled softly with incredulity.

"Betrayal" was the word that came to mind. There had,
after all, been an explicit assurance given by the Chinese
nearly fourteen years before, that the first Chief Executive
of what in *putonghua* was called Xianggang would be
drawn from within the Hong Kong community. Whoever it
was would be—or would probably be, for this, it had to be
admitted, was never stated specifically—a person of Cantonese stock. But this Mr. Mao of the telegram, far from
being Cantonese, far from having any links at all with the
Hong Kong community, far from being in any sense the
choice of the five million who still lived in the territory,
was a total outsider.

Mao Ren-chin came from Dalian, in Liaoning province,
south Manchuria. He spoke not a word of the Cantonese dialect. He was seventy-four years old, a former soldier, reputed to be a hard-line member of the Party. He had done
much, it was reliably reported, to help organise the suppression of the Chinese student movements in 1976, 1989, 1993
and 1996. He was, in short, the very antithesis of the kind
of person that Hong Kong, even in its politically emascu-
lated state at the time of the handover, wanted to have

preside over its first months and years of post-colonial life.
It was an appointment, Harbinson felt sure, that would lead
to disaster.

He instructed Bates to awaken his deputy, Brigadier Rex
Tomsett, and the young Major, Julian Berry, who had been
sent from London six months before to help organise the
handover ceremonial this coming Monday night. The General was in no mood for small talk. "Meet me at my car at
zero three fifty," he told each man as he came to the phone.
"We have a problem. There is a meeting at Government
House at four. Top Secret Rules apply. That is all."

The three men met downstairs, outside the steel grilles of
the gates to the Prince of Wales Building. The two junior
officers saluted the General, who climbed into the back seat
of the armoured Jaguar. Tomsett, who carried a sheaf of
briefing papers, sat beside him. The driver, a corporal from
the 6th Gurkha Rifles, the General's former regiment, shut
the car's door, and waited while Berry got himself and his
briefcase into the front seat. Then, checking to see that all
the bullet-proof windows were properly closed, he drove
off through the triple chicanes, past the sentries and the
sandbags that marked the perimeter of Tamar, and out into
the confusion—ebbing somewhat, given the hour—of the
Hong Kong night.

The city did look in a hellish state. There was little
enough traffic about, except for army and police vehicles.
But small groups of agitated people were still milling
around the Star Ferry concourse, spilling out of the MTR*
exits—not that the trains themselves were running—and
were joining groups already in Statue Square and the streets
around the old Legislative Council building. A few held up
banners, and chanted. From one group came an eerie, ugly
growl of anger. Suddenly this group charged as one towards
a police car which, with the sound of screaming tyres,
promptly sped away. A water-cannon lay in wait up an alley by the Bank, with helmeted troops beside it. Some were
smoking. A few looked half asleep.

*Mass Transit Railway, the Hong Kong version of the Underground.

Even with the windows closed, the onion-smell of tear gas filtered in through the car's air conditioning system, and the eyes of the four occupants began to smart. And there was another more acrid smell of burning tyres. A number of fires had been set. Half-way up Garden Lu a police LandCruiser was on its side in flames, and from the flyover the group could see the orange glow of fire from shops and offices at the base of Furama House and on top of the car park at Murray Road. There had once been secret police offices there—"J" branch had worked from above the park in its early years—and there were said to be files and computer tapes stored in what had become a big police godown. Probably that was why it had been set alight. In fact, as the officers all knew, most of the files were on computer disc, stored in the vaults out at Chung Hom Kok, where the old GCHQ monitoring station had been; in the coming days they were supposedly to be loaded on to a destroyer that would be waiting behind Po Toi—doubtless the Annexes to the night's message had some further details from London about that. Exactly what would be done with the files was anyone's guess. Someone had estimated that 3 million personal records had been accumulated by "J" branch in the past two years: doubtless there would be some great material for an entire battalion of historians and blackmailers.

The Jaguar, its two-star general's badge gleaming in the light of the fires, turned into Upper Albert Road and pushed its way through the crowds that, for the previous week, had assembled nightly beyond the barricades in front of the Government House walls. There were a series of checks and searches here, even for so well-known a group of visitors as these. The sergeant who performed the final inspection was, his cap badge declared, a member of the 2nd Battalion, The Queen's Regiment—the final British unit that London had seen fit to have garrisoned down at Stanley Fort.

It was a decision that had prompted some wry comment in a number of Messes and in a letter to *The Times* about the irony—a deliberately contrived coincidence, it was thought sure. For the Second Battalion, a complicated amalgam of other units that was first formed as a consequence of the end of Empire, and then made even more necessary by the steady reductions in the number of soldiery after the end of the Cold War, had subsumed into its immensity a relic of what was once called the Royal East Kent Regiment—a unit that was once rather better known simply as the Buffs. And this regiment had listed among its battle honours (though not in bold type, for in truth it was no great victory) *"Pekin, 1860."* The Buffs and their sepoys had, under the command of Lord Elgin, taken part in the sacking of the Chinese emperor's Summer Palace—an adventure in which *The Times* correspondent, Bowlby, had been captured, and died (a point which, the letter writer felt certain, would see his missive into print). To send as its final military gesture to Hong Kong a unit that had been intimately involved in the destruction of old Peking was, if nothing else, cheeky. If, that is, it had been deliberate.

Furthermore, Brigadier Tomsett was a Royal Scot—and back in the days when the Scots were dignified by the title of First of Foot, the Scotsmen too had been making war on Peking. A Brigadier and a battalion—it was too much of a coincidence, *The Times* letter writer had suggested.

This was no time to ponder on such an amusing twist. Once the sergeant had, unsmiling, scrutinised all the passes and saluted those whom he now was certain were his superiors, there was a short wait while unseen hydraulic jacks pushed down the anti-terrorist blocks, after which the car drove through the great white gates and around the lawn. Richard Adaire was waiting, grim-faced. The general nodded for him to lead the way, and the three soldiers went in to the study.

"Gentlemen," began Sir John, once everyone was seated. "I am afraid what we have here"—and he tapped the paper on his desk—"looks very much like the beginning of the end. I don't mean to sound dramatic, but I'm angry. And frankly, I'm afraid of the implications of this. Not just for Hong Kong but for China herself. And not even just for China. I fear, quite candidly, for the whole region. The implications of a decision like this are very grave indeed. As I assume you all agree?"

The soldiers nodded. The men were briefly silent. Outside the sound of shouts and cries and breaking glass had died—dawn, after all, was less than an hour away. But the weather radar at Tamar had shown thick clouds boiling up from the east, and this night would be peculiarly long, and dark. A sudden crump of thunder sounded in the distance: the beginnings of the storm that threatened to spoil the ceremonial which would mark the beginnings of true Chinese rule over this tiny territory. The Governor looked up at the sound, as did the General. They grinned at one another, but sardonically.

QUEEN'S ROAD EAST, HAPPY VALLEY, HONG KONG

BEFORE DAWN

During the night some thirty-six men were assigned to be visibly guarding the red marble entrance to the New China News Agency on Queen's Road East. This had been the People's Republic's centre of operations in Hong Kong—its embassy, if you will—since the early Eighties, and it was to be guarded rigorously from any threat to which the Hong Kong government might unwittingly play host. Its head was an Ambassador, in both rank and regard: if the officers had ever housed a true News Agency, then it and its editors and writers had long gone to more down-at-heel quarters far away.

On this particular night the guards were especially vigilant. A small detachment of British infantrymen formed the outer ring—there had been bamboo knife-rest barricades set up on Queen's Road itself, and others with razor-wire trimmings established on the approaches from Wanchai and the Aberdeen Tunnel. Large blue signs propped up by sandbags ordered night-time motorists to extinguish their headlights and submit to searches and ID checks. A short line of cars waited: drivers were warned that they could spend some minutes waiting too, while a young infantryman from the London suburbs tried to work his way around the linguistic complexities involved in persuading a Cantonese driver to offer some proof of who he was and why he was abroad at this hour.

Beyond the lines of soldiers, and assigned specifically to the task of checking on any pedestrians who might be making for the eleven-storey building, was a detachment of ten men from the Hong Kong Supplementary Force. There were 3,000 such individuals now assigned to duties around the territory. They had been recruited in Britain in 1995 after the manning levels in the Royal Hong Kong Police had fallen to what was considered a dangerous low. According to the Kirby Inquiry's Report on the 1995 riots, those recruited for the HKSF "are not men who had derived overmuch benefit from their training, if indeed they undertook it at all," and, moreover, "were drawn generally from that seemingly bottomless pool of security employees who had, for one reason or another, failed to qualify for entry into any United Kingdom police force." One newspaper, seeing them in action at a political rally a year before had called them "louts," and compared them unfavourably to the "B" Specials, Protestant bully-boys who had once been attached to the Royal Ulster Constabulary, called out to whack Catholic heads in times of trouble in and around Belfast.

The men of the HKSF, known generally as "Suppers" and kitted out in dark blue serge tunics and battledress trousers, lounged against the Agency's walls. Each held a long truncheon and carried a gas-gun in a holster; from each belt dangled a tear-gas mask and every man wore a dark blue helmet, the visor down. On this occasion they were not carrying side-arms: these would only be drawn from the armouries at moments of extreme emergency. But both individually and collectively the men of the HKSF looked tough, and full of menace.

Behind them, standing actually at the Agency's iron-bound gate, were four regular police officers—their jungle-green uniforms crisp, their silver badges of rank glittering in the street lamps, their radios chattering and squawking with the noise of distant messaging. All were Chinese: the last Britons to take junior operational posts within the RHKP had been eased out the year before. Pressure from Peking, it was said. Senior officers were permitted to remain until retirement, though the Commissioner had by agreement been a post reserved for a Chinese since 1988. The only remaining Britons in senior posts were the Regional Commanders in Hong Kong Island and the New Territories, five of the District Commanders and eleven Divisional Commanders. There were no junior British officers other than in administration and training.

The men's uniforms had been changed at China's request too. The dark blue winter wear and the pale desert khaki of the summer strip had given way to a uniform that was chromatically consonant with that worn by the men of the People's Armed Police across the border, though the men of Hong Kong were distinguished by the immeasurably better cut of their tunics, by their possession of radios and badges of rank, and by their caps, on which the old dragon-and-pearl icon of Hong Kong had been allowed to remain. The prefix "Royal" had been officially dropped six months before: it would cease to be used in all official communications from midnight on the final day of June. The fact that the word was still in common unofficial usage stemmed partly from custom, partly from defiance.

At this time of night—it was shortly before five, and a faint stain of morning could be seen on the clouds looming over Mount Collinson—neither the police, nor the Suppers, nor the infantry had a great deal of work to do. Earlier, things had been quite active. The remains of a stolen sixteen-seat minibus still smouldered on its side in the roadway, the rubber of its tyres reduced to smoking white powder. Shards of glass and broken masonry littering the road were being kicked aimlessly into the gutters by soldiers. There were also dozens of empty gas cartridges, lying as testimony to the volleys that were fired some six hours before, when a mob had roared up from Wanchai, well on in drink, its members—all Cantonese, and probably part of the local Triad gangs—eager to get their hands on any of the

Chinese mainland officials who had long since retreated behind the marble bastions of Agency protection.

At five-thirty, a careful observer would have noticed, there came a sudden increase in the volume and frequency of radio transmissions to and from the four police officers. Almost simultaneously the lieutenant in charge of the army platoon ordered the opening of one of the barricades; and within moments of that having been accomplished the iron blast doors at the front of the Agency were unhasped and opened wide. Then, over the brow of the low hill by the Ruttonjee Sanatorium, came a stream of police motorcycles and Land-Rovers, their blue lights flashing, their sirens uncannily silent. Four motorcycles, headlights blazing; then three, four, five white police cars—and then a lone black Mercedes, with darkened windows, flying two flags of the People's Republic from its front bumpers. Further police cars brought up the rear.

The convoy sped down the hill, through the chicanes. The army lieutenant turned towards the cars, and saluted. Beside the Agency the police vehicles braked to a sudden stop, fanning out to afford still further protection while the Mercedes itself eased to a stop beside the gates. For a few seconds there was total silence, and nothing moved—not a man, not a car, not a light, not a door.

But then, like a snake flicking its tongue from above its fangs, a small Chinese man darted suddenly from inside the Agency and opened the rear door of the car. The Hong Kong Police moved forwards, perhaps to protect the recording of this scene from any inquisitive telephoto lens. All that could be glimpsed was the momentary passing from car to building of the type of blue cloth cap commonly worn by Chinese senior cadres and, for an instant, the grey-haired head of an elderly man. And then the car's door was slammed, and the car and escort vehicles started for base. The twin iron gates of the Agency were clanged shut, and one could hear bolts being rammed home, and keys twisted in the locks. The policemen stepped away, the Suppers commenced their lounging once again, and the men of the

2nd Battalion, The Queen's Regiment, shifted the barricades back into position.

A number of lights were snapped on in adjoining rooms on the building's eighth floor—a floor invariably reserved, according to Security Branch Intelligence, for the truly senior of their visitors. The events in Queen's Road East on that hot Saturday morning had seen the arrival, unnoticed by almost all, of the man who had just become known to the Foreign Office as the next Chief Executive of Hong Kong. Mr. Mao had come down from Peking to take up his post a few days early. Now he was installed, and not a soul knew of it.

THE MINISTRY OF FOREIGN AFFAIRS, PEKING

MID-MORNING

Madame Zhang was a little late, her assistant said, and would Mr. James like to wait in her office? The Reuters man, who had long since had his breakfast, agreed to tea, and watched idly as the assistant unplugged the soft old cork from the vacuum flask and sloshed near-boiling water on to a layer of black leaves in a cracked mug. The leaves rose, forming an island of vegetation, through which the tea now had to be drunk. Strange, he mused, that the inventors of the drink can never make it properly. He waved away a cigarette from the cylindrical tin of fifty.

He was not entirely sure why he had been summoned. Zhang Xiaodi was the senior spokesman for Sino-European Bilateral Matters at the Foreign Ministry, had held her post for the past three years, and was popular with the five other Europeans—excluding the *Tass*, *Pravda* and *Izvestia* correspondents, who had their own briefing officer—who remained to work as journalists in Peking. (The clamp-down on the foreign press in 1993 had drastically reduced the number of Western news representatives resident in Peking, from more than ninety to less than twenty. The number of academics and students at Chinese universities and institutes had been similarly slashed, all in the name of limiting foreign influences on Chinese attitudes.)

Since Madame Zhang's given name *Xiao* meant "little" and *Di* "flower," they called her Daisy, and the man from Agence France Presse was reputed to have briefly enjoyed a near-liaison with her. Shortly after this it was made known that she had been divorced from a chemical engineer who, those who had met him at Great Hall cocktail parties reported, smelled strongly of green onions, and rarely shaved. She was still, however, known as Madame, and was generally thought of as untouchable.

But as to why her office had called to summon him, and him alone, Richard James did not know. He had to assume it had something to do with Hong Kong which, after all, was only three days away from repossession. The BBC had reported a fairly rough night, and the Reuters wire spoke of three deaths in a shooting incident at Tuen Mun. But there had been no suggestion of behaviour by the British, at least, that warranted criticism. So why this meeting? An appointment to be made? Not that of the Chief Executive, though: there had been a well-reported leak just the week before that it was likely to be David Lam, the Chairman of the Bank of North Asia, and matters had briefly stabilised once the reports had gained wide enough currency. Lam, a rather colourless man who sat on the boards of a dozen of the colony's *hongs*,* and who belonged to all the right clubs and had all the proper connections, was the ideal choice. There could be no question of the Chinese attempting to veto that.

While Richard James, two years as the Reuters news agency man in China, and with just another one in Peking to go, pondered on all these matters, staring out on to the shadowless greys of the street beyond, the door opened quietly and Madame Zhang and one other man, in uniform, filtered in. He heard her, fortunately, and stood: he was startled to see that she was dressed in deep grey, and that

*The big trading companies such as Swires, Jardines, Hutchison, Inchcape, etc. Not to be confused with the "Hong" of Hong Kong which means fragrant (Kong means harbour).

she looked almost frumpish, and was not smiling. He decided not to refer to her as Daisy. She bade him sit down and followed suit. The uniformed man, who looked like a People's Liberation Army officer, did not.

"I hope they have given you tea. We are sorry to ask you to come here so early this morning. I shall now explain. This is an official meeting, but one the occurrence of which you will not report, Mr. James." She paused, and looked at him. He nodded.

"I have a brief statement to make to you, and I will then offer you some background guidance. You will not take notes. I will have no further explanation. There will be no questions. It is to be firmly understood that you will not report the sources of the following remarks, and that you will make no report of the contents of the remarks until thirteen hours, local time, today. I have to ask you if you understand these rules?" She looked up again.

"I accept them, Madame Zhang," Richard James replied, embarrassed and puzzled by the formality.

"Are you using a tape recorder?" she asked, suddenly.

"No," he said. But he took a small Sony from his pocket—it was switched off—and laid it on the table. The uniformed figure stepped out from the shadows and picked it up. "It will be returned later," the man said, stepping back into a dark corner of the room.

Madame Zhang cleared her throat, spitting into a brass pot beside the sofa. She put on a pair of dark-rimmed spectacles.

"This, then, is the text of the Statement. 'The Hong Kong and Macau Affairs Office of the State Council of the People's Republic of China is pleased to announce the appointment of State Councillor Mao Ren-chin to the post of Chief Executive of the Special Administrative Region of Xianggang—Hong Kong—with effect from 1 July 1997. Mr. Mao, who is seventy-four, presently advises the Council on legal and constitutional matters. He is a Hero of the Revolution, and has a distinguished career spanning many decades. The Foreign Ministry joins with the Hong Kong and Macau Affairs Office in offering Mr. Mao its salutations for this most auspicious post, in which he will be aided nobly by all compatriots in the new SAR.' That is the end of the Statement.

"I now have a few words of guidance to add." Madame Zhang spoke shakily. Richard thought she sounded nervous, almost frightened.

"It may come as a surprise for you to learn of Mr. Mao's appointment." Richard James nodded his assent, vigorously. "I believe our Hong Kong compatriots had been expecting that Lin Zhou-ming* would be appointed. But after considerable thought it has been decided that it would be more appropriate to appoint a man who is distinguished throughout China, rather than a man who, however notable his achievements, is known principally for his work in and around your colony—or rather your former colony, as it will soon be. There are other considerations too. But it was felt that in the interests of a fuller dialogue between Beijing and the newly re-acquired Region, the appointee should have a direct line, if you will, to the State Council in the capital, as well as a presence in the Region itself. The custom for the last two decades has been to appoint a representative with strong Beijing connections to the Xinhua—the News Agency—office. It has also been the custom to select senior representatives holding similar qualifications to act as provincial governors. The Government of the People's Republic is thus maintaining a tradition of governance of many years, and is extending it to cover the special situation in our newly regained region of Xianggang."

Madame Zhang took off her spectacles and looked across at the correspondent. "That is by way of background. I will have nothing further to say on this matter." She rose.

Richard said: "There are a number of questions," but Madame Zhang waved him down.

"That is all I can say—really," she replied, looking

---

*The Chinese character which in the Cantonese dialect is pronounced *Lam* sounds like *Lin* when spoken in Madame Zhang's tongue, *putonghua*. Lin Zhou-ming is the same person as David Lam.

across at the soldier, who was readying himself to escort her from the room. "You must understand. These are sensitive times."

The soldier handed Richard his tape recorder, then stood at Madame Zhang's side and led her quickly out into the corridor. By the time Richard reached the door the passage was dark and empty, except for a cleaner who was aimlessly buffing the floor with a five-foot mop. Mustering his primitive Chinese he asked the woman if she had seen a soldier and a female cadre pass by a few seconds before, but the woman grunted and kept her face to the ground, pushing the dirt back and forth, grinding it still further into the cement.

JIANGUOMENWAI, PEKING

BEFORE NOON

Ten minutes later the correspondent was in the Embassy. He had asked the Press Secretary for an urgent and immediate meeting with Sir Peter MacDuff, the ambassador, and was not surprised to be shown upstairs and into the private office without delay. He related to the two men, and the Military Attaché, whom Sir Peter had invited, the gist of what he knew. He asked for some further information, some guidance.

There was a long and pregnant silence. The ambassador looked at his watch. It was fifteen minutes before noon, China summer time. He looked at the carpet, then at his Press Secretary, then at Richard. He cleared his throat.

"I cannot, of course, expect you to tell me how you heard this information?" he asked. Richard shook his head.

"Of course. I will draw my own conclusions. I will assume for the purpose of what I now have to say that it came as a secret briefing from an official of the Foreign Ministry. I don't expect you to confirm or deny this. But we are all well aware that some departments in the Ministry take a view somewhat at variance with the official one. I will expand on this in a moment or two.

"What I have to say first—indeed, everything I will say to you now—is completely and utterly off the record. Is that understood? I mean, seriously understood?"

Richard nodded, adding, for posterity and formality, "Yes, of course, Sir Peter."

"Right. I'm going to have to speak to London about this—though it looks as if I'll not get any sort of sensible answer before you file your piece. And on this point I've got to be candid with you—I'd be very much obliged if you'd delay filing this for another couple of hours. Perhaps you'd tell me whether you're able to at the end of what I have to say. I know I'm in no position to ask. But there are considerations—lives at stake, basically. A delay would be helpful.

"But whatever. This appointment is something we've known of for about three days. That an appointment might be made along these general lines is something we have known for almost a year, and which we have lobbied hard to reverse. In vain, seemingly. I am not permitted to tell you exactly how we heard first. If I say that we are well connected in Washington, and that the new President, Mr. Benson, has trenchant views on the situation in this corner of the world, you might understand. If in addition I say Cheltenham, and if I remind you that we have a station in Hong Kong at Chung Hom Kok, then perhaps you can draw your own conclusions. But anyway—we heard, and we confronted the Chinese Ambassador in London with what we knew.

"You can imagine what we said. Direct contravention of the letter and the spirit of the 1984 Declaration, the 1991 Agreement, and the 1993 Letter. A move likely to cause serious social disorder. A move which, if known about before the handover, when getting out might be possible, would cause panic. And all kinds of other implications. We told Ambassador Li how we felt about it, in no uncertain terms.

"We were given a formal reply about ten hours ago. This confirmed what GCHQ and the Americans had said. It also went on to say that in view of the probability of social disorder in the territory if the announcement was made before the moment of handover, no announcement would be made until the moment of the change of sovereignty itself, on Monday night.

"Her Majesty's Government then took certain prudent and precautionary measures, including one that I will only tell you as background and which you must absolutely not report." He looked pointedly at Richard.

The Reuters man winced. "I think you know the rules, sir. If you tell me, I must report it. All I can do is accept what you say as unattributable. That's how it is, I'm afraid."

"Well, in that case I can't tell you what the precaution might be; you will have to speculate. I suppose it is more a matter for the history books, anyway.

"I was formally informed of these decisions about seven hours ago. So was Sir John Courtenay. So was General Harbinson. So were our embassies in Washington and at the UN.

"Frankly, I had expected the Chinese side to stick by their agreement not to make any announcement. But now they appear, by their briefing of you, to have broken that agreement. They have, of course, sought to distance themselves from the briefing by winning your assurance of confidentiality and have informed you as a representative of Reuters. I will have to inform the government, and steps will have to be taken. If you report this now, it will have the most severe consequences for the people of Hong Kong. That is all I can say on that matter."

Richard looked pained. "Once again, sir, I know you know the rules. Of course I will have to report what I've been told, and on time. That's my job. Of course I know it is yours to try to persuade me otherwise. But we have different tasks here. You have to deal with trouble. I just have to report it. And anyway—you get a knighthood and a fancy house for that sort of thing." He got on well enough with Sir Peter to be able to say so, though on this occasion, with the ambassador in what seemed the grimmest of tempers, he thought he might be sailing close to the winds. The Press Secretary, a rather weak-chinned man named Treadwell, stepped forward in protest. Sir Peter waved him back.

"You're right, to an extent. But I want you to consider one other matter—something the Sinologists will make much of in the next few days. And that is what I was talking about at the start of this lecture—*just why did they choose to announce it*?

"It is difficult for me to guess, since you won't tell me who told you. But let me suppose, as I did at the start, that it came from a branch of the Foreign Ministry. Let me suppose that this particular branch is in some way closely connected with the army. There might have been some army involvement in your briefing—yes?"

Richard said nothing, and tried to look as impassive as a poker player with a single pair and a great deal in the pot.

"Be that as it may. One has to begin with the single presumption that there is going to be one hell of a lot of trouble in Hong Kong as a result of this move. The Cantonese will be furious, blindly furious, at being let down this way. By tonight there'll be riots the like of which you've never seen before. I expect that within half an hour of your bulletin going out on the radio, there'll be a dozen people dead.

"Now who will those people be? If the announcement was kept until next Tuesday, then the whole thing is a matter for the Chinese alone. *They'll* have to clean up. If anyone tries to play the heavy-handed law enforcement card, it's the Chinese.

"But now, with the statement coming out on Saturday, who'll be there to take the brunt of it all? Right—*we will be*. Who have we got down there—a battalion of infantry, some Gurkhas, some reservists, the Suppers, the police? They'll be in the middle. They'll be firing the gas grenades. They'll be smashing in a few heads. And if the mob gets angry at anyone—who'll they be getting angry at? Why—*us*, of course. And that'll give the Chinese a bit of breathing space. Not much, mind you. But for a moment or two, a day or so, the British colonialists will be the villains—appointing a northern Chinese to run Hong Kong! They're just asking for trouble.

"And when I say trouble, I mean real trouble. I mean civil war type trouble. This is really big stuff. You know how angry the Cantonese are, how vicious they can get. Well, this kind of a decision is going to whip them up—and not just in Canton. They'll be angry in Canton and Xiamen and Guilin and Macau and Kunming. Everywhere in the south, they'll be angry and anti-north. It really has the makings of major trouble.

"So someone, some branch within the Foreign Ministry is wanting to head it off. Someone—I'm still assuming you were told about this by the Ministry, and probably by that little girl, Daisy Zhang or whatever you call her—someone wants the British to be blamed, not the Chinese. Someone, in other words, realises what's going to happen. Someone, in other words, is a pragmatist.

"And if there's war, it is going to be pragmatists against the dogmatists. So you can see the splits developing. Right under their very noses. Right here in a senior ministry. And you can bet they leaked it to you to show you that there was a split. After all they could have simply put out a statement over Xinhua. No need for anyone to be personally involved doing it that way. So ask yourself for a moment why they didn't.

"I only wish you'd tell me if there was a soldier present. I wish you'd give me some idea of which one, so I can get some idea of where the army stands on this? Not that it would tell me much. It'd just be a hint."

But Richard remained mute. He looked at his watch. It was just after noon. He had to leave, and he had to file.

And so Sir Peter showed him out, promising him there'd be no hard feelings about the meeting. "Only just think how well you'd have been treated if I were Chinese. But here I am showing you out—nearly even offered you a glass of sherry. If I were a Chinese official asking one of your Xinhua colleagues for information, and he refused, it'd be round the back with a bullet in the neck, don't you think?"

Back in the empty office Richard James wrote his story. He switched on his computer terminal, punched in his access code, and typed a crisp and effortless 300 words, as he had done countless times before in a career that had already covered eight countries. He slugged it for the urgent attention of the Foreign Duty Editor in London:

PROMELUNSKY FOREIGN
EXJAMESPEKING 280350z note embargo 280400z strict
FLASH FIRST PARA
In a surprise move the Chinese government today appointed the Long March veteran Mao Ren-chin to be the first Chief Executive of Hong Kong, which passes into mainland control on Monday night.
ENDFLASH PARA RESUME
Mr. Mao's appointment, made known through highly placed sources in the Chinese capital, is expected to provoke a serious adverse reaction in Hong Kong. The British government, which has known about the appointment for the past three days, is said to be taking "prudent and precautionary steps" to limit any consequential disturbances in the colony. There have been serious anti-British and anti-Communist demonstrations and riots in the past week.

Mr. Mao, who is seventy-four, comes from Dalian city, in southern Manchuria. A State Councillor and adviser to the Chinese leadership on legal and constitutional affairs, he is reputed to have assumed a strong stance against students involved in the various anti-corruption and pro-liberty movements in China in the last ten years. He is known to have been personally behind the public execution of the so-called "Shanghai Six" after the Shanghai University disturbances of 1995. (++NB TO PIX EDITOR: MAO SEEN IN FRONT ROW OF EXECUTION AUDIENCE ON 13 AUGUST 95 REUTERS STAFF PICTURES AVAILABLE++)

Hong Kong had expected the popular 53-year-old North Asia Bank chief David Lam to be appointed as first Chief Executive. Mr. Lam is not only well liked and respected in Hong Kong, but has the ear of the Chinese ruling élite. He is Cantonese—which Mr. Mao is not. The 1984 Joint Declaration signed by the British and Chinese leaders spoke of the need to appoint the territory's Chief Executive "from within the local community," and, until today, it had been assumed that the Peking government would stick to this undertaking. The British government is expected to make its feeling known to the Chinese ambassador in London later today.+++

SVCMELUNSKY +++Analysis piece follows in fifteen minutes. Above should do for the flash+++

RGDS JAMES PEKING

Richard looked over the piece, tinkered with it briefly, then set his machine into XMIT mode. He looked at the clock. It was ten minutes to one. Outside the sky was leaden. The streets were empty, except for a few cyclists and the occasional passing bus. Four members of the People's Armed Police, assigned to guard the entrance to the compound, stood at attention by the gate. The clock's second hand swept up to mark nine minutes before one, China summer time—nine minutes before four in the morning, Greenwich Mean Time, nine minutes before noon, Hong Kong. Richard pressed the green transmit message key.

A box flashed onto the screen, with a dial indicating how long it took the story to be sent, and to arrive, checked for transmission errors, on Jacob Melunsky's desk. Four seconds, the dial said.

And nine minutes after that the message was dispatched around the world. Down in the Hong Kong Reuters office, over in the London offices of a dozen newspapers, across in New York, and down in Sydney, the same clangour of ten bells would announce the arrival of a major story. It arrived back in Peking, too, with barely a word changed:

FLASH FLASH FLASH+++0400gmt 28 June
Mao Named First Chinese Hong Kong Governor

By Richard James, Peking, Saturday 28 June
In a surprise move the Chinese government today . . .

Richard James sat back in his chair and lit a cigarette. He inhaled one long, deep breath. And now, he said to himself, all hell breaks out.

QUEEN'S ROAD, HONG KONG

MID-AFTERNOON

Twenty of the protected two-ton Bedford trucks, dark blue, with their steel grilles clicked down over all the windows, had been deployed in the rain down every side-street by two o'clock, after urgent orders had been transmitted from Police Headquarters in North Wanchai. Four hundred constables from the regular police and 200 additional Suppers, issued with side arms and, in a few cases, with automatic rifles, were at the ready. Two police helicopters, flying high, were overhead. The windows of the New China News Agency were shuttered, and the doors were firmly closed.

The Reuters dispatch had been broadcast first by the Chinese-language pirate commercial station, the Catholic-Church-backed Radio Freedom, *Chi Yao Ding Toi*, at three minutes past twelve. By half past the hour—by which time even the government-controlled radio and TV stations were (somewhat reluctantly, it was later said) issuing statements about Mao's appointment—small crowds were out on the streets. The Xinhua office in Sha Tin, which was not well guarded, had been briefly attacked by a pair of young men wielding crowbars and choppers. The doors of the offices of the Ever Light Company in Yuen Long, a trading concern with long-established connections across the frontier, were spattered with black paint. The police and army were fully expecting trouble directed at any mainland Chinese institution—the New China News Agency being a natural prime target—and they believed themselves to be well prepared.

The speed and efficiency of the organisation of the subsequent vocal and violent opposition to Mao's appointment led to the assumption by police intelligence—a correct assumption, as it later turned out—that it was principally the work of Hong Kong's major Triad gangs, acting in concert.

Before relating the particular effects of the Triad-led disturbances in the territory during the closing days of British rule, it is perhaps appropriate to offer some brief background information.

For the previous two years, ever since the signing of the so-called Warwick Accord in April 1995 between the Sun Yee On and the 14K gangs after their meeting at the Warwick Hotel on Cheung Chau Island, the Triads had emerged as a powerful political force—the only powerful political force, in fact—in the territory. The various democratic organisations that had been founded with such optimism in the early part of the decade had all foundered, their early antipathy to China becoming ever more muted, their popular support in consequence becoming ever more limited. The only groups who were consistently regarded by the ordinary working-class Hong Kong Chinese as having both the muscle and the willpower to stand up for the entrepreneurial "rights" of the Hong Kong public, and to be standing firmly against the sombre tenets of Marx and Mao were, as it happened, utterly illegal: this network of rigidly organised and historically romanticised gangs of criminals, loan sharks, drug-peddlers and racketeers, who had been a running sore on the face of most Chinese communities around the world for many decades, but who had only achieved a degree of cohesion, and the consequent political muscle, here in Hong Kong.

Although for the previous half century all of the Triad societies in Hong Kong had directed their individual energies towards crime (while at the same time enjoying the same kind of cosy, seemingly respectable relationship with slum society as was projected by the Sicilian Mafia) their leadership had reason to remember that their roots had little to do with thievery and pimping. The very name, Triad, is a semantic contraction of the organisation's original title,

The Heaven and Earth League—in Chinese an ideographic trinity forged of the characters for words pronounced in Cantonese as *San*, *Ho* and *Hui* and standing for heaven, earth and man. And the original purpose of the group thus gilded was—two centuries ago—the extirpation of the hated Manchus, the barbarous foreigners who had ruled China since 1644.

Such a grouping had, of necessity, to be utterly secret; the numerous clones met in covens: their members were the subject of witchhunts and victims of terrible revenge. The political ambitions of the League within China were not to be realised until the revolution of 1912; and those of its brother organisations continued long after. The 14K, which was to flourish quite openly (though illegally) in Hong Kong until the end of British rule, had been established in Canton City as a nakedly political operation, aimed at consolidating popular support behind the Kuomintang of Chiang Kai-shek, and against the growing power of Mao Tse-tung. It was only when the members of 14K realised they had failed in this particular aim (Chiang having being forced by the overwhelming military superiority of Mao to run to Taiwan and establish his nationalist government there) that the gang moved down from Canton to Hong Kong and, preserving their secrecy, their rituals and their symbols, started on the more infamously predatory side of their career.

A survey early in 1996 showed there were some forty-three Triad societies at work in Hong Kong. This was well down from the fifty-four whose existence was acknowledged by a police study in 1991—an indication, the police then concluded erroneously, that they were "winning the war" against what they considered to be the most nefarious of organisations. But rather than "winning" any war, the police—who years before had managed not only to infiltrate the Triads, but who had then actually been a singularly corrupt extension of them—were becoming progressively less and less competent to understand them, or even to find them. Police informers within the gangs were brutally dealt with: one such young man who was found dead in an alley

in Sham Shui Po in the late summer of 1995, after the signing of the Accord, had been skinned and scalped. A deafening silence thereafter protected the organisations from the
police. The Accord, which involved the signing of blood
oaths by some thirty-eight of the major groups, similarly
protected most of the gangs (for they had been, of course,
arch-rivals) from each other.

The hierarchy within any of the major Triads—the Sun
Yee On, the Wo Sing Wo, the Won On Lok, the Big Circle
Boys, the 14K, the Four Seas, the Bamboo Union—is invariably the same. The leading members are given titles
that are both evocative and, hinting to many foreigners at
the strangeness of Chinese society, numerical. The clan
chief is known as the Dragon Head or, in this more familiar
terminology of the streets, the 489. Beneath him is the Second Marshal, the 438. Below him in status, the Red Pole,
Number 426—the man to whom is allotted the disagreeable
tasks of skinning and scalping and meting out other punishments for members' acts of malfeasance, treachery, or
worse. And then the White Paper Fan, 419, and the Straw
Sandal, 432 (who is a less than amiable individual usually
involved in protection rackets). Finally come the legions of
junior members known as the 49 Boys who are recruited
direct from school, and who are on probation awaiting their
ritual tattooing, their granting of passwords and all the rest
of the paraphernalia that goes with the *lam dang long*, the
so-called *hanging of the blue lantern*, the youngsters'
formal initiation into the tribe.

The numbers of Triad members grew almost exponen-
tially following the signing of the Warwick Accord. Under
this agreement all of the individual "regiments" in the Triad
pantheon would remain, recruiting where they were best
known, carrying out their own internal disciplinary functions, indulging in the relatively small-scale activities that
kept their income streams flowing healthily. The individual
regiments would, however, cease all competition between
one another, and borders for the individual gangs' territories
were rigidly set by the rulings of an official Boundary
Commission. (The head of this Commission, a 426 in the

Sun Yee On named Mr. Law, had previously worked as an Assistant Registration Officer in the Constitutional and Electoral Affairs Division of the Government Secretariat, and thus had some experience in these matters. Police intelligence concluded that he did not give any obvious favours to his own gang, which in any case had innumerable territorial claims in most of the major urban areas and housing estates.)

In addition to these arrangements for internal regimental management, the Accord resulted in the promotion of a senior hierarchy of members who would coordinate the political activities of all of the membership. This new leadership, well aware of the fate that would befall identified members once the mainland Chinese had established their rule, remained shadowy indeed. Few names have ever been credibly reported. British intelligence was in this respect somewhat more accurate and reliable than that provided by the Hong Kong Police Special Branch, who were caught wrong-footed on many of the Triad developments after the signing of the Accord. The one name that emerged was that of one Peter Heung Way Yeung, who had as his cover job that of solicitor's clerk in a firm of Kowloon tax lawyers. Mr. Heung is thought to have been appointed the "Super 489," with overall political authority over the Hong Kong Triad membership, with some limited authority to define policy and, in an emergency, to order the deployment of regiment members.

By the beginning of 1997 it was thought that 245,000 men and boys aged sixteen and over had been recruited into the forty-three known Triad gangs. The 14K was still the most prominent, with an estimated membership of 47,000, and an annual income in excess of $1.8 billion. The total amount of money taken in by the various illegal organisations in 1996, the last year for which reliable figures are known, was $4.7 billion.

One further factor needs to be explained. In the immediate aftermath of the signing of the Warwick Accord Mr. Heung and a number of his most politically adroit lieutenants sought a meeting in Shenzhen City, immediately across the border fence, with senior officials in the Guangdong Provincial Administration. In particular they had asked for an interview with W. Y. Yip, the Administration's political officer, to see if some measure of co-operation might be achieved once the British authorities had vacated the territory of Hong Kong. It was assumed that the enthusiasm for corruption found among middle levels of the Chinese bureaucracy would enable such an alliance—informal or otherwise—to be founded. But in the event Mr. Heung's group was rebuffed. No meeting ever took place, and radio intercepts and wiretaps on both sides of the border suggest that any desire for union or association remained moribund. Observers in Hong Kong and London have long regarded this as puzzling; although one possibility, that the Cantonese-speaking officials who were approached by the Heung team were fearful of having their complicity discovered by those Peking-based cadres who were assigned to the Guangdong Administrative Service, was thought to provide a reasonable explanation.

It is against this complicated background that the involvement of the Triads in the final days of Hong Kong's British administration needs to be regarded.

News of the appointment of Mao was first given to Peter Heung at 1215, at his headquarters on the penthouse floor of a new commercial building at 230 Shanghai Street, Kowloon. A number of his 49 Boys had heard the broadcast on the Catholic station, and had relayed it back through their various Straw Sandals. Heung, knowing the extent of the wiretaps on his phones and radio intercepts on his mobile phones, sent alarm messages, in a specially developed code, to his deputies by fax. The first messages were sent at 1255, and were dispatched to gang deputies in Aberdeen, Shek O, Wanchai, Kennedy Town, Western, Causeway Bay and to that very small group in Repulse Bay on the South Side of Hong Kong Island.

This signal, which was duly intercepted by Special Branch engineers working at the facsimile switching centre in Causeway Bay, said simply, and in Chinese characters, DRAGON MOUTH EIGHT. There was no great difficulty to the decoding: the phrase DRAGON MOUTH clearly signified the headquarters of the New China News Agency; and EIGHT was, in line with the Thai linguistic conceit of adding six to everything, an indication that something would happen there either at two, or in two hours.

The Branch Senior Duty Analyst concluded that, given the logistical difficulty that various Second Marshals might have of rounding up significant numbers of members in just sixty-five minutes, the number related to two hours. A signal marked Most Immediate was thus sent to the Police Operations Room, the HQ Police Tactical Unit (Fan Ling), the HQ Supplementary Force (Hong Kong Island) and to the Royal Hong Kong Regiment's barracks at Happy Valley, where a number of regular soldiers from 3 Queen's were billeted, advising them of the probability of a confrontation near the New China News Agency on Queen's Road East at 3 P.M. Commanders were then advised by secure telephone that there could well be serious violence, and that all available defensive means should be taken to minimise it.

A subsequent directive to the Commander British Forces and the Police Commissioner, marked "For Your Eyes Only" and sent from the Political Adviser's Office at Government House, timed at 1330 local, underlined the need for the police, the supplementary force members and all army units, both local Volunteers and the British garrison, to maintain discipline and to exercise restraint.

"There is the possibility," the directive concluded, "that this news has been deliberately leaked in Peking by factions, presently unknown to us, who would not react unfavourably to the British and colonial disciplined services becoming intimately involved in last-minute disturbances. It is our desire to keep our involvement in any civil disorder problems to a minimum.

"However, in view of the potential new dangers to life and property, and in view of the possible instability and questionable loyalty of the RHKP in dealing with this particular problem, and in view of possible discipline problems within the HKSF, two army battalions equipped for civil order work, 1KOSB and 2 Para, which are presently standing by at the airfield at Bandar Seri Begawan, Brunei, can be made available to you at short notice. It is our hope that deployment of additional forces will not prove necessary. It cannot, however, be impressed upon unit commanders too firmly that the necessity to protect key personnel and buildings in these final few hours of British Administration remains paramount."

Helicopters, flying low because of heavy clouds and mist, reported the first significant gatherings of crowds near the Aberdeen Tunnel and in Central District, and then of a very large crowd—of as many as 3,000 people—massing on Hennessey Road, Wanchai, and still growing. Police spotters on the roofs of nearby buildings said most were young men, often with red bands tied around their foreheads. Many pushed or pulled small handcarts on which were piled bottles—probably Molotov cocktails—and fragments of paving stone. The carts, of a type well known for their use in making local deliveries, appeared to have been stored, awaiting such a moment. A few banners were in evidence, all of them outspokenly condemning the mainland Chinese. These, too, appeared to have been prepared beforehand: none specified the appointment of Mao as central to the popular disquiet. The organisation of the coming riot—for there could be no doubt that the confrontation would result in rioting—was clearly most sophisticated.

The police and Supplementary Force units took up their positions around the NCNA building. Three companies of soldiers were held in reserve, waiting for the Governor's permission before they could be called in formally to assist the civil power in the suppression of a riot. On many occasions in the past two years such sanction had been given: there seemed little likelihood it would be withheld today, and so the company commanders had already broken out the tear gas and the live ammunition, and the soldiers were waiting fully equipped to do battle.

Advance picquets of police across the approach roads

confronted the crowds of demonstrators as they came within a quarter mile of their target. Officers with megaphones formally warned them, in English and Cantonese, that they were breaking the law, specifically the Public Order Act, and that they should cease their illegal assembly and disperse quietly. The warnings had little effect. By 3 P.M. a crowd of men estimated to number 6,000 had converged on the scene: 4,000 had come up Morrison Hill Road from Wanchai, 800 had spilled out from the tunnel entrance and were descending the flyover exit ramps, and a further 1,000 were streaming down Stubbs Road and along Queen's Road.

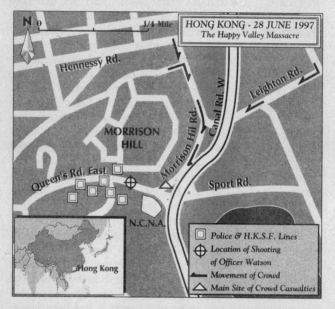

The police and Supplementary Force units, numbering no more than 600 armed men, had to face in three directions an angry crowd that outnumbered them by ten to one. The Hong Kong Island Regional Commander, George Clovis, a man widely known for his trenchant views and his bushy moustaches, was to say later that it would be difficult to heed the Political Adviser's warning about the need to keep use of force to a minimum.

"This was a huge Triad-organised mob that was bent, quite simply, on sacking the news agency and on tracking down Mr. Mao, whom they had good reason to believe was inside the building. Our use of minimum force, in compliance with the advice of a Foreign Office official who had little experience in operational matters, would only have served to frustrate and delay the efforts of the mob.

"I believed at the time and still believe today* that to delay and frustrate a mob organised by Mr. Heung's group would have enraged them to such an extent that there would have been many casualties among the disciplined forces guarding the building.

"Accordingly, I instructed the individual force commanders to make use of such means as they deemed necessary to protect the building and its occupants, and to protect the force members themselves; and I further requested that the regular army would be deployed only in the event that the building was itself under direct threat. I felt, in short, that we would handle matters satisfactorily providing we were permitted to employ proper firepower.

"I regarded any political consequences of our success in handling this temporary emergency as being of secondary importance, compared with my immediate need to protect life and limb. Besides, it was clear that any political considerations for the British side would inevitably be limited by time: at the moment of the outbreak of violence outside the NCNA on the Satur-

*Commander Clovis's remarks were part of a deposition made before the All-Party Parliamentary Committee Inquiry into the circumstances surrounding the final handover of Hong Kong and related developments in south China, and were published in the Committee's final report (Cmnd 5611, October 1997, HMSO).

day Britain had just fifty-seven hours' of tenure remaining. So my decision to use deadly force was, in my view, correct."

Strong popular support for Mr. Clovis was expressed in Britain at the time of the Parliamentary Inquiry, and no vote of censure for his conduct was thought necessary. John Wildways, a Conservative Member of Parliament who had not sat on the Committee, remarked that "We made a mistake with General Dyer. We weren't going to make the same mistake again."

By the time the three mobs had assembled, the rain that had started the day had eased and the weather was warm and misty. "Good tear-gas weather," as police were wont to say. Accordingly, tear-gas launchers mounted on Land-Rovers, and Supplementary Force officers armed with gas guns, were pushed to the front of the defensive lines. Loud-hailer announcements exhorted the crowds to disperse, but were shouted down.

A number of speakers—young, vocal, well-educated— then began to harangue the "colonial forces" for conspiring, as they put it, to prevent the crowds of Hong Kong people "making clear their feelings about having a Communist from Peking" as their new governor. With each of a series of emotive phrases, the speakers began to whip the mood of the mob into one of extraordinary anger, and experienced police officers were later to say they had rarely witnessed such passion among any group of the Hong Kong citizenry. The mood during the pro-communist riots of 1967 seemed muted, compared with the fury that was building on this Saturday afternoon.

"There was a feeling of bitter desperation," one of Clovis's junior officers told the inquiry. "I had seen anger before—anger at the British, at the local government, over building projects, over a variety of decisions announced since the Joint Declaration. But the mobs' attitudes and actions had always had a sort of Confucian respectability to them—rather as if this was the crowd's duty to show the government the error of its ways. This was something very, very different. It was naked fury."

The first missiles began to rain down on police lines at 3:50 P.M.—bricks, paving stones, pieces of iron, marbles, ballbearings fired from catapults. All lines held until 4 P.M., when the first of a wave of petrol bombs was launched—huge numbers of bombs, coming from all three crowds, exploding with near simultaneity, and causing severe disruptions. Clovis ordered a massive cannonade of tear gas, and during the first half hour of the confrontation more than 400 canisters of gas were fired into the crowd or lobbed behind it with grenade launchers to cause maximum confusion.

But the gas essentially failed to move the mob—particularly the Wanchai crowd which, according to helicopter estimates, had grown to some 5,000 by 4 P.M. And the missile batteries increased furiously, with wave after wave of axe-heads, iron bars, chunks of concrete and glass spikes rained down on the men. By 4:10 P.M. some thirty-one police and Supplementary Force members had been injured; and it was at 4:12 P.M., according to later reports, that the first indication came of the employment of firearms by the rioters—with the corollary that some firmer action was going to have to be taken.

In this incident a Special Supplementary Officer, Patrick Watson, attached to "B" platoon, 3rd HKSF, was hit in the chest by a 9 mm bullet and died almost immediately. The reaction from within the Force was immediate. Their commander, John Oakes, demanded through the police senior officer on site, who was the District Officer (Eastern District), that his men be permitted to use live ammunition to repulse further attacks. This police officer, who was later to report noticing some reluctance on the part of the younger Chinese recruits to be involved in a serious confrontation with the rioters, supposed that a wholly British-manned unit would have, as he stated later, "more fire in its belly," and would probably deal positively with the disturbance. He then gave immediate assent to the request, as he had the notional authority to do, and as a matter of record and courtesy passed his decision up the line to Commander Clovis.

The shootings that occurred as a direct consequence of this District Officer's explicit instruction can be regarded, with the benefit of today's hindsight, as the true beginning of the wave of violence that was to engulf China for the following years. If not exactly the first shot of China's still continuing civil war, it was certainly the first exchange of fire of any consequence, and one that precipitated a series of actions, political, diplomatic and military, that have brought China and its neighbours to their present parlous state.

Because of the enormity of the consequences of his action, the District Officer himself, who is married to a Hong Kong Chinese woman, has never been officially named. But records published at the time identify the DO (Eastern) as a Mr. Christopher Green; and a Mr. Green of the same age and background is now known to be working as a police adviser to a former British colonial possession in West Africa.

Immediately upon receipt of the order—some accounts suggest some minutes before its receipt—men of "B" platoon opened fire on the mob in Morrison Hill Road with their automatic rifles. Ten men of this platoon fired continuously, reloading several times; and they were joined by men of "C" and "D" platoons shortly thereafter.

In all, over a period of the eight minutes between 4:15 P.M. and 4:23 P.M., some 431 rounds of high-velocity ammunition were fired directly into the crowd. Although the fire arms training of the Supplementary force was limited, at best, the concentration of fire and the enormous size of the crowd which retreated in panic down a narrow road dictated the very considerable scale of casualties. A total of 102 males, many of them little more than schoolchildren, were shot dead; a further 240 were injured—some badly burned after a trolley-load of petrol bombs was hit and caught fire. Almost all the casualties, save for those hit in the very opening moments of the firing, were shot in the back.

By 4:25 P.M., when all shooting had stopped, the streets in the immediate vicinity of the NCNA building were cleared, though Morrison Hill Road itself was the scene of terrible carnage. Scores of bodies lay where they had fallen, and the pitiful cries of the wounded, dragging themselves to shelter, were especially affecting.

The Supplementary Force members were ordered not to take part in clearing-up operations, but were to remain guarding the NCNA from a now much-diminished threat of attack. Heavily armed police, who summoned dozens of first-aid units to the scene, moved cautiously down into Wanchai, sealing off roads as they did so, and taking care of survivors as best they could. The British Army remained scrupulously in the background, the battalion commander reasoning that members of the Chinese population "would not welcome the sight of any more white faces," as he put it, "because of what we are now going to be accused of having done."

WEST KOWLOON

EVENING

The Colonel's decision was founded on a shrewd judgement but one that was to prove, mercifully for the British, somewhat shortsighted. Later that night, as renewed rain lashed down on the territory, the leaders of the united Triad organisations met in the Shanghai Road offices of Mr. Heung, to review the situation. They all, with a solemnity and concern that others might find uncharacteristic of loan sharks and drug dealers, professed themselves stunned by the enormity of the tragedy. They seemed particularly puzzled that the British, who now had little more than two days of administrative tenure left to run, would commit so grave a tactical error. "They seem to be siding with Beijing," was a remark heard and echoed many times. "They feel obliged to protect this Mao, and are willing to kill large numbers of us to do so. What a terrible end to their rule here. What strange ways they have of saying farewell."

But Peter Heung, their supreme leader, took a different view, one which coincided, not entirely unexpectedly, with the view being taken during similar analysis sessions held late that evening at Government House, at Police Headquarters and, over pre-lunch sherries, across in Downing Street in London. It was a degree of insight and foresight that showed just why the Warwick Accord signatories had named him as their principal spokesman and policymaker.

"The events of this afternoon," he told his brother office-holders in carefully measured tones, "were indeed tragic. The scale of the killing appears to have been extraordinary. At the time the figures were not fully known; it was thought that more than 80 bodies had been recovered, and the local hospitals had accounted for 156 living casualties. The total may have exceeded the casualty figures from the Tienanmen Square incident of 1989, and of the Wuhan People's Park incident of 1993. There will no doubt, be hostile commentaries from Beijing, and I have to assume there may even be an offer from the Chinese to bring troops or People's Armed Police into the territory before the handover, to protect the citizens from the British.

"But my belief is that all this has been contrived by the mainland government—or at least by sections of the Chinese government—with two principal aims. First, they want to blacken the names of the British just as they are leaving, to ensure that international opinion reacts positively to the Chinese takeover. They want to have the British leave with the reputation of imperialists, with all that that implies. And second, they want to divert public hostility away from themselves. For just remember why we organised the marches this morning. Who were we opposing? Was it the British? No, it was not. Was it the Hong Kong Government? No, it was not. It was China—the mainland Chinese. They had broken the agreement. They had decided to appoint this old communist to rule over us. So we decided to get our people out on the streets to show them how we felt.

"Now if we had only learned of Mao's appointment on Tuesday, when we were probably expected to, we would have done the same thing—made a protest—but we would be up against the Chinese authorities. *They* would have been guarding the NCNA or Government House, or wherever Mao chose as his headquarters. But in fact, as we all now know, we learned of his appointment three days early. And that being the case, we had to deal with the *local* authorities, the colonial authorities, who were bound by duty to guard the premises of the Chinese.

"Now, under ordinary circumstances, if only the police and the British were on the streets, matters might have ended peacefully. There would have been a riot. They would have operated with a lot of gas, a lot of arrests, and everything would be over. We would have made our point. The television would have covered it. The Chinese would be condemned for what they had done, for how they had broken their word, and that would be that.

"But instead we had these part-time soldiers—a lot of scum, recruited from the worst parts of Britain, men who wouldn't care how many of us they shot. And they reacted badly, and fired at us. So we had a massacre—done by the British. So now we all hate the British again, and we've forgotten that it's the Chinese who caused it all!

"So whoever leaked that story to the press this morning in Beijing was acting very shrewdly. It was a clever move. It was one that worked exactly as they had wanted. We've now got to think more cautiously about our next response. We've played into their hands once. We mustn't be caught like this again. We made a mistake, Brothers—next time, we'll be more clever."

GOVERNMENT HOUSE

EVENING

The Emergency Committee convened at 7 P.M., in the main conference room on the ground floor. As throughout most of the mansion, evidence of impending departure was all around: paintings had been taken down from walls, tea-chests filled with books lay everywhere, much of the nonessential furniture was covered with dustcloths. But

Government House continued to function with decorous efficiency. Richard Adaire was on hand beneath the *porte-cochère* to meet the individual participants: General Harbinson; Brigadier Tomsett; the Police Commissioner Sir K. H. Poon; the Director of Special Branch Leung Ping-lok; the Information Services Director Mary Chung; the Political Adviser Robin Moore; and a representative from Composite Signals Organisation, who was, as usual, unnamed. The seven arranged themselves around the conference table; they stood when Sir John arrived shortly after 7:15 P.M.

The meeting was brief. It opened with a discussion of the casualties that had been tallied on both sides: the civilian death toll was now known to have been finalised at 102; there was one known death among the KHSF, Patrick Watson from Toxteth, Liverpool; and a further twelve casualties caused by fire bombs and a single pipe bomb which exploded near the picquet outside the Sikh gurdwara on Queen's Road.

Commissioner Poon, who had overall responsibility for civil order in the territory, expressed his formal regret for what he called the "mishandling" of the situation. He did not name the District Officer (Eastern) for giving permission for the Supplementary Force platoons to open fire; but in his defence he noted that the officer was unaware that one of the platoons had taken a casualty, and that the mood of the men could be fairly described as "vengeful." He accepted that Commander Clovis, a man of much experience in colonial police conduct, was only told of the permission after the fact; and that the Commander had informed him that, had he been asked for permission, rather than presented with a *fait accompli*, he might have been reluctant to give it.

"Rather shutting the door after the horse has bolted, don't you think, Commissioner?" said Sir John. "There's not a great deal of point in justifying what has happened, or analysing the events on the ground. What's happened has happened. We've got to work out what to do next."

The discussion that followed considered various possibilities. Central to the options was the fact that two fully equipped army battalions were presently waiting for orders at the Brunei international airport. They could be brought in at night, landed at Sek Kong in the centre of the New Territories, and deployed at various key posts before dawn. The Police Commissioner was eager for this to be done, and argued that it would take some of the pressure off his men, who were suffering from severe morale problems, and amongst whom there were already mumblings of grave discontent.

"I have to report," he said, "that there has been actual mutinous talk. The Messes at Yau Ma Tei, Ho Man Tin and Kwun Tong Districts are filled with disgruntled men who are muttering about their unwillingness to fight Chinese in the streets. And the commanders both in Frontier District and the Border Division are reporting actual attempted defection—men going north across the fence and into Shen Zhen, to get away from what is happening. I regret I cannot offer you the comfort of a police force which is necessarily going to be able to hold the line. It depends on the task we are set. If we have to guard key posts, if we remain a final line of defence, then I think maybe we can do it. If we are to be used offensively against our own people, against people as well organised as Mr. Heung's, then I am afraid we will break. It is as well you know this."

Sir John gave, very briefly, what those who knew him well recognised as a slightly contemptuous smirk. He neither liked nor admired Commissioner Poon, and he had opposed his being given a knighthood. But Downing Street had countermanded; honouring the Commissioner would be a device for displaying British faith in the police force at a time of crisis, a private memorandum had said.

But the sardonic expression faded rapidly from the Governor's face. He waved down any further comment from Poon. He looked instead to the end of the table. "Let's hear of the situation to the north of the border. The gentleman from CSO: perhaps you would give us the benefit of your knowledge to date."

The Composite Signals Organisation maintained a number of foreign signals intelligence-gathering stations around Britain and around the world, all reporting to GCHQ, Cheltenham, and with selected reports passed on to the National Security Agency in Fort Meade, Maryland. Since the late 1970s the principal Far Eastern collection station had been sited on the headland of Chung Hom Kok in southern Hong Kong island. Arrangements had been made in 1996 for the dismantling of the major receiving antennae and radios and associated computers, and their shipment to Darwin, in Northern Australia.

However, it had been decided by the Joint Services Intelligence Evaluation Committee (JSIEC) in London that a small but selected array of equipment would remain in place, for the monitoring of events in China and North Korea, until the end of British administration. According to this arrangement a number of Royal Navy helicopters would remove the final equipment and files to a waiting destroyer, which had been on station in southern Hong Kong waters for the previous week. London had insisted that it wished to enjoy maximum intelligence-gathering abilities for as long as was practically possible: a number of cryptographers and Chinese-language specialists were already on the ship, HMS *Dorsetshire*, and were decoding signals passed between all the major Chinese organisations. GCHQ's pride in being able to monitor telephone conversations held by members of the Chinese leadership in their command headquarters at Zhongnanhai, beside the Forbidden City in Peking, was undiminished by the lowering of activity at Chung Hom Kok.

The CSO officer was able to report what both Sir John and General Harbinson wished to hear: there was absolutely no indication of any new military activity in the Guangdong Military District, nor of any particular heightened activity throughout the whole of the Guangzhou Military Region. Indeed, the only significant developments in the region had come in April, when the Political Commissars at Regional Headquarters in Canton City, and at Divisional Headquarters there and in Guangxi, Hunan and Hainan Island, had been changed, all at the same time. This had been a puzzling development, and the CSO representative was not able to offer any explanation—certainly none that would have any likely bearing on the incidents that had just taken place in Hong Kong.

"Our only suggestion of a development that may be of real interest is that from Zhanjiang. Some of you may remember this place—it is a port on the gooseneck of southern Guangdong Province, down near Hainan Island. You may remember when it was a French treaty port named Fort-Bayard. Anyway, we hear this afternoon that Vice-Admiral Gao, the Commander of the South Sea Fleet, has ordered a number of his transports and a number of commandeered passenger vessels—we think eight, but we are waiting for the pictures—to be moved closer to Hong Kong waters.

"Our suspicion is that these vessels are loaded with troops and vehicles, and members of the Armed Police and the Auxiliary Police. We also feel that they are bound for Hong Kong, although they are keeping radio silence. We have a P. & O. container ship, the *Cape Carmarthen*, near by and on a parallel track, and she had been asked to listen out with particular care. She is also looking for light-signalling between the flagship and the convoy.

"We had always suspected that this would happen. The emotive impact of Chinese troops and vehicles coming across the frontier itself would have been too great. We have anticipated that they would establish themselves by sea: they could make landings in small boats at the outer islands—on Lantau, Lamma, Peng Chau, Cheung Chau—and secure those places; and they could land at the airport, in Aberdeen, at Kwun Tong, at Castle Peak, at Tai Po, and secure much of the island, Kowloon and the New Territories. No one would be much the wiser. Only when they wanted to stage something public would they need to moor one of their vessels at Stonecutters Island, or by the Star Ferry landing, or at Ocean Terminal, or down the road at HMS *Tamar*; they would have a great deal more control of the impact of the changeover, and they would be able to gain real control that much more quickly.

"So we don't see anything particularly sinister. Not even the timing. The departure from Zhanjiang began at 1600 local time—that was 3 P.M., Hong Kong time—and they are about a day's sailing away. Our information is that they will stand off Fan Lau lighthouse, in the Pearly River estuary, until about 9 P.M. on Monday night. Then they'll move.

"I would like to stress one thing—to the extent that SIGINT officers like myself can stress anything without committing *lèse majesté*." The Governor motioned to him to continue.

"We do not think the dispatch of this force—if we can call it such a thing—is in any way connected with the events this afternoon. We do not think it is linked in any way with the Foreign Ministry's decision to brief the Reuters man in Peking. We think this move has been long planned, and has been fully approved by the Central Military Commission. Unlike the briefing, which we do not think had the approval of the CMC. We don't know about that. We're still checking.

"So in our opinion—and I suspect you will find that this is the opinion of the JCIEC—the reaction of the civil order institutions in Hong Kong should not take these developments into account. We should not react, lady and gentlemen. This is irrelevant to our immediate problems.

"And my second suggestion is simply that we do not allow this news to be publicised. If we add the news to that of Mr. Mao's appointment, local feelings are sure to be inflamed still further. Nothing, I think, need be said, or even alluded to, suggesting Chinese naval manoeuvres." Here the CSO man, and indeed all the conferees, looked across at Miss Chung, the tough and respected former head of Radio Television Hong Kong, who now headed the entire information department of the colonial government. (She would be leaving on Monday night, for retirement in Vancouver.)

"I will of course do my best," Miss Chung replied, acidly. "But if Peking decides to leak this one too, there's not a great deal that I can do."

The CSO officer took off his glasses, and rubbed his eyes. "Which brings me to one final point. And before I go on, may I express the wish that everyone here will forgive me for what I accept is a particularly gross example of a signals officer exceeding his remit. It is simply that I am currently in possession of particular and particularly sensitive information, of which I need to inform you. I believe I am right to doubt whether, under these most exacting of circumstances, matters of departmental protocol will prevent my forwarding this information to the committee and commenting on what my training suggests is its significance. May I, despite the lapse, go on?" He glanced around the room. The Governor signalled at him to continue.

"Very well then. We in the community do not believe that this news will be announced, publicly or privately, until after the handover is complete. We believe the Chinese will wish to keep it a total secret, to avoid any complications. We base our assumption on a small piece of information we received less than thirty minutes ago, from an operative in Peking.

"We understand that the official in the Chinese Foreign Ministry who summoned the Reuters reporter was a Madame Zhang Xiaodi, the Western European Senior Desk Officer. Madame Zhang was well known to our Embassy in Peking, had travelled to London on a number of occasions and had, moreover, developed a reasonably intimate personal relationship with our present Minister of State, Lord Inverdonald—and Lady Inverdonald, I might add. We have considered her to be a friend of the British, though no more than that.

"At first we found her decision to leak the information on the Mao appointment somewhat perplexing. It would deflect criticism of the move from China, and towards ourselves—which is just what has happened. Why she—a friend of ours, as I mentioned—should do such a thing, was, as I say, perplexing.

"But we considered the longer-term implications, as she and on whoever's behalf she was acting must have considered too. And we concluded, as they probably did, that the reaction in Hong Kong to what has happened today would in fact calm, very quickly. Our suspicion is that Mr.

Heung's groups will not cause trouble tomorrow, but will wait until we leave. They will reserve their fire, if they have any, for those who are coming, not those who are leaving. Madame Zhang's group, if I may call them that, and whoever they are, seem to have counted on that too.

"They assumed it would alert the Hong Kong population to the duplicity of the mainland Chinese, and it would give them fair warning; and that the price in lives that they—and us, the British—would have to pay would be worthwhile, they thought, so long as the ultimate goal, that of enabling the groups to coalesce and to marshal their anger while they could still do so, was achieved. So long as Heung's officers are thinking along the same lines as we are, then a formidable anti-Mainland resistance group has been born today, and will provide the nucleus for further activity in Hong Kong and south China in the months to come.

"That, I believe, is why the news was leaked. The army officer who was in the room with her—we have seen all the Reuters service messages to London, of course—was probably part of the group that, we guess, wants there to be an anti-Mainland organisation set up and working inside Hong Kong. In other words, Madame Zhang's act was, in the eyes of any shrewd and dogmatically loyalist cadre in Peking, one of profound disloyalty.

"It seems, lady and gentlemen, that there are indeed shrewd and dogmatically loyalist men in Peking. We heard half an hour ago that Madame Zhang had been removed from her office, summarily tried, and that she has now been shot. We have no information on the army officer who was with her. But she, poor woman, is definitely dead."

CHAPTER FOUR

Entr'acte

THE GOLDEN DEER RESTAURANT
SHAM SHUI PO, HONG KONG

Sunday, 29 June 1997

DIM SUM

Peter Heung, who had remained in the Shanghai Road offices all night (a bunk had been set up for him in an inner office after the long nights of the previous year's rioting) had received a telephone call shortly after dawn. It came from a man he knew quite well, a British Army captain named Richard Margerison.

The two had first met socially two years before, at a cocktail party given by a local insurance agent named Derek Thomas, who had connections deep within the territory's government. (His father had been a senior Appeals Court justice; his stepmother was a member of the Legislative Council, and sat on many company boards.) Thomas and Margerison were old friends; and Thomas knew Heung (and Margerison was aware of this) because of the latter's job as a solicitors' clerk with Appleby, Rowling and Munke, the tax lawyers.

Margerison knew, in addition, about Heung's other connections. Richard Margerison was a very considerable enigma in the British Army. He held an American green card (but, not being a citizen, was permitted to serve in an army loyal to his late father's nationality). He had as one of his principal homes a large dairy farm south of Watertown in upstate New York, and he had a socially celebrated sister who worked as a fashion model with the Click! agency, and lived in Greenwich Village. He was said to be comfortably well-off, was handsome, a bachelor of remarkable eligibility, and he spoke several languages including Korean, which had helped when he asked to be posted as temporary head of the United Nations Honour Guard that accompanies the Commander-in-Chief of UN and US Forces in South Korea.

There had never been any certainty about his precise duties either in Korea or in Hong Kong. In the colony he occupied offices on the twelfth floor of HMS *Tamar*, conveniently close to those of the Commander, British Forces, to whom he was said to be an adviser. He did not answer to the Foreign Office men who worked three floors above, and who were the colony's more visible spies. He travelled frequently, and those with whom he socialised said he was often away for inexplicably long periods, in countries and places of which he spoke little.

And he knew a great deal, as it happened, about Peter Heung and the Warwick Accord. The party at which he expected that Heung would be present took place just three weeks after the signing: Margerison thought, very much on his own initiative as subsequent papers have indicated, that he might strike up a relationship with Heung to find out something, however little, about the agreement between the 14K and the Sun Yee On—to see whether it encompassed other Triad groups, and whether it presaged the birth of a real political entity. It was Margerison's report, dated 14 July 1995, that gave Her Majesty's Government its first insight—an insight that the Hong Kong government was never able to duplicate, nor was ever told—into the rapidly growing new power structure in the territory, and beyond into south China. It was this report that laid the basis for the development of a whole new sense of *realpolitik* among the British: the development of an unspoken assumption, and one that was never to be translated formally into a policy, that these gangsters were, in fact, to be regarded both as spokesmen for the working people of Hong Kong and as a group with whom Britain, however distasteful it might seem, could do some kind of business.

This change of heart, this development, this recognition of a certain political congruency came about largely because Richard Margerison did indeed strike up a friendship with Peter Heung. It would be idle to say they two were intimate: there was too little trust between the two sides in those years for close friendship to develop. But it was evident that there could be, in time, a communion of interests, if not of spirit, and the two men were content to deal on that basis. Both sides had a common foe in the mainland Chinese; both sides had indifferent relations with the Hong Kong government, which they regarded as contemptibly inept; both sides claimed they favoured the retention of the capitalist system in the territory, and its extension well beyond, into all of the China that wished to enjoy its benefits.

But it was here, in matters of interpretation, that they differed. Margerison wished for the full flowering of the free-market system to be nurtured within the framework of law (though he was willing to debate the philosophical implications of that wish); Heung had bolder, more ambitious, less scrupulous means of making money—means that not unnaturally included the comfortable feathering of his own nest.

The two men saw each other every two or three months, usually alone, usually in restaurants. Those who saw them and did not recognise them took them for homosexuals, for there was a certain furtiveness in their manner. But Heung invariably saw to it that lieutenants were near by, and on call, so within the Chinese community it was probably fair to say that the relationship was one that was known about, and probably approved. One must assume that the mainland Chinese, whose agents were well positioned throughout the territory (though probably not deep within Heung's organisations: the scalpings and skinnings appeared to have taken care of that), knew of the relationship as well.

Very early on Sunday morning, 29 June 1997, Margerison was briefed by the General. The details of this briefing have never been fully discussed: one can only speculate on the basis of what happened subsequently. The first direct consequence of the briefing came at 8:15 A.M. when Margerison telephoned Heung and arranged to meet in the Golden Deer Restaurant, over early dim sum. Heung, heavily guarded, was the first to arrive. He left four of his men outside the restaurant, and scattered another three at other tables. He was reading the *Ta Kung Pao* when the officer walked in—a small joke between the two of them, since *Ta Kung Pao* was a rabidly left-wing paper, espousing views with which neither man was in accord.

On this occasion neither man was disposed to be amused. Heung, after all, had lost a great number of his young recruits during the shootings of the previous afternoon, and he was under considerable street pressure to have his forces retaliate against those Britons who had perpetrated the killings. That he should instead be sitting down and dining with one of these very people would, in ordinary circumstances, seem heretical, wholly incredible. But Peter Heung was a man of considerable authority over his troops. Those lieutenants who knew of the meeting with Margerison were the same men who had attended the previous evening's strategy session, and who thus knew—and approved—of the more cautious and restrained approach that they were planning to take in the final remaining hours of British administration. They acknowledged that the mainland government—or some unidentified group within the mainland government, acting for reasons they could not entirely fathom—had tricked them into the fight with the British. And they knew they would not be so tricked again.

So although these lieutenants did not know the full extent of Heung's relationship with Margerison, they were content with what they knew. They supposed that such discussions as had taken place before, as well as these brief discussions scheduled at the Golden Deer today, would prove to be of ultimate benefit to the organisation, and through the organisation, to the people of Hong Kong. Such synergies may have seemed improbable had they been revealed at the time: from today's perspective—when there is universal recognition of the commonality of enemies—they seem rather more credible.

The meeting was brief, and simple. Since both men had anticipated, in a very non-specific sense, the possibility of some serious breakdown in civil order on the eve of the handover, and since Margerison had the sympathetic ear of thinking British diplomats when he insisted on the importance of the Warwick Accord, some "arrangements," as the Foreign Office had instructed, had been made. Margerison was here to tell Heung of the nature of those arrangements.

They were far from generous. A few dozen Chinese-made automatic rifles. A hundred or so side-arms, all, via roundabout sources, from North Korea. A quantity of a reliable Pakistani-made plastic explosive, and a quantity of detonators. Sufficient ammunition from a supplier in Israel to keep a few small cells going for a month, at most. No radios. No codes. No names of any contacts.

Margerison gave Heung a list of six-figure numbers, the grid references of the points where the twelve packages had been cached, some days before. Most were concealed in the network of old British trenches that had been dug into hillsides all around the territory during the Forties, just before the Japanese invasion. Although some thought had been given to transferring the arms directly, and so ensuring that they got into the right hands, this method ensured secrecy—that no connection between donor and recipient could be discovered. The only link was this Golden Deer meeting, and the slip of paper with the grid references, which would become an irrelevance once the caches had been found and removed. And this, Margerison suggested, should happen quickly—within hours. The trench hiding-places would be easy for Heung's men to find; the weapons dumps were individually of sufficiently small quantities to ensure that they could be moved with ease and without suspicion.

"But is that really all?" Heung asked, once Margerison had told him the news. "We have a massive task. You know how massive. We are dealing with a hugely powerful force, one with excellent intelligence, with vast networks of spies and informers. To have any hope of dealing effectively, we need many weapons. What you have arranged is simply not enough."

Margerison had anticipated the man's plaint. There was no possibility of obtaining more, he explained. Downing Street knew of the arrangement, and had given its assent on the firm assurance that all involved would be at pains to see that no possible connection to the British authorities could ever be either suspected or established—this instruction being surely understandable, he said to Heung, who nodded. To meet this requirement, the weapons had all to have originated in places that would arouse no suspicion if the mainland Chinese did ever discover them, before or after they had been collected from the caches. And collecting weapons and explosives from North Korea and Pakistan was not a matter wholly lacking in complication, Margerison went on. Only limited numbers could be found and brought into Hong Kong without either the Hong Kong government or the mainland intelligence operators coming to know.

"All told, you'll have to accept that we've done the best we can. You know how to turn these into many more. You don't have to be a genius. You just have to be tactically shrewd. But I can't say any more. I won't say any more. You have the references. I leave it up to you."

Margerison got up to leave, and extended his hand to the Dragon Head. "A great deal depends on what you do now. I wish some of us were staying behind to give you a hand. But we can't. So I'll just wish you all the best. I dare say I'll read about you. Stay out of trouble. They'll be looking for a reason to pull you in—ten minutes after they've taken over, I expect. I'd keep low. Very low."

Margerison left, walked to the MTR stop, and merging into the crowds took a train back to Tamar. Heung pretended to study the *Ta Kung Pao* for a few moments more, and then left for Shanghai Road. He was on the telephone for the next ten minutes, and then disappeared.

CHAPTER FIVE

Recessional
(CONCLUSION)

Monday, 30 June 1997

LATE EVENING

The green Bedford trucks grumbled slowly through the city, halting at their prearranged points to collect the men and their belongings for shipment home. The task of clearing the barracks, formally set in motion some weeks before, had been completed a few hours earlier. Four transport ships on three-month charter to the Royal Navy and one ammunition supply ship were assembled in the harbour to take on the last remaining stocks and men. The thirty trucks that would take the final sentries and their equipment to the docks would be handed over to the Hong Kong government.

The Chinese authorities had been firm in demanding that the British military make what they termed a "proper" exit from Hong Kong. By this, they had told the Joint Liaison Group, they meant that no weapons or ammunition or "militarily significant equipment" of any kind could be left in the territory by the departing British forces. Furthermore, the 1,000 men of the Royal Hong Kong Regiment, known in the territory as the Volunteers and regarded in British operational terms as part of 38th Gurkha Rifles, would have to be disarmed. This was a suggestion that was greeted with dismay in the territory (dismay that was reinforced by the seeming alacrity with which the British agreed to the demand), and there were angry demonstrations outside Government House when the rules were promulgated in the summer of 1996.

Most of the protesters were elderly expatriates—even though the Volunteers were overwhelmingly Chinese—who saw in the Hong Kong Regiment a relic of Empire that, they felt, should not be permitted to wither and die. An army unit without weapons was valueless, they said; and a wreath of white roses was suspended outside the main gate to the Happy Valley barracks, the headquarters of the Volunteers for the previous forty years. The commanding officer did not order it to be removed; but pressure from Government House, to whom complaints had been made by the New China News Agency, saw that it was taken down after a day.

The result of these agreements with the Chinese was the arrival in early June of the ammunition ship HMS *Andromeda*, which remained in the Dangerous Goods Anchorage taking on cargo and mysterious crates day and night for the duration of her stay. The British authorities never allowed the mainland Chinese to know precisely what equipment was maintained at the various British barracks, nor at the two small Ordnance Stores at Stonecutters Island and at Sek Kong. Nor did the Chinese balk at the refusal of their request, since they had consistently agreed to the sovereign status of British military bases on Hong Kong soil.

But the Chinese did post observation craft alongside *Andromeda*, ostentatiously taking photographs and filmed records as the boxes and crates were loaded aboard. The nature of some of the cargo surprised even such members of the Hong Kong public who came to know of the loadings: a number of heavy artillery pieces, three self-propelled howitzers, ten armoured personnel carriers and six small tanks were taken aboard the ship on the first day—equipment that was testimony to a rather more con-

siderable amount of firepower than had even been suspected. Hong Kong, after all, was officially described as
only "a small garrison, akin to those in Cyprus, the Falk-
lands and Belize."

The ammunition boxes were counted out daily by the unsmiling and assiduous Chinese observers, as were the jeeps
and lorries and engine parts and helicopters and bowsers
and small cranes, rubber boats and radio transmitters and
receivers and uniform stores and NAAFI equipment and all
the other accoutrements of empire and far-flung military
power. By the morning of 30 June, all was safely squirreled
away in holds and under canvas awnings on deck. The
quartermasters reported to the Commander, British Forces,
on "the satisfactory clearance of the Hong Kong garrison,"
and 4,200 of the remaining forces had, on that final Monday morning, been put aboard ten Royal Air Force flights
for Brize Norton, and redeployment. The Supplementary
Forces had also embarked on fleets of chartered British Air-
ways jets; by 9 P.M. all were said to be outside colonial jurisdiction, having been paid off, and given a letter formally
thanking them for their duties.

Those wounded on Saturday afternoon were taken aboard
one of the transport ships, which had excellent medical fa-
cilities. The coffin holding the body of Warrant Officer Patrick Watson, late of 3HKSF, was in the hold of one of the
aircraft. He was to be the only British fatality of the
handover, and though his widow and two children naturally
regarded his death as the most dreadful of tragedies, it was
to be the considered judgement of British military historians
that, all things considered, the British side "got off pretty
lightly."

By 10 P.M., little remained of a British presence in Hong
Kong. The offices and barrack-blocks were empty, guarded
by groups of police and awaiting the anticipated inspection
of the mainland Chinese. And all the while, during this eerie period, the old British Bedford lorries ground slowly
from depot point to depot point, collecting the last groups
of men and their kitbags, dismantling the barricades, or
handing over the sentry duties to the men of the Hong

Kong Police who were, it is worth noting, permitted to continue to wear their side-arms.

Occasionally small groups of Chinese civilians would gather beside the sandbag emplacements in the streets to bid farewell to the British soldiers—farewells that were more notable for the nervousness with which they were expressed than for their particular warmth. The small public gatherings were illustrative, however, of the profound change of mood that had seized the territory over the previous twenty-four hours: a Chinese population that could have been expected to rise up and attack and destroy all that was British, as revenge for the mayhem of Saturday, was now reported to be docile, almost submissive, almost friendly.

The explanation, it is now known, was quite simple: the Heung officers had put out the word to their men and boys that there should be no further reaction to the killings and the violence of Saturday afternoon, and that word was being almost universally obeyed (a degree of compliance that was helped to no small degree by the activities of large numbers of Straw Sandals directed to police the order). Moreover, there was no evidence of any "freelance" reaction from Chinese unconnected with the Saturday disturbances. Once again, members of the Triad group worked to ensure calm throughout the territory's population, those associated with their political aims and those who were not. There had been a brief upsurge of activity in Kowloon late on Saturday night, when a police barracks was burned to the ground and two Hong Kong policemen were killed. But a force of Suppers firing tear gas had put paid to that by 3 A.M. on Sunday, since when there had been no reports of significant violence directed against either the British or the mainland Chinese. In a report to the Governor made at midmorning on Monday—his last officially scheduled commentary since the General Declaration of Emergency three months before—Commissioner Poon noted with surprise the passing of "one of the most serene nights Hong Kong has known in the past thirty years," and went on to mention with wistful irony how pleasing it would have been if the colony had always been so tranquil.

As had been decided on Saturday, Government House had made no announcement about the Chinese naval convoy that had left Zhanjiang that afternoon. However, in view of the contact made between Captain Margerison and Mr. Heung, and in view of the likelihood that large numbers of mainland Chinese would soon be deployed throughout the territory, a further and final discreet connection was made in which the British side made it clear that no time should be lost by Heung's organisers in the collection of the various packages located at the grid reference points. The British side was relieved to be assured that all the collections had indeed been made, that the packages were in safe custody and that the paper with the grid references had been destroyed. Mr. Heung's associates wondered aloud why the urgency, and one was reported to have asked a British representative direct if the hurry related to the likelihood that the Chinese would arrive *en masse*, perhaps by helicopter or by sea. The British representative replied that he assumed that under the terms of a gentlemen's agreement reached at the Joint Liaison Group meeting in March, the very small number—"a token force"—of Chinese PLA (People's Liberation Army) and PAP (People's Armed Police) members who would be stationed in Hong Kong would arrive by land over the Lo Wu, Lok Ma Choi and Sha Tau Kok border crossing points. The reply was disingenuous; but was apparently believed.

Meanwhile the Marine Department, with the assistance of coded radio signals from the *Carmarthen Bay*, had been tracking the Chinese fleet continuously since Saturday. It had not, as expected, waited off Fan Lau light on Lantau Island, just beyond the limit of Hong Kong waters that was closest to its point of departure. (Passengers on commercial boats passing between Hong Kong and Macau knew Fan Lau well: they knew that once the light was square on their starboard beam, they could commence gambling since they were no longer under colonial jurisdiction; similarly, on the return journey, the appearance of Fan Lau on the port beam meant that the chips had to be cashed in, the roulette wheel silenced and the playing cards shelved for another day.)

Instead of parking there the convoy of four naval transports and eight former passenger ships, including an old Danish-built cruise ship that had for many years been used as a floating hotel off the city of Xiamen, had divided into three, and had manoeuvred into position at noon on Monday. One transport and four liners—designated Group Alpha—had turned north up the Pearl River, and then had wheeled about and had held position off the Castle Peak power station. Group Beta, consisting of two transports and two liners, had heaved to and was lying uncomfortably in very choppy waters behind the Waglan Island lighthouse at the eastern approach to the territory. The remainder of the force, Group Gamma, was off Lamma Island, to the south.

At 10:30 P.M. the Marine Department telephoned to inform Government House—which was now preparing for the flag-lowering ceremony—that the three groups of vessels had simultaneously passed into territorial waters and were steaming rapidly towards their supposed landing-points. Group Alpha had passed down the Urmston Roads and was lying off the main container base at Tsing Yi; Beta was about to pass through the Lei Yue Mun gap and could be expected to be off Kai Tak airport runway by 11 P.M.; and Gamma had moved in close to the Aberdeen typhoon shelter. Observers in accompanying small vessels had reported that a number of Chinese Army and Navy Mi6 Mikhail heavy transport helicopters were visible on the converted afterdecks of the liners, and that their rotors were turning in evident preparation for take-off.

Protocol officers from the British and Chinese sides had met three weeks before to decide on the detailed provisions for the final ceremonial. Perhaps the most important practical result of the talks was that the British had been given six extra hours after the official handover deadline—which was midnight local time; 1 A.M. Chinese Daylight Saving Time; 5 P.M. British Daylight Saving Time in London; and 4 P.M. GMT—to clear up and leave. This meant that the final collection of sentries, the destruction of papers, the establishment of radio links and so forth could continue past the actual deadline. The legality of doing so and the necessary indemnifications had been covered both by a Note from the Chinese Embassy in London and the passage of a brief Enabling Act at Westminster: the British expressed their gratitude to the Chinese for their forbearance.

The ceremony surrounding the lowering of the Union flag and the raising of its Chinese counterpart was said to have been adapted from that used at the end of British rule of their last Chinese colony, that at Port Edward in Shandong Province in 1930. At that time the British flag was left flying at sunset on the evening of the retrocession; at midnight the Chinese flag was raised alongside it; and by dawn the British flag had been taken down and all British diplomatic and military personnel had been embarked on a battleship, which then bade its farewell with sirens at sunrise, and set sail for the Royal Navy base at Esquimault in Canada.

Much the same was supposedly due to happen in Hong Kong. The British and Hong Kong flags flew together in the garden at Government House, without having been struck at dusk as was customary. The Chinese flag was due to be raised at midnight, in the presence of a group of dignitaries who would arrive from the New China News Agency a few moments beforehand. Sir John and Lady Courtenay would then fly to the cruiser HMS *Manchester*, and the support staff would fly on a later Navy helicopter to the destroyers HMS *Calliope* and HMS *Hermione*, which were waiting in Junk Bay, ready for a speedy departure. It had been arranged that all remaining military personnel would be embarked at the same time, and that all British military men and materials—and vessels—would have cleared what would then be Xianggang Chinese territorial waters by 6 A.M. on Tuesday, 1 July.

In the event the ceremonial was even less ornate an affair than the stripped-down version approved by the protocol officers; and the departure by the British was hurried and—according to participants—undignified. The following reconstruction comes largely from the diaries of the author, who was permitted access to much of the closing formalities. A British newspaper journalist, a Mr. Ralph Upton, supplied additional details.

The Governor and Lady Courtenay walked out of the Government House kitchen and through the empty dining-room. A couple of naval ratings were collecting the last boxes and bundling them up to go off on the tender to the *Manchester*, the cruiser which would speed the senior colonial officers out to sea. The pair emerged into the brightly lit foyer, looked around for the last time at the paintings that had been left behind—nothing of note, someone had assured them—and went out into the heat of the night.

The three klieg lamps which local television had set up to provide coverage for the BBC immediately flared into life, dazzling the group. Six Royal Marines—a lieutenant and five of his men—came to attention. The officer saluted as the group emerged: Lord Inverdonald (the Foreign Office Minister of State with Special Responsibilities for Hong Kong), then Sir John and Lady Courtenay, General Harbinson, Brigadier Tomsett and Richard Adair.

Inverdonald stepped up to the podium. The rest of the party stood grouped around him. The Marine lieutenant barked a command, and from beneath the monkey-puzzle tree stepped a soldier in full Highland dress with bagpipes. Pipe-Major Duncan Kennedy, from the band of the 2nd Battalion, Royal Scots, had been flown from Edinburgh only days before, to perform the simple act of playing the lament *St. Kilda*. It must have been evident to those who were watching the broadcast that Lady Courtenay, who was of Scots origin, found this lament—a soliloquy on the abandonment of another small and distant island—intensely painful. She and her husband looked straight ahead, almost at attention, willing the piper to stop. Which he did, at three minutes before the hour, with a trailing note left in the air, swept away by the wind, and the sound of Inverdonald clearing his throat. He looked in the direction of the main gate. He had but two simple sentences to utter.

"In the name of Her Majesty, and of the people of Hong Kong, I invite our honoured guests to join us in the celebration of arrival. Please enter these precincts, as welcome friends."

And with that, and with a strangely menacing silence that was punctuated only by the sound of twenty-four motor tyres crunching on to gravel and the occasional grating of branches against one another in the wind, six long black Mercedes limousines moved slowly in through the gates. They had been parked on Upper Albert Road for the past few minutes, protected by a detachment of British troops. Each of the cars had darkened windows, and each flew two red flags of the People's Republic of China. The convoy moved around clockwise, behind the television camera, heading towards the podium, the lead car coming to rest beside the main doorway of the house.

The Royal Marine lieutenant opened the passenger door of this car, and his men, each of whom had been assigned to stand at a point where each following car would halt, opened the doors of the others. From the lead car stepped two men: Zhang Nan, the rather disagreeable negotiator who had been head of the News Agency for the past seven years, and a small, plump, busy-looking man with bushy eyebrows and bad teeth which were displayed in a fixed grin. He was unknown by sight to many of the party. But the BBC commentator knew, and the commentary could be heard coming from a television set somewhere near by.

". . . and now, confirming all the rumours of the last few hours, we see stepping from the first car, the man all Hong Kong has feared to see appointed as its new Chief Executive—74-year-old Mao Ren-chin. The agreement of thirteen years ago had spoken specifically of the people here having some influence over the choice of their immediate ruler. But this man, who comes from Dalian in northeastern China, who speaks English but no Cantonese and who is known as a diehard party member with enormous influence in the ruling hierarchy of Hong Kong. . . . If, as we suspect, Zhang Nan is going to introduce him as Chief Executive—in effect, the replacement for Sir John Courtenay—we can expect the new territory to become, rapidly, a very different place . . ."

From the other cars stepped two dozen or more Chinese men, some familiar, some not, some in Western suits, some in baggy outfits of dark blue serge or grey duck. Two soldiers and a sailor from the People's Liberation Army were among the throng too—unarmed, as the orders had specified. They moved towards the podium.

Lord Inverdonald grasped Zhang Nan's hand and shook it warmly, then took, with considerably less warmth, the hand proffered by Mr. Mao. He made to introduce the others, but Mao waved him down. "No time," he said. "Raise the flag."

Sir John looked down at his watch. A minute to go. The Royal Marine Lieutenant—history records his name as Roger Moorcock, a 24-year-old bachelor from Kendal, in Westmorland—then stepped forward and took from a leather box beside the front steps, and with due reverence, a single and apparently very large Chinese flag. Aided by Sergeant Michael Firth, Corporal Peter Ransome and by the unidentified Chinese sailor, he then clipped the flag to its halyard, secured all, and waited.

From a radio set inside the doors the chimes of Big Ben, 6,000 miles away in London, sounded the preamble to sixteen hours, Greenwich Mean Time, seventeen hours, British Summer Time, and midnight, Hong Kong time. The sixteen notes tumbled out of the ether, pleasing in their primitive melody, raising the tension to an unbearable quivering, as though every soul and every mind and every heartbeat was touched by a tuning fork, humming with expectation.

The first peal of the great thirteen-ton bell finally crashed out of the silence. A shouted command, one in Cantonese, one in English, and the huge Chinese flag was rushed effortlessly up to the top of the pole, and the halyards lashed and knotted below to assure its security. Everyone looked upwards as the hot winds swiftly unfurled it and sent it waving lazily, even in the gale, with a vast imposing dignity, beside the jauntily tattered Union Jack a few feet beyond. Inverdonald, the Courtenays, the General, his ADC and Rex Tomsett stood with respectful rigidity, while the remaining peals of the bell thundered through the night.

And then they stopped, and from down below in the streets came a sudden huzzah of activity: a surge like the roar of an immense wave, sucking back the beach before it came crashing down again. It seemed to be a mixture of cheering and wailing, of distant firecrackers and explosions, of gunfire and sirens and the sound of tyres turning at high speed. It was not, in short, a pleasant sound, nor one that augured well for a night of peace.

Then another sound started from beside the tennis courts. The sudden low whine of the starter motor, and the slow thwack of a Sea King's rotor blades, as the Governor's helicopter fired up, ready to take Sir John and his party off to the waiting *Manchester*.

The party, including Ambassador Zhang and Mr. Mao, walked around to the perimeter of the helicopter pad. As they waited, Sir John tried small talk. "We've prepared a small gift for you, Mr. Zhang," he said, and turned to let Richard Adaire hand him a flat red morocco case, about the size of a large magazine, with a royal crest engraved in gold. "It's an original Chinnery, a watercolour, a picture of Hong Kong in 1841, the year we—well, the year that this ceremony seeks to have forgotten." He handed it to Zhang. "I hope you like it, sir. And may I congratulate you both— congratulate you all."

Zhang waved his gesture away, and grunted at an aide to take the box. Mao then said, in surprisingly good English: "You won't want to miss your machine, I think," and with a gesture more usually reserved for bouncers in Kowloon nightclubs, made as though to usher the Governor across the tennis court to where the helicopter crew was waiting to board them.

And so, with a few kisses and handshakes of farewell, but with less real ceremonial than has probably ever attended the concluding moments of any part of the British Empire save perhaps that of the island of Southern Thule, in Antarctica, His Excellency the Governor, Lady Courtenay, the Minister of State at the Foreign and Commonwealth Office and the Commander and Deputy Commander, British Forces, clambered into the helicopter with as much dignity as the wind and height of the Sea King's steps permitted them, and, at precisely 300 seconds into Chinese rule, left the soil that they so recently had governed.

At first the dark blue machine clattered upwards just a few feet, then it moved forward, then back, put its nose down and began to move ahead and upwards out over the tennis courts, before turning left over Upper Albert Road. At a height of no more than fifty feet it hovered above the flagpoles, setting the two banners streaming wildly. The machine then rose again, with a deafening roar, until it was level with the top of the Japanese turret above the Governor's study, climbed high above the azalea bushes of the great gardens, and finally, its red lights winking on and off, looped up and away over the huge skyscrapers of Central to where HMS *Manchester* was even now steaming at ten knots, down the western roads. Soon the sky was silent, with just the lights twinkling on and off; and then these, too, had vanished into the darkness. The Colonial Presence, in the persons of this small group of men and a woman, had left for ever.

The agreement with Peking had the British governor and his party beyond the limits of territorial waters within ninety minutes of the raising of the Chinese flag. London had insisted that all would be done strictly by the book, and that matters of pride were no longer of any consequence. "Leave in a timely fashion with dignity," was the order of the day.

Meanwhile some thirty men had poured from the other cars and had swarmed inside Government House within moments. Sentries—by now well armed, with machine-guns—took up positions by the doorway. Two trucks drew up outside, and two dozen more men in fatigues, carrying rifles with fixed bayonets, took up positions along the driveway. There was the crackle of instructions shouted over the radio—in *putonghua*, not Cantonese. Five more soldiers were posted at the outer gate, and in the sentry-boxes from which they were already hustling the British soldiers into their own Bedford trucks. "All right, you bastard," Upton heard one voice say, in broad Lancashire. "I'm getting out as fast as I can. Don't bloody push me or I'll clout you."

Two soldiers came quickly across to the flagpoles, looked upwards to see from which the Chinese flag was flying, and undid the halyards of the other. One of the remaining Britons tried to protest, but a third soldier blocked his way. "You stay—no interfere," said the man, an officer. The Union Jack came down, and a soldier took it away, presumably as a souvenir. Another soldier was seen with the royal crest, torn from the lectern.

There came the clattering of rotor blades again, sounding directly above the remaining party. It was only twenty past—and the first of the helicopters due to take the ancillary parties to sea were not due until twenty *to*. What on earth was happening?

The leading soldier caught up to *The Times'* correspondent. "Mister Upton," he said roughly. "Mister Adaire? This helicopter for you. You must go now. No time for more. You must leave. This official residence."

Those final five minutes remain confused in the minds of all who took part. The helicopter settled down, the door was thrown open. Chinese sentries were pushing people roughly towards the Lynx, pulling them down under the rotor blades. Hands reached out of the helicopter doors and hauled the last pair on board. Even as they did so the machine was lifting up and turning around, blowing some of the Chinese soldiers to the ground. There was shouting, anger, confusion.

They flew high above Central, the Fleet Air Arm pilot cool and composed. "Six-oh-one turning for *Hermione* now with six souls aboard, ETA one six three five Zulu."

"Roger six-oh-one, *Hermione*. New orders received, so we are presently under way some two nautical miles east of Junk Bay. Come direct to our beacon and prepare for under-way landing."

"Roger and Wilco, *Hermione*, see you soon."

From the air the city was as staggeringly beautiful as ever, with the orange fires and the blue flashing lights of emergency vehicles adding immeasurably to the scene. But the machine was speeding out over water, and before long the lights of Central and Kowloon were well behind them, and the airport approach light gantries slipped below, and then the islets to the east, and finally, picked out in the blackness of the open sea, they saw the running lights of the little frigate, heading as rapidly as possible away from Hong Kong. The pilot was well trained, and put them down on the after-deck with little fuss. By twenty minutes to one they were in the wardroom, being handed large glasses of gin by the captain.

"My apologies," he said. "Bit of a fright all round. They changed the rules the moment they took charge, it seems. They weren't going to have an ambiguous night where no one knew where they stood—not with all the bother in the city. So we got orders, exactly one minute after midnight, telling us to be out of their waters no later than *Manchester*—and she's got until one-thirty, I believe." He looked across at a lieutenant, who nodded his assent.

"They warned us they might shoot at us if we didn't so we had to scrap all the best plans and get out. All sorts of things have happened. Radio's off the air. They shut down the BBC feed. We don't have a working consulate for another week. And I was just told they've cut the phones, so we can't patch in to any of our friends who're still there. We just won't know what's going on until they've secured things."

Everyone then gathered under the soft red nightlights of the bridge, and gazed out into the blackness. Waglan Island Lighthouse—the Light at the End of the Empire, it had once been called—slipped by to starboard. The captain ordered a turn, to a southeasterly course, and rang down for full speed ahead both.

Richard Adaire stepped out on to the starboard bridge wind. Hong Kong was but a reddish glow on the horizon now, aside from a few islets that loomed up blackly against the beam of the lights. They passed a shoal of fishing junks, and a small cargo ship, inbound. But otherwise, as the colony slipped ever further astern, the sea darkened and became more deserted still. And a swell, struck up by the passing storm, began to lift the little ship up, and dump her down heavily. It was going to be an uncomfortable night.

Then there was a cry from the bridge. "Vessel dead ahead one mile, stopped in the water." The captain ordered a cut in speed to half ahead, and a turn of ten degrees to starboard. He came on to the wing. "The sentry boat. Just making sure we're out the door on time. And we will be!"

The captain looked at his watch, the luminous figures pulsing in the dark. It was twenty-five minutes past. He peered ahead, holding on to a stanchion to keep his balance as the vessel turned into the swells. There was a black shape ahead, probably the guardship. He could just make out the faint riding lights, before suddenly an Aldis lantern came on, and he could hear the shutters rise and snap shut, as they tapped out their morse signal.

The lookout read off the letters. "They're saying farewell, sir," he said, and read out: "Have safe voyage. Don't come back. This belongs to China now. Goodbye."

At the same time, and with the same apparent speed, the soldiers and police of the People's Republic came ashore to retake their longest-sought possession. The huge Mikhail troop-carrying helicopters and landing craft brought men to all the piers and docks in and around Hong Kong and Kowloon, in Aberdeen and Silvermine Bay and Tai Po and Tuen Mun and Yuen Long and at every village on Lamma and Lantau and Cheung Chau and Ma Wan and every other centre of population reckoned to be of potential challenge. By three in the morning there were sentries posted at all the major junctions in Central, Tsim Sha Tsui, Mong Kok, Sham Shui Po and Sha Tin; all the British Army barracks were secure; the airport was closed; the Navy was in full control of the waters and there were political officers manning the radar rooms at the Marine Department. Government House, from which flew the red banner with its golden stars, was protected by scores of soldiers; and on

Queen's Road East the lights blazed fiercely from the red marble building that now sported a brass plaque reading "Central Organising Offices—Xianggang Special Administrative Region."

A guard had also been placed outside the offices at 230 Shanghi Street, Kowloon, and a search made of the premises. But, as might be expected of a small China trading company at three in the morning during this most turbulent time in the Region's history, there was nobody to be found in the office; nor were there any documents to be found that were of any interest to the detectives from the People's Armed Police who conducted a thorough search.

ROOM 4231, DEPARTMENT OF STATE WASHINGTON, DC

Thursday, 3 July 1997

It was the eve of the long Fourth of July weekend, and everyone in every quarter of the United States government—like everyone else in the country—was wanting to get away early. Mercifully for most of the people at State, the world was in a generally placid mood—except, that is, for the troubles in Hong Kong, which had kept everyone in the East Asia Department awake for the past week or so. These people were not, by the looks of things, going to be able to get away early.

The events in South China had been the principal story on CNN every day since the Happy Valley riots. Some of the racier aspects of the story had even made it onto the network shows. Moreover the BBC coverage of the handover ceremony had been watched live by many millions of enthralled people—even though noon, Eastern Time, on a summer Monday was not the best time to catch the American public in front of its televisions.

By then China—and the plight of Hong Kong—had captured the American imagination once again. It was a peculiar phenomenon: the apparently imperturbable villainy of the Chinese Communist leadership was political anathema to all Americans, of course. But China, as in Cathay, Old China, the Middle Kingdom, the land of Imperial Yellow, of concubinage, of bound feet, of silk, of Squeeze and Face—that was something different, and America was currently infatuated with it. All over the country there were now China Tea Clubs, decorated in the style of Thirties Shanghi. Cantonese dining was back in fashion, and people were rediscovering the small triumph of eating with chopsticks. The *cheongsam* had come back into some sort of vogue. Mature women in suburban Dallas and Grosse Pointe and Westchester County were spending afternoons playing mah-jong, and there were said to be fan-tan tables in Atlantic City and down on Paradise Island. The novels of Amy Tan were all the rage, and late night television was managing to offend everyone by showing Charlie Chan and Fu Manchu mysteries, and being accused of presenting a stereotypical China, which the viewing public naturally loved. The May 1997 issue of *Vanity Fair* had written a cover story on the television star Pu Ching, who lived in Los Angeles and who laid claim (accurately, genealogists concluded) to being the Empress of China-in-waiting. Barber shops in Los Angeles reported that the queue had taken over from the ponytail, for men.

Many analysts said the phenomenon had much to do with—and was indeed a reaction to—the wave of anti-Japanese sentiment that had begun to sweep the country in the early and middle Nineties, and which had let to the abrogation of the US-Japan Mutual Security Treaty in June 1994. (That American troops, airmen and warships had been withdrawn from their bases in Japan during 1995 was inconvenient—and would prove decidedly so during the mounting of Operation Eastern Union, the defence of South Korea, in February 1998. The leadership on both sides of the Pacific agreed, however, that in the face of ugly domestic realities in their respective countries, annulling the Treaty had become an absolute political necessity.)

Contacts between an increasingly aggressive Japan and an economically battered United States remained correct and formal during the latter half of the decade, despite the abrogation of the Treaty. But the old intimacy had evaporated. And with this intimacy went part of a grand and historic American connection with the Orient—a connection that had been a part of American life ever since the establishment of the first Chinatowns in San Francisco, ever since Lieutenant Pinkerton met Cho-cho-san in Nagasaki City.

Hence, it is thought, the deliberate rediscovery of an idealised China. It was of no consequence that today's China was still ruled by the Communist gerontocracy. What the American of the late Nineties needed was to assuage the thirst that had been caused by the departure of Japan. An obsession with China, in some shape or form, and with things Chinese, did just that.

But obsession or not, it was irritating in the extreme to the members of the HK7 Committee when, as they had each feared, the call came at noon on Thursday from the Assistant Secretary of State's office, scheduling an extraordinary meeting of the Committee in the fourth-floor conference room at five that evening. Most were planning to leave town: one—the man from the European Affairs Bureau—had been scheduled to leave on the 7 P.M. Air Russia flight to Moscow, for a long weekend with his fiancée.

It was an ill-tempered group that assembled under the portraits of President Benson and Secretary Crowther that evening. Hugh Charlesworth recognised the mutinous mood, and apologised.

"I really would not have scheduled this meeting, ladies and gentlemen, had I not felt it to be most urgent. But I had a telephone call today from Miss Waters at the Agency. She is to blame, if anyone is. She feels she has something to report."

Jillian Waters, who had been the CIA representative on the HK7 Committee for nine of the last twelve regular meetings, was both well-liked and well-respected by the group. Yale and Stanford and one of the first doctorates to be granted at the new Shaw Institute of Chinese Studies at Oxford. Her special subject at Langley was the tracking of political personalities in China, and her analyses were said by all who received them to be invariably factually spot-on and analytically shrewd. The looks of ill-temper thus slowly faded from the faces of her six colleagues, to be replaced by expressions of keen interest.

"I have rather little to say in terms of facts. But the little I have gleaned sounds kind of interesting." Miss Waters glanced up, and looked around the room over the top of her spectacles. "This meeting is, by the way, classified Top Secret. We all know that. But it is perhaps worth repeating on this occasion.

"I have firm information that suggests three things. First: within the next few days we are going to see the outbreak of a full-scale campaign of social disruption waged in Southern China. There will be strikes, riots, assassinations—and the forces that are organising the campaign are well equipped, and will soon be better equipped. Second: at least three well-known political personalities in southern China now believe they have enough latent popular support to encourage an attempt to break away from the main Chinese union.

"And last—and this will cause problems for the sceptics among you—is that I have what I believe to be good and reliable information that elements of the People's Liberation Army based in the region are becoming unstable. They could prove unreliable in the event of a major outbreak of disorder. Their loyalty to central authority, in short, is in question."

Peter Chin, Deputy Director of the People's Republic of China Bureau, laughed incredulously. The other five looked stunned, well aware of the implications of Miss Water's news. There was a sudden barrage of questions. Hugh Charlesworth raised his hand for silence.

"Peter is right to doubt this information," he said. "I found it difficult to believe. But I think it is fair to say that your reporting from Canton City has been rather poor of late"—Peter Chin nodded in response, and remarked that he had had nothing to do with the appointments to the

Consulate-General there—"and these reports all came from Canton, or thereabouts, and from impeccable sources.

"They need to be checked, but using all the normal procedures that will not alert anyone to the suggestion that we have any information whatsoever. This—if it is true—is for the development of policy. Not for the development of reaction. So no word to our missions in China, or elsewhere. This is one for Washington—and it would be as well if Canton and all the Chinese missions are allowed to be surprised by whatever happens. Maybe nothing will. But if it does, and if their normal diplomatic channels have told them nothing, then I want them caught off-guard. We don't want anyone in Peking having any idea of the level of our information.

"So, everyone—go back and double-check with your own sources. I'll expect a report in forty-eight hours. And after that, if it's good, it's for the National Security Council. This deserves an airing in the White House. Things could get out of hand in China pretty quickly. And the implications of that—the implications for Japan, for instance— well, I'm sure I don't have to spell it out."

Thus was the Fourth of July weekend spoiled for seven American bureaucrats and their families, and for a young woman, a Russian translator living in Moscow. By the Monday, however, a report was on Charlesworth's desk; it was on Secretary of State Crowther's desk by mid-afternoon; and by evening had been circulated to the core personnel on the National Security Council's East Asia Coordinating Committee. A copy was also sent to the NSC's Interdepartmental Groups for Defense Policy, Foreign Policy and Emergency Planning.

The United States government was, in other words, fast becoming aware—and at the very highest level of policy making—of the gathering storms in China. A complex series of policy options for dealing with a number of long-term eventualities was constructed. Very few of these options have ever been made public.

It is significant to note, however, that at a meeting held in late August 1997, members of the Joint Chiefs of Staff were briefed secretly on matters relating to southern China and its neighbours, and that as a result they ordered the formal commencement of Phase I of the Joint Chiefs of Staff Crisis Action System. Under the Crisis Action System Phase I order, a military plan would now be developed for the management of one or two of the most likely outcomes of the China situation—a plan that would involve the possible deployment of American forces into the region.

It is of further significance to note that, according to available records (and there are very few, since all these operations were conducted under a need-to-know Top Secret basis) the staff who were assigned to the Crisis Action System planning effort included, as well as the expected specialists on China and Taiwan, a number of intelligence and military analysts who were familiar with three other nations not presently involved—South Korea, North Korea and, somewhat surprisingly, Japan.

The inference is clear: that even as early as the late summer of 1997, the United States was beginning to express concern at the possibility, however slight, that Japan might in the longer term become a party to the gathering crisis; and, further, that the United States of America might have to exercise some kind of military option to prevent such a situation from developing uncontrollably.

CHAPTER SIX

Intimations of Anger

CANTON CITY

Thursday, 10 July 1997

China is a country where superstition still plays a vital role in the lives of its 1.5 billion inhabitants, and in the summer of 1997, to judge by contemporary accounts in the *People's Daily*, there was much to be superstitious about.

The astrologers, whose utterances are still given considerable weight, especially in rural China, had all long before predicted adverse combinations of astral conjunctions, planetary alignments and elemental combinations. A cow with two heads had been born on a farm outside Zhuhai. There was a mysterious wave of sickness, which involved the eruption of unsightly boils, among the ferrymen who worked on the lower reaches of the Pearl River. On 9 March there was, for the first time in scores of years, a total solar eclipse, which could be seen from Mongolia to Manchuria. And, in early July, a typhoon which had threatened to dampen Hong Kong's midnight handover celebrations recurved, as the Western Pacific's summer storms are apt to do, and struck the southern Guangdong coast with immense ferocity, drowning an estimated fifty-two people, bringing down several hundred houses and matsheds, and spoiling the stores of rice in a score of riverside godowns.

The first sign of real trouble came in Canton City, on the morning of 10 July. A young and recently arrived member of the People's Armed Police named Wan Zhu'er was bicycling to his point duties when he was shot through the head in the main city market, as he passed the edible birds section. It was said that the owls, which were on hand to be trussed for the pot, since a particular variant of the brown fish owl is regarded as a great delicacy in southern China, boiled in soup, gazed down with interest at the body. The constable died quickly, and though his bicycle was left untouched his gun, a small automatic pistol, a Type 54 copy of the Russian Tokarev made in Shanghai, was taken from its holster. A clip of 7.62mm ammunition was taken as well.

Constable Wan had been assigned to surveillance and guard duties close to an unmarked Party building beside the Shamian north bridge. But it was not his specific duties that lay behind his violent death. That, as subsequent developments confirmed, came about partly because of who he was, but principally because of where he came from.

His colleagues said he was from a village up in Shandong province, near the town of Weifang in northeastern China. He spoke heavily accented Mandarin, and some Cantonese. He had been assigned six weeks before to guard duties in Canton City because, firstly, he was tall and looked daunting, and secondly because there was an official campaign—fruitless, as it later turned out—to persuade northern PAP officers to take assignments in the south to learn the dialects of southern China.

The truck drivers who passed Comrade Wan at his post seemingly knew, or had a fair suspicion, that he was a northerner. The people of Canton City had long been accustomed to seeing Northerners in their midst, and were well able to recognise them. As a provincial capital city, Canton sported scores of official institutions that were laden with *bak fong yan*, as those bureaucrats from "the north direction" were known. All the locally-posted officials of the central government were from *bak fong*, as were most of those who worked administering the railways, many of the officers in the army and the police, the senior men in the telegraph offices, banks and customs houses. And all these hundreds had, until quite recently, been tolerated by the Cantonese of Canton—not exactly liked, but accepted as part of the enormous patchwork quilt that was China, and which had been stitched into some semblance of a harmonious whole by the efforts of the Party.

In recent years, however, that tolerance had started to wear a little thin. More and more often the classic veiled insult—"you steamed bread eaters"—was heard snarled at northerners.* It was a development that was both slow and subtle, and which requires some background explanation.

For a long while there had been some suspicion and distaste—others might claim it could be more properly described as a downright loathing—expressed for the Northerners by the Cantonese *of Hong Kong*. These, it should be remembered, are not the same as the Cantonese people generally. They are a people who, thanks in part to the astonishing economic prosperity of their colonial home, steadily developed marked differences in attitude and outlook from their ethnically and linguistically similar colleagues who lived to the north of what in colonial times was the border fence. (This fence, built by the British to keep would-be immigrants out of the colony, still existed for a long time after the handing-back of the territory, though the subsequent events that are retold in these pages rendered it a wholly irrelevant structure; a second, electrified, chain-link fence some miles further into China had also been built by the Chinese as further insurance against the contagions of Hong Kong ever entering the ideologically uncorrupted bloodstream of China proper: it, too, was to prove quite useless.)

As long ago as the Seventies the residents of Hong Kong began to be referred to by their Chinese compatriots, by

*The reference is to the climatically induced diet of northern Chinese, which tends to be based on dry-farmed wheat—hence buns, bread and noodles. Southern China, on the contrary, is wet and hot—hence rice. Since southerners tend also to be darker and shorter than northerners, the reverse epithet is "southern monkeys."

politicians, even by anthropologists, as *Hong Kong-ese* people, a group who were now so different from the Cantonese that they had become almost a distinct and separate race. They were taller, heavier, healthier, they lived longer lives, and immense new lexicons had intruded into their (already very colourful, slang-filled) mother-tongue. They were, indeed, a race apart—and it was this race who, in the Seventies and Eighties, began to run out of trust and patience for their fellow Chinese from the north.

For the rest of the world and China, a great many things may well have been true. In the years following the Great Proletarian Cultural Revolution, after the death of Mao Tsetung, the arrest of the Gang of Four and the ascension of the seeming pragmatism and openness of Deng Xiaoping, it may have been true that the whole world trusted the northern Chinese. It may have been true that the Americans, the French, the Germans, the Italians—everyone of consequence, in fact—accepted without question that some great sea-change had come over China, and that she had, after all, returned herself to the community of nations for ever. It may have been true that the British, who were after all renowned for their diplomatic wisdom and caution, had decided that they could place their trust in the essential goodness of the Peking Chinese. And it may have been true that in this spirit they dealt away the future of their tiny colony of Hong Kong, and gave it into the hands of the Pekingese with little more than a fond hope that all would be well.

It may have been that all these things were true for the rest of the world. But for the Hong Kong people they were never true. The Hong Kong people never gave the Chinese their trust. Communist China was, after all, the country and the system from which they had fled. Communist China was the country which they remembered only too well, which they knew only too well, and which seemed to them to behave still with pitiless inconsistency. Torture, assassination, massacre, official corruption—a whole catalogue of sins of which Hong Kong had been mercifully purged still flourished in China. And Hong Kong wanted none of it.

So while the rest of the world took comfort in the appearance, as they saw it, of the "new" China, and of an entity with whom they could do business and treat as an equal, so the Hong Kong people became steadily more and more cynical. They tried to fall in with the rest of world opinion. They tried optimism, and buoyancy, and—being from Hong Kong, where the dollar was an all-powerful juju—they tried to make as much money in business as they could before the deadline as they saw it, of 1997. But underlying all of their attempts was a profound sense of unease, mistrust, and distaste, all of which they expressed by the simple expedient of leaving the colony, in huge numbers. "Voting with our feet," they called it.

This exodus began as a trickle in the Eighties, soon after the publication of the Joint Declaration. Perhaps 100 people were leaving every week. It was a relatively insignificant figure regarded by the government as statistically insignificant, and was little noticed. But a decade later the stream had widened to a flood. In 1992 people were fleeing Hong Kong at the rate of 1,000 a week, for Canada, Australia, the United States. By 1995 some 300 of them were leaving every day—most of them skilled professionals, the qualified, the intelligent. By now they were going anywhere that would take them—to Tonga, Belize, Singapore, Uruguay. The people who had hoped, who had done their best to try to trust those who would soon take them over, now just wanted to get out, to somewhere that offered them and their children some suggestion of stability. The unskilled and the ill-educated who were left behind soon became easy prey, as we have already seen, for the blandishments of the territory's well-organised and politically adroit criminal gangs.

But also during the Eighties there came, unrecognised at first, a further stealthy development, and one of profound importance to the way in which China was later to disintegrate to its present anarchic state.

The suspicion, the distaste, the distrust, the loathing—whatever it was; a precise characterisation of the antipathy expressed towards the northern Chinese comes very much from the reading of individual sets of runes—was up until that point peculiar to, wholly restricted to the Hong Kong people. It was almost wholly non-existent in China itself. To the north of the border fence the Chinese, whether they were Cantonese or Pekingese, Manchu or Szechuan, were of essentially similar outlook, once conditioned by decades of propaganda. It was an outlook which had little in common with that of the people of Hong Kong.

The Hong Kongers may have been ethnically Cantonese, but they were spiritually capitalists. The phrase "running dogs" was often used by ordinary Chinese to describe them, those greedy semi-barbarians south of the fence. And up until this point during the Eighties there was no apparent mistrust—at least, no mistrust that was ever publicly expressed, though Sinologists have claimed to have detected it many years before—ever expressed by the Cantonese of China for their northern compatriots. There was, in fact, much more mistrust for those to the south, in Hong Kong.

The date of a shift in attitude can hardly be fixed, but it probably started to occur between the time of the Joint Declaration in September 1984, which dealt with Hong Kong's future, and the Tienanmen Square incident of five years later. At any rate, some time during the mid-point of the decade the mood started to change and the suspicion that was being expressed by the Hong Kong people started to infect the minds and attitudes and expressions of their colleagues over the border, the 80 million inhabitants of Guangdong Province.

Slowly a new kind of cross-border sympathy began to be forged, one that conjoined these people into a broad ethnic and ideological communion. At first it was the Hong Kongers with just their Cantonese-speaking confrères, and then with those who lived in the provinces near by, in Fujian, Guangxi and Hunan. There were many reasons for the development. There was prosperity, for a start: ever since the formation of the Shenzhen Special Economic Zone in 1980, and of its three neighbour zones along the coast at Zhuhai, Xiamen and Shantou, there had been a tremendous influx of foreign money and foreign ideas. Skyscrapers had been built, with revolving restaurants on top, in which *cheongsam*-clad waitresses would bring bottles of Burgundy to the table. A huge four-lane expressway had been built to link Canton City to Hong Kong. Most southern Chinese watched Hong Kong television, and those who could not at least listened to Hong Kong radio.

It was still true that the peasantry of Qinghai Province, the farmers of Heilongjiang Province, and the desert-nomads of Xinjiang had no knowledge of such developments, and were thus insulated against the influences of capital and greed. But in general the provinces of southern China were fast gaining a solid apprehension of the world outside, and of the possibilities that could be open to their own people. South of the Yangtze River there was indeed a "new" China developing—but one that was evolving not, as Party cadres once had hoped, into an immense ideological communion, but into an ethnic whole that was united by a common hope for modernism and prosperity and individual freedom. South of the Yangtze River, in short, the Chinese people wanted what they saw their colleagues in Hong Kong already had.

The Cantonese were, of course, at the forefront of these developments. By the early Nineties, under the relentlessly seductive influences of Hong Kong, the Province of Guangdong had become, in the view of Party ideologues in Peking, "tainted." The word first appeared in a commentary in the *People's Daily* of 26 December 1993—the centenary of Mao Tse-tung's birth. The paper's editors wrote at length about the legacy of the esteemed founder of the People's Republic, and concluded that there was much of which all China could be proud. But the condition of the nation was judged by the editor still to be, in some quarters, imperfect:

There is concern, however, at recent anti-progressive trends that have been detected among certain uninformed quarters of Guangdong and Fujian Provinces, where the triple contagions of avarice, corruption and landlordism are once more rearing their heads. These pathetic human traits have long been known to exist—and indeed to have been fostered by the colonial elements—among our compatriots in Hong Kong. Now, in part because of the huge infrastructural developments that physically link Hong Kong to our mainland provinces, we have seen some of these evil tendencies start to taint the less personally courageous of our people in Guangdong. It will take bold action on the part of our glorious Party to root out this evil. But the Party has never flinched from its duty, and there is great confidence among the guiding influences of our nation that these cancers can be purged from our midst. It is important that, in the coming months of this struggle, we all be on our guard and see that, while work is being undertaken to rid these influences from our midst, they not be permitted to infect other nearby quarters of our glorious nation. The imperialist capitalist-roaders who will soon, and mercifully, be absolutely gone from our shores must not be allowed to leave influences behind that may pose a danger to our nation and its people, and lead them to practise the decadent ways that will yet prove and accelerate the downfall of these aged imperial states.

This warning, blunt and uncompromising though it seemed, was taken less seriously than it perhaps should have been. The Hong Kong newspapers wrote about it at length; the local stockmarkets (including the market established in Shenzhen in 1991—another indication of "taint") fell heavily.

But a day or two later Mr. Gilbert Hu, a Hong Kong–based businessman with immense interests in building new roads and rail links in southern China (he had built the four-lane Canton–Hong Kong Highway, for example, and was involved in a consortium to build the Canton City Beltway) made a series of reassuring statements on local television (which he knew would be heard throughout Guangdong Province) to the effect that the success of southern China in no way threatened the primacy of the nation's political system, and that the economic benefits that proximity to Hong Kong brought to southern China would inevitably trickle through to the entire country, helping to make the nation as a whole richer and more up to date. Mr. Hu's remarks, which were reaffirmed by the Provincial Governor, Zhu Senlin, helped to stabilise the situation; and for more than two years following there was no further public statement from Peking, and no signs in southern China that anyone had taken notice of the remarks.

In the summer of 1995, however, there were further signs that all was not well in relations between the ruling north and the ideologically wayward south. Governor Zhu, an amiable but compliant figure who had been appointed to his post four years before, came into a heated and public confrontation with his immediate predecessor, Mr. Yi Juan Ling.

Mr. Yi was, crucially, a native of Guangdong province. (Technically he was a Hakka, but he was on record as saying that his heart was in Guangdong.) He was the son of Yi Jianying, a venerated Marshal in the Chinese Army and a Long March hero. He had been appointed by Peking in 1993 to run Guangdong Province: by all statistical reckonings he had succeeded fabulously. He was much liked, too—and not least because of his local roots.

Too often a Chinese provincial governor was, like the commanding general of a military region or his political commissar, a figure deliberately selected to be from ethnic and linguistic stock far removed from the province he was governing or the army he was commanding. While this rarely produced any actual resentment among the population, who were either persuaded by propaganda or too cowed by other means to think of protest, they were never exactly exultant about it. But in 1993 the people of Guangdong had reason to celebrate: Yi Juan Ling was one of their own, rewarded for meritorious service in the trenches by being given command over people he knew, and who drew pride from his appointment.

But after only a few months Peking started to worry: the very success that Yi was overseeing was producing, they thought, a cuckoo in the nest. Internal memorandums— many of them intercepted by the SIGINT interceptors at Chung Hom Kok—showed that conservative elements in

Peking were becoming increasingly concerned at the way
Governor Yi seemed to be building a "mountain stronghold" in south China. There were privately expressed fears
that he might be creating a power base for himself, that he
was becoming in short, the economic version of a warlord.

So after only a year Governor Yi was retired, and his
post was taken by a man from a more traditional, conservative and non-Cantonese (actually Shanghainese) background: Mr. Zhu Senlin. Mr. Yi, however, refused to move
out of his mansion near Canton City, arguing that, as an old
man of great distinction, it was both improper and inconvenient for him to leave.

The situation was at first of little consequence. Governor
Zhu was found a palace of equivalent splendour, and Mr. Yi
was generally ignored. Or would have been ignored had he
not embarked on a strenuous programme of self-promotion
by giving, over the following three years, a series of
lengthy interviews to the Hong Kong press, in each of
which he drew attention to the scale of his success, based,
as he put it, on the "keen friendship" which he was able to
enjoy with "my local people." He expressed his concern
that the same intimacy might not develop with the "less
well-connected" Zhu regime. He pointed out that all the reforms he had instituted in Guangdong were carried out with
the full support of the Peking government—he was thus at
pains to demonstrate that there never had been any intention on his part to create a "mountain stronghold"—but
went on to issue what others interpreted as veiled protests
at what seemed to be a gradual easing of the pace of reform
in the south.

"I am naturally fully supportive of the great leaders of
our nation," he told *Asia Week*. "Those who think otherwise
have been indulging in incorrect speculation based on certain superficial phenomena. The tide of events in our nation
has changed, that is true. It is naturally unwise to check the
flow of that tide. I have no doubt this view is shared by the
great majority of those who are placed in positions of great
trust by the people, and whose wisdom is central to the suc-

cessful management of our ancient and complicated nation."

Few would take issue with such remarks. But in the summer of 1995 Governor Zhu did, and challenged his predecessor in a signed article in the Canton City *Workers' Daily*.

There are those no longer in public office who shared the responsibility for taking our region of China along perilous pathways. Now that the folly of their ways has been demonstrated, now that the tainting of our way of life has been treated and the restlessness which briefly characterised our country has been stilled, it would be as well if such former office-holders were to keep their own counsel. It would be most unfortunate if the passions which once gripped our people are permitted to visit us again: should they do so, those former office holders who speculate on such matters and who wish for the old days and the old ways would have to be held responsible.

Mr. Yi left public view three days after the publication of this editorial, and was not seen again for some months. Signals Intelligence reports indicated that he had been briefly placed under house arrest. By September he was released from whatever privations he suffered, and though he gave no further interviews with any member of the press, and became somewhat difficult to see (diplomats from Hong Kong had long been in the habit of taking tea with him as part of their scouting ventures into the south Chinese hinterland) he was said to be alive and well, still in his old house, and a figure of some note on what passed for the Canton social scene. The fact of his silence was taken as a victory for Peking, but a sign as well that the anxiety over the "tainting" of the region had not eased. Peking was indeed still very much on its guard.

This was the situation that prevailed when Constable Wan Zhu'er was shot dead on 10 July 1997.

It has to be remembered that the shooting of a policeman

in China is an event of extraordinary rarity. The premeditated defiance, in any form, of the state, of authority, is extremely infrequent. Chinese people do not, generally speaking, go on strike. They do not carry banners of protest. They do not walk out of public meetings. Heckling is a virtually unknown phenomenon. Graffiti is rare. Vandalism never takes place. Instructions are followed. Orders are obeyed. The individual never acts alone. Only the mob turns mean.

Many times in recent years the mob has tried to defy authority. In Peking in 1976, Shanghai in 1987, in Peking again in 1989, in Wuhan four years later, crowds of students, joined later by workers did battle with the police and in the two last incidents, with the soldiers of the PLA as well. The demonstrators always came off much the worse, and retreated to lick their wounds and think again about mounting other protests at a later date. Scores of them died or were injured in the confrontations; and while it was true that in several of the incidents police and soldiers and other authority figures died and were injured as well, it can fairly be said that they died or they suffered at the hands of the mob, in the heat of battle, and that their fate was decided in an impromptu fashion and never once premeditated. Although Chinese records on the committing of individual acts of criminal violence are difficult to discover, it seems likely that Constable Wan was the first policeman to die by an assassin's hand in a decade, at least. His murder caused, without a doubt, a major sensation—one that echoed all the way to Peking.

Within minutes of the shooting, which was logged as having taken place at 7:17 A.M., police from the depot on Shamian Island sealed off the road where Constable Wan lay. In addition other police and security men closed all the entrances and exits to the Qingping Market. Crowds of housewives and workers who were making early morning visits on their way to their factories and offices, or who were buying the ingredients for their lunch, began to build up in front of the police barricades. Long lines of cars and buses accumulated on Liuersan Lu, the road running along the waterfront between the market and Shamian.*

The noise of car horns, the shouts of angry drivers, the querulous protests of the gathering crowds, the insufferable heat of a damp July Thursday—all of this led to a growing fractiousness, and a potential for trouble that was quickly spotted by Police Commissioner Zhou. But instead of attempting to placate the crowd by reopening the market, say (for the scene of the crime occupied only a very small section of its outer rim, just off Qingping Lu) or devising a de-

---

*The name Liuersan Lu, "6-23 Road," commemorates the shooting of striking Chinese workers by British and French soldiers on 23 June 1925, an incident that did much to strengthen the hand of the anti-Imperialist movement and the so-called United Front coalition of Communists and Kuomintang. There is no evidence that those stranded in the traffic jam more than seven decades later were aware of how history was repeating itself.

tour for the stranded motorists, the Commissioner ordered a large detachment of armed police into the area to impress the crowd into silence and forbearance. By mid-morning there was an uneasy standoff: some 20,000 people in the side streets around the market, some 600 vehicles caught between the barricades and, surrounding them all, two battalions of the PAP, armed with rifles and side-arms and in no mood to let the situation get further out of hand.

The investigation into the shooting, meanwhile, had produced some interesting facts. Constable Wan took the single bullet in the right side of his face: it had entered below his cheekbone and spun upwards through his brain, emerging through the scalp and blowing almost all of the top left side of his head away. He would have died instantly. The single bullet used in the attack was a 9mm Parabellum, and from comparison with photographs of other bullets it was speedily agreed among the police that it was a bullet that had been manufactured in Israel. The weapon that fired it was probably, the detectives then concluded with surprising rapidity, an Uzi sub-machine-gun, set to fire single shots.

Given the trajectory of the bullet and the characteristics of the weapon—which was somewhat difficult to aim, and best fired at close range—it was likely that the assassin was hiding in a car or a lorry parked on Qingping Lu. The bullet's upward path suggested that the assassin was lower than the target, probably in a car, rather than a lorry. Investigators thus began questioning all those who were in the market at the time. Had they heard the shot? Had they seen a vehicle—probably a car—leave the area in a hurry, after the shooting? In fact, had they seen anything at all unusual that morning?

Qingping Market is a place where a Western visitor would regard almost everything as unusual. That the constable was shot while cycling just beside the parade of owls—eagle owls and brown fish owls being the most favoured for the pot—hints at the menagerie beyond. On a normal day one can find, in the slimy alleyways of Quingping, such delights as leopard, golden monkey, the seven-banded civet cat, pangolins rolled tight into defensive balls, the slow loris, the giant salamander, a bagful of banded kraits, a cage of Peking robins, and legions of unremarkable cats and dogs, all waiting to be butchered, skewered and served up roasted for dinner.

Against such a background—of strange animal cries, the pandemonium of the crowds of shoppers, the traffic noise and the thunderclaps (for the day had begun with a vicious summer storm)—could anyone be expected to remember hearing a gunshot, or seeing a car lurch off in an unexpected hurry or the constable fall to the ground? At least, such were the excuses that those questioned all offered. After four hours, during which the crowds grew larger and more restless and more angry, it turned out that no one had seen or heard anything. No one in the market that morning was able to help the police carry the investigation any further than their own forensic examinations had taken them. There was, it seemed to the frustrated and irritated officers, almost a conspiracy of silence abroad. One detective even claimed to his superiors later that he had heard two men in the market laugh and say they were glad that the policeman had died. "Wretched scum from Peking," was the phrase that was used—a remark that may have been geographically inaccurate (since the constable had come from Shandong Province, 300 miles south of Peking), but which probably summed up the sentiment of the crowd.

By lunchtime the mood on both sides was dangerously hostile. The detectives had achieved nothing, and, under pressure from their officers to find some clues to the killing, their questioning was growing ever harsher. The shoppers and passers-by, who were by now clearly unwilling to be of any help to the police, had been detained for much longer than any one of them was willing to tolerate. The crowds outside the police barricades began to jeer at the police, and to shout sympathetically to those detained inside.

Then suddenly half a dozen of those who were being held for questioning decided that they had had enough, and broke away from their questioners. They ran at full speed through the slippery halls of the market and straight into the backs of the policemen who were keeping the curious crowds out. Their speed and determination allowed them to break the police line and, in the momentary confusion, they succeeded in getting through to their colleagues outside. A huge cheer went up, and the crowd began to pelt the police with vegetables and chunks of sugar cane and the contents of dozens of large straw baskets of refuse that were waiting for collection in a gutter.

Two companies of armed police were ordered to hurry around to the northern side of the market, where this irruption of violence had broken out, and to take up defensive positions. They were ordered, as a precautionary measure, to fix bayonets; the sight of this formidable array of men marching towards the alleys where the mob had accumulated caused immediate panic and dismay. "Another Wuhan!" a woman screamed, and there was a chorus of anger from the mob. "You cowards!" "Why turn your guns on us?" "Have you no shame?"

However, the boiling black clouds which had been circling the city all morning chose this particular moment to explode in thunder and lightning, and great drops of rain began to pelt down. A brief but violent tropical storm lashed down on the city once again, as it had earlier that morning. Within five minutes the streets were awash with torrents of dirty water coursing its way down to the canal and the Pearl River. The crowds melted away home and the tension was instantly relieved.

The Police Commissioner, after consulting his officers on the spot, decided there would be little value in pursuing further interviews, and allowed all those remaining in the market to go home as well, once they had given their identity card numbers and their addresses to the officers.

But Peking was not satisfied. Later that evening Commissioner Zhou—who had made a full report on the incident to his superiors, and to the office of Governor Zhu Senlin—was telephoned personally by an (as yet unidentified) official at the headquarters of the Public Security Bureau. The precise contents of the message have never been revealed, but it is believed that it was made brutally clear to the Commissioner and his senior colleagues that such

signs of potential disorder as had manifested themselves in
Canton City that morning and afternoon should be dealt
with immediately, the results promulgated with equal speed,
and the population left in no doubt that neither the central,
provincial nor city governments would tolerate such aber-
rant behaviour.

The Commissioner did indeed act swiftly. Late that evening he ordered two dozen men from the PSB to enter, by
force if necessary, a number of rooming houses in a slum
area close to the market at Zhoutouzui Wharf, from where
the Pearl River boat services to and from Hong Kong are
operated. The houses, gloomy and foetid places notorious
for harbouring smugglers and drug users and the cheaper
kinds of prostitutes, were often raided when politicians demanded a quick arrest or a scapegoat for an unsolved
crime, and the police were confident, on this occasion as in
the past, of netting someone on whom they could pin this
killing.

By midnight three men were in custody. Two—Leung Ka
Tan and Leung Wan—were from Hong Kong; the third,
Lam Wang Fook, was from the city of Foshan, about
twenty miles west of Canton. None of the three had satisfactory identification papers, the police said later, and one
of the Leungs was in possession of a rusty automatic pistol
which might have been fired recently. It was of 7.62mm
calibre, and so could not be directly linked to the murder of
Constable Wan.

None the less the men were taken early next morning to
a public hearing of the Canton City People's Court. Each of
the men was held tightly by the arms—which were hand-
cuffed behind the back—by two members of the PAP. They
looked dazed, and several observers in court said later they
appeared to have been drugged.

A tribunal of judges sitting for twenty minutes heard the
evidence against them. Eyewitness accounts were read out,
indicating that all three men had been seen in a red Toyota,
evidently a former Hong Kong taxicab, parked in Qingping
Lu at 6:45 the previous morning. Forensic tests were read
out, showing that wax impression samples taken from the

hands of suspect Lam showed evidence of cordite burns that matched the known chemical characteristics of the type of cordite used in Israeli-manufactured ammunition. A scrawled note was produced with the characters for "police" and "Quingping Market" and a time "7 A.M." clearly legible. All this evidence, a prosecuting lawyer said, proved beyond a shadow of doubt that these three men had conspired to murder Constable Wan. It was regrettable, the lawyer told the court, that the eyewitnesses were unable to be present that morning, and that the forensic scientist who had conducted the tests on Lam's hands had been ordered to another case in southern Guangdong; the calligraphy expert who had compared the characters on the handwritten note with samples of Leung Ka Tan's writing, pronouncing them "of identical origin," could be called back from holiday if necessary. The tribunal replied that it did not feel such drastic measures were called for. The three men were clearly, on the basis of the evidence so painstakingly assembled, guilty as charged, and would be sentenced to death by shooting.

Accordingly later that morning, a hot and sunny Friday, the three men were placed, standing, in the back of three open police trucks, to be driven to their place of execution. The chosen spot was a small park named Dongshanhu to the east of the city. During the five-mile journey from the courts on Jeifang Beilu, in the north of the city, loudspeaker announcements informed pedestrians and motorists and the crowds of cyclists that the men responsible for the appalling crime of the morning before had been successfully apprehended, and were being dealt with according to law. Large posters hung around each man's neck also stated, in large red characters, the nature of the crime and his guilt. Since the journey was a slow one it is estimated that in the order of 1 million people came to know of the impending act of retribution.

The act itself came at five minutes after noon—nearly twenty-nine hours after the murder. The lorries bumped across the waste ground into the park. The backs of the lorries were opened, the men were pulled down and marched to a spot on a small hillock near the riverside. They were forced to kneel beside each other.

The policemen guarding them moved back, and one senior officer stepped forward with a pistol. He went up to Mr. Lam, placed the snout of the pistol beneath his right ear, angled upwards, and fired. Lam fell forward, dead. The officer then moved to the two Leungs, and did the same. Another officer with a stethoscope examined the three for any sign of life and, finding none, ordered the bodies placed in the back of one of the open trucks. The policemen then left the scene. A park attendant with a brush of bamboo strips tidied up the area and brushed earth over the pools of blood.

Later that day large posters went up outside the city police stations with the names of the three men, an account of their crimes, the court's verdict, and the nature of the sentence. Across each of the names was drawn a distinctive red tick mark, indicating that the sentence had, in all cases, been carried out. Justice had both been done and, as was most important in what the Police Commissioner was later to say were "these volatile times," had been seen to be done. The people of south China had been warned.

CHAPTER SEVEN

Onset of Rage

THE SOUTH COAST OF CHINA

July 1997

The southern Chinese summer grew steadily hotter and more sultry, and an unusual number of powerful storms battered the coastal towns and villages. The rains spread into central China too, the Yangtze and the Yellow Rivers flooded catastrophically, and hundreds of people were reportedly drowned in Sichuan and Hubei Provinces, which suffered this year even more miserably than was customary.

Hundreds of thousands of refugees (perhaps scores of millions, the number could never be reasonably estimated) joined the annual trek south—workless and hungry peasants leaving their hardscrabble farms and their mud-ruined fields in search of work, or even for the opportunity to beg, in the industrial cities of Guangdong. Such unfortunate people could be seen everywhere in the city: they were smaller and darker skinned than their Cantonese comrades. They were invariably dressed in rags, showed no shame in their appearance, and had an almost feral energy for hard and dirty manual work, for panhandling, or for villainy.

Outside the main railway station, which was in any case perpetually thronged with masses of filthy, sweaty and unkempt men and women, hundreds of such refugees would lie in wait for arriving or departing passengers. One young woman, who serves as an example of the mood of eco-

nomic desperation of the times, would sit outside the Main
Line exit from dawn until late at night, an undersized and
almost lifeless baby clutched firmly to her naked and shriv-
elled breast. Any passenger who evidenced even the slightest hint of prosperity—by carrying a suitcase instead of a
sack, or if one article of his clothing that he wore looked
clean, or even moderately new, or if he carried a newspaper
or a magazine or some other sign of having recently parted
with small change—any such hapless individual was her in-
variable and immediate target.

She would launch herself at him with the speed and
venom of a snake. She would fasten herself to him with a
single bony claw, and she would screech at him in some
barely comprehensible rural tongue, demanding that he part
with a few *renminbi* for the child she held clamped tight
under her other arm. He invariably would look bewildered,
disgusted and embarrassed by turn. He would try to beat
her away, as would a man enveloped in a swarm of bees.
But it was of no avail. She would shout even more loudly,
and she would berate him for his lack of decency, his lack
of charity, and for his assault on her and her defenceless
child. And eventually, under so withering a barrag he
would give in, and dig deep into his pockets for one or two
from a small bundle of creased and dirty notes that he was
in no position to afford to waste, and he would hand them
to the woman who, without even a word or a gesture of
gratitude, would sidle back into the crowds, and wait for
her next victim, the next unsuspecting arrival in the city of
Canton.

By 1995, according to a study made available from the
American Embassy in Peking, there were no fewer than
340 million peasants—more people, in other words, than
lived in all of the United States—who could officially be
classified as so deeply underemployed that by Western
standards they would be regarded as literally unemployed.
And in 1997, driven by poverty, hunger, frustration, desperation, anger—and then the floods—they were on the move.
It mattered little to such people that China had strict rules
to limit labour mobility—rules that prohibited anyone mov-

ing to another town without a Residency Permit, a document rarely granted, and then only to those with a guaranteed job (which, as might be expected of so controlled a state, could not be acquired without the production of a Residency Permit). These people moved in an unstoppable flood, and when they arrived in the chosen city— Chongqing, or Changsha, or Canton—they knew they had already flouted the rules, and were thus outlaws, and could suffer no worse than imprisonment, which would at least ensure them a small amount of daily food, work, and shelter.

The social order of Canton, rarely stable in the best of times, and maintained in less good times by strict policing and force of arms, was to deteriorate sharply in the summers of the Nineties. As the numbers of workless peasants increased, as their summer migrations accelerated in scale and boldness, as climatic conditions forced more and more of a deeply dissatisfied rural population to infiltrate the city populations, so the distemper of the city became ever more pronounced. An Oriental version of Boyle's law seemed to operate: the temperature went up, the numbers of people climbed, the volume available for their accommodation remained unchanged, and so the pressure increased steadily, inexorably, fatally. Sooner or later something was bound to burst.

Hindsight shows us now that the events of 10 and 11 July 1997—the assassination, and the hurried retribution— provided the needle that was to release this pressure. But other contributory factors were to come into play in the following days, ensuring that the explosion, when it finally came at the end of the month (to coincide, not unexpectedly, with the celebrations called to mark the 76th anniversary of the First Congress of the Chinese Communist Party) was all the more extreme.

The principal factor was the knowledge both in Peking and Canton that the three men hauled from their shacks near the Zhoutouzui wharf had nothing at all to do with the shooting of Constable Wan. The public security apparatus felt that the execution of the three men might still any latent local volatility, and remind any dissident forces of who exactly was in control. But the act was only an expedient. The reality remained that some vestigial anti-social organisation now existed in Canton, and that it was an organisation equipped with, at the very least, an Uzi sub-machine-gun from Israel and sufficient ammunition from the same source, and was possessed of a car, a willing driver and a good marksman, together with the constable's own side-arm and a clip of 7.62mm bullets. This unit alone, if it remained undetected, could be dangerous: the likelihood was that many more members, and many more weapons, were secreted around the city. The police had to find them, and find the source of both the men and *matériel*, and put a swift and decisive halt to whatever anti-social agency had started to operate.

Emergency conferences held by senior PSB officers during mid-July drew on their very limited resources of street intelligence (which had gone unaccountably silent in recent weeks) and concluded that the most probable source of the trouble was Hong Kong. However, a Policy Directive from Peking dated 4 July ordered that the "serious social unrest" that had followed the departure of the British (and which had resulted in fires, destruction of many buildings and the deaths of some 300 people evenly divided between the civilian and armed populations) "should now be allowed to dissipate." Thus any "interference in Hong Kong's internal government," which invariably led to "grave expressions of anger among the local population," should be "kept at a minimum for the time being, to permit Chief Executive Mao to enjoy a period of stability."

The corollary to this instruction was that officials from the PSB should not undertake major criminal investigations inside the territory, other than with the permission of Mao's office. A formal approach seeking such permission was turned down flat. A senior PSB officer from Canton accordingly flew to Peking to win the sanction of higher authority. He returned on 17 July with permission to send his officers, in plain clothes, into the Special Administrative Region and to make "such discreet investigations as are deemed vitally necessary." Before his men left he added a warning to the effect that "the normal procedures used by the Bureau to conduct investigations may not be wholly suited to the sensitivities of the people of Hong Kong."

The next day twelve Bureau officers travelled by train to Kowloon and, to use the slang of the time (and completely ignoring the warning from Peking) "slapped some beancurd" in the slums of Mong Kok. The arrest and subsequent torture—for this is what the "slapping" implied—of three men whose names were in the Mong Kok police files of known arms smugglers produced little that was of use or interest, other than to confirm that Uzi submachine-guns had been freely available "shortly before the end of July," and that a number were known to be circulating now.

The dealers themselves had not seen any of these weapons, though they admitted under severe "slapping" that they could provide suitable 9mm American-made Parabellum ammunition from stock. But none had been ordered in the previous week, the dealers said: everyone "in the business" was clearly intimidated by the Chinese Communist presence, which was much larger and more overwhelming than had even been expected.

The leader of the PSB group, fearing that their continued stay in the Region would leak out and further excite local passions and embarrass the local leadership, then ordered a retreat. To limit any likelihood of the news of their questioning becoming public, the three arms dealers were promptly strangled to death in circumstances that made the killings appear to be the result of criminal rivalry.

On their return to Guangdong Province the police ordered strict new controls to be placed on all movements through the two barriers. At the southern frontier—the old Hong Kong border—there would henceforth be a thorough inspection of all northbound vehicles and their occupants, all of whom would now have to disembark and be subjected to a body inspection; the northern frontier, which had recently been equipped with electric fencing on which two young men (trying to get into the Zone from the north) had already died, was thought to be adequately secure, though new mirror-sticks were to be provided to vehicle inspectors to ensure that no goods were smuggled into China underneath any northbound cars or trucks.

Peter Heung had by this time vanished underground. To maintain his invisibility he had a simple set of rules. He would not spend successive nights at the same address. He never used the telephone. He communicated with his lieutenants in code, on scraps of paper. Such meetings as he attended were called at short notice, with those attending ignorant of which of their colleagues was likely to be present. But in spite of these inconveniences he was still surprisingly able to organise his White Fans and his 49 Boys to perform the bidding of the gang hierarchy. The three nights of heavy rioting that greeted the arrival of the Chinese and the departure of the British colonial administrators was testimony to his tactical genius. Furthermore, there was no indication that Chinese intelligence knew either his name or his whereabouts: as part of the agreement with Margerison struck some weeks before, all Special Branch files relating to the Warwick Accord had been either destroyed or removed to vaults in London.

It did not take Heung very long to find out about the visit of the PSB officers from Canton City, nor to ascertain the "release" (to use bandit slang once again) of the three men they had interrogated. He and his colleagues had expected the visit, and had expected they would lose men as a consequence of it. That only three had suffered was not, in the group's view, particularly distressing since these particular three had no knowledge of the Margerison arrangements, and no knowledge (aside from the inevitable rumours) of the fate of the new weapons.

As it happened, more than 80 percent of the weapons had already been sent into Chinese territory. They had gone, by train, by car, in individual pockets and in plastic luggage bags, during the chaos of those first few days of July. Border security for southbound travellers was exacting; but for northbound visitors there was very little. (It only became strict in the immediate aftermath of Constable Wan's death on 10 July, and then again following the visit of the PSB officers on 18 July. For the first week of July the searching of passengers and vehicles passing up to Shenzhen and beyond was perfunctory at best.)

Heung's view of the need for such movement of arms stemmed from two thoughts: first, his uncertainty that he could maintain the total operational security of his Hong Kong forces, and second, and most important of all, his and his colleagues' firm belief that, in the long term, *it was more valuable for his organisation to try to help foment discord and trouble in Canton in southern China than it was for him to reinforce the resentment and dissent that already existed in Hong Kong*.

The task of turning the population against the northern Chinese was, as has been explained above, already complete in the former British territory. But the growing dissatisfaction in the main cities of Guangdong and Fujian Provinces—Canton in particular, but in Zhuhai, Foshan, Huiyang, Shantou, Zhanzhou, Xiamen and Quanzhou as well, as outlined in the previous chapter—suggested to Heung's group that there was sufficient potential to produce, one day, and with their help, a pan-Cantonese, pan-Fukkienese political communion, a southern resistance axis, or whatever else one might term it: in short, a coalition of men and forces south of the Yangtze who perhaps might, one day, be able to help direct all of southern China along the same path that had, until very recently, been followed by the people of Hong Kong.

Captain Margerison had mentioned the point to him idly some months before. Now, with the acquisition of a limited amount of weapons, there was the opportunity. He could perhaps help nudge his colleagues across the frontier in the proper direction. So he directed both the bulk of the weapons, the explosives and the ammunition and more than a hundred of his best men, all of them former natives of Canton City or of Xiamen, and frequent visitors to their relatives there, with orders to blend into the population and await detailed instructions.

Their general occupation in the meantime was to arrange and complete a small number of assassinations, as a way of testing the authorities' mettle and competence (an order which they started to carry out—with the shooting of Constable Wan—with dispatch); and to assist in finding and organising groups who might, at appropriate moments, stage acts of disobedience and defiance to excite and irritate the authorities. Only after these probing devices had been completed and their effects noted would more serious and concerted activities begin.

The second and third of such "probing" incidents took place simultaneously early on the evening of Tuesday, 22 July. Both took place in Fujian Province, a coastal region to the east of Guangdong which enjoyed a prosperity similar to that of the Pearl River delta area. According to Heung's operations officers in China there was an important tactical purpose in staging the events in these two separate areas: firstly, it would enable the rebels to gauge the level of popular sympathy in two ethnically dissimilar but equivalently prosperous and "tainted" parts of south China; and secondly, it would enable a comparison of the government's response to incidents staged in two adjoining military regions, for although Guangdong and Fujian Provinces are linked by a common border, and are, like all provinces, separate military districts, they happen also to belong to different Military Regions. Guangdong Province is a part of Guanzhou Military Region, which—commanded by a full general based on the outskirts of Canton City—includes six Military Districts, each commanded by a lieutenant-general. These six are Guangdong, Guangxi, Hainan Island, Hubei, Hunan and, since 1 July, Yianggang. Fujian, on the other hand, is part of the Nanjing Military Region, which has its headquarters in the city of Nanjing. The Region administers five districts, which include Fujian, Anhui, Zhejiang, Jiangxi and Jiangsu and is associated with the Shanghai

Military Garrison Command, which (like Peking and Tianjin Garrisons) has a high degree of military autonomy.

It is important to note also that Fujian Military District has notional responsibility for "protecting" the mainland from Taiwan. The forces there had, ever since the Fifties, been on the alert for any hostile acts that might be mounted by the forces of the Republic of China, which lies directly east of Fujian—and indeed of Xiamen City—across the 100-mile-wide Taiwan Strait. So Heung's group supposed that the response, if any, of the Fujian military commander to what he might see as an incipient rebellion, would be likely to be very much more robust—because of the perceived "foreign threat" from Taipei—than would be the response to similar problems arising elsewhere in any other districts. (Although it was perhaps true that the action of commanders in Tibet and the extreme north of Manchuria, who would have reason to suspect foreign threats of a different kind from the Tibetans, the Nepalese, India, forces loyal to the Dalai Lama, or the Russians, respectively, might be equally swift and strong.)

Which makes the boldness of the Xiamen incident of 22 July, and the tenor of the reaction, all the more interesting.

It will be recalled that in late July the country was scheduled to celebrate the seventy-sixth anniversary of the staging of the First Congress of the Chinese Communist Party. The anniversaries were generally lavish affairs, with each provincial capital vying with its rivals in the scale and grandeur of its parades, with special editions of the newspapers, adulatory documentary films on television and in cinemas, and self-congratulatory banquets where the local party grandees would toast the achievements of the past year and look forward with professed enthusiasm to the triumphs awaiting.

This year the celebrations were due to be even more heartfelt, since the Party could now give thanks for the welcoming into its fold of one further piece of real estate—Hong Kong—and a further 6 million new comrades, to take the total population of China over the almost unimaginably massive figure of 1,500 million. It remained only for the

Portuguese-held enclave of Macau to join the family—an event which was formally due to happen in two years' time—and then for Taiwan, which it surely would, but at some date as yet unstated—before the entire realm of the Middle Kingdom could all be safely joined into an ideological one. This anniversary, therefore, would be particularly joyful, marking the first of the final steps that the nation was taking towards becoming the state for which all the Chinese yearned.

There were two dozen elderly Party cadres in Xiamen and the neighbouring counties who were due to be singled out for honours at the 1997 celebrations. The formal banquet at which citations were to be read and plaques presented was due to take place on Friday, 25 July in the famous Bagua Lou, "The Building of the Eight Diagrams" on the island of Gulangyu. The building, with its distinctive dome, had been a merchant's mansion; during the cultural revolution it had been an electrical factory; and then in the Seventies it had been restored, and opened as a museum of Xiamen history in 1993. It was the finest building in the city, the natural setting for a ceremony of this splendour.

A final planning meeting was organised for the evening of the Tuesday before. It would be attended by the Assistant Party Secretary, Mr. Wei Chunwa, four of his secretariat, and a group of ten officials from the Xiamen Municipality and from Hui'an County, who were planning to stage a tableau. This meeting, which had been little publicised, was also to take place in a grand building—in this case the former trader's mansion complex that had been taken over by the Municipality in 1978 and was now known as the Gulangyu Guesthouse. This assembly of three large houses lay in a park, once the old Foreign Concession Parade Ground, near the northern end of the little island, and suitably close to the much-visited museum to Koxinga,* the region's favourite son.

*Koxinga was the nickname for the famous and revered General Zhen Chenggong, who used Xiamen as his base for his numerous fruitless attacks on the Manchus after the fall of the Ming Dynasty in 1644. But his

The guesthouse, once owned by a businessman named Mr. Huang, had managed to keep all its old furniture—old clocks (one made by Hamilton in New York in 1911), a fine billiard table (made by a company in London's Soho Square in 1925), leather Chesterfields and grimy oil paintings. The place had the look and feel of a rather down-at-heel gentlemen's club—and with the fine old banyan trees and the scrubby lawns, a colonial watering-hole in some distant corner of the tropics.

The men arranged themselves around the main dining table at 6 P.M. Mr. Wei, who was the guest of honour, was seated at the head of the table; two of his four assistants were beside him, the other two at the far end of the table. The men from Hui'an and Xiamen were in between. At 6:07 P.M.—the hands of the Hamilton clock stopped at this point—there came a huge explosion. A bomb, estimated to contain at least four pounds of a plastic explosive, exploded beneath the table no more than two feet from where Mr. Wei was sitting. He was almost decapitated, and died instantly, as did his two closest assistants, three of the men from Xiamen Municipality, a waiter who had been pouring Mr. Wei's tea, and another unidentified man. The remaining members of the group were all savagely injured, with two of them requiring the amputation of both legs, and all suffering severe abdominal injuries.

Devastation in the room was extraordinary, and the fact that two large crossbeams were blown out and crashed down on the injured delayed the removal of the men to a hospital. In addition, none of the clinics on the island was capable of handling such an emergency, and the injured had to be taken by boat across to the city's piano-shaped tourist

defeat at the hands of the northerners is less well remembered by modern Chinese than is his single triumph—his attack on the Dutch in Taiwan, and his success in driving them unceremoniously off to Japan. Koxinga's little army—strong men, selected, it was said, only if each could lift a 600 lb. stone lion on to his back—is an army of heroes, even today. And among the gifts that each of the cadres was due to be given at the Friday celebration dinner was a small stone lion, an exact hand-carved replica of that still kept in an honoured place in the Gulangyu shrine.

pier, and sped to Xiamen Number Four Hospital. It was not until midnight that the injured had all been removed from the ruined building, and forensic examination did not start until dawn.

There had been an initial suspicion that a liquefied gas bottle from the kitchen, inadvertently left beneath the table, had somehow caught fire and exploded. But the discovery, shortly after first light, of the remains of a timing device, with a Seiko digital watch seemingly used as part of the triggering mechanism, indicated beyond doubt that the incident was an act of sabotage. One, moreover, of which its organisers could be justly proud: seven men, five of them leading local members of the Chinese Communist Party, had died. It was probable that the Friday celebrations would have to be cancelled.

This probability increased further when local police were told of another unprecedented outrage that had occurred in the nearby town of Shitsze, also known by its nickname of Xiao Xianggang, or "Little Hong Kong."

The town, which ten years before had been no more than a gaggle of crude shacks, had blossomed into one of the country's most astonishing success stories. It had neither a railway nor a port, and until 1995 had been connected to the rest of Fujian Province by a single-lane track. And yet—for reasons which were never explained, but were thought to have been due to a large measure of official corruption, and the fact that a very large number of the local residents had wealthy relations living abroad in the Philippines and the United States—it boomed, like nowhere else in South China, with more than 10,000 privately owned businesses.

It was possible to obtain anything in Shitsze City. There were BMW cars for sale, and Honda motorcycles, CDs of the latest Japanese pop singers, CDI players, cases of Australian Chardonnay, pornographic holograms, See's chocolates, Love Flower Brand silk underwear (which was made in a privately owned factory), Jade Horse Brand Cigars (owned by the Tabaqueria Filipiniana of Manila, and exported around the world) and Xiao Xianggang Brandy, rebottled as "Tall Man" French VSO, and marketed very successfully in Macau.

Occasionally the local authorities were ordered, by Public Security Ministry fiat from Peking, to try to clamp down on the plethora of illegality in the town. Such clampdowns usually manifested themselves as executions, which followed widely publicised show trials. Such a trial had taken place on 20 July, when two men, a Mr. Hua and a Mr. Dong, were put on show in Shitsze's half-completed basketball stadium, accused of smuggling Hitachi television sets from a Manila-registered freighter which was, at the time of its supposed sighting, hove to ten miles east of Quemoy Island.

The men were duly sentenced to death and were marched off to a patch of waste ground a mile outside town. However, as they were being helped down from their transport there was a brief and efficient ambush: five armed men stepped from an unmarked van and, according to eyewitness reports, spoke to the police escorts. One of the policemen clearly objected, there was a struggle, and a single shot was fired. The policeman fell to the ground, injured. The remaining officers dropped their weapons and fled, whereupon Mr. Hua and Dr. Dong, collecting up the half-dozen rifles and pistols left behind, were bundled into the van and driven away. The policeman who had been injured had not been badly hurt, and survived: he said later he believed the assailants had Hong Kong accents. The other policemen, at the time news of this incident was telegraphed to Xiamen, had not been found.

The authorities were, in essence, panic-stricken. The police and Public Security Bureau had long been under standing orders to notify the army if anything untoward and "of possibly Taiwan-inspired origin" occurred in the area. Acting under these instructions the Xiamen authorities informed the Fujian Military District Commissar, Chen Shuqing, at his headquarters camp near Drum Mountain, east of the provincial capital city of Fuzhou. Chen conferred both with his military commander, General Shen, and by telephone with Region HQ in Nanjing City. They concluded that enemy interference was probably behind the two incidents, and suitable precautions had therefore to be taken.

The Drum Mountain Early Warning Station was thus put on full alert. Two squadrons of Shenjang J8 fighter aircraft based at Xiamen and Fuzhou were told to be ready for immediate action. Armed patrol vessels of the East Sea Fleet were ordered to set out from Dinghai Island near Shanghai, and from Xiamen naval dockyard, and to stand to in the Taiwan Straits. Two Anshan-class destroyers were ordered to proceed north from Hong Kong, to join the patrol vessels.

In addition, two entire infantry divisions from the 63rd Integrated Group Army based near Quanzhou were ordered into full battle gear, and six coastal artillery batteries were issued with quantities of 155mm ammunition and instructed to be on close watch for any potential invaders from across the Straits. The two islands of Quemoy and Matsu, the former so near that observers on Gulangyu could see the Taiwanese flag with only moderately powered glasses, were kept under particular surveillance.

It was against this background of the most extraordinary military readiness that the Fujian Provincial PSB began the investigation into the most serious acts of criminal violence and defiance to have occurred in China for twenty years.

For the Gulangyu inquiry the island was completely sealed off: the ferry-boat that normally shuttled to and from the mainland was halted, and only official police boats were permitted to land. The fishing harbour was shut. Policemen fanned out over the island, telling all residents to remain indoors.

A number of clues were found in the debris. Fragments of the Seiko digital watch timer were dug from the mess of plaster and brick soon after dawn. Then a number of charred fragments of paper were found which were cylindrically curved, probably wrappers from sticks of explosive. The detectives were able to recognise two types of writing on the paper, one English, the other probably Urdu. More careful examination that followed the piecing-together of a number of these paper fragments indicated that the explosives had come from a well-known but illicit munitions factory in a town called Darra, in Pakistan's North-West Frontier Province. To import from such a source would not be difficult: ever since the opening, ten years before, of the Karakoram Highway between Gilgit and Kashgar there had been justifiable anxiety about the possibility of what were called "tribal guns" being brought into China. One of the consequences of the Gulangyu investigation was an immediate tightening of the frontier inspection, much as had been ordered on the Hong Kong–Shenzhen border: the dangers of allowing weapons into the country were self-evident.

Other clues emerged later in the day. A worker in the grounds of the old Catholic church—not a Catholic himself, but a gardener who had long been in the pay of the PSB and had been assigned to keep an eye on the activities of the elderly priest—reported that a week before he had seen three men, who at the time he assumed were tourists, talking in hushed tones to a man known to be a cleaner from the guesthouse. He assumed the men were tourists because they were speaking in Cantonese, a language which he did not understand.

Enquiries showed that the cleaner, whose name was Li, had left the island by boat on the afternoon of the explosion. The guesthouse manager said he had been working in the main dining-room that afternoon. He also reported that Li was from Canton City, and that while he spoke *putonghua* and some Fukkienese, his mother tongue was Cantonese.

All of this information had been gleaned before noon on 23 July, the Wednesday. It seemed clear to the investigators that the conspiracy involved at least four men of whom at least three came from either Canton or Hong Kong. The word "tourist," when used by a Chinese, usually refers to someone from an evidently very different community— someone whose appearance and dress and manner look most unfamiliar. The fact that the three men who spoke to the cleaner were evidently very different in appearance from the cleaner—who did come from Canton—suggested to the investigators that they were looking for a group from Hong Kong.

Messages were sent to all hotels and guesthouses to check their records. Surveillance at airports and liner ports was stepped up. Xiamen University, which was still open for summer classes, was ordered closed, and the students told to remain on campus. The single bridge linking Xiamen to the mainland at Jimei was cordoned off by troops. Later that afternoon house-to-house searches were ordered in two districts of the city known to be favoured by overseas Chinese—particularly the Taiwanese who trickled up from Hong Kong, and those who lived in Manila, and returned to see relations in the region.

The only effect of this hurriedly and clumsily organised cordon and search operation was to alienate at least two sectors of the local population—the students and the fishermen. Neither of these groups of people, amounting to nearly 4,000 each, was permitted to leave. By early evening the students had become dangerously restless and the leader of the student body, a third-year anthropologist named Duan Kun, organised a protest march out of the university grounds. The march got under way at 7 P.M. and had reached Daxue Lu, the main coast road that leads to the city, when it was confronted by a double line of men from the People's Armed Police.

At about the same time, and one has to assume by pure coincidence, a crowd of several hundreds squid-fishermen whom police had forbidden to take their craft out for the night also gathered on Daxue Lu about a third of a mile west from where the students were facing their lines of policemen. Here a similar double line of PAP, all armed with rifles, halted the fishermen. There was then a great deal of shouted protest from both groups—protest which might have ebbed away during the evening had not one of the more observant students, alerted by the noise of distant shouting, noticed, some few hundred yards down the hill, the lines of police and the distant crowd of brother protestors.

The students then took up the cry of the fishermen, and within minutes hundreds of them had broken through the police lines and had run down the incline to confront the other police line from the rear. The fishermen began to push against the policemen from the front; students were jeering and catcalling from the back; and the PAP officer in charge, finding that his radio did not work and that he had little chance of calling in reinforcements, panicked. He screamed to the front line of his men, who had fixed bayonets, to stand firm; and to the rear line to reverse and, if necessary, to ward off the students with force.

For a few moments this tactic worked, and the students retreated. But Duan Kun, aware of the power of his rhetoric, climbed up on a boulder and started to scream an attack on the authorities. He had just shouted the current student rallying-cry of "Remember Wuhan!" when one of the soldiers, probably acting without orders and fearing for his life, fired a single shot at him, hitting him square in the chest. Mr. Duan spun backwards from the rock and landed on his head in a jumble of sharp granite riprap that made up the footwall at the rear of the bathing beach.

The fishermen, seeing the shooting, roared into action as one, and began to fight the policemen with their bare hands, tearing the rifles from their grip, punching, pulling hair, kicking, biting. The rear line of police turned to help their colleagues, whereupon the students rushed at them, laying about them and disarming all of the police in a matter of minutes. Before night had fallen the thirty policemen had been stripped of weapons, ammunition, uniforms and the broken radio, and were standing forlornly by the roadside in their underwear. Two of them, however, marched off with the victorious students, three others with the exultant fishermen.

These five men will come to be remembered in history books throughout the world as the first of the turncoats, in what was to become—from the point of view of the Chinese authorities—a summer of traitorous and disastrous be-

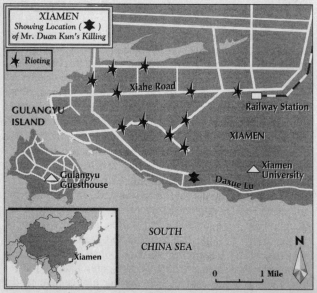

haviour. And one that essentially began with a night of ugliness and mayhem in a city that was shortly to become wayward and virtually ungovernable.

Crowds of students and factory workers roamed through the city streets all that night. There was one major organised protest, when the body of Duan Kun—for the young man never responded to treatment, and died at 8:30 P.M. in the University medical department—was carried in procession along Xiamen Road, towards the railway station. The students took the longer route in an attempt to generate as much local sympathy and publicity as they could. Hundreds of other workers, alerted by swiftly spreading rumours, joined the cortège and followed it to the Municipal Court, and there set up a huge, impromptu protest rally.

Large four-character posters denounced the authorities' actions in shooting at the student, and other observers recorded seeing banners attacking in turn the corruption and anti-Chinese attitudes of the local Party leaders, the insulting behaviour of the police, the selfish outlook of the Municipal officials, the lack of press freedom and freedom to stage public meetings, and—perhaps most interesting of all—the swingeing measures that had been taken against "our fraternal partners in the newly liberated territory of Hong Kong."

Police patrols were spat at and insulted, and one police car near the Xiamen Guesthouse was overturned and set on fire, its occupants forced to flee and to leave their weapons behind. Indeed, it has to be said with the benefit of hindsight that an unusually large proportion of the police and public security officials who were caught up in most of these early incidents seemed to flee, almost without hesitation.

The conclusion that has to be drawn from the alacrity with which they fled, especially in the light of subsequent events, is that many in the rank and file of the police both recognised the feelings of the mob and, moreover, were in many cases not wholly out of sympathy with them. China's police forces and their less well-organised bands of auxiliary colleagues were by custom nearly all recruited locally (the appointment of the late Constable Wan Zhu'er in Canton being part of a nationwide programme to attempt to reverse this policy). In Xiamen City on the night of 23 July and, to judge from the mood at the Qingping Market days earlier, these locally recruited guardians of authority harboured feelings that were in broad accord with those of the people they policed. By the middle of that July week no single unit had broken. But it was becoming perilously clear to the local commanders that it would not be long before a police battalion would defy its officer cadres, and defect to the students and workers against whom they now stood guard.

The temper of that Wednesday evening grew ever more ferocious. By midnight some sixteen shops and offices had been set alight by the mob, and trucks had been used to barricade entrances to the grounds of the ten-year-old ultra-luxurious Xiamen Guesthouse, which the students decided to sack and occupy as their temporary headquarters.

A small group of leaders, all anthropology students and friends of their slain colleague, decided to use the long-distance telephones in the hotel's management office to help rally support. Calls were made to student colleagues in Canton (Duan Kun's home town: the students were asked to convey the news of his death to his parents, who lived in a suburb to the west of the city), in Shanghai and Peking. In addition the Xiamen students telephoned the office of the Reuters correspondent, Richard James, who was known locally since he visited the university campus during the last period of unrest two years before. James, who was unable to obtain any confirmation of the events from the university authorities, was none the less able to file a short story based on what the students had said, on his telephone calls to a Swedish factory official staying at the Xiamen Mandarin Hotel, and on his own sources in the diplomatic community. After detailing the night's events his piece continued:

A spokesman for the Xiamen Municipality was not available for comment last night. In Peking a spokesman for the Ministry of Public Security said there had been reports of a minor outbreak of "hooliganism" which had been dealt with appropriately.

Meanwhile there were persistent reports from within the diplomatic community in the Chinese capital that units of the country's armed forces had been put on heightened alert following an unexplained "event" that also happened in Xiamen yesterday. The Defence Ministry denied that any forces were at an unusually high state of readiness, and accused foreign embassies who were repeating such reports of "mischief-making." The ambassadors of Pakistan and the United Kingdom were both summoned to the Ministry during the day, but both described their visits as "routine."

There were firm denials also that there had been any "incident" in Xiamen on Tuesday; nor that another reported "breakdown in discipline"—notified by students in Peking—had taken place at the small town of Shitsze, also called "Little Hong Kong," some eighty miles east of Xiamen. "Such reports are quite without foundation," the Public Security Ministry spokesman said. "The only report I have that might be of interest is that an execution of three convicted smugglers in the town of Shitsze, due to have taken place on Tuesday, has been postponed. New evidence in the case has been put forward to the Examining Magistrate, and a decision on the men's future will be made in a day or two. With that single exception there is nothing taking place in Fujian Province that would be of any interest to the outside world."

The Reuters desk in London, interested in the disruption of public order on the streets of Xiamen, was however insistent on having further news of troop alerts. These, after all, had potential international consequences. Within minutes of his sending his first story Richard James received an urgent service request:

PROJAMES PEKING EXFOREIGN DNE 231730-ZULU MOST URGENT: FCO HERE CONFIRMING STATE OF READINESS ALERT BY SELECTED

TROOPS AIR AND NAVAL UNITS IN NANJING
MILITARY REGION STOP THIS SUGGESTS IMMI-
NENT ATTACK BY TAIWAN STOP ADVISE US
LEAD SOONEST STOP ENDS MELUNSKY+++

By 3 A.M., when the rioting in Xiamen had started to
subside, Peking—which had become aware of the Reuters
request—decided to make a statement in order to clarify a
matter that now seemed to be of such urgent interest to foreign embassies. Since it seemed evident to Peking itself that
there was no actual threat from the Kuomintang on Taiwan,
and thus there was nothing occurring in southeastern China
that had any international consequences, it was thought important to say so. Accordingly—and with an eye on the
timing of the London and New York newspaper first
editions—Pang Weiqang, a spokesman for the Foreign Ministry, summoned reporters to a 4 A.M. briefing, at which he
read out, without elaboration or taking questions, the following hastily written single paragraph:

The Government of the People's Republic of China,
wishing to allay any unjustified concern, is pleased to
confirm that, for a period of eighteen hours yesterday, a
limited number of troops, patrol vessels and fighter aircraft attached to the Nanjing Military region and the East
Sea Fleet took part in a routine training exercise in and
off the coasts of Fujian and Zhejiang Provinces. These
exercises have now been successfully completed, and the
results are being evaluated. The troops and associated
forces will remain at training readiness during the evaluation period. There is no reason for alarm at any of these
moves, which are purely intended to test and examine the
strength and capabilities of the forces of the People's Republic of China.

The only puzzling matter, Richard James was later to
write, was that Madame Zhang had not given the briefing.
This was normally her task, even at this unseemly hour of
the morning. Mr. Pang, of whom he knew little, declined to

answer any questions, either about the status of troops or, during those normally friendly, off-camera moments that follow a briefing, about Madame Zhang. "I know nothing of her," was all he said and left the room.

Later that same morning the body of Duan Kun was driven to his parents' house in Canton City.

There was no mention of the "routine training exercise" in Thursday morning's vernacular papers. There was, however, one significant paragraph tucked away at the bottom of the main news page in the Canton City *Workers' Daily*. It referred to the actions of certain *liu mang*—the word means hoodlums—in Xiamen city, who had been on a "drinking spree" after the success of a local football team. A small crowd of these "drunken and carousing young men" carried out "a limited number of wanton acts of vandalism" before being "apprehended by socially responsible members of society and handed over to the authorities." It was likely, the newspaper concluded, that the courts would deal strictly with this outbreak of "youthful boisterousness."

The customary code words and phrases—"hoodlums," "vandalism," "socially responsible members of society"— were all there, readily apparent to those few foreign readers who had developed the cryptological skills necessary for the full appreciation of the Chinese press. But it has to be assumed, too, that the paragraph was principally designed to be read by any potential *liu mang* in Canton. The local police, the item was clearly warning them, would crack down harshly on any further disturbances. Canton City was where the authorities anticipated the next rebellious blow would fall.

They were entirely accurate. The rebel leadership met late on Wednesday night in a safe house in Shenzhen— conveniently close to the Hong Kong frontier, but with excellent road communications both north and east, to both Canton and Xiamen. They decided that the arrival of Duan's body and the rites associated with his funeral could provide the necessary excuse for a massing of crowds.

Some incident, it was felt, would almost certainly occur between the crowd and the authorities who were sent to police them; if not, the leaders decided, then there should be agents present who could easily ensure an outbreak of trouble.

The Duan family, who were Christian and by Chinese standards quite comfortably off, lived in the *xiguan*, the western quarter of the city. Mr. Duan senior was by all accounts a most remarkable man, seen in retrospect as one of the quiet heroes of modern China.

Like so many notables, from the famous Admiral Cheng Ho onwards, he was not a Han Chinese. (Admiral Cheng, whose fourteenth-century sailing fleet reached as far as Mogadishu in East Africa, was a Muslim, and moreover a eunuch.) Mr. Duan came from Kunming, in western China, and he belonged to a Tibeto-Burman minority group, the *yi*. He looked different from the majority of those around him. He was not a strong believer in such Confucian concepts as "face." And he was extremely clever mathematically, having won a doctoral degree from the Shanghai Mathematical Institute. At the time of these events he held a post as the local under-manager of a Hong Kong–based bank.

It would have been incorrect to describe Mr. Duan as politically active. It would have been folly for a man in his position, and one who had that cherished privilege of a passport, to have voiced his opinions or to have become involved in any group that was under the watchful eye of the PSB. But he was evidently a man who harboured strongly held views about what he saw as the injustices of contemporary Chinese rule. He had long been a strong private supporter of what were regarded as the "young" reformers in Peking—men like Hu Yaobang and Zhao Zhiyang—and he had been bitterly angered by the crushing of the Tienanmen and Wuhan protests. He maintained a good personal friendship with his former patron, the elderly former Guangdong governor, Yi Juan Ling. But other than this vaguely "dangerous" association—for Yi, as has been mentioned, was something of a maverick figure in Canton City society—

Mr. Duan said and did nothing, except to counsel his children on his long term hopes for an improved China.

His frequent visits to Hong Kong before the British handover had convinced him of the merits of the free-market economy—though it was remarked unkindly in the Hong Kong Special Branch files that he was thought to have developed a particular friendship with a junior bank official in the territory, a relationship which may have accounted in a large part for his fondness for the place. He told his children that he had been disillusioned by the way that China had dealt with both Hong Kong and Britain over the future of the territory, and he had rightly regarded both the Joint Declaration of 1984 and the Memorandum of Understanding of 1991 as allowing China almost unfettered rule there.

He was accordingly not in the least bit surprised when Peking announced that Mao Ren-chin had been appointed to the post of Chief Executive; but he was sufficiently diplomatic to hold his tongue, and he said nothing untoward during his only post-handover visit to Hong Kong in early July.

Both he and his wife had encouraged their son's student enthusiasms, and while they were devastated by his death, they saw him as very much of a martyr for a cause which they and their late son had so vigorously espoused.

The couple were, in short, and fortuitously, everything that Peter Hueng's group could possibly hope for. It was no surprise to learn that the Duan family were thus visited by two members of the group early on that Thursday morning. And although details of the conversation have never been made available, subsequent events suggest that it took little persuading for them to agree that Duan should address the protest rally planned for later that afternoon and evening.

The bank reacted sympathetically when he telephoned to say he would not be coming to work that day. The rebel leaders, together with Mr. Duan and, through the good offices of a child messenger, old Mr. Yi himself, were thus locked in meetings all day. They were planning the direction of protests later that evening—protests that were to assume a profound importance in the development of modern China.

It is useful at this point to summarise the positions of the various sides as they were known to stand at noon on Thursday, 24 July 1997.

Thus far three cities in two provinces of China were affected by the disturbances—Canton, the capital of Guangdong Province, and Xiamen and Shitsze, both situated in Fujian Province. (Disturbances were also continuing sporadically in Hong Kong; but the focus of the rebels' activities, as had been made clear by Peter Heung's meeting in early July, was to be south China itself. Events in Hong Kong, though historically seminal in their early stages, were now of less immediate relevance.)

In all three cities there had been as massive call-out both of police and People's Armed Police. In Fujian Province—which came under the authority of the Nanjing Military Region—there had also been what can be reasonably described as a fairly comprehensive alert of troops and naval units, to meet what was suspected of being a Taiwanese threat.

There were three Integrated Group Armies assigned to Nanjing, the 1st, 12th and 63rd, under the leadership of the elderly General Nie Kuiji, a man brought in to command in 1994 and reputed to be of strict conservative bent. The political commissars in headquarters—certainly the chief commissar and his two senior deputies—were also men of considerable age and seniority who had no known sympathy with any reform group. The same was also thought to be true of the military command in Fujian Military District, although there had been some suspicion voiced in Western embassies that one of the deputy commanders, the 56-year-old Major-General Chen Shengkun, held political views that were not wholly in tune with those of his senior colleagues in Nanjing and Peking.

The military situation in Guangdong was, from the point of view of the Peking political authorities, considerably less certain. The reorganisation of the PLA that followed the

1993 Wuhan Incident, and various border problems with India (1992), Turkestan (1994), Mongolia (1994) and Laos (1995), the ever-present potential for problems with Taiwan and the continuing internal security disruptions in Xizang (Tibet) had prompted the dispatch of the most experienced and hard-line commanding generals to the western and southern border areas and the southeastern coast, as well as to Hubei, where the Wuhan students were still in an occasionally rebellious mood.

Hubei, it should be recalled, is in the Guangzhou Military Region, and outsiders might therefore have thought it logical that those men selected as commanders of the region should have been particularly resolute individuals who would deal firmly with any disturbances or threats of disturbance in this northern outpost. But due to some oversight—or perhaps to a deliberate act of policy in Peking—it was thought that while the commanding general in Hubei Military District itself should be such a strong and uncompromising figure, the rest of Guangzhou—and indeed, the overall Guangzhou leadership—need not be so restrictive. After all, recruiting was performed locally: to maintain a high level of morale among Cantonese soldiers, and to keep them in good fighting trim, it was thought more suitable to appoint a Cantonese commanding general, even if he occasionally erred on the side of ideological flexibility. Should he ever be found to be doctrinally wanting, his ideological needs would be supplied by a team of firm Peking-approved political commissars.

This, as it turned out, was to prove a fatal error of judgement. General Tang Zhu Hou, a Cantonese who had been transferred down from the cold plains of northern Manchuria six months before, was a man whose divided loyalties became swiftly apparent. His chief commissar, a Shanghainese named Gu Zhi, had once been chief of the political department of the Peking Garrison, and was known to be excessively hard-line. But Mr. Gu aside, all the ranking officers down the chain of command were southerners. This included most of the influential figures at Guangzhou regional headquarters, the generals and the brigadiers and staff colonels in the Canton City district headquarters, and the great majority of the field officers out at regimental and battalion level. This particular set of forces—and in particular the 40th Integrated Group Army based outside Canton itself—was almost entirely led by men from South China, men who were theoretically liable to be "tainted."

It has never been wholly clear just why Peking permitted this situation to develop—for it evolved over a number of years, rather than resulted from a sudden change in policy. It can only be surmised that the posts which these southerners filled were not thought by the Peking authorities to be vital to the defence or the internal security of the realm. The politically hard-line officers, those who could be sure of keeping the revolutionary flame alive, were needed in Tibet and Turkestan. The men who were, or were suspected of being, of marginally more flexible stance could be kept in "soft" posts like those in the relatively risk-free south. The error—the fatal flaw in this thinking—was the supposition that Guangzhou and its neighbouring southern provinces were in any way "soft."

In Canton, on the hot and sunny afternoon of Thursday, 24 July, approximately 2,500 police and PAP auxiliaries were on street duty. The Police Commissioner had warned General Tang of the possibility of civil disorder in the city, and that his men should be prepared for a call-out request. Accordingly, three battalions of the 123rd Infantry Division and most of the 44th Light Armoured Regiment were put on standby in the barracks.

Across in Fujian the military alert of the previous day was still in force. But the situation on the streets was quiet, and the general assumption among the field officers was that they would soon be stood down. Peking, indeed, was about to order such a relaxation of duty, to allay the international anxiety which was still simmering. The General Political Department of the Ministry of National Defence cautioned, however, that it might be more prudent to wait to see how matters developed in Canton, in case any military assistance was to be needed there. Hindsight shows that was about the only prudent move that the Ministry was to make during the next twenty-four hours.

Crowds began to gather in mid-afternoon at the Memorial Garden to the Martyrs of the Canton Uprising, on Zhong-shan Lu. The Duan family, and the Heung rebel organisers, thought this an ideologically suitable venue. The gardens commemorate those Cantonese activists who, led by Sun Yat-sen, organised the first proper uprising against the ruling Manchu dynasty in April 1911. It was an insurrectionary act that failed (seventy-two young rebels died) but for the Qing forces who routed the small force it was very much a Pyrrhic victory. They themselves were swept from power just six months later. The seventy-two Cantonese fighters of 1911 are regarded as heroes still: it was Peter Heung's view that the Cantonese fighters of 1997 would earn a reputation that would be just as glorious, and might enjoy an even longer life.

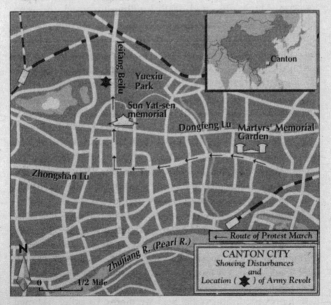

← Route of Protest March

CANTON CITY
*Showing Disturbances
and
Location (✴) of Army Revolt*

Chinese Communist authorities—like communists in most countries—have rarely been fully competent to deal with public demonstrations other than by the sudden deployment of disproportionately massive amounts of force. Dealing with the curious routines and feints and diversionary tactics of sophisticated street opposition, such as that being planned by the Heung rebels, presented an acute problem for the police, for they lacked the relevant skills and in consequence made many blunders. The first blunder of this particular incident came early in the afternoon when Police Commissioner Zhou decided to send the bulk of his forces to entirely the wrong location.

He supposed, for no obvious reason, that the demonstrations—which were ostensibly planned to offer public sympathy for the Duan family, and to condemn the killing of their young son by the Xiamen police force—would be staged in Yuexiu Park. This large expanse of grassland to the north of the city was the site of the much-visited Sun Yat-sen Memorial, and traditionally attracted the few government-approved rallies that took place in the city.

Zhou had accordingly placed the bulk of his men there, and it was nearly 5 P.M. before radio messages from Zhongshan Lu alerted him to the need for a change of plan. By the time the bulk of his forces arrived and were properly deployed on Zhongshan and Lingyuan Roads, and by the time barricades had been erected at the front and east gates of the park so that police could check that no weapons were being brought inside, at least 25,000 people had assembled. It was thought, on the basis of information from the plain-clothes surveillance officers who had issued the alert, that some of those already in the park carried weapons and stocks of Molotov cocktails.

The mood of the crowd, once the police vehicles were heard and then seen approaching, became increasingly militant. Marshals inside the park had to urge restraint on a number of young tearaways, who wanted immediately to launch an attack on the police before they were sufficiently well organised to repulse it. By 5:30 P.M., however, calm of a sort prevailed, and organisers were able to bring Mr. and

Mrs. Duan in through the front gate—though not until the police had searched and (Mrs. Duan complained later) insulted the couple for "mingling with agitators and trouble-makers."

When it became known that the Duans were in the garden there was a giant roar of approval. There was an even greater roar of appreciation when a young man climbed to the podium that had been erected in front of the Martyrs' Memorial and announced that he had been asked to broadcast a message of sympathy for the bereaved family from no less a luminary than the former Guangdong Provincial Governor, Yi Juan Ling.

There were several minutes of almost uncontrollable cheering, and shouts of "Marshal Yi's son can see the good sense of our ways!", "The old governor is a fine champion of our rights!" and "The people respect your attention to their problems!", before the crowd organisers, urging the mob to be respectful to the memory of the fallen student, caused a hush to fall on the huge assembly. Hundreds more protestors were still filtering in through the police lines: by 5:45 P.M. probably 40,000 demonstrators were jammed in front of the memorial.

Two Gazelle helicopters stuttered overhead, presumably with Army observers aboard. Outside the railings hundreds of city police looked on, unsmiling; behind them were scores of helmeted Armed Police in close order formations, each man with his rifle, bayonet unfolded, clasped tight before his chest.

The young man placed a small tape recorder in front of the microphone, and the unmistakable voice of Governor Yi, speaking in Cantonese, thundered out over the stifling evening air. It was a brief address. But it had a heretical, accusing tone that few who heard it would ever forget. The crucial final passage, which triggered burst after burst of loud and wild cheering, has been translated as follows:

The events of these past few weeks have saddened all the people of southern China. Our compatriots in Hong Kong have been betrayed. Citizens of our own city have been snatched from their beds and punished savagely for crimes they have not committed. Our friends in Xiamen have suffered much, and there are parents here with us tonight who have lost a young son, a man whose brilliant future was snuffed out by the arrogant action of unprincipled men of power.

There comes a time in a people's history when they must begin to realise that they, the people, have the power, and that the state, those who claim to have the power, do not deserve to have it and to wield it with such cruelty and barbarism. It has become clear to me and to many of you in recent months and years that the hopes and aspirations of those of us who have the good fortune to live in the warmth and rains of southern China have the potential to enjoy a good and happy life, with prosperity brought about as the direct result of our own labours.

Sadly there are those in authority in China today—those who have been in such authority for many, many years—who will not believe that a people have a right to enjoy a good and happy life based on the fruits of their own labours and the expenditure of their own energies. But I believe, and I hope that many of you believe, that this right does exist. I believe that this is a right worth struggling for. I believe that we should light a beacon here, a beacon that will be seen by all our friends along the whole of the southern coast of this wonderful land, so that they will rise up and turn back the repressive forces that seek to deny us what is no more and no less than a God-given right.

And I use the phrase "God-given" advisedly. Many of us here in this city are not, or have not been permitted to be, followers of a God. But the young man in whose memory we meet, Duan Kun, was a follower of the Christian God. His father and mother, who are here in this time of sorrow, find strength in that same Christian God as well. They believe that their God instils certain rights in the human spirit—rights to be free, to be happy, to live without fear. I believe in those rights too, and I hope you will also. And I believe and hope that you young people of Canton, and of all the neighbouring cities that will sight the beacon we light today, will strive for this belief and for all these beliefs in the right of the individual—and will fight for these beliefs and for these rights. If this fight is undertaken by you, and if you prevail as prevail you must, then young Duan Kun will not have given his life for nothing. Rise up! Overturn the tyranny! Rise up!

The student switched off the machine and stepped down from the podium, and the park erupted in an ocean of sound. Cheers, cries of "Rise Up! Rise Up!" and "You are with us!", and jeers at the watching policemen rang out for more than ten uninterrupted minutes. Outside the park the streets were now thronged with the curious, people drawn as if by magnetism to the vast and endless roaring sound. They were the ordinary Canton citizenry, passers-by and shoppers, and workers on their way home from the factories in east Canton.

The police tried to move them on, the officers becoming ever more desperate to avoid having their men trapped, caught between two mobs. Just outside the East gate a burly middle-aged policeman was very nearly run down by a cyclist who—like so many Chinese cyclists—was looking at the view and not the road. The officer lashed out with his rifle butt, knocking the cyclist to the ground. Six or more others—including two middle-aged women workers—crashed into the first. Within seconds an angry knot of people had crowded around the policeman cursing him for his clumsiness, his lack of concern for the people. Other police rushed to help him, and soon a boiling mob of police and cyclists and housewives and shoppers and schoolchildren and ever more curious bystanders had accumulated in the centre of Zhongshan Lu. People were shouting and waving their fists, and at the outside of the mob young men could be seen pushing and shoving.

Across in the park Mr. Duan had begun to speak, and after the exuberance that was stimulated by Governor Yi's address, a respectful silence had fallen on the crowd. But Duan, despite his soft voice and the curiously pleasing *yi*-accented Cantonese, turned out to be something of an orator as well. The deeply felt nature of his grief, his passionate denunciation of the "cruel and wanton actions" of the Xiamen police, his simple, intelligently stated sincerity all roused the crowd once again. And when Duan, too, began to take up the cry "Rise Up! Rise Up!", the mobs, both the vast one inside the iron fence and now the fast-gathering crowd outside, started to howl their protest, and catcall and jeer at the police.

The first of the inevitable hail of missiles were thrown not from the rebel crowds in the park, but by the workers out in the street. The knot of men and women who had gathered in front of the park entrance withdrew—shouts urging them to do so were heard coming from an alleyway that ran southwards down to Donghua main road. Parked in the alley, it turned out, was a construction lorry, and beside it a pile of cobblestones that had been ripped from the street earlier in the month. The men in the crowd seized hungrily at the larger stones and began to pelt the policemen, aiming particularly at the burly officer who had first knocked the man from his bicycle.

The police tried to run, but were hemmed in by stone-throwing crowds. They looked terrified, huddling together against the park's iron bars, cowering as fusillade after fusillade of jagged chunks of granite and concrete rained down on them. One had a radio and could be seen shouting into it before he was knocked to the ground by a stone. But he had evidently managed to get his message across, for no more than a minute had passed when, jogging silently from another side street, came at least a hundred Armed Police, helmeted, wearing white gloves. They streamed out, running in a perfect loping lockstep until, with a cry that sounded like a war-whoop, they suddenly began to sprint forward, directly towards the main stone-throwing group.

The mob broke and scattered back into the alley. The police stopped their running and, turning briefly back to their previously surrounded colleagues, ordered them to run back to the protection of the main police group, 200 yards to the west. This they did, carrying their injured away with them.

At the same time, however, crowds of excited youngsters who had been at the park meeting began to stream out of the exits and on to Zhongshan Lu. Here they joined up with the workers who, as they became bolder, poured out of the alleyways and doors in which they had been sheltering. The police reserve surprise squad who had just been brought in to break them up now melted back westward, having completed their assigned task of rescuing their trapped colleagues. The pattern of confrontation was thus now quite simple: a mass of police and Armed Police were at the southwest corner of the Memorial Gardens, near the junction with Lingyuan West Road; and the rebels and their worker colleagues occupied all of Zhongshan Lu. And it was from here that the rebels decided to advance. With ten young men in the lead, all wearing red headbands bearing the characters "Rise Up!", and with Mr. and Mrs. Duan behind them, the first of what must now have been 80,000 people, angry, excitable and unpredictable, began to march westwards, towards the building they had now declared as their goal—the headquarters of Canton Public Security at Number 863, Jeifang Beilu.

"We must destroy in order to rebuild!" one of the hastily scrawled banners proclaimed. The police who made the initial attempt to stop the mob reported back to their commanders that the final line of defence would probably have to be the PSB office. "It is not possible to hold back so many angry people with the forces we have available," a police commander was recorded as having shouted into his radio. "You will have to hold the PSB office as a last resort, and with much force of arms."

At the park's corner the police did their best to halt the progress of the mob. Two Russian-made water cannon that had been brought up from the police barracks in the north of the city, and which had not been used for more than a decade, fired into the centre of the slowly moving tide of people. But this was a hot, unbearably sticky evening: the cool clouds of water—even the jets that, at close range, knocked down a few of the young men—seemed refreshing, and only spurred the crowd to greater enthusiasm. And when the police fired tear-gas, the youngsters were ready for it.

Within the mob was an extraordinarily sophisticated degree of good tactical organisation. At every tenth row of marchers there was one strong young man designated to carry a large red nylon bag filled with strips of vinegar-soaked cloth. At the moment that the first platoons of PAP gas-gunners appeared at a street corner near Yuexiu Park, the marchers stopped briefly. Each of the red bags was opened, the cloth strips were handed out, and by the time that the first volleys of gas canisters and grenades thundered down on the mob the rebels were prepared. Only a few young men and women broke rank and ran away from the billowing white clouds: the police, falling back into the park reported with astonishment that as the smoke cleared away the march continued steadily, menacingly. Four drummers had by this time joined the head of the procession, and they beat out a steady and sinister rhythm. It was, one Western observer later remarked, "like hearing the procession of the tumbrils. It was terrifying. The atmosphere was electric. You knew this could never end peacefully."

Shortly before 9 P.M. the head of the march turned north into Jeifang Beilu, and approached the PSB headquarters. The marchers had moved slowly and deliberately through the city, their leaders occasionally stopping to exhort them to "defy and destroy the vicious apparatus of the state machine," urging them to meet the enemy—the police, the Armed Police, the Army—with "a firm eye and a straight back." They made their steady progress westward despite frequent police attacks with gas-guns and water cannon, and despite the speedy erection of more than a dozen barbed-wire barricades that were swept away by the crowds as though they were made of balsa wood.

It was 9:15 P.M., and by now dark and still very hot, when the leading demonstrators finally ordered the procession to halt. Before them, looming up like a vast impregnable medieval border fort, with turrets and razor wire and spiked railing, was the PSB headquarters. Scores of powerful searchlights illuminated its tall, faceless walls, and cast an eerie white light back down on to the tens of thousands of faces in the crowd.

The light also caught in sharp silhouette the figures of what seemed hundreds upon hundreds of helmeted figures, each showing his bayonet up above his left shoulder. The men stood with imperturbable immobility. These, as anticipated, were the men of the Chinese Army—men whom regimental history now records as belonging to the 46th Battalion of the 123rd Infantry Division, based at Xicun Barracks in the northwest of the city.

They had been brought into the city by truck three hours before after Commissioner Zhou had formally requested General Tang Zhou Hou to provide support for the civil power because of "an urgent and imminent threat to the city's security." The soldiers, mostly young men from the rural rice-growing areas of the province, had been instantly deployed to protect the PSB headquarters. They were under command of a Lieutenant Colonel Li Guo-hong, a man whose role in his country's history will not easily be forgotten.

Two entire companies of troops had been deployed to guard the PSB offices, and a third was held in reserve. A line of open Army trucks could be seen in the background, near the China Hotel and across from the Statue of Five Rams. Beside them, in the centre of Jeifang Beilu, was a group of six armoured personnel carriers, the Type YW 309 ICVs that had been in use for the past decade, and could carry eight men at speeds of 30 m.p.h. for more than 300 miles. Each armoured car had a small machine-gun and a much larger 73mm cannon, and three of them had multiple tear-gas grenade-launchers. They looked menacing under the bright street lamps, with their diesel engines revving up and blowing clouds of blue smoke into the street. Helmeted soldiers stood in each turret, seemingly waiting for the order to move.

The immediate attention of the demonstrators was fo-

cused, however, on the solid phalanx of soldiers who
blocked their way. There were three lines of them, all carrying automatic rifles. Most had the new light Norinco CQ
guns, which fired 5.56mm bullets at a rate of three a second, in ten bursts. Others carried the more traditional Type
68 assault rifles, while up on the roof of the PSB were
marksmen with Dragunov sniping rifles and light-machine-
guns. It was certainly a formidable demonstration of firepower, and there was no question that it checked the
advance of the marchers. They gathered silently under the
lights, the massed marchers behind them coming to a halt
so that, within a few minutes, the street was filled with a
vast mass of silent humanity. Perhaps 100,000 were now involved. To the helicopters still stuttering overhead the confrontation must have appeared especially dramatic: a throng
of humanity kept at bay by three thin lines of green, and six
small toy-like armoured cars.

The rebel leaders decided that, for the moment at least,
further northward progress would be imprudent. Their goal,
the hated PSB office, was within shouting range and probably Commissioner Zhou was inside. So they would give
voice to their dispute, and shout their protests over the
heads of the soldiers, hoping that Zhou and his fellow intelligence officers would hear, and, as a student was later to
say, "Be properly ashamed of what they have done." The
leaders set up a chorus of shouts—"Rise Up!", "Shame on
the forces of repression!", "Down with the old men!"—
until the voices of the mob swelled into an immense cathe-
dral roar, peppered only with the bass thrumming of the
helicopters 200 feet overhead.

The soldiers stood stony-faced, their rifles tightly
clutched before them. Their officers, who were identified
by their shoulder flashes and by the fact that they held
9mm machine-pistols (snub-nosed black guns with folding
stocks that were now snapped into the ready position) stood
beside their men, looking over to the command post, where
Colonel Li stood waiting for his orders. The noise of the
crowd grew thunderous, intolerable. A few stones soon began to rain down—all of them thrown into high arcs so that

they went above the heads of the soldiers and crashed into the PSB compound.

The helicopters swooped lower. The radios crackled ever more urgently. Sounding over the roar of the mob there came a sudden electric hum, then a buzz, and the roar of stentorian voices from several loudspeakers began to echo down and along the street.

"Comrades, be attentive. This is an urgent message to you all!" A chorus of hisses and catcalls greeted the introduction. "We are not your comrades!" one voice returned. "Crawl back into your holes, you cowards!" screamed another. And "*diu lei lo mou*"—you motherfucker! The cantonese have access to the coarsest of all Chinese vocabularies, and the crowd made ample use of this talent that night.

But the loudspeakers boomed still louder, until the voice seemed less than human, more some terrible feral howl. "Go back to your homes, dear comrades. Go back now!

"This demonstration of yours is absolutely forbidden. Some of you have behaved most irresponsibly. A small number of you have committed wanton acts of destruction. By doing this you have insulted the dignity of the Party. The Party is the people. You are insulting the people of China. You must stop these insults.

"You must now go peacefully to your homes, or else a terrible tragedy will befall you all. This is your last warning.

"The People's Army is here to protect our dear city from any further acts of vandalism, and it will use its might to protect the city as instructed.

"The People's Army is your friend, and the people love their Army. Only deranged people do not love the People's Army. This is China. This is not some foreign nation, where the people behave with stupidity. This is our dear country, and it must be orderly.

"So take urgent notice of this announcement, dear comrades. There will not be another. You must go to your homes, or else dreadful and unforgettable things will happen here tonight!"

The loudspeakers then buzzed for a few moments more, and there was a sudden loud burst of martial music, crackling with interference and the burning of overloaded cables. A rattle of sharp detonations set off a wild frenzy near one edge of the crowd: someone had thrown a string of firecrackers, and they popped and fizzed and banged their way across the roadway. Some of the soldiers instantly levelled their rifles towards the disturbance, and glanced with fright towards their commanders, waiting for the order to go.

Then, without warning, all the lights in the street went out. The music from the speakers faded and died. A strange and eerie calm descended, as if the entire crowd and the forces opposing them were collectively holding their breath. From the rear of the mob came the sound of flagstones being broken, the better to make ammunition. And from the very front on the left there was a sudden flash of flame as the rags of four petrol bombs were lit from a match. The four bombs soared up into space and crashed, spreading huge gobbets and pools of fire at the base of the walls of the PSB compound. But then the scene fell silent, and dark once again; the street breathed in, and echoed with the vague thump of a huge communal heartbeat.

Suddenly there was more radio noise—quick, urgent commands being given, their staccato echoing between the buildings. The sounds became more and more confused, there was the amplified noise of argument, then a strange screeching, followed by the thump of scores of steel-shod boots, but not in unison.

The rebel leaders were accustomed now to the blackness that had fallen since the failure of the power. They supposed the police had cut it deliberately, as had been the case in Tienanmen Square in Peking, and on the Wuchang Bridge in Wuhan, a precursor to the rampage and the killings. So the young men were prepared to have to run, to dodge and weave through a hail of bullets and the roaring chase of armoured cars. They expected it to begin at any moment; but instead there was some apparent discord in the lines in front of them, and whatever the movement of soldiery presaged was not an attack on the students. They could see vaguely now: the soldiers had moved back 100 feet, and some were facing—it scarcely seemed possible— were facing backwards, *towards* the PSB.

In a fraction of a second they realised what seemed the unimaginable enormity of what had happened. *The soldiers had changed sides.* This single unit of the People's Liberation Army, perhaps amounting to the three companies of the 46th Battalion, 123rd Infantry, had rebelled. For some then quite inexplicable reason they had turned against the men of the Public Security Bureau and the People's Armed Police, they had turned against Commissioner Zhou and his men. *They had taken the side of the students and the workers: they were in open rebellion against the government of China.*

For a few moments, while the rumour went racing wildly through the body of protestors, there was confusion, suspicion, doubt and fear. The crucial question was the extent and solidity of the rebellion: was it just the men who had mutinied? Did the officers acquiesce? Did they, perhaps, foment the rebellion? The answer came dramatically, moments later.

The buzz of the loudspeakers was heard. The lights snapped on up and down the street. The PSB office, now surrounded by scores of soldiers, all pointing their rifles towards its walls and up at its sentry-posts, was illuminated by searchlights once again. The speakers crackled into life.

"People of Canton," said an unfamiliar voice, quavering with nervousness at first, but rapidly gaining strength and authority, "do not be afraid. This is a night of victory!"

My name is Li Guo-hong. The post I have the honour to hold is commanding colonel of the 46th Battalion of the 123rd Infantry Division of the People's Liberation Army. We have been sent in to Canton City to give support to the civilian forces of law and order. As you see, we have been assigned to give protection to the senior officers' headquarters of the Public Security Bureau.

Fifteen minutes ago we were given very solemn news. We were issued with orders to attack you people and drive you back towards the river. We were told to use any methods of force to make you return to the river and go to your homes. We were ordered to fire our guns at you to make you move your position.

But I have now to tell you that, in my position as commanding colonel of this battalion, and being a son of Guangdong, and commanding men who come from this province of ours, I could not order the firing of guns at my Guangdong compatriots and comrades. I conferred briefly with my company and platoon commanders, and they graciously informed me that this decision would be well received by the men in my battalion. I therefore ordered them not to fire at you. I am ashamed to report that I disobeyed my commanders. This is a Cantonese unit. It will not fire on Cantonese people.

The crowd, stunned by what they were hearing, cheered wildly, but were cut off immediately as Colonel Li continued to speak.

I therefore informed the Police Commissioner, Comrade Zhou, that I would not carry out the order he had transmitted to me. I also sent a radio message to the Commanding Generals of the Guangzhou Military Region and the Guangdong Military District, informing them of my decision. I have had no reply from them. But I have just been informed by radio that at least three of the Municipal Police groups who have been monitoring the progress of this protest demonstration of yours have agreed to join with me!

I cannot speak for long. The situation is very dangerous. But I have to tell you that the only way for us to succeed is to rally behind an organised army. This situation will never improve if the rule is placed in the hands of the masses. There must be leadership. There must be direction. There must be discipline. All I say to you now—in words which the heroic Mao Tse-tung declared in other, very different circumstances—is this: To rebel is justified! Bombard the Headquarters! Let us now go forward and do these things!

The crowd surged forward, hugely excited, the popular mood suddenly stoked with adrenaline. But sentries with loudhailers urged them back. "This is a task for the soldiers. This is too dangerous for the people. Let them fight. Let them succeed."

The two helicopters that had been circling above all the while suddenly gunned their motors and raced northwards, presumably to the Army air base out near Baiyun airport. The six armoured cars raced their engines, too, and a thick cloud of blue smoke suddenly obscured them. Between them and the crowd, the soldiers were busily taking up positions on the east side of the road, taking cover behind the trees that grew thickly in this part of Yuexiu Park. Only when all the soldiers had vanished, and the PSB office, brightly lit, was quite isolated, did the megaphone start broadcasting. This time it was a different voice, and it was speaking in *putonghua*, not Cantonese. Those with authority inside the building were men from Peking: these were the architects of the policy that had brought Constable Wan Zhu'er and his like to Canton, a policy which provided the first excuse, if excuse were needed, for the terrible instability of this seemingly endless hot July.

"The People's Liberation Army wishes you to know that your barrack block is quite surrounded," the voice announced, slowly and calmly. "It would be wise for you to come to our side, to put down your weapons and to permit our forces to take you into custody. You will come to no harm. You will be sent back to your homes in Peking. If you do not do as we wish and as is undoubtedly wise, you will be fired upon. The forces on our side have an overwhelming superiority. Come out now, and surrender. In the name of China, come!"

The answer was a single burst of rocket fire. With a tremendous whoosh! an anti-tank grenade shot out from a lower-floor window. It smashed into the front of the leading armoured car, there was a huge explosion, the car was thrown violently up into the air and landed, a flaming ball, a dozen feet back. Soldiers rushed forwards out of the trees and tried to beat back the flames; but there then came volley after volley of rifle fire from the windows at the same level. Two of the soldiers fell, their steel helmets clattering on to the road, while the rest withdrew.

Colonel Li's forces soon struck back. Two machine-guns mounted in the woods started to fire, the bullets raking the front of the PSB, smashing glass, tearing chunks of masonry from the walls, shattering wood. At the same time the five remaining armoured cars moved in and began firing their 73mm cannon, their commanders aiming them at the upper windows and the roof. There was a small forest of radio antennas on the flat roof of the building, probably being used at this very moment, relaying sounds and news of the disaster back to Regional Command and then on to Peking itself.

The radio aerials fell within seconds, their support structures smashed apart by the fusillade of cannon-fire. At the same time, a shell from another APC smashed through an upper-floor window, and flames began to lick hungrily from within. There were angry shouts and cries from the men who had been in the room, and figures could be seen at the windows, frantically trying to get out. But heavy steel bars, tangled from the gunfire, prevented their escape, and the crowds could only watch as the men clawed frantically, flames spouting around them, until they slumped back, out of sight.

Machine-guns inside the PSB started to chatter in reply, and from a courtyard at the rear, mortar shells began to rain down on the roadway, exploding in bursts of orange and green. But the barrage was not intense, and not strong enough to halt the steady onrush of the remaining armoured cars, which chugged their purposeful way across the wide expanse of road and up to the heavy steel gates of the compound. The small convoy halted momentarily. There was a sustained burst of firing from the two lead cars, and a huge hole was blown in the roadway and, behind it, the gates. The cars headed into the crater, tipped down, then up, and pushed through the broken entrance. Within seconds they were all safely inside the compound, within the wall, and hundreds of Colonel Li's men were running fast behind them.

The remaining action lasted less than two minutes. There was another burst of cannon-fire from the APC, and a few replying rifle shots. But only a very few. The crowd, who had by now pressed right up to the limit set by the sentries, and were watching the drama with rapt but disciplined fascination, could hear the battle tailing away. When silence fell the crowd pushed forward, straining to hear anything—cries, running footfalls, radio messages, licking flames, the crunch of heavy tyres on broken glass. And then a sudden cheer went up. A single phrase in Cantonese was being repeatedly shouted from an upstairs window. *"Ngau dei tau hong—ngau dei tau hong!* (They've surrendered—they've surrendered!) The PSB men have given themselves up. The first battle is over. The first battle is won."

His cry came shortly before midnight on Thursday, 24 July. In a few moments more it would be Friday, and the nation would be marking with joy and tears, with fireworks and parades (or so the China News Agency had forecast) the anniversary of that first Communist Party Congress, more than three quarters of a century before.

In Peking and Shanghai, Lanzhou, Shenyang and Kunming—in every Chinese city, from Mohe in the icy north of Manchuria to Yulin in the tropic south of Hainan, from Kashgar among the deserts and peaks of the west to Tongjiang, thousands of miles away in the birch forests of the east—everywhere across this immense nation of 1,500 million people, the Party would be celebrating. Everywhere across the vast expanse of China—except, now, for this one southern city.

For the Party would not be celebrating in Canton. The city where the Chinese revolution had first really begun, nearly ninety years before, and where the first blows were struck against the despots and the tyrants of the Qing regime—this city was now about to see the birth of a new

Chinese revolution. On the eve of the anniversary of Communism's Chinese birth this city and thousands, perhaps even millions, of her people were busily and eagerly putting Chinese Communism to its death. What started with the death of a single Christian student—who did not even come from Canton—turned into a massed protest of angry people. The protestation of this anger turned, in a matter of a few short hours, into the rebellion of a single Army regiment. The conversion of this one of the People's Army units—however small and insignificant it was in terms of numbers, however fated its action was to be the later cause of destruction and tragedy—in its turn released a flood of pent-up disaffection among the other forces of discipline and the State.

Within hours, quite literally hours, the Canton Municipal Police force had fallen in with the wishes of the crowd, had turned away from its leadership. The People's Militia, and most of the rank and file of the People's Armed Police had, with a speed and scale not witnessed since the Eastern European revolutions of ten years before, reversed their loyalties and become a mirror image of themselves. And overnight, this city of 4 million became a tiny island of freedom, a pinpoint of light in the grey miasma of Maoism that had spread over China for the previous forty-eight years. Its immediate fate was certain: the fate of the nation and the system that surrounded it has not been settled yet. The only certainty of that heady Thursday night lay behind the cry of the victorious infantryman, hauling down the red flag from in front of the police headquarters.

"The first battle is over," he had cried. The battle for Canton may indeed have been won on that steamy night, but it was certainly only the first of very many battles yet to come, not all of which would be won by these same victors.

CHAPTER EIGHT

Descent into Chaos

CANTON

July–August 1997

The rebels in Canton consolidated their hold on the city with a remarkable swiftness matched by the tardiness with which Peking reacted to the crisis. The State Council did not meet to discuss the situation until Saturday, and a series of bitter and complex internal wranglings, which will be discussed in more detail later, delayed a decision for almost a full week. During these final days of July the revolution, once secured in Canton, was able to spread to nearby towns and cities, so that by the beginning of August almost all of Guangdong Province and parts of neighbouring Hunan—and—crucially—Fujian Provinces were affected as well.

The speed with which the Republicans—for this was the name the rebels gave to themselves—took hold of the administration of their southern bastion was so great, and there was such widespread confusion, that an accurate reconstruction of the events has proved difficult. The account that follows, though falling victim on occasion to these limitations, is probably a reasonably reliable, if brief, narration of the historic days that followed the attack on the PSB on Jeifang North Road.

The heroes of 24th July were Colonel Li Guo-hong, the eloquent father of the slain student, Mr. Duan Keda, and, from his sickbed, the former Provincial Governor Yi Juan

157

Ling. Shortly after midnight, while patrols of soldiers from the 46th were securing the PSB, and while the crowds of demonstrators were still roaming the streets in search of any counter-revolutionary activity, these three men, accompanied by three young student leaders, a Mr. Gu, a Mr. Ng and a Miss Wong, organised a brief meeting to discuss what to do next.

The meeting was held at Governor Yi's home, the former gubernatorial mansion from which he had declined to move following his dismissal three years before. A maid served scalding cups of chiu-chow tea in an effort to keep everyone awake. The old man, who was described later as "excited but calm," sat up in his bed, and acted as chairman. The four other men sat at the foot of the bed with Miss Wong taking the role of secretary.

Her notes serve as the basis for this short account: she remarks at the opening of her record that the meeting, convened at Colonel Li's request, took place on the morning of a day that was reckoned by the Communist Party to be most auspicious. She had crossed out the character for auspicious, and replaced it with the word "unlucky."

There was little time for formality. Colonel Li, grim-faced and grimy from the brief fight, outlined the military situation as best he knew it. He first explained that in and around Canton City itself—he nodded across to Governor Yi, who would already know these details from his terms in office—there were now approximately three infantry divisions. Four more divisions made up the total strength of the Military Region. The total number of men under arms in the Region (which stretched 1,000 miles from the sea to the mountains of northern Hubei) thus amounted to some 100,000. Colonel Li's battalion, from which the headquarters company had been detached to remain in the Xicun barracks that night, had a strength of no more than 600 men.

The arithmetic, Li went on, was sobering. Just one half of 1 per cent of the Army in just one of the seven regions of China were with them. As a fraction of the total Chinese Army the numbers would have seemed still more depressing; just two hundredths of 1 per cent had turned. Miss Wong noted: "Members assumed expression of great misery."

But the young colonel brightened. Before he left the barracks that afternoon, he explained, he had been summoned to a private interview with his divisional commander, a Major-General Lan. Like the colonel and most of the other senior line officers in the District, Lan was a southerner, born in Zhuhai. He had distinguished himself fifteen years before in the border war with the Vietnamese, and bore a vivid scar across his right cheek as testimony to the ferocity of the battles.

Lan, who conducted the brief meeting in his private quarters, spoke somewhat elliptically—nervous, as Li soon realised, that the political commissars who were attached to the division might have some means of listening in to the conversation. The message, however, was abundantly clear to Li, who had worked under Lan for some years, and knew of his private disaffection from the Peking leadership.

"Should you decide," Lan said, "to permit your battalion to side with those whom you have been ordered to subdue, then you may count on full practical support from me, from my division, and in all probability from the divisions commanded by Generals Hu Dai-fang and Yang Xuchu as well. Whether you decide to use this occasion to stage rebellion is wholly up to your political and tactical judgement. We have discussed this subject on many occasions during the last year: you may decide, such is the ferment of the city at present, that this is the moment to strike."

It was left simply to work out a simple and unambiguous set of signals that would need to be sent to Xicun Barracks and then on to the Baiyun Divisional Headquarters if indeed the rebellion had taken place. General Lan decided that three messages should be prepared, each one of them plausible in its own right and unlikely to draw the attention of the commissars monitoring the signals traffic. "Returning to barracks immediately" would denote an attempt that had failed or was clearly about to fail. "Delayed by unexpected opposition" would indicate that help was needed, but that with such help there was little doubt that the revolt would succeed. "Operation concluded" would tell Lan and his brother generals that the battalion had managed both to revolt and to defeat those limited number of forces arrayed against it in the police and public security barracks.

"I naturally sent the message 'Operation concluded' at 2344 hours," Li said. "It was acknowledged with congratulations and a foreign phrase, "three cheers." While I have had no time for confirmation I have taken this message to mean that all three divisions are now ours. I believe that the security of Canton City is thus internally absolute. Our principal threat is now from outside. Our purpose at this meeting will be to decide on our short-term strategy. Long-term is not my business. We have concluded a small victory. We have effective support. We need to know we can survive, before we establish how we can fight."

Governor Yi smiled. "This is the beginning of a very interesting period in our country's history," he said. "I am only sorry that this opening meeting is taking place in such insalubrious quarters. The Communists, I think, did rather better in that regard when they first met in Shanghai." Everyone laughed, their mood lighter now that they realised there would be relatively few problems within the city itself. The testing time would come in a day or so—though at this meeting no one was aware of exactly how much time would elapse before the first response from Peking. No one knew there was likely to be any breathing space.

"We need to secure the city," the Governor said, warming to the theme, suddenly assuming his old mantle of authority. "First, all the obvious. The radio station. Television station. All transmitters. The power stations. The Party headquarters. Railways. Civil airport. Military air bases. That means a large number of soldiers and police. The deployment should begin immediately. We need a spokesman—either me or Duan here. We need to tell the people what has happened, and ask for their support. I suggest we secure all points now, then make radio broadcast at 5 A.M. and repeat it every fifteen minutes thereafter. We need to have a curfew, a state of emergency, and the closing of all roads in and out of the city. If we have your colleagues, Colonel Li, this will be quite easy to organise. We can manage without but their help will be of inestimable value. And of course, not having them fighting us is of inestimable value too." There was a gale of good-humoured laughter once again. The mood was optimistic; there was a scent of triumph in the air.

Duan Keda volunteered to be the spokesman. It was arranged that he would travel, under police escort, to the broadcasting station, and prepare an address for the early morning. He would stress in his speech that he was simply a conduit for information, and that the leaders of the rebellion would appear later, once the situation had become more stable. According to Miss Wong's notes, Duan then asked what the movement should be called? "We must have a name. We must be able to say in whose name, under what ideological flag we fight. What do I say this morning?"

Governor Yi smiled. "I hope we can all agree that we shall call ourselves—the Republicans. Our name must be simple. It must mean, as our friend Mr. Duan remarks, exactly what we stand for. And it must be recognisable as an idea around the world. For one thing must be understood here: our movement, which has its beginnings in this small room, will be known throughout the world. We will be spoken of in America and England and in faraway places. We must be known by something that they know too. And I have one further thing to say on this subject too—but may we first agree? We are the Republican Party of China? Yes?"

One of the student representatives, Mr. Gu, rose, his face flushed with tension. "But we should be the Kuomintang, surely? We follow the path of Sun Yat-sen. We have our origins in the south. We started our demonstrations at the Martyrs' Memorial Garden. Are we not fighting in the traditions of the Nationalist Party? Should we not call ourselves this?"

His was a lone protest, and the force and eloquence with which it was rebutted suggests, from scrutiny of the historical documents, that he may have well been required to ask the question so as to provide an opportunity for a policy statement to be placed firmly on the record. The argument that both Governor Yi and Mr. Duan put to the young man was simple: the very concept of nationalism was, to this new entity, intellectually repugnant. Mr. Yi then went on to explain, in a speech which Miss Wong was to capture in full, and which remains the most eloquent testimony to the early ideas of the Republican Party—almost, one might say, the Party Manifesto:

I have thought about all these questions at length in the years that I have been away from centre stage. I and a few of my colleagues who you will come to know in the months ahead have considered this before. We have known this day would come. We suspected it would come, just as it has done, in the aftermath of the return to us of our beloved Hong Kong. We have had contacts with men and organisations there who share our ideas, even if they organised themselves along lines that seemed to some of us to be ethically unacceptable. But that is no matter now. They have helped put us where we are now. You will meet them soon.

My argument is basically this: if we can accept nationalism as our by-word, as the guiding light of the movement we have started here today, then our policies would be directed by the idea of nationalism, and this idea is one that would lead us and our nation into further chaos.

I say further chaos, because we must all understand that what has happened today is certain to lead to chaos within China, a total breakdown of all our established ways, for what could be many months and years. There are old hatreds in this land of ours. There are old hatreds in the lands that surround ours. People exploit hatred. They exploit weakness. Nations that are in chaos are weak. There may be attempts at exploitation from both within and without. All of the old wounds will be bound to flare up. Old scores will have to be settled. That is all inevitable, and it is important that we recognize what is going to happen.

I am an old man. I may not live to see this through. But you are younger. You have the power. You must also have the vision and the wisdom to know just what it is that you have started, and to have the courage to fight on, no matter how great the damage to you and all you have known and loved. For you must recognise what I believe Sun Yat-sen realised, but which few have been able to realise since—and that is that you, us, this idea *has right on its side.* Has, if you like [and here he looked over at Mr. Duan, whom he knew to be a Christian] *God on its side.*

So there will be a terrible chaos. But we can try to alleviate it, even though it is us, and our ideas, that have begun it. We can try, I believe, by at least assuming a mantle of moderation. And that is why I believe that the concept of republicanism is right for us—simply because it is and always has been a neutral, moderate concept. What does it mean? It simply means that the people are sovereign, and that the nation is theirs, and that there is no figurehead promoted to leadership by divine right, or by tradition, or by reasons of class or cleverness or wealth. The people say who is their leader, and they are thus the masters of their nation.

Nationalism, on the other hand, would place us instantly in conflict—with the outside world, with all the new nations that have been born on our frontier. Or else there would be attempts at union, at the forging of links between people beyond and inside our frontiers to form yet new nations, still unknown. So our border would be in turmoil for many years to come.

Within our nation, especially such a richly complex nation as ours, the idea of nationalism would be sure to lead to racism. See what has happened in India, a neighbour with whom we have better relations than once before. All their religious and racial groups have sought national status. They are at each others' throats. They fight in the name of nationalism, and have become Balkanised, weakened, impoverished. Look at the Balkans today, the terrible breakup of Yugoslavia, the difficulties in Italy, in Ireland, even in America again. No, my friends, nationalism promotes sectarianism, and we need the wisdom to be able to see that now, and not fall into a trap of naming ourselves after the idea.

The world has changed greatly since the collapse of Communism in Eastern Europe in the late 1980s, and we have seen with horror and dismay how the spectre of nationalism has risen to replace it—particularly in Yeltsin's short-lived Commonwealth. We have seen so many new nations that have risen, and in some cases fallen, with frightening speed, as people after people, freed from the crushing yoke of Communism, have declared their nationalistic ideals, their desire to be "free," to be "themselves." In China, the danger is the same. There could be a Manchu nation. A *yi* nation, Mr. Duan. A Tibetan nation. A Cantonese nation. This, surely, is what we all want to avoid. But it will be difficult to do so.

I see the nightmare of banditry rising again—and I, you must know, remember what the time of the bandits was like. I see warlordism. I see a civil war of terrifying proportions and length. But I see us, those of us in this little group, as being in possession of another force, and that is the force of moral leadership. Because although it will be said that we are just southerners fighting against northerners, you know, I know, that we are much, much more than that.

The south is rising not because it is southern, but because it, more than any other region of China, has some knowledge of the power and possibilities of freedom. There are people in this area of our nation who have seen and tasted its goodness. There are people who have seen it in Hong Kong. You have seen it, Mr. Duan. You have been there, and you have seen how much finer life is down there, how backward our people, our attitudes, our lives are here. It may be changing. It probably is. We must start our movement here to help to rescue it, before it is too late.

I have seen the workings of freedom. I have been overseas, and I have seen Paris and London, and I have seen Hong Kong. So I know what is possible. I know what happens in a system where any man is allowed to try to reach his own potential, to strive for any heights his abilities and his energies permit. And it is for these ideas, rather than the fact of our being southern Chinese people, that we fight.

To call ourselves nationalists, to align ourselves from the beginning of our movement with our compatriots in Taiwan, is to make, in my view, a fatal mistake in what the outside world knows as public relations. What we stand for is freedom and the people—all the people of China. The people must be sovereign. The people must be free. The party must be the Republican Party of China. Republicanism must be our guiding principal. And this the name we must adopt.

Of course, there will be much more substantive meetings than this. We have only been in a state of rebellion for a matter of hours—though some of us have been considering such a move for many months and years. It is impossible to chart a path for an organisation that is but a few hours old. All I have just said is to give some direction and impetus—some sense of organisation, if you will—to our young movement. For unless we know where we are going, even those few of us who are here, then this movement, like any other directionless movement, will filter away into the sand. So nothing I have said is carved in stone. Proper meetings, with debate and discussion, and elections and votes, will decide our ultimate direction. This is just to get matters under way. I hope you respect and understand that approach.

Mr. Yi then fell back on his pillow, exhausted. He took a sip of tea. Mr. Gu, who had stood throughout this oration, his expression changing from dejection to elation as he listened to the old man speak, clapped his hands in a sign of appreciation, and sat down. He had been defeated, or converted—the notes do not reveal, though as we have seen, Miss Wong noted his appearance, which is suggestive. Colonel Li spoke next: "If that matter is settled—and I take it we all agree—then we have some things to attend to urgently. I shall make contact with my senior officers and return with some of my men to Baiyun headquarters, to ascertain the situation. No doubt we shall be ordering the police under our control to take the various actions you recommend, Governor. Mr. Duan, as spokesman I wish you formally to notify the foreign consulates in this city of the situation. We will draft a brief statement here, and we shall make sure the foreign powers are aware of the development. We may need assistance. I also recommend that we make contact now with our compatriots in Hong Kong, to inform them of the situation and to open a channel of communication with them. We are unaware so far of the loyalty of the border security forces at Shenzhen. It is my expectation that they will not be on our side of the argument, and there may have to be some fighting. We shall also make contact with our colleagues across in Fujian Province.

"From now on, gentlemen and Miss Wong, I shall fade into the background. I am, after all, only a colonel, in charge of one very small percentage of the Army— although a percentage that has been at a pivotal point in our nation's history. From now on the decisions in this conflict will be made by the general officers and their staffs, and by the political leadership. I believe you will regard it as appropriate, Governor Yi, if there is no resurgence of the cult of personality that has so often sullied our nation's record. My name will be remembered, perhaps. But from now I will return to my regiment and, until some future appropriate moment, to my rank.

"Our tasks are clear, then? Mr. Duan—to write the statement, to deliver it, and to broadcast it. You will have an escort of soldiers to guarantee your security. Mr. Gu and Mr. Ng will go to the telephone exchange and attempt to make contact with Hong Kong, telling them of the situation. Miss Wong will remain here and write a record of these events, and provide a central telephone number which any of us may call to relay messages to one another. And Governor Yi, dear Governor Yi, you may now try to go to sleep. It will have been a very testing day for you. You have done much to bring this movement to life. You will be able to watch it grow. But I hope you will be able to do so in some comfort and peace."

The colonel rose, clicked his heels in what Miss Wong took to be a most un-Chinese fashion, and left the room. His escort was waiting, and those remaining in the Governor's bedroom listened to the APC's engines roar into life, remaining silent as the soldiers took off into the city.

The brief statement—which was written in English as well as in Chinese—took them only a few moments to prepare. When Miss Wong had completed writing it, on a single sheet of white vellum, it was datelined "Canton—25 July 1997," and read as follows:

The Republican Party of China has today been established, and has taken control of the city of Canton as a first step to gaining control of all of China. The aim of the Party is to restore to the people of our great and beloved nation the freedoms and happiness and prosperity that are common to most other nations in the world, and which have been taken away by the evil machinations of the Chinese Communist Party. The Republican Party recognises the sovereignty of all the people of China, and is against only those who are the enemies of the freedom of those sovereign peoples. The Party has already been given the unqualified support of the People's Liberation Army and the People's Armed Police, the People's Militia and the Municipal Police of the city of Canton. The Party will seek to make contact, probably through third parties, with the Communist authorities in Peking, to ascertain the position of the leadership in our nation's capital. The Republican Party of China calls on the nation to support its aims in the coming struggle, and asks respectfully for the sympathy and understanding and succour of the like-minded nations around the world who, it is hoped, will support our goals in our nation's coming time of need. All honour and blessings to the people of China!

The statement was signed and dated, with a red ink chop-mark, simply "Yi Juan Ling, for the Republican Party of China." James Gahan, Her Majesty's Consul for South China, had not slept at all that night. The disturbances in town during the previous afternoon and evening had, he later confessed, caught him somewhat by surprise. He had, of course, been aware of the Reuters report of an outbreak of violence the day before in Xiamen, and he knew that the body of the dead student would be brought back to Canton for the funeral. He had also heard rumours that the violence in Xiamen had been the consequence of a ham-fisted police investigation into an apparent explosion on the island of Gulangyu—an explosion in which, he had heard, a number of Communist Party officials had been injured, or had died. But he had not reckoned on any kind of popular demonstration in Canton City—and certainly not a popular uprising on the scale that he was shortly to learn had taken place.

He was later to say (and the Foreign Office was sympathetic to his explanation) that he had only just taken up his post, sixteen days before. There had never been a Canton Consulate: this office had been established as a direct result of the retrocession of Hong Kong, and was a subsidiary of the Consulate-General that had been set up in Hong Kong itself, to monitor the passport situation of those British subjects and protected persons who remained in the Special Administrative Region. The Chinese had gained two new consular offices in the United Kingdom as a result: where now the British had offices in Peking, Shanghai, Hong Kong and Canton, so the Chinese had consular offices in London, Cardiff, Glasgow and Belfast—the first being the Embassy, the last being a Consulate, and the two others being formal Consulates-General.

Mr. Gahan, a 50-year-old trade specialist who had not had a China post before, but had been, successively, a Middle East Floater, Third Secretary Djakarta, Third, later Second, Secretary Madrid, Second Secretary (Commercial) Caracas and had then been seconded to the Department of Trade and Industry in London immediately before his Canton posting, had been given a Chinese interpreter-cum-secretary. But because of the perceived relative unimportance of the post, he had been given few other tools with which to carry out an effective intelligence-gathering mission in this part of China.

The *Parliamentary Inquiry into Circumstances Surrounding the Final Handover of Hong Kong and Related Developments in South China* (op. cit.—HMSO Report Cmnd 5611, October 1997) was later to be severely critical of what members regarded as "this severe lack of foresight in British planning policy for UK-China relations."

Mr. Gahan, despite his lack of information that night, was awake when the Consulate's doorbell rang. He assumed there was no security problem: the police guard outside the Consulate was impressive, and had been doubled the previous night. Whoever had managed to penetrate it at this time of night—his bedside clock said 3 A.M. which he automatically calculated was 6 P.M. in London, on Thursday—would be bound to be on business. So without hesitation he went downstairs, and opened the door to find Mr. Duan Keda, a man he had not previously encountered but whose name he knew as that of the father of the dead Xiamen University student. Mr. Duan was holding a message clipped to a board.

He was to say later that he found Mr. Duan a most impressive individual—stoic, dignified, sincere and, crucially, very credible. The visitor handed him the single sheet of paper, and asked the Consul if he could possibly either photocopy it—since Miss Wong had only typed the one sheet—or transcribe it in longhand. He said he understood that at this hour it would be unlikely that a secretary would be on duty. Gahan accordingly sat down at his study desk and painstakingly copied out the statement. He handed it back to Mr. Duan, who checked it for accuracy. Mr. Duan then thanked him, said he would have to make a similar visitation to the United States Consulate, and left.

Once he had gone, Gahan tried to telephone Peking, but found that the lines were inexplicably down. It was the same with Hong Kong, and with London and, most irritating of all, he found he could not get through to the American Consulate. The telephones were still working, but there seemed to be some fault on all the lines he tried. He telephoned the White Swan Hotel, to check: the operator there said that a city-wide emergency had been declared, but did not know why. He then decided to walk to the American Consulate but when he turned into Zhongshan Lu—the Consulate was on the outskirts of Liwan Park, in the west of the city, close (as it happened) to the pleasant suburban area where the Duan family lived—he found to his astonishment a constant stream of armoured cars grinding into the city from across the Pearl River Bridge. Heavily armed soldiers were taking up positions at street corners. Large guns—they looked to him rather like anti-aircraft weapons—were being set up in the park, with soldiers piling sandbags around their supports.

Before he had made 100 yards an infantryman pointed a sub-machine-gun at him and shouted angrily. The soldier was joined by two others, all wearing helmets, and the three gestured at him. He fancied he heard the words: "Go your home!"; but even if he had not, Her Majesty's Consul had to assume that some kind of curfew had been put into effect and it would probably be imprudent for him to go further. He turned tail and scuttled back into the Consulate, heading for the radio room.

Here, thanks to the rapidly reducing costs of modern technology, was his single—though unsecured—link to London: a Casio hand-held satellite link radio-phone, with a long-life battery and a small dish aerial. He took the device on to the lawn, examined the built-in compass to find north, and then pointed the tiny dish aerial east forty-one degrees and south thirteen degrees, and switched on the power. Tiny motors then aligned the dish ever more finely, until it was locked on to the Marisat III Pacific satellite, hovering in geostationary orbit 22,000 miles above Hawaii and, on securing an answering signal from the Marisat's Foreign Office transponder, demanded "Dial Number."

It was 3:25 A.M. in Canton—6:25 P.M. at the Foreign Office. Given the likelihood that the Far East Department had left for the evening, and adding to that the uncertainty over the radio-phone's batteries and the possibility, however remote, that the consulate's garden might at any moment be overrun with Chinese soldiers (a terrifying prospect for most people, let alone a man recently on secondment to the DTI) Gahan decided to speak directly to the Resident Clerk. The Clerk—one of six First Secretaries who took turns to work a week of night shifts in a flat at the top of the Foreign Office, in case of a faraway crisis just like this—began his duties at 6 P.M., and remained beside his bank of phones and faxes and telex machines until 10 A.M. the next day. He effectively directed the running of British Foreign Policy from the apartment overlooking the Horse Guards: he could telephone almost anyone at the core of the British establishment; he had the illusion of near-total power.

He picked up the telephone instantly. "Resident Clerk here," he said.

"This is Gahan, Consulate-General Canton," said the diplomat, unsteadily, and then added the word "China," for good measure. "I am speaking on a non-secure line. We have a situation here that I believe is very grave. So I am going to give you a brief report. We may be cut off."

"Wait a moment, Mr. Gahan," replied the Clerk. He tried to assume a reassuring tone. Here, he realised swiftly, was a low-flying diplomat who was probably out of his depth, alone, and frightened. But at the same time, in a tradition that went back to the days of Richard Burton and beyond, he was being resourceful, and probably trying to do his very best. Goodness knows he was managing to send this report. (The Clerk was a suave man named Woodhead who was said to be in line for the post of Head of Chancery in Paris. He was not to find out for many more months that a colleague he would never come to know intimately was at the time kneeling by a radio transmitter on a muddy lawn, with the screech of armoured-car tyres, the grinding of tank-tracks and the occasional rattle of sub-machine-gun fire coming from all around. But he said that his measured response that night stemmed from his belief that "Gahan was probably in a rather tight situation," and it would be "sensible to listen carefully to everything he said, and then to thank him most sincerely for his efforts and let him know that we cared.") "I'm just going to switch on the recorder, so I don't miss a word. Right—go ahead."

Gahan, sounding more reassured by the pleasant voice at the other end of the (remarkably clear) line, then reported what he knew. He spoke of the telegrams he had sent the day before, and of the growing tension that he had felt in the city ever since the shooting of Constable Wan Zhu'er two weeks before. (That incident—with its probable Hong Kong connections—had happened just two days after he had taken up his post. A China specialist at the US mission and an old friend at the Hong Kong Consulate-General had told him of the immense significance of the shooting and the authorities' violent reaction to it: he had written a telegram two days later that forecast severe trouble that summer in the city—a telegram that would stand him in good stead during the Parliamentary Inquiry later that year, and which would do his career prospects no harm either.)

He went on to outline with speed the events in Xiamen and such additional rumoured details of the explosion in the Galangyu Guesthouse as he had omitted from his telegram. (He had not originally said that any Party officials had died, but the rumours had been ever stronger during the Thursday, and so he repeated them now: the line was good enough for him to be able to hear Woodhead's rapid intake of breath.) He spoke of Wednesday's riot at Xiamen University, the confusing events of Thursday, the visit of Mr. Duan and the apparent founding of a new political entity named "The Republican Party of China."

"In summary, though I say this with the benefit of a little more than a fortnight in this country, it seems to me as though Canton is in the grip of a serious insurrection involving instruments of armed authority at the very highest levels. It would perhaps be accurate to say that there has been, in this part of southern China, if I may mix my languages rather inelegantly, a *de facto coup d'état*. I can only imagine now that Peking will seek to reverse this situation with speed and resolution. Depending on the ability of these Republicans to muster the support of the people and of other forces in adjoining regions, we may have the makings of a major disruptive situation in this country. I hesitate to use the words civil war. But you should be aware of the potential for some grave events here."

Gahan then went on briefly to mention the communications difficulties, and that he was unable to copy this message to Peking or Hong Kong, nor to raise his colleagues in other missions. He knew that Duan, who was escorted by a number of police, would be making a similar visit to the US Consulate-General, and assuming that he made it safely through the streets he would imagine that a report similar to his own would at that moment be arriving in Washington. He told Woodhead that he was physically all right, that the Consulate had stocks of food and water and its own generator (although he doubted that any staff would make it to work next day), that the Republicans were unlikely to be hostile to the presence of foreigners in their territory, and that he felt certain he could manage to man the office without problems for some while. He knew of 128 British citizens who had registered as living in the consular region and he would attempt to get in touch with them as the situation allowed. His own advice was that they remain at home and keep out of sight, and he wondered if such a message could be broadcast by the World Service.

Finally he asked that the Clerk telephone Mrs. Gahan in Gillingham in Dorset to inform her of the situation and to suggest that she postpone her planned arrival in China until the situation clarified itself. At this state the Battery Low light on the transmitter began to blink, and the transmission of the first report made to the outside world of these remarkable events in Chinese history—and, it was to turn out, in world history—came to an end.

Although it would be unsurprising to learn, in view of Mr. Gahan's very recent posting, that the British were the last to learn of the uprising they were, in fact, the first. This had much to do with Mr. Duan's choice of the British as the first to receive a copy of the Republican Party Statement, which in turn had to do with the closeness of the Consulate to Governor Yi's house and to the fact that, as a worker in a Hong Kong bank Mr. Duan had had cause to visit the new Consulate only three days before. He had gone not to see Mr. Gahan, as it happened, but to ask advice from a clerk about a quantity of funds that had been frozen in Hong Kong by the new Chinese Banking Commissioner there, under the complicated new Exchange Control rules. The clerk had not been able to help, but had been sympathetic.

The relative speed with which London knew of the uprising also had much to do with circumstances at the US Consulate, which had recently moved to a large compound near its old offices in the Dong Feng Hotel and very close to the PSB. Its staff, unlike Mr. Gahan, had a fair appreciation of the situation—or at least, of the call-out of the Army to deal with the protest march. They had not however, heard the statement from Colonel Li (despite his announcement being made no more than 200 yards from the Consulate wall: the State Department was later to blame "unfavourable wind conditions" for the statement's lack of audibility) and were unaware of the storming of the PSB headquarters by Colonel Li's battalion. Telephone and telex communications were then cut, and all Canton was able to report to Washington over its own portable cellular network was that there had been "serious disturbances" in the city, with a considerable amount of gunfire from a "bewildering variety" of weapons.

By the time Mr. Duan arrived at the Consulate gates—even though he arrived with a police escort and other trappings of formality—the Marine guards refused to let him in. From behind their bulletproof windows the pair on duty (normally only one was stationed at the entrance, but the guard had been doubled in the wake of the disturbances, with the rest of the eight-man squad armed and in a ready-room inside the building) ordered Mr. Duan and his party to be escorted away from the Consulate's walls, and they refused to accept the proffered piece of paper. It was not until one of the marines called a duty political officer to inform him that "a suspicious individual escorted by a number of uniformed and armed men" was waiting on Liuhua Road and refusing to leave that some attention was paid to him. The letter was eventually accepted and, as Mr. Duan insisted, photocopied and returned to him.

The Consul-General, a long-serving career officer named Meisel, was on the radio-telephone to Washington for more than an hour during this period and it was only when he finally broke the connection, after being assured of further security assistance from Peking, that he was asked to assess Duan's photocopied statement. Not having seen Duan himself, and relying only on reports from his Marines, he did not at first pay much attention; it was only after the Department had radioed back to alert him to reports from both the US Embassy in London and from the NSA's own intercepts from Fort Meade, Maryland, that he reread the statement, considered anew its signature, and reacted with the energy that such a development warranted. He was later to be reprimanded, and was not to serve in an overseas post again.

In London, the Foreign Secretary James Hogge was holding a reception for a visiting Iraqi trade delegation at his official London residence in Carlton Gardens. Peter Woodhead had, as protocol demanded, tracked down the relevant Minister of State for the region, Lord Inverdonald—he was at a reception as well, for the departing South Korean ambassador—and told him of the news from Canton.

Inverdonald, who had presided over the flag-lowering ceremony in Hong Kong just four weeks before and whose experience allowed him readily to appreciate the likelihood of a major breakdown in civil order in both Hong Kong and South China, immediately called Hogge, and suggested a meeting. Together with such other assistants as were found—including the Head of the Far Eastern Department Robert Folkes, the Head of News Department Peter Mayhew and the Head of Defence Department Roger Whittham—an emergency meeting was held in the Foreign

Secretary's office just two hours later at 9 P.M., when presumably dawn was breaking in southern China.

Details of the meeting have remained highly classified. Certain relatively trivial facts have emerged, some from a special meeting of diplomatic correspondents that was called just before midnight. These include the fact that after a series of unexplained disturbances involving the People's Liberation Army, communications appeared to have broken down inside China, and that the British missions in Peking and Shanghai had been told of a particularly critical situation that had developed overnight in Canton by means of radio messages direct from London; that the British subjects resident throughout China—including the newly constituted Xianggang SAR ("which Correspondents will recall," said the Head of News, with a sardonic grin, "was until lately the Crown Colony of Hong Kong")—were being asked to keep off the streets, and to listen to the World Service for instructions since messages to this effect had been passed for broadcast to Bush House; that two of the British warships that had taken part in the evacuation of Hong Kong and which had then proceeded to Australian waters, HMS *Manchester* and HMS *Hermione*, were being called back north to await orders while on what the diplomat quaintly referred to as "the China station"; that other Allies, who were unaware of the China development, had been informed; and that from the evidence of the last two weeks in Canton and from around the rest of China, with additional recent information about possible "serious and possibly profound disagreements" breaking out inside a number of key ministries in Peking, including Defence, Foreign Affairs and Internal Security, China appeared to be headed for a period of "serious instability." It was, therefore, probable that a meeting of the major Western powers and the Russian Federation would be called within the coming days to assess the situation: the American Secretary of State Mr. Richard Crowther and his Moscow counterpart, Mr. Akhrimov, had both been informed that night.

What was never made clear in the briefing with the correspondents was exactly what Britain's policy might now be. Neither was it made clear whether there was any probability of a common allied policy—and if there was, what that was likely to be.

But some hints of a possible British attitude—which heavily influences today's general Western thought on the calamitous situation in the region—could be discerned some months before. Close reading, for instance, of the proceedings of a confidential Chatham House Conference entitled *The Political Structure of North-East Asia in the Twenty-First Century*, held the previous January, and attended by Lord McLean, a former Permanent Under-Secretary at the Foreign Office, and now Professor Emeritus of Asian Studies at the University of Leeds, would have enabled a reasonably astute analyst to have drawn a fair outline of at least the potential for new ideas; and the *New York Times* was actually bold enough to recognise and to write, albeit briefly, about a new "tilt" in Western attitudes suggested by the similarly close scrutiny of a series of lectures given at Harvard in the spring of 1997 by Professor the Lord Wilson, the Director of the Shaw Institute of Chinese Studies at Oxford, a former British diplomat and acknowledged specialist on modern Chinese political history.

Both McLean and Wilson, who, as advisers to the British government were the principal navigators of this new direction, appeared to hold, basically, that in the event of any conflict within China's borders, the Western powers should display a discreet tendency *to favour the hopes and aspirations of the southern Chinese* over those of the Communist old guard in the north.

There was no doubt, the pair reiterated in separate interviews early in the year (stressing at the same time that both were retired, and were now officially "out of the loop") that the failure of Communism in Europe and the former Soviet Union, and the resulting fragmentation of both blocs into quarrelsome micro-states, would eventually happen in China. The fact that Communism had survived for so long in both China and North Korea was a puzzle, and had many probable reasons. It was, for instance, a measure of the relative lack of public discontent in both countries—of the existence of a bovine acceptance of the *status quo* that arose from the enduring sub-Confucian trait of respect for authority and the popular acceptance of the wisdom of elders, as well as from the very poor communications, the absolute control of the press, radio and television and of popular movement within the two countries, and from the extremely harsh and imaginatively cruel public penalties that were imposed on any would-be rebels within the system.

Banishment, exile, bamboo slivers under the fingernails—the spectrum of punishment was vast, and appalling. "While both the Chinese and the North Koreans can be the most gentle and kindly people in the world," one of those attending the Chatham House conference wrote, "there is a capacity for cruelty and repression within both societies that is quite chilling. It is nothing like the animal savagery of Amin's Uganda, nor is it akin to the crazed butchery of some of the Middle Eastern despots we have seen in recent years. In China and in North Korea those in power appear to sit down and think: how exactly do we inflict the most awful pain on a man? How many volts do we give him, where, and for how long? How finely should the wire be sharpened before we insert it? To how many degrees do we heat the iron bar? For how long can we strangle someone before we release the noose, and then start it up again? The cruelty here is precise, it is measured to a fine art, it is carried out coldly and with clinical ritual. It is therefore infinitely more terrifying than any cruelty based on anger. People know what is coming to them if they stray—and they know that they never know how dreadful it is going to be. So they almost never stray. Just to be afraid to imagine what will happen is enough to keep a society straight."

But having said that, the academics concluded, there was a weak spot in the Chinese armour—the influence, steadily growing in the south of the country since the late 1970s, of the entrepreneurial ways of life that had proved so successful for the southern Chinese in Hong Kong. The potential for the "tainting" of sub-Yangtze China by the "triple contagions of avarice, corruption and landlordism" and other capitalist excesses had been condemned by the Peking authorities as far back as 1993, in the famous *People's Daily* editorial written on the centenary of Mao Tse-tung's birth. (Further details of the extent of this influence, and of the dismay of the Communist authorities, were outlined in Chapter 4.)

In the eyes of the West—particularly in the eyes of Western commercial interests—it was these same capitalist influences that offered the chance for the making of some massive fortunes. Businesses in the West had, of course, looked hungrily at the possibilities offered by a China that, since the opening up of the country to foreigners in the early 1970s, had nearly doubled its population of potential customers. It was a delightful coincidence that personal liberties and democracy tended to go hand in hand with market-led economies. From the simple view of the unreconstructed business leaders in the West, for China to be turned capitalist—to be tainted by the southern influences, in other words—would be little short of ideal.

The British academics naturally enough shared this view, and took it further by hoping for the encouragement of personal freedoms in China. And, finding little resistance to this view within the infamous "China Mafia" of the Foreign Office, it became an essential plank—though a very secret one—of British and then American foreign policy. The "infection" of southern China was thus, during the remaining years of British rule in Hong Kong, to be systematically encouraged; limited but significant assistance was to be given, *sub rosa*, to a would-be dissident movement that seemed likely to have the ability both to grow in Hong Kong and to become, eventually, rooted in Guangdong and Fujian Provinces (hence the meetings between Captain Margerison and Peter Heung, outlined above); and, if such a movement produced a serious rebellion, it should be supported.

The procedures are very delicate whereby a foreign power is able to support a rebel movement, without seeming to violate that cardinal rule of international diplomacy which forbids meddling in a nation's internal affairs. Under conditions of the greatest secrecy, weapons and ammunition can be supplied. Men can be trained. Your own soldiers, specially schooled, can be inserted. Where diplomatic breakdown can be risked, rebel governments-in-exile can be harboured. Regional regimes newly established in captured enclaves can be recognised. Leaders can be welcomed. Conferences can be organised. Mediation can be offered. Peace can be brokered. Support can be given to the stripling regime.

Britain—and, it was to be assumed, the United States— almost certainly favoured a comprehensive approach to the Canton rebellion, following this basic outline of what has become known as the McLean Formula. Since the situation in China has not yet been wholly clarified it is not possible to be certain. But the covert foreign military support given to the Republicans has been ostentatiously welcomed in London and Washington and there is a distinct iciness in relations between London and Peking.

But to enlarge on these matters is to skip ahead too far in the narrative: suffice to say that at the first meeting of what was soon to become known as the China Crisis Committee, the CCC, the decision to tilt in favour of the Republican Party of China was probably made. (Similar recommendations had already been made by Mr. Charlesworth's HK7 Committee in Washington.) The success which the Party and its military allies has subsequently enjoyed is owed in large measure to the decisions that were initiated, on the one hand by Hogge, Inverdonald and ffolkes—the so-called "Holy Trinity"—after taking advice from the "Heavenly Twins" of Wilson and McLean, and on the other by Hugh Charlesworth, and his ebullient new Secretary of State.

However, other grave events in the Western Pacific have recently taken place, all undoubtedly consequent upon the situation in China. Whether responsibility for those events can be laid at the door of any Western government's China policy is a matter that will have to be debated for many years to come.

By dawn on Friday Canton was almost totally secure. The Guangdong Communist Party headquarters had proved troublesome, and it took several hours of negotiation—though no gunfire—to persuade a group of diehards to give themselves up and to hand over their weaponry and, more crucially, their files, to the rebel leaders. But, as Colonel Li suspected from his "three cheers" message, the three divisional commanders, Lan, Hu and Yang, had all pledged allegiance to Governor Yi and, moreover—and in the most significant shift of the latter part of that crucial night—so had General Tang Zhu Hou, the General Officer Commanding Guangzhou Military Region.

Discussion on the matter had been mercifully brief. General Lan, who it will be remembered had spoken to Colonel Li in his quarters immediately before the skirmish outside the PSB barracks, had—without the company of his political commissar—visited his brother generals shortly afterwards, to tell them of the situation. He was careful to see that their ever-vigilant commissars were not present at the meeting either. He took care to say, truthfully and in case there was any surreptitious monitoring of the conversation, that he had not specifically conspired with Colonel Li to persuade him to "turn" his battalion.

His view was that the other major-generals, although broadly sympathetic to the aspirations of the Cantonese non-Communists, would not be so disloyal to the tenets of a proud and disciplined army as to incite junior officers to treasonable behaviour. Such a move should come from below—from the colonel level, invariably the locus of discontent in any army. The colonels were close enough to the rank and file to detect the popular mood, and they were on terms of sufficient intimacy with the staff to be able to transmit that mood upwards.

All that General Lan had done, he told Hu and Yang with great care, was to indicate to the colonel that if in his duties that night he detected a mood among his men that might persuade him to disobey an order or orders that were genuinely repugnant to him as a patriotic Chinese, then any act of defiance that he committed would in all probability not encounter disfavour at staff level and above.

General Hu and General Yang agreed, instantly. It remained now to neutralise the commissars—by cutting off their communications links rather than by the drastic but possibly necessary means of killing them, it was thought— and to alert the two most senior officers in the chain, Lieutenant-General Wu, GOC Guangdong Military District (who was in any case on leave) and, most important of all, General Tang, the GOC-in-C of Guangzhou Military Region. These two latter officers were based at the Army headquarters near Baiyun airport: to get Tang's *imprimatur* was vital to the military success of the coming operation.

The two black Red Flag limousines that left Xicun barracks for Baiyun at 1:30 A.M. that Friday morning took only fifteen minutes to complete the vitally important journey. General Tang was in any case expecting them: his commissar Gu Zhi, had received a coded message from a subordinate at Xicun, warning him of the possibility of trouble within the senior ranks of the local detachments. As the three divisional commanders were announced, Gu was in the process of angrily lecturing his general—in *putonghua*, which was both Gu's and Tang's second language, Gu being from Shanghai, Tang from Zhuhai—on the lunacy, as he put it, of the move.

"Of course, like you, I am aware of the discontent that has been spreading. I am not blind, nor am I unfeeling. But to take a step like that which has been reported to me is madness. It is also, if I may say so, quite extraordinarily insulting timing. Today, as you know, is the anniversary of the Party's first congress. Next week is the seventieth birthday of our glorious People's Liberation Army. Yet now I hear that you are seriously thinking of acquiescing to the demands of a small clique of back-sliders, of corrupt and greedy criminals, influenced by gangsters in Hong Kong . . ."

General Tang motioned him to be quiet, and welcomed his three junior officers into his study. "I have heard what is going on. I have been monitoring the radio traffic. I believe Colonel Li is about to send you a message from Jeifang Beilu. The signaller will bring it to us presently. Meanwhile my friend Mr. Gu here is raising objections. He accuses me of being a traitor, of not having enough patience. That last is indeed true. But we need not talk of this now."

The Army signaller entered, with a handwritten note. Tang glanced at the name of the addressees, and handed the paper to General Lan. The General read it, then instructed the soldier to make a reply to Colonel Li immediately. It was to read "Your message acknowledged. Felicitations on your achievement." It was to be signed simply "Lan, Commander 123rd Infantry." Then, just as the signaller was leaving, Lan called him back, and instructed him to add the phrase "three cheers" to the message. "He will appreciate the significance," he said, and looked pointedly at his two colleagues and at their senior commander.

Commissar Gu then tried to leave the room, but was stopped by a sentry. "You will be placed under arrest, I regret to say, along with all your fellows," said Tang. "You must not be permitted to make any attempts to communicate with other units of the Liberation Army or with other cadres. Should you succeed in doing so by any means, you will be shot. There is to be no question about this. This movement will succeed. We have right on our side, whatever you may say." More sentries were called, and Gu, screeching abuse in Shangainese, was led away to the cells. Others later joined him; telephone messages to the Xicun barracks and the remaining camps in and around Canton City instructed line officers there to locate all the political commissars and place them under close arrest.

In the meantime the two remaining infantry battalions and the single armoured unit that had already been placed on alert, the 37th and 38th Infantry Battalions and the 44th Light Armoured Regiment, all of which were attached to the 123rd Division, were ordered to deploy with immediate effect to the Baiyun civil and military airports, to the main railway station and the port and to the Communist Party headquarters and, in liaison with Colonel Li of the 46th Infantry, to carry out the procedures which they knew all too well, having studied in great detail the document *Standing Instructions for the Comprehensive Security of the City*. (The circumstances in which they were now putting the *Instructions* into effect were, however, somewhat different from those which had been assumed by the document's authors.)

Hundreds of soldiers and light armoured cars then started to pour into the city and its outskirts. By dawn the operation was essentially complete. Canton City was, except for a few small pockets of resistance, in the hands of the Republican Party, and was now waiting for the rest of China to flex its mighty muscles and strike back.

PEKING

Friday, 25 July 1997

No comprehensive account of what took place inside the Chinese leaders' apartments in Zhongnanhai during this critical period is ever expected to be published. The old men gathered around the equally elderly and enfeebled President Yang Shankun are unlikely to write their memoirs; nor are there allies—like the Bulgarians, in the old days—who were privy to the internal machinations of the Chinese power élite, and who would, at some later date, recount what they knew. Peking and Pyongyang were almost wholly isolated in the world—a handful of minor African states and a cluster of unvisited island nations were their only friends; and though both France and Germany supplied weapons and defence technology to China, its diplomats were never among the inmates who enjoyed real access to those at the centres of power.

The events in Peking that followed the rebellion in Canton can only be sketchily reconstructed from the reports of some Western diplomats, the few journalists operating in the city, and from that most useful of information sources, the electronic intelligence intercepts captured from the three satellite monitoring stations at Darwin in Australia's Northern Territories, at Wakkanai in northern Hokkaido, Japan, and the recently completed monitoring base operating under the cover of the new BBC short-wave transmitter near Chiang Mai, in Thailand.

The British Ambassador at Peking, Sir Peter MacDuff, had been told of the apparent rebellion in a Flash telegram which arrived shortly before dawn. He tried to call Gahan in Canton, but was told by the Embassy operator the lines were said to be "temporarily down." He then convened an immediate meeting in his study with the Military Attaché, Colonel Robert Strange, and with his Political Counsellor, Simon Hughes-Lockhart. He told them of Gahan's extraordinary report to London—which, he now gathered, had been confirmed by a much later but apparently substantially similar report passed to the State Department by their Canton consular office. The entire military organisation based in Canton City had seemingly rebelled, and had pledged its loyalty to an organisation about which nothing was known save its name, the Republican Party of China, and its titular leader, the former provincial governor Yi Juan Ling. He declined to say what British policy was likely to be in the event of a full-scale Chinese civil war. This was clearly a major crisis, one which threatened the stability of the region and perhaps the world. He asked if either of his colleagues had any further news or thoughts.

Hughes-Lockhart was able to report on what he thought was the development of schisms in a number of Peking Ministries. He had, in fact, been writing a minute on the subject in the office the day before, and was due to present it to the Ambassador that very morning.

He had discovered that there were in particular, in his phrase, "ominous cracks" developing within the Ministry of Foreign Affairs. That something exceedingly peculiar was happening had become clear in the wake of the summary execution by shooting of Madame Zhang three weeks before. Exhaustive interviews with the Reuters correspondent, Richard James, and attempts to have him recognise from Colonel Strange's massive library of mug-shots the Army officer who had accompanied Madame Zhang to that fateful last interview, had eventually produced a name: the soldier was in all probability a Captain Wong Hao-tian, an English-language specialist who was working as a documents translator at the Chinese Military Academy at Shijiazhuang, south of Peking. Captain Wong had been seconded from a post in an infantry regiment attached to the 123rd Division, based in Canton.

Colonel Strange nodded, adding that the Chinese captain had not been seen since, and it was assumed that he had returned to his original post in Canton. (He certainly did not return to Shijiazhuang Academy that Saturday afternoon, and an informer working for a British government agency at Peking airport hinted that he may have been spotted boarding a jet of China South Air Lines later that afternoon.) The Military Academy had been closed to all foreign visitors, diplomats included, for the previous month. It was not known exactly why the officer had accompanied Madame Zhang to the meeting with James, though the natural assumption within the Embassy was that the directive for leaking the news of Mr. Mao's appointment as Chief Executive of Xianggang SAR (Hong Kong) came not from within the Ministry of Foreign Affairs itself but from a rebel group within the Army, and, moreover, one that had powerful connections inside the Ministry.

The Political Counsellor had been able to find out who had authorised the execution of Madame Zhang. The Head of the General Political Department of the PLA, Mr. Yang Baibang, who was the younger step-brother of the Chinese President, Yang Shankun, conducted a swift investigation once he heard of the release of the news. He summoned the Foreign Affairs Minister, who angrily denied all knowledge of the maverick news leak: the scapegoat was Madame Zhang, and she was picked up by PAP officers at 5 P.M., taken to the Political Department fifteen minutes later, then taken to a remote spot behind the Daiyuotai Guest House and shot in the back of the neck.

Hughes-Lockhart said he had learned that a small group of middle-ranking Western specialists—all of them former colleagues of Madame Zhang—had been removed from their posts and sent to a language training school in Shenyang, in Manchuria. Day-to-day contacts between the Ministry and a number of European countries had been badly affected as a result. Three ambassadors—those to Iceland, Tadzhikistan and Sri Lanka—had been recalled in the past week; and there was a rumour circulating among the diplomatic compounds of Sanlitun and Jianguomenwai that the Deputy Foreign Minister, Li Jiwei, had been removed from office.

"My conclusion," Hughes-Lockhart went on, "is that a group of Ministry officials knew of this coming Army rebellion, and supported its aims. Some of these people have been slowly and quite carefully removed from positions of influence. At least one—Madame Zhang—has been executed, as an example to others. But I expect that this dissident movement within the Ministry is in fact quite large, and I very much doubt that the powers that be have the ability to contain it. Not now, at least."

Colonel Strange, who had only been on-post for three months, admitted that he was not well enough grounded to have heard much about dissidence within the PLA. He had followed up the disappearance of Captain Wong, as Simon Hughes-Lockhart had just noted; and he had been aware of "mutterings" among reformist officers, most of them assigned to forces based in southern China, that were suggestive of serious unease within the PLA command structure. He had anticipated trouble—indeed, a minute from his predecessor, Colonel Peterman, had indicated the "mutterings" among a reform group of younger officers had begun in the aftermath of the violence of the Wuhan Incident. But neither Peterman nor he, Strange, had the slightest idea that matters were to move with such speed. All he could do now was to sketch, very broadly, the known military dispositions, and, from the point of view of a disinterested foreign military officer, advise the Ambassador on how matters could possibly develop. He looked at the Ambassador for agreement, and Sir Peter nodded.

"The Chinese have, ever since the breakdown of Communism in Russia and her satellites, been most fearful for the security of their national borders. As everyone now knows, the country is surrounded on all sides but one by non-socialist countries—some of them old, some others of them very new and the consequence of the explosion of nationalism that followed the collapse of the Marxist experiment. With the single exception of the Yalu River boundary, where China abuts on to her lone ideological friend and ally North Korea, the entire length of her land border is inhabited by non-Communists who, in most cases, have ethnic connections with the people living as neighbours across inside China.

"Consider. Vietnam has not been Communist since 1994, and Laos held popular elections last year. Myanmar, Burma, is in the hands of a military clique, but one that is now aggressively right wing, and which no longer subscribes to the beliefs of Ne Win, who is generally thought of as a madman. India, of course, is perpetually troublesome, but is no longer specifically non-aligned and nowadays generally sides with the United States. Bhutan and Nepal are manifestly non-socialist, and have been since their two monarchs offered democratic reforms to their people—there was some flirtation with Marxism in 1991, it is true, but it was pretty short-lived.

"Pakistan and Afghanistan are of course rabidly antisocialist in their outlook. The Kazakh Federation is brutally militaristic, and the neighbouring state of Tadzhkistan is unstable and illiberal. Kirgizia is free and independent again. Even old Tannu Tuva is back on her feet again. The Mongol Republic is heartily anti-Marxist, though barely stable. The Russian republic, with the exceptions I have noted, is stable, though there have lately been stirrings, as you know, among several of the ethnic groups in Eastern Siberia—most notably the Buryat groups east of Irkutsk, who have been forging links with the Oroqen minorities of northern Manchuria.

"The Chinese have good reason to be worried about their frontiers. There are Vietnamese and Lao Burmese minority groups living in Yunnan and Guangxi Provinces. There is quite a strong Yao opposition group in Yunnan, particularly. Then again, Xizang—Tibet—is terribly unstable, and there is much cross-border assistance from the Nepalese and the Indians. There are various Turkic groups in Xinjiang who

The Chinese People's Liberation Army

Basic Organization

The Chinese Army, the Chinese Navy, the Second Artillery (the strategic nuclear forces) and the Chinese Air Force are known generically as the forces of the People's Liberation Army. While they are technically subordinate to the Ministry of National Defence they come under the overall supervision of the two Central Military Commissions, that of of the Communist Party and (since 1982) of the National People's Congress. The Army is thus regarded as a force that 'belongs', as it were, both to the Party and to the People.

The Army itself, which had a strength (in 1997) of 2,450,000 (of which 1,400,000 were conscripts) is organized into some 24 Integrated Group Armies and, geographically, into seven Military Regions (MRs), 29 Military Districts (MDs) and three Garrison Commands.

The Military Regions (indicated on the map below) are each headed by a full General, with a Political Commissar of equivalent rank serving alongside. The Military Districts and Garrison Commands are headed by Lieutenant-Generals. Each of the Integrated Group Armies, commanded by a Lieutenant-General, is approximately equivalent in size to a US Army Corps, with a strength of about 44,000 troops. A Group Army usually has three infantry divisions, as well as associated tank, artillery and air defence units. Armies are assigned to the various Military Regions as required. Defence ministry recruitment policy attempts to discourage 'regionalization' of fighting units, though this has not always been successful, especially (and crucially) in South China.

The upper chart on the next page shows the regional and district organization of the PLA in July 1997, with a further indication of the identity - where known - of the Group Armies (GAs) and some Divisions assigned to various geographical units.

The lower chart shows in rather more detail the situation that obtained in two of the more acutely affected PLA units by mid-1999, with the units and the unit leaders who were known to have gone across to the Republican government, or played some otherwise interesting part in the story, indicated.

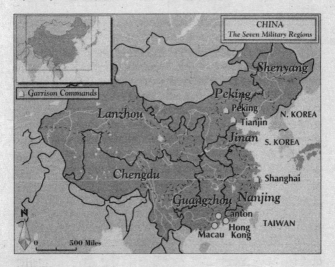

CHINA
The Seven Military Regions

Garrison Commands

Shenyang

Peking
Peking
Tianjin   N. KOREA

Lanzhou

Jinan   S. KOREA

Chengdu

Shanghai

Guangzhou Nanjing
Canton
Hong TAIWAN
Macau Kong

N

0   500 Miles

P.L.A. Organization, July 1997

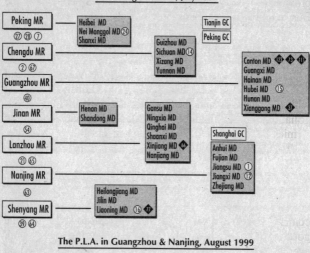

The P.L.A. in Guangzhou & Nanjing, August 1999

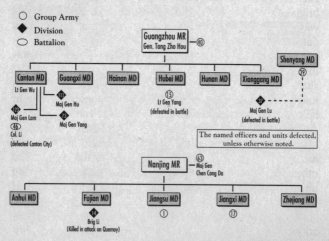

have much to do with their brothers and sisters across in the Federation. The people of Inner Mongolia are being stirred up by those in Outer Mongolia. The Manchus are reviving their strength in Dongbei—the three North East provinces—and are being egged on by the Siberians and the Buryats and the other minority groups.

"So the Peking authorities have seen fit to handle this by placing their best Armies and their best men out in the frontier regions. The élite corps are there—the 2nd and the 67th Armies in Chengdu, dealing with the Vietnamese and the Burmese; the 21st and the 65th in Lanzhou, dealing with the Tibetans and the Tadjiks; the 24th in Inner Mongolia; the 16th, 39th and 64th in Manchuria; and four whole Armies in and around Peking, just in case there's any assault on the capital.

"But the Armies that are not so hot, and particularly the commanders that are not so totally reliable, have been assigned to the centre and the south—where the trouble has broken out. The 15th and the 40th in Guangzhou Region—commanded by General Tang? It's difficult to know why he got the job. There have always been mutterings about him, ever since Tienanmen Square, when he was an armoured brigade commander. He did as he was told. But it was always rumoured that he did it with bad grace, and he was out of the picture for four or five years.

"Then again, the 1st Army in Nanjing—buttressed admittedly by the 12th and the 63rd—seems to have its fair share of troubles. General Nie, who runs the show, is a tough old man, a real died-in-the-wool conservative. But he's old, that has to be remembered. Not entirely with it. And one of his deputies who was operational commander of the three divisions of the 63rd Army based at Quanzhou has long been suspect. He was involved in the call-out the other day, when Peking thought the Taiwanese were stirring up trouble in Xiamen. He was at Sandhurst for a while, if that means anything.

"Speaking off the top of my head, then, we have a situation where the upper echelons of two of the lesser southern Armies have rebelled. I don't know for sure that all of the troops under General Tang's command are with him. I have strong reservations, for instance, about the airborne divisions based at Wuhan, part of the 15th Army in Hubei. I know the general in Wuhan, a wild man named Yang, and I think there's a fair chance he'll side with Peking, no matter what his Regional command orders him to do.

"But I would imagine that some of the Nanjing Military Region officers will come over to the side of the rebels. By the end of the next few days we will probably see four and maybe five armies, more or less totally on the side of the Republicans. Who will attack whom, I can't rightly say.

"Then I would expect some of the new independent states on the Russian side of the frontier to stir up trouble, and the Indians do the same on theirs, so that the border armies will be too occupied to be able to deal with this insurrection. Peking will thus have to use its capital forces to attack. That probably means the 27th Army, which is the most loyal of all, and has a great deal of internal air support and a great deal of mobility. But to move forces out of the capital—well, for the old leaders here it is a risk, a very grave risk.

"From the rebels' point of view there is one thing that must be done, and I imagine they can do it, and will want to do it quickly. And that is secure Hong Kong and bring it into the fold.

"If they have Hong Kong on their side, then they'll have the port, the airfields, the railways links—the perfect logistical tail for whatever they do. They'll probably get their hands on the Shenzhen airport, which will be useful for them. It would be nice for them to have the ports and airfields in Shantou and Xiamen as well, but Hong Kong is the crucial one. I can't pretend to know what British policy is. I think I know what I'd like it to be. But if there was any possibility of us siding with the rebels, then the fact of Hong Kong being in rebel hands would clearly make it a great deal easier for us to help, with covert resupply and that sort of thing.

"We know two things about the military situation in Hong Kong. The first, obviously, is that the population is going to be very much on the side of the rebels. And the second is that the troops which have been sent down to occupy the place are detached from the 39th Army, from Manchuria. They're really tough—real so-and-sos. They've seen a lot of fighting. Their commanders are true died-in-the-wool conservatives. Their troops are peasant boys from the remotest and roughest of regions, and they have been taught to loathe the Cantonese. I suspect they'll put up quite a fight.

"But the Republicans have got to engage them, and quickly, and gain those airfields and ports. It is absolutely vital. So I'd imagine that the fighting will begin in earnest inside Hong Kong within the next few hours. I could be wrong—but if I were a betting man . . ."

Later in the day there were reports of "unusual activity" within Zhongnanhai compound, with many vehicles entering and leaving through the gate beside the Forbidden City. However, the complicated network of tunnels beneath Peking—many of the tunnels restricted to the use of senior members of the Chinese government—would have enabled officials to ply between the various ministries and commissions without ever being seen by the public; it has to be assumed, given the magnitude of the crisis, that the "unusual activity" seen at the surface was but a fraction of that actually experienced.

Among those few who were both seen entering the compound and were recognised was General Li Huan, the Commander of the Second Artillery Corps. Since the Corps is the division in charge of all China's atomic weapons delivery systems it is assumed that the leadership was trying to make certain that, no matter what happened between the land forces in southern China, no rebel group managed to lay its hands on atomic weapons. The Political Commissar attached to the Second Artillery, a Mr. Yin, was also called in to the meeting. What was said can only be surmised.

The Commander of the Chinese Air Force was believed to be in Hong Kong at the time of the rebellion. His deputy, a General Ri, is thought to have attended the Zhongnanhai meeting.

A brief statement was then issued through the China News Agency that Friday evening, over the dual signatures of—somewhat unexpectedly—the Ministry of Railways and the Director of the Civil Aviation Administration. Referring to "unauthorised disruptive acts" by "a limited number of hooligans and mobsters" in "a small segment of Guandong Province," it had been decided with immediate effect to halt all rail and air traffic links between Canton City on the one hand and the cities of Peking, Shanghai, Nanjing, Wuhan, Kunming and Xian on the other; and, in a second case, between the city of Xiamen on the one hand and Shanghai, Peking and Nanjing on the other. Moreover, frontier security police at the road crossings between the Provinces of Hunan and Hubei, Anhui, Zhejiang and Jiangxi, and Guangxi and Guizhou were being instructed to make strict checks on all vehicles and people passing between provinces; and it was suggested that, to minimise personal inconvenience, citizens in the affected regions stay at home "until a normal situation has been restored."

Two things that might have been expected to happen on that Friday did not, however. First, there was no formal convening of either the thirteen-man State Council, nor of the Central Military Commission, the rather smaller and more exclusive body that acts, during events of the utmost gravity, as the supreme authority in matters relating to the nation's civil discipline.

The only explanation to be put forward by those Peking-based diplomats who make a study of the minutiae of Chinese politics was a rather colourful one: that the problems clearly affecting the middle-level bureaucrats within the Ministry of Foreign Affairs were now leaching into the upper echelons of the highest policy-making bodies of the nation. Dissent within either the CMC or the State Council was unheard of since the days before the Cultural Revolution; but at the same time, there was an apparent lack of firm and decisive action that day, and although later events suggest that the two bodies have since pulled themselves together (and that there have been several rumoured changes in the membership of the CMC), only dissent could have accounted for the dithering.

The second event that did not take place that Friday was the staging of any attempt to reverse the deteriorating military situation. The cancellation of domestic air travel, the closure of selected airports and the shutdown of most of the southern railway system admittedly did clear the way for the rapid movement of soldiers if and when that was reckoned to be necessary. But none was actually moved. None of the main northern Group Army commands, so far as could be ascertained, was even put on special alert. Moreover—and in view of the developments of the next few hours, crucially—no signal was sent (or at least, none was ever intercepted: and all intercept stations had been ordered to listen intently for code traffic out of Peking) to the Commander, PLA Sub-Regional Headquarters, Xianggang.

Major-General Lu Chuanzhi, who had his temporary headquarters at the former Royal Naval base on what used to be Hong Kong's Stonecutters Island, was wholly ignorant of the developments in Canton. He was thus caught quite unprepared by the events of the few hours between breakfast and dinnertime on the following, highly eventful, Saturday.

XIANGGANG SAR

FRIDAY MORNING TO SATURDAY NIGHT

The rebel generals had acted precisely as Colonel Strange had anticipated. At their barracks meeting early on the Friday morning they had mapped out their immediate stratagems. They had two principal concerns. The first was based on the lack of response to radio messages from General Yang up in Wuhan. All of the other military district commanders and the scores of various outpost commands within the massive Guangzhou Region had been told during the night of the developments; and all had reacted enthusiastically to the situation, giving their unqualified backing to Governor Yi and the Republican cause. All, that is, except General Yang, Commander of the 15th Group Army. Not a word had come from him, and further attempts to make contact even with his signals units had been in vain.

General Yang, who was reportedly the son-in-law of the President of the Supreme People's Court, and was from Shaanxi Province, had a particularly mobile force at his disposal. He had paratroopers and transport aircraft, and—coming under his tactical command in time of crisis—he had two squadrons of modern, Russian-built MiG 29 jet fighters, which were given by Moscow in 1992 after the Chinese pledged several hundred million dollars' worth of construction loans to the then crippled Commonwealth of Independent States. The fighters were normally assigned to the Chengdu Military Region, to assist troops in the event of cross-border skirmishes in the southwest; but they had been seconded to General Yang's territory three months before to enable him to stage a series of exercises.

If Yang decided to stay loyal to Peking, his forces would surely be the first to be utilised to weaken Tang's hold on the far south—and in Tang's view, they would present a formidable problem. Orders thus went out to ensure that the rebel units and key locations were given full anti-aircraft protection, including the deployment of all of the region's available batteries of surface-to-air missiles.

The second concern expressed that morning at Baiyun was the need to acquire, and quickly, the shortest of supply lines, and to accomplish this by seizing a port.

The obvious choice was Hong Kong. The other possible candidates, Shantou and Xiamen, both fell under the operational control of the Nanjing Military region which, in the aftermath of the mysterious events on Gulangyu, had been ordered to effect a wide-ranging programme of alerts against possible actions by—fanciful though it now sounds—the forces in Taiwan. One effect of this order was to ensure that the coastal and anti-aircraft defences of both cities would be much more active than usual; and in addition warships from the East Sea Fleet would be on patrol in the Straits.

Of course, it was always possible that the Nanjing command would pass to the rebels—Tang had good enough contacts to suppose that this would, in time, happen. But he could not be sure, and so reasoned that to attack Shantou or Xiamen now would be imprudent and premature and, though the prize was very great, would present a very considerable risk.

By contrast, Hong Kong was exceptionally lightly guarded against outside attack. That, the authorities had mistakenly believed, was a near-total improbability. The troops who had been selected for posting to the SAR were there principally to maintain civil order. They were men from the far north of China; they had been told that the Cantonese who they were there to guard were troublesome, awkward, anti-Chinese. Their foremost task was to subdue the local population, to bully them if necessary, to keep them cowed, and thus to ensure by force of arms and numbers their continued loyalty to the regime of their new Chief Executive, Mr. Mao.

It will be recalled that troops had been dispatched to the former colony by ship. They had been taken by rail to Zhanjiang in southwestern China, and then embarked on a fleet of vessels—both warships and commandeered passenger craft. The actual landings on Hong Kong territory, made either by small craft or from helicopters, were comprehensive, sophisticated and well-organised. Nearly one complete division was involved in the operation—and from all the lightly armed 37th Infantry, a unit originally assigned to the 39th Army in Harbin, in north Manchuria. They, in particular, had been selected because of their unfamiliar ethnic origin, and because of their near-total ignorance of the ways and the language of the people they had to police. But the price that the designers of this cunningly unpleasant form of suppression had to pay was that they were very lightly armed. They were not equipped to deal with what was least expected—an attack by heavily armed and airmobile divisions of rebel soldiers, coming from a few miles to the north.

A plan for the attack on Hong Kong had to be devised quickly, before any messages of warning or, more dangerously, any suitable reinforcements, were sent from Peking. Accordingly General Tang directed that the attack be made by Major-General Hu Dai-fang's 111th Division; that a formal plan be devised and agreed by that evening; and that the operation be commenced on Saturday morning and completed by Saturday evening.

Hu and his staff officers spent the rest of the day in secret conclave, emerging at about 4 P.M. to brief General Tang. Approval was formalised at 5:30 P.M., whereupon the first detachments of infantrymen—all wearing bright Imperial-yellow arm-bands—were sent south, by truck, and told to await orders on the Shenzhen airfield. Operations would commence at first light. Tang's principal concern was now whether the 15th Army would mount an aerial attack on him in Canton while he was one division short, and before he had the supply-lines he needed. He doubled and trebled the radio and radar watch, searching for any signs of activity from the barracks in Hubei Province; he slept little on Friday night, though all was quiet.

Sunrise officially came to Shenzhen airport at 6:36 A.M., China summer time. General Hu's men had been moving fast for more than an hour before first light, and most of their trucks and their eighty medium tanks had been massed among the skyscrapers of Shenzhen City by the time startled workers started to trickle into the factories and offices.

The plan was simple enough, and depended on speed and surprise and sudden annihilation. Given the need to keep the local population on the Republicans' side, orders had been issued to all platoon and section leaders to use their weapons selectively and to cause only the very minimum of collateral damage and casualties. If it were possible to confuse the opposition and to force a surrender without a shot being fired, so much the better.

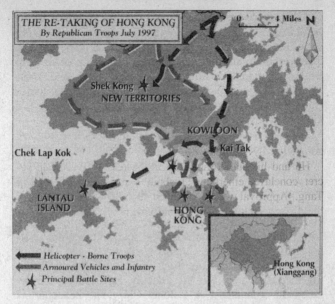

THE RE-TAKING OF HONG KONG
By Republican Troops July 1997

0   4 Miles   N

Shek Kong
NEW TERRITORIES

KOWLOON

Chek Lap Kok   Kai Tak

LANTAU
ISLAND

HONG
KONG

Helicopter - Borne Troops
Armoured Vehicles and Infantry
Principal Battle Sites

Hong Kong
(Xianggang)

During the night the very small number of Type 77 amphibious vehicles that were available to General Hu had been used to ferry all 135 members of the 111th Division's Reconnaissance Company across to the Mai Po marshes. From here they had fanned out across the territory, using stolen and commandeered vehicles and a variety of other special forces' tactics, and by 6 A.M. were already comfortably close to various key points, from where they were due to mount a series of sudden ambuscades. At 5:55 A.M. specialists from the signals battalion had cut all communications lines with Hong Kong, and had set up portable electronic jamming equipment to frustrate the internal communications of the Manchurian infantrymen—the frequencies having already been determined during the night by the Recon force.

The attack proper began at 6:15 A.M., with the launch of three separate operations. First, a force of twenty-two Mi6

Mikhail troop-carrying helicopters—each capable of carrying thirty men and their equipment—flew low over the New Territories with the three goals of securing the Kai Tak airfield, surrounding the main northern regimental headquarters in the countryside at Sek Kong, and, most symbolically important of all, reinforcing the special forces troops who were scheduled to commence their attack on Government House at 6:40 A.M.

The first wave of machines crossed the eastern edge of the border near the village of Sha Tau Kok, and apparently escaped detection. The first ten helicopters then swung right and landed in the grounds of the Sek Kong barracks, where they arrived at 6:35 A.M. The men—approximately two companies' strength—then deployed tactically towards the HQ building, but meeting no resistance approached in force, behind a Chinese flag. The four gate sentries challenged them, but were summarily disarmed, and thirty of the invading soldiers fanned out inside the building, capturing the radio room and the armoury, and locating the detachment commander, a Colonel Chin. The headquarters was thus totally secure by 7 A.M., and the men of the 111th spent the following hour collecting prisoners and detaining them in the barracks stockade.

Capturing the Kai Tak airfield proved to be an equally easy task. The helicopters flew below the radar shield and landed on the apron—five beside the cargo building, five near the control tower. Sentries guarding the tower were disarmed with astonishing speed, and by 7:15 A.M. Kai Tak was safely in rebel hands. (The much larger Chek Lap Kok airport, which had been the source of so much delay and argument in the 1990s, was still not complete at the time of the invasion. The island itself, well secured by razor-topped airport fencing, was to be used later that day for detaining the prisoners from the 37th Infantry Division.)

These two victories were secured without the need for the firing of a single shot. The same was not true, however, of the raid on Government House. As had been planned, some fifty men from the Recon battalion made their first contact with the enormous number of guards close to the front gate at 6:15 A.M. Resistance here was far stronger than had been imagined. An élite unit, later determined to be men of the 37th's fabled 104th Mechanised Light Infantry, had been assigned to guard the territory's Chief Executive, and they fought hard, using a large number of very sophisticated weapons.

The Republican soldiers, a section of whom were also spotted by sentries (or by electronic warning devices; it was not made clear in the Report) as they approached Government House from the northeast corner, took a huge amount of automatic weapons fire. During the first two minutes of the fight they were hit by no fewer than eight fragmentation grenades. Six men were killed outright and four others were gravely wounded: the remainder withdrew.

A few minutes later the two remaining helicopters from the twenty-two that had set off from Shenzhen settled on the rear lawn—under heavy automatic gunfire that the Recon battalion had not been able to prevent—and disgorged some sixty well-armed troops. One of the helicopters was hit by a lucky bullet and caught alight—creating a massive pall of smoke from behind which, fortunately, the invading troops were able to mount a swift operation to get inside the mansion itself.

Once there they fought, hand to hand, with the Manchurian defenders. There was much use of the bayonet and, in one case, of a portable phosgene gas generator, which sent some 100 defending troops retching and screaming out into the fresh air. The remaining men from the Recon unit had by this time also regrouped, and mounted an attack on the sentries by the Government House front gate.

By 7:30 A.M. rebel soldiers had fought their way up to the third-floor bedroom of Chief Executive Mao Ren-chin, had broken down the door with their rifle butts and placed Mao—so terrified he was about to be shot that he was reportedly found cowering beneath his bed—under arrest. Mao Ren-chin, the man from Manchuria whose appointment had caused such turmoil and, already, so much suffering, had ruled over the Special Administrative Region of Xianggang for just 25 days. The best that could be said about his tenure was that it had stimulated this particular revolution: in the eyes of those who care for the future of China, however, whether that Revolution was to be a good or an evil thing depended essentially upon its outcome. If it ever succeeded, then Mao Ren-chin would probably become at least a footnote, though probably nothing more in the long history of the nation.

At the same time as the helicopter and Recon battalion attacks, three very large convoys, each comprised of approximately sixty lightly armoured cars and trucks, sped down the three main highway links from China into Hong Kong. The regiments involved secured in turn the Lo Wu to Tai Po Highway, the Castle Peak Elevated Road and the Canton Expressway Feeder Road, and then poured southwards in strength. Some, about 4,000 men, would peel off to secure areas of Kowloon; helicopters would ferry smaller detachments—perhaps a total of 1,000—to clean up the pockets of loyalist resistance in the outer islands, particularly on Lantau; the remainder, 2,000 soldiers, would continue south until they reached the mouths of all three of the Cross Harbour Tunnels. Tanks would follow, and some 3,000 infantrymen behind them, marching in double-quick time.

With both the Sek Kong regional headquarters seized, and the territory's Chief Executive under arrest, there seemed little point in resistance. But the Manchu-based soldiers are tough men, and they fought hard to retain some redoubts—especially, and at first somewhat mysteriously, an area of central Hong Kong Island between two mountains, which in colonial times were called Jardine's Lookout and Mount Butler.

The Republican troops were first aware of this resistance when, shortly before noon, one of their convoys was moving slowly up Wong Nai Chung Gap Road. The battalions were under orders both to secure the communities of Aberdeen and Repulse Bay, to take control of the satellite earth stations at Stanley and Chung Hom Kok, and to install (two engineer companies were accompanying the infantry) a set

of coastal defence and air defence batteries to secure the
colony from any surprise attack from the South China Sea.
But as the vehicles ground their way up the steep hill, they
suddenly and catastrophically came under heavy artillery
fire from the east.

At least five trucks were hit by what was almost certainly 152mm shellfire, probably from the most modern
Type 66 towed artillery; as many as eighty soldiers were
killed. It was a brutally disruptive attack—the more so because the regiment's officers could not exactly understand
what the Manchu artillery was attempting to defend at the
top of this ridge. Close scrutiny of the maps showed an essentially barren hillside, with one area of granite quarries,
now disused.

General Hu's men promptly regrouped, and summoned
up elements of the artillery regiment, which were equipped
with fast-moving howitzers. Spotters in a number of Gazelle helicopters—which had been taken on the ground at
Kai Tak airport—located the enemy as being well dug in
just to the north of the ridge at Jardine's Lookout, where
there were a maze of trenches and tunnels dug by British
defenders in 1941. It could take a considerable time to prise
the men from their grasp of the hillside—for whatever reason, they were clinging on to it.

Heavy bombardment of the enemy positions began at 1
P.M., with the eight howitzers lobbing shells into the hillside
at the rate of one every five seconds. The enemy replied
fitfully—clearly they had little ammunition, and were probably out of contact with their battalion headquarters, which
had almost certainly been seized. But they did not give up
easily: by 3 P.M. machine-gun and sniper fire was still raking the hillside, and the howitzers were unable to make
their way across the ravines and dense undergrowth that
covers so much of the Hong Kong countryside. Shortly before 4 P.M. the regimental commander ordered in the infantry for mopping-up, together with a chemical company
equipped with flamethrowers: an hour later the hillside was
quiet.

Inspection of the area quickly showed what the artillery

had been trying to protect. Immediately below the quarry was the entrance, closed by heavy concrete gates, to a series of large chambers that had been tunnelled into the base of Mount Butler. Originally the chambers had been constructed by the Royal Hong Kong Police Force, and were used to store emergency vehicles, ammunition, tear-gas, communications equipment and other vital spares for use in times of emergency. But since the arrival of the mainland troops—by which time all these items had been removed, and had been loaded on to HMS *Dorsetshire* together with the secret decryption equipment from the CSO station at Chung Hom Kok—all manner of other paraphernalia were stored there.

The engineers placed demolition charges on the gates. Troops entering the caverns found vast quantities of costly goods, apparently looted from museums and private houses all around the territory. Some were in the midst of being crated before, presumably, being sent up into mainland China itself. Twenty civilian workers were discovered, and were arrested. There were large quantities of jade, porcelain, paintings and calligraphy scrolls, as well as high quality antique furniture, jewellery and precious stones. Papers indicated other collections that were due for confiscation: several names of prominent Hong Kong businessmen and elderly aristocrats who had decided to remain in the territory and welcome the "return" of the mainland Chinese, were indicated—marks against some identified the type of collection in which each was known to have specialised.

There were other small pockets of resistance, though the fighting was not so savage as at Jardine's Lookout, given the relatively low value of the positions the soldiers had been instructed to protect. On Lantau Island there was a spirited firefight at the old Shek Pik prison on the southern coast; on taking it the Republican soldiers discovered that some forty Chinese men and women had been detained there under the terms of what they said were hastily imposed security regulations. All the prisoners were Taiwanese. Then again, in a former Vietnamese refugee detention camp near the High Island reservoir, Republican troops came across a bedraggled and demoralised group of more than 300 Indian nationals.

They were apparently all Sindhis, and were among the small number of Indian passport holders who, for one administrative reason or another, had not managed to obtain alternate passports or residency permits before the Chinese took over. They had thus been officially classed as stateless persons and, the Manchurian troops not taking too kindly to them, they were placed in detention camps while the new administration decided their fate.

They expected to be eventually deported to Pakistan, where they or their parents had originally come from (though when they first journeyed to Hong Kong, or when their parents had taken jobs in Shanghai, there was no such entity as Pakistan). Nearly all of them were Hindus: it would be "socially impossible," as they had kept insisting to their Chinese captors, for them to return to a nation that had been established on the basis of being almost wholly Islamic.

Their experiences in the previous month had been horrendous. Almost all of them spoke Cantonese, and a few had some Mandarin or *putonghua*. But the new soldiers, who were different in appearance and in manners, spoke none of these languages—or else their *putonghua* was heavily accented, and almost unrecognisable. They were most unfriendly, and seemed to regard the Indians as beneath contempt until many of them had begun to fear for their lives.

Now, while they were in the depths of depression, they were to be still more confused by the sudden appearance at the camp gates—and after a brief exchange of gunfire with their sentries—of a new detachment of Cantonese-speaking troops, all of whom were wearing yellow flashes on their uniform sleeves. General Hu's orders to keep good relations with the civilian population were also being rigorously observed so the Indians were given rations, and told that they would be free to return home after a few days of administrative checks. The relief on their faces was evident—all the more so when one of the Republican soldiers told them of the rebellion in Canton, and that in his view "we will now see the end of Communism in China."

As the mopping-up operations continued, so contact was initiated between Peter Heung and his organised triad groups. One might wonder why contact was not made at an earlier stage—perhaps even during the planning of the operation to take the territory. The group would have proven most useful in providing local knowledge to the invaders, and in taking part in psychological operations and sabotage, to help the arriving troops. But it was not until late on Saturday that contact was made, and it appears from the records that the contact came from Heung's group to the men of the 111th Division, and not vice versa. The explanation offered by General Hu is certainly plausible.

His incoming army certainly knew some details of the existence of the Triad group. The Guangdong provincial government, through its agents working in colonial Hong Kong, had had access for the better part of a year to intelligence reports relating to the Warwick Accord. But these reports were confusing and inconclusive, and in retrospect they seem to have been deliberately contaminated with locally generated black propaganda.

It is now known that a top-secret unit buried deep within Headquarters British Forces, identified only by the number of the room from which it operated, G-13, did disseminate confusing information in selected quarters of the territory, in the hope that it would be picked up, and then confuse, the mainland Chinese. A Ministry of Defence "D" notice was issued in June 1997 asking editors of British newspapers to refrain from discussing even the existence of this unit. No such obligation rests with the present author, however; and it is now possible to reveal that the unit had six members, all fluent Chinese speakers, and headed by a psychological warfare specialist from the Ministry, Dr. John Gurdon. Dr. Gurdon had been placed in the colony some five years before, under the cover of "Attached Commander British Forces Hong Kong" and with the public position of adviser on cross-border developments to the various brigadiers who headed the colony's small garrison. He made particular efforts to cultivate excellent relations with local left-wing groups, leaders and newspapers in the territory; he was on notably good terms with one of the writers on one such opinion-forming paper, the *Ta Kung Pao*. He is believed to have given misleading information on the identities of the signatories of the Warwick Accord, as well as on the group's aims and abilities; he is known to have fomented rivalries between two groups of left-wing publishers; and he is said to have given to a Taiwanese journalist, whom he suspected of being a double agent, a series of bogus tape-recordings that he said resulted from telephone taps between the New China News Agency and a Western reporter. His record for spreading confusion and dissent among the large army of Chinese secret service personnel working under a variety of covers in Hong Kong in the closing months of British administration was, London colleagues later admitted, most impressive.

It was a testimony, therefore, either to the excellent security of Heung's group—who were well practised in the local version of *omerta*—or to a signal degree of G-13–assisted incompetence on the part of the Chinese agents, that little specific was known about the Heung group. General Hu had no knowledge, for instance, of the meetings between Heung and Margerison, nor of the small arms dumps left behind by the British forces. There is no indication that the Chinese forensic scientists working either on the cases of the murder of Constable Wan, the explosion at the Gulangyu Guesthouse, or the escape of the men due to be executed in the town of Shitsze, had any proof of links with any gangs operating in Hong Kong, or with any arms or explosives left behind by the departing British. The extent to which this lack of progress by the Guangdong and Fujian authorities was due to their local incompetence, or whether they were in any way further frustrated by G-13 or similar groups, is still unknown. It remains singularly fortunate, from the point of view of the Republican rebels, that no such discoveries were made during the days before the events outside the Canton City PSB headquarters.

The contact made between the 111th Division officers and Heung's men was cordial, and produced an informal agreement that men of the latter group would be able to play a part in assisting with the policing of the territory, with identifying and locating locals who had collaborated with the Manchu forces, and with agents of the Peking government who had been operating before the British departure. The agreement seemed a convenient one at the time; but local Hong Kong residents have since complained that the untoward degree of graft and corruption that has plagued the territory since the date of the Republican takeover indicates that it was an imprudent move, and may limit the possibilities of a swift return to real democracy in the territory.

The final fight—which was mercifully brief—was at the Stonecutters Island Garrison headquarters. General Hu wished to lead this assault himself. The Xianggang Commander, Lu Chuanzhi of the 37th Division, was known to him as a classmate, though not as a particular friend. They had served in adjoining regiments twenty years before during the Vietnam border wars, and General Lu had taken part in many of the suppression operations in Tibet.

He had also played a prominent role in the 1989 Tienanmen Incident—it was indeed believed, though it was never confirmed, that he was the officer who, from a helicopter hovering above Fuxingmenwai and West Changan Avenues, gave orders for those soldiers then advancing to clear the Square of protesters to fire at will. PLA files on the incident had apparently been destroyed less than a year after the event, and other senior Army officers had conspired to protect the identity of those who were directly responsible for the killings. Persistent rumours had long connected General Lu to those orders: since Hu Dai-fang had lost a niece—student of Peking Normal University—in the massacre, he had long felt a sense of acute bitterness about the affair. It could fairly be said that it was Tienanmen, and the later Wuhan Incident, that first triggered the sentiments that led him to take part in the Canton Rebellion: taking General Lu's surrender here would, therefore, have a particular sweetness to it.

In the event the confrontation was neither prolonged nor spectacular. The 37th Infantry Division's headquarters held about 1,200 troops, with a 120-strong guard company, a small number of armoured cars and machine-guns. There had never been any expectation of an attack from the north: such defences as there were assumed either insurrectionary activity from the local population, or an attack from the air or water by enemy forces assembled in the South China Sea. Two companies from an anti-aircraft battalion and a number of fast patrol boats moored beside the base offered protection from such eventualities.

Opposing them on this Saturday afternoon was a highly organised force, in high good spirits. One half of the force had moved southwards, down the main highway from the Kwai Chung container base—once the world's busiest—and the other had come from the east via the main Boundary Street Expressway. The force was comprised of some 60 tanks, 40 armoured cars, two dozen self-propelled howitzers, dozens of pieces of towed artillery and any number of mortars, and some 5,000 heavily armed infantrymen. To have resisted would have been pointless, as General Hu pointed out in a megaphone address to the loyalist troops. He had sufficient foresight to have a graduate of Shenyang Foreign Languages Institute, a former resident of Heilongjiang Province, address the headquarters troops in their own dialect. The young man, standing atop a personnel carrier, spoke as follows:

"As you may know from foreign broadcast sources, forces loyal to the former governor of Guangdong Province, Mr. Yi Juan Ling, have lately taken control of the city of Canton and of the surrounding region. These troops, our brothers in arms, are committed to assisting Governor Yi and other democratically minded people to restore liberty and the rights to personal happiness to the people of all of our dear country.

"The entire civilian population of Canton is with us. And we have received messages from all over southern China, from Yunnan in the west to Jiangxi in the east, indicating that we now have the masses on our side. I am now pleased to be able to inform you that the armies based in all of the Guangzhou and Nanjing Military Regions have come over to Governor Yi's view. Our position is therefore impregnable.

"Our military leaders recently arrived at the wise and understandable decision that, to enable our troops to have at their disposal the very best possible logistical advantage, it was necessary for us to take control of a major port and aviation centre. We were aware that the indigenous population of the Special Administrative Region of Xianggang—which is to be formally known again now by the name by which its inhabitants have long called it, Hong Kong—was likely to concur with Governor Yi's view of the developments in southern China. We felt it prudent, therefore, to make as one of our movement's priorities the securing of Hong Kong to our cause.

"A strong force of men led by the heroic General Hu Dai-fang thus crossed into Hong Kong this morning. In the past ten hours we have succeeded in securing the city and its key positions and in detaining the entire 37th Infantry Division, all of whom are now on their way to a detention centre off Lantau Island.

"In the name of Governor Yi Juan Ling, and in the fervent hope of a peaceful and dignified end to this conflict, I thus call upon you men, on your officers and on your general officer commanding, to come forward without delay and indicate by customary means your total surrender to our forces. I can offer the assurances that all will be well-treated, and that you will be permitted to return without delay to your homes, providing the situation permits it. I look to the immediate display of a white flag of truce, and to receiving emissaries from your leadership. That is all."

There was an uneasy pause. Then an upstairs window was opened in the main headquarters building, and two soldiers could be dimly seen draping a white sheet from the sill. There was a ripple of pleasure from the waiting troops, and one or two of the tank commanders turned off their diesel engines, thickening the silence of the evening.

A door opened, and three Army officers, each carrying a white banner, marched out across the parade ground and up to the triple wire fence. "We have come to offer the surrender of the entire remaining force of the 37th Infantry Division," their senior officer, a major, announced stiffly. "Emissaries from your group will be welcome. Our men prefer not to engage in battle with other compatriots, no matter from which part of China they come. Our desire is for a peaceful end to this struggle."

By dusk the entire headquarters battalion had formally surrendered and laid down their arms, and General Hu's soldiers were consolidating their position. Yellow quarantine signal flags—for now the only flags available to the Republicans, and to be their symbol for the coming several weeks of the campaign—were hoisted above the barrack blocks; another had been raised over Government House, from where temporary administrators were already working, principally to see if there were records of any further detainees who had been picked up by the soldiers of the 37th.

Radio Television Hong Kong had been secured early in the afternoon, and its transmitters had been putting out a steady diet of Cantonese popular music. But at 8 P.M. General Hu appeared in a simultaneous radio and television broadcast. Speaking in Cantonese he announced the establishment of the Republican Party of China, the need for the speedy capture of the territory and the success of his mission. Everyone who co-operated would be safe, he said. Furthermore, the establishment of "a civilian Administration that finds favour with the local people" would be carried out promptly. He would be holding urgent talks later that night with the British Consul-General, Peter Williamson, and with officials from the US Consulate, to ask for advice on the running of the territory. And he went on to make a further series of reassuring remarks, to the effect that the new administration would abide by the letter and the spirit of the major promises that had been made thirteen years before in the Joint Declaration on the Future of Hong

Kong. But then he added some further words, which must have sent a chill down the necks of many of his listeners.

As all of you who have lived here in the last thirteen years must be aware, the British colonial government placed many restrictions on the citizens of Hong Kong in the closing period of their rule to ensure that the people did or said nothing that was likely to insult or to anger the Communist government of the People's Republic of China. Many times British officials made statements declaring that Hong Kong "will not be used as a base for subversion" against the People's Republic. It was regarded by the British as crucially important that relations between China and Hong Kong were, on the surface at least, amicable.

From today, all of that is to change. The illusion of amicability ends here. The Republican Party of China has been established specifically to rid China of the scourge of Communism. The movement has as its emotional base the City of Canton—a city that has played so vitally important a role in revolution and rebellion in the past.

Now, however, we need a practical base—a site with peerless communications, with access to high technology and transport, with expertise and knowledge. Hong Kong is the natural centre of such excellence. From today onwards, therefore, all talk of Hong Kong's unwillingness to assist in the overthrow of the Communist régime ceases. This is the paramount headquarters. From this single bastion of capitalism and freedom will grow a revolution that will inevitably spread across the face of the entire nation. For the first time we can say with pride that the Cantonese people, and especially the Cantonese people who live along the banks of the Pearl River between the two mighty cities of Canton and Hong Kong, will take up the torch and the sword, and fight for a new China. We have the energy, the pride and the will. We will not stop, until China is free!

The broadcast was monitored in Peking that night. The State Council was called into emergency session in the Zhongnanhai Compound just before midnight. The telephone call summoning the thirteen members warned that decisions of the utmost gravity, relating to matters of national and international importance, had to be taken without delay.

In the West, too, a sudden air of emergency gripped the leadership. In London a Cabinet meeting was called for Sunday morning, local time. In Washington there was an emergency secret meeting of the Charlesworth Committee and, at the urging of Secretary of State Crowther, a meeting of the National Security Council's Deputies Committee late in the evening. Both meetings were scheduled to hear disturbing evidence of strange and inexplicable warnings about other, seemingly unrelated military activities that were now affecting two of China's eastern neighbours.

CHAPTER NINE

Dominions of Fury

PEKING

Sunday, 27 July 1997

News of the loss of Hong Kong, and the stated intention of its interim rulers to permit a speedy return to democracy and freedom, triggered a sudden and terrified panic among the elders in Peking. The State Councillors—the nation's cabinet, headed by the premier, Li Peng—converged on the Zhongnanhai Compound in the small hours of the morning. One member who has since crossed to the Republican side, the 61-year-old Shanghainese hero of the Vietnam War, Li Lizhi, later described the scene.

The meeting took place underground, in a room harshly illuminated by neon tubes and guarded by helmeted sentries from the élite Peking Garrison Command. The men who assembled from their homes to the north and west of the city came through a steel door that led into the network of tunnels running below the city. None came in from the lift that led from the upstairs world. The attendees were all ashenfaced, angry and puzzled.

The premier and the Ministers for Defence, State Security and Civil Affairs led the brief discussion. The situation was offered in outline: the Army in Canton had rebelled, and had gained control of Hong Kong; there was a growing likelihood that Army units in Fujian Province, and perhaps throughout Nanjing Region, would join the rebellion. The

People's Republic of China was facing the greatest threat ever known to its internal stability. Harsh measures needed to be taken quickly to stamp out the rebellion, before it was allowed to infect the rest of the nation.

A little-known councillor, Qian Hanxiong, who had been gazetted head of the equally unfamiliar Bureau for the Establishment of Correct Socialist Attitudes, an offshoot of the State Security Ministry, was first asked to make remarks about the identities of those who were known to have seized power. He said that in his view the ringleaders of the operation were Governor Yi, General Tang and three or four of his subordinate generals, together with a number of figures in Hong Kong including "figures well-known in organised anti-socialist criminal movement," including the colony's best-known barrister and former political activist, Martin Lee Chu-ming. Subsequent information has shown that particular surmise to be incorrect: it is probable, once again, that the propaganda put out by the British G-13 unit had had some influence on Peking's muddled thinking.

Qian announced that he had already instructed Radio Peking and its foreign language satellites to commence broadcasts denouncing these men individually and by name, and for all national radio and television stations to commence immediately a programme of massive discreditation of "these guilty individuals and bandits." He was confident, he said, that "among the peasants and workers at least, any temptation to believe the lies of these southern monkeys will vanish quickly," such was the persuasive nature of the broadcasts his Bureau had formulated.

The Minister of Defence angrily waved him down. "Propaganda is not what is needed right now," he said, thumping his fist on the table. "We have a crisis that could spread to critical units of our beloved Army in a matter of days. It must be halted by military means immediately. The peasants are for the moment irrelevant in all of this. The key is the loyalty of the Army.

"We have atomic missile units that are close to the rebels, and it is vital to our nation that they be secured and protected. There are many institutions holding weapons of unparalleled ferocity—and if they fall into the hands of these vandals and outlaws, the country will be in even greater peril.

"I have information, gentlemen, that this rebellion has been fomented by Kuomintang forces in Taiwan." There was a chorus of shouts of disbelief and anger from many of the assembled councillors. Some of the older men present, survivors of the Long March and of the brutal civil war against Chiang Kai-shek's armies, bayed from their wheel-chairs, hammering their sticks against the floor. It was some minutes before the Premier was able to restore order, and the Defence minister could continue.

"I urge our Council to give me the necessary permission to go after the source of this insurrectionary madness, by striking at the heart of the Kuomintang military machine it-self." There was a further eruption of shouting, with cries of "Yes, let him do it! Kill the traitors of the Kuomintang! End the division of our country! Kill all those who are loyal to the bandit Chiang!"

"Our brave forces in Fujian," he went on, rising to the mood of the occasion, "who at this moment are being sub-jected to the most brutal propaganda attacks by the rebel forces, should be allowed the honour of making the strike against the capitalist warmongers in Taipei. But if those for-ces are of uncertain loyalty—and this may happen, council-lors should be fully prepared—then we must make use of the Shanghai Garrison Command and the destroyers of the East Sea Fleet to make the attack.

"This is for you to decide, as it is a matter of foreign policy, and may have repercussions that go far beyond these concrete walls. But whatever you do instruct, I must first have your immediate unanimous agreement and authorisa-tion to move regiments by air to protect the nuclear forces of our Second Artillery, and to take similar steps to protect the chemical and biological warfare bases and nuclear re-search institutes that have been set up in a number of dis-tant provinces known to you all.

"Secondly I request permission for an immediate air and paratroop assault on the rebel headquarters at Baiyun and

Hong Kong. I am pleased to be able to tell you that the airborne elements of the 15th Army in Wuhan have remained loyal, and the officers and men, to whom I spoke only a few minutes before coming down to this meeting, are now eagerly awaiting permission to strike at the cowards and desperadoes who are in control of the southern part of the nation. That operation must begin now, this very night.

"And thirdly, I request permission to begin planning for this recommended assault on the Kuomintang force. Such an assault will have, in my view, a dual effect—both of neutralising the source of this rebellion and of providing a stimulus for our patriotic people, a symbol of our resolve around which they can rally in this time of uncertainty."

Several councillors rose. The premier waved them down, and stood himself. "There must be no argument. I authorise immediate moves to secure the atomic and chemical weapons bases. I authorise an immediate airborne attack on Baiyun and Hong Kong. I also instruct you to make contact with our forces in Fuijan to see if there are officers sufficiently reliable and loyal to add to this attack, so that the Canton forces find themselves under fire from two separate army groups.

"But I cannot give sanction yet to a move against our compatriots in Taiwan. Only after the most exhaustive proof of their complicity in this rebellion, and which I would wish to have demonstrated before the United Nations Security Council, can I engage in warfare with the Kuomintang. You know full well of my hatred for these villainous people. My own father was murdered by them when I was a small child. But the consequences of our attacking them now without the proof that I demand would be too horrendous to contemplate. So for that, I cannot give permission."

A storm of shouting and bellowing broke out, and so many members who were able to stand, did so, and started waving fists at one another in argument that sentries entered the room to ensure that the rebellion itself had not penetrated this supposed fastness of loyalty. The premier struggled to calm his deputies and, gesturing to the soldiers to leave the room, eventually succeeded in doing so.

"Gentlemen," he said finally, "we have work to do. Let us meet again in forty-eight hours' time. By then, I feel sure, I and our colleague Ministers will have encouraging news for you all. But for now, we have work to do. The nation must be composed. The Army must be stabilised. The crisis must not be permitted to spread. To achieve all of these goals we need to act, not to argue. So let us go from here in agreement, and meet in two days' time, and see where the actions we have taken this day have themselves taken us." He looked directly at each of the councillors—the more particularly at those, mostly seated, who represented the troublesome old guard of the Party, those who feared most that their grip on power might be faltering. "Have no fears," he said to one, whose face was suffused with anxiety. "We will prevail. We shall see each other again in two days' time."

It was in fact nearly two weeks before the State Council was to meet again, so dire and fast-moving were the developments of the following days. It would be misleading to assign a particular priority to the occurrences, since all of them contributed in one way or another to the beginning of the awful ebb and flow of a classically complicated civil war. The order in which the events are recounted here is not necessarily chronological: all had their beginnings in the August of the war's first year, but each incident overlapped in time and had eventual effects on the outcome of each of the other incidents—as, once again, the occurrences of war are likely to do. The picture that emerges from this *tour d'horizon* does present the quiddity of the situation that summer—of a nation decaying rapidly into uncontrollability, fast presenting that phenomenon that has terrified world-watchers' nightmares for centuries past: China—on the loose.

FUJIAN PROVINCE—
THE COAST OF THE TAIWAN STRAIT

On the beach road not far from the city of Xiamen, where so many of the events that triggered the first battles of the civil war took place, is a small bluff, topped by a structure known as the Huli Mountain Fortress. This is a venerable and not unlovely complex of brick barrack and granite battlement, a sort of Chinese Martello Tower. It was built in 1823, at a time when the Ching emperors were starting to become restive at the way that foreigners—particularly the British—were landing huge quantities of Indian opium at their seaports. The drug was seriously debilitating to the Chinese peasantry, and the Forbidden City was grumbling, quite properly, that so vile a trade should be halted.

The construction of Huli Mountain Fort, from which cannon could be trained across the mouth of Amoy Bay and so restrict ships' access to the port that was then known as Amoy (but which is now Xiamen) just predated the appearance on the political scene of Canton's infamous Commissioner Lin, the bureaucrat whose formal campaign against the British export of the drug to the Pearl River ports started the Opium Wars—which had such disastrous and humiliating repercussions for all of China.

So it is yet another pleasing historical irony—like the commencement of Canton's July riots at the Martyrs' Memorial—to find that this very same fort, which was built to help in a war that then itself decimated China and the dynasty that ran it, and helped in no small way to found and aid the early prosperity of the Colony of Hong Kong, should play a part, nearly two centuries later, in events that were so savagely to injure the nation on which it stood. China, though, is so rich in historical association, and has so long a lineage, that barely an event can take place, nor a site be chosen for one, that has not played a part in the story before. And Huli Mountain Fortress played a part of no small significance in the summer of 1997.

Since the mid-1980s the fortress had been abandoned. The barracks were empty, their windows broken, their doors broken from their hinges. But at the cliff's edge, protected by embrasured buttresses of yard-thick cement, was a huge old gun. It had been made by Krupp in 1895, and could hurl half-ton shells for twenty miles. But in the early summer of 1997 it stood as it had for nearly fifteen years, silent and rusting, locked on a trajectory of fifty-two degrees, and a bearing of 92 degrees, a fraction south of east.

It had been one of a number of guns that, just twenty years earlier, had been active almost beyond an artilleryman's imagination. A glance through the rusting gunsights would explain why. Not five miles away from the Huli Mountain Fortress, and on a bearing of 092° magnetic from its gun, is a rocky island, perhaps eight miles long and, so the maps indicate, seven miles wide. There is a small port at the southern end called Shuitou, and near by a town of 40,000 people—the town of Quemoy. And though the dialect names of the island are various—Chinmen Tao, or Kinmen Tao are those most commonly heard in Xiamen City—the world knows the island by the name of its tiny capital, Quemoy.

For although Peking will not tolerate the remark, the island is legally not a part of the People's Republic of China. It may be only five miles away from the coast; it may be possible, on a calm day, to hear conversations from fishermen on the coast, or hear music wafting from radios in the island villages; but this island of Quemoy basks under the invigilation of a red flag quartered with blue, with a twelve-pointed white star. The flag, in other words, of the Republic of China, of Taiwan. The flag of the Kuomintang, fluttering within easy sight of a child's spyglass, just a short swim across the Bay of Amoy.

Back in the 1950s, the sight and sound of the hated Kuomintang—for more powerful glasses would reveal Taiwanese soldiers patrolling the Quemoy beaches—so very close to the Chinese mainland was utter anathema to the loyalists of the Communist government. No matter that Taiwan and the few offshore islands held by Chiang Kai-shek were visible signs of his defeat—a reminder to all Chinese people that a man who had once wanted his flag to fly from Manchuria to the Annamese border, could fly it only a few chunks of rock off the nation's eastern coast. To the diehards, the very sight of the flag was too insulting; and so a violent campaign to purge the vision was initiated.

Every day during the mid- and early-1950s heavy

guns—of which the Krupp monster at Huli Shan was one—pounded and pounded away at Quemoy (and at Matsu, a similar though smaller island off the town of Fuzhou, to the north). The Taiwanese responded both with anger, and *sang-froid*: they protested in 1954 that they would demand implementation of the terms of the newly ratified defence treaty with the United States (and indeed the 7th Fleet was deployed, and the world was briefly plunged into a diplomatic crisis); and at the same time they ordered their soldiers on the outpost to plaster immense banners along the most visible beaches, bearing the ideographs, in red on white, of one of Sun Yat-sen's best-know aphorisms: "people's democracy, people's rights, people's livelihood."

The crisis eventually stilled. The mainland Chinese, under discreet pressure from the Great Powers, lost interest in the islands; most of the guns were hauled away for other tasks, or for scrap; and the Krupp cannon at Huli Shan Fortress which had been manned by full-time soldiers of the PLA, was then handed over to ratings from the Navy's East Sea Fleet. In 1984 it was abandoned, and left to the wind and the damp oxidising agents it carried to reduce it—like the idea of the forcible conquest of Taiwan—to history.

All of which would have probably continued, had not a Brigade Commander named Li Guang, based with his troops in the barracks just a few hundred yards from Huli Shan, decided to attempt to revivify a patriotic fascination with the fate of the island of Quemoy. He was in command of a tank brigade, part of the battle-hardened 14th Tank Division. He planned to use his not inconsiderable military assets for what he thought would be one grand and splendid patriotic act—a move that would unite all China behind him and enable it to purge, at a stroke, those elements of cowards and madmen who, he understood, were now trying to destroy the fabric of the nation.

Brigadier Li was manifestly part of no gerontocracy, being just forty-seven years old. He had, none the less, something very much in common with the old men of the Central Committee and of the Central Military Commission: a perfervid enthusiasm for the Communist system, one that had brought him many times to the notice of the authorities and of his senior officers. Long before he had won the First Grade of the Wartime Hero and Model Soldier Medal, for what the citation proclaimed were "patriotic actions beyond the call of duty during the Counter-Attack for Self-Defence against Vietnamese Aggression along the China-Vietnam Border." Precisely what those actions were has never been revealed.

But it is known that Brigadier Li, when still a young captain, was head of the "Lei Feng Squad" that had been formed within his tank battalion. He was its natural leader: he had long been well-known for trying to follow Mao's instructional slogan "Learn from Lei Feng," and his barracks room was awash with well-thumbed copies of biographies and magazine articles about the famously courageous little soldier Lei, whose exploits—although quite probably fictitious—did so much to stimulate patriotism and zeal within the ranks of the Chinese Army. And Brigadier Li is said by his men to have followed the example of Lei Feng in at least one particular respect—by offering to wash out the socks of soldiers who had become fatigued by the jungle fighting. But it was always hinted that some particular act of military heroism, and not his enthusiasm for laundry-work, had won him the Wartime Hero and Model Soldier Medal. It remains something of a mystery that the Chinese authorities chose never to publicise it.

One explanation perhaps lies in the acute embarrassment—not to say the heavy military loss—that was suffered by the Chinese authorities as a direct consequence of Brigadier Li's extraordinary and unilateral actions of August 1997. For, taking a far more extreme and improbable step than even Lei Feng's biographer might imagine, Li Guang decided to take it upon himself to do what no Chinese had tried to do seriously since 1958—to liberate Quemoy from Taiwanese hands.

He had planned his move to come shortly after the celebrations—which were naturally cancelled this year because of the crisis—that were scheduled to mark the seventieth anniversary of the Founding of the PLA. He had

planned with some care: and he began with placing sixteen
men from his signals battalion—fourteen soldiers and two
officers—inside the offices of the local branch of Xiamen
Central Radio. They informed the quite credulous station
director that they had been dispatched there to act as additional sentries, bolstering the existing Militia force to help
guard the station and its transmitter against possible seizure
by Cantonese rebels.

Leaving a statement behind with his signallers, and a series of precise instructions for its broadcast on receipt of a
prearranged signal, Brigadier Li then ordered the placement, under cover of a moonless night, of more than a
dozen of his heavy artillery pieces and 140mm rocket
launchers, into positions along the coast between Xiamen
City and Huli Shan, and for a mile beyond. He also, for
what is assumed to have been emotional reasons, arranged
for ammunition to be brought from the reserve amoury for
the old Krupp cannon, enabling that ancient weapon to be
added to his notional list of assets for the planned bombardment.

It needs to be said that he took all of these remarkable
steps entirely on his own initiative, without reference either
to his divisional commander (who in any case had been
summoned up to Nanjing for "urgent consultations" about
the fast-developing situation), nor to his political commissar, who accepted the unusual number of movements of
men and *matériel* from the barracks as part of an "emergency exercise" that had been ordered in response to the
heightened tension in the Taiwan Strait.

The guns and rockets were all zeroed in on the well-
identified targets—gun emplacements, barracks, a small
communications centre and (for its symbolic value) the
huge Taiwanese flag that could be seen along Quemoy's
western coast. They could not be seen at night, of course;
but the aiming coordinates had already been constructed in
Li's planning department some days before, and the gun
crews had simply to ratchet their weapons to predesignated
compass bearings and trajectories, to be certain their ammunition would do the necessary damage.

At the same time he ordered some 2,000 of his most skilled and courageous infantrymen to embark on a flotilla of landing craft and zodiac boats that had been driven down to the shore just after dusk. By midnight he was ready for his daredevil operation; and shortly thereafter, following the firing of a series of green flares, he order his artillerymen to commence a withering cannonade, all directed at enemy positions in Quemoy. A coast that had been quiet for the previous forty years erupted in a sea of flame and fury as the shells and rockets arched out over the water with furious frequency. The roar and shudder of the guns was like the beginnings of an earthquake. In Xiamen near by, and in towns as far away as Jimei and Shitsze—which had itself played a small part in the events leading to this catastrophe—residents were rudely shaken awake, many reportedly thinking that this was the end of the world.

The barrage went on for more than an hour. All the while, under cover of the streaking gold parabolas of shellfire, the boats and landing craft sped forward at full tilt. By the time they were within hailing distance of the coast the gunfire slackened, then stopped. It remained only for them to gain the shore and, so Li's brother officers had planned, the island of Quemoy would be theirs. Resistance had surely been crushed like eggshells: no force could withstand so fierce a bombardment, especially without a breath of warning.

And so, as the scores of ships manoeuvered into position to wait for the flares ordering the landing of their soldiers, the signal—somewhat unimaginatively, a telephone call and the uttering of the name "Lei Feng"—went out to the radio station. The "sentries" then took control of the station and its transmitters; and one of the officers, speaking in perfect *putonghua,* made the following announcement:

> People of Fujian. People of China. This special announcement, a matter of pride and joy for you all, is made with the authority of the People's Liberation Army stationed in Xiamen City.
>
> For the last forty-eight years, as you all will know, the

treacherous bandits of the Kuomintang have grasped with cowardly hands our beloved island of Chinmen Tao, and have waved in our faces the wretched flag of their bastard-like nationhood. For forty-eight years our People's Republic has borne with valour and stoicism this gross insult, and we have watched with pain and torment the flying of the symbol of their treachery across so short a stretch of sea.

But today, after an heroic struggle that was mercifully brief and cost our glorious fighters little by way of sacrifice, I am honoured to announce to you that moves are even now under way to recover the island of Chinmen Tao, and return it to its natural place alongside all the other lands and dominions that are so dear to all our hearts.

By the time the golden sun rises over our nation tomorrow, this dear island and our compatriot brothers and sisters will have been freed from the corrupt tyranny of their evil gaolers, and will be welcomed back into the arms of the motherland. All praise and honour to our glorious fighting men, and to the bold and imaginative plan that has enabled them to right this most despicable wrong of recent history.

The Brigadier had given orders that this message was to be broadcast every fifteen minutes, throughout the night, and that it was to be replaced at dawn by an even more stirring announcement of triumph. But in the event it was only to be heard three more times during that night; and no other message of similar bent ever replaced it. For within one further hour, and with tragic results, the Taiwanese military struck back.

Within moments of the halting of the artillery barrage, dozens of F-5E fighters came roaring south of the Quemoy headland and fired salvoes of Sidewinder missiles directly into the mass of boats beneath them. The pilots were clearly using laser aiming devices and other smart electronic homing aids, for within no more than ten minutes the attacking force was in total disarray, with over twenty boats sunk or sinking, and the waters thick with struggling and screaming men. Machine-guns on the shore opened up, firing into the blackness at near point-blank range adding to the carnage in the water. Sheets of flame occasionally illuminated the scene; but otherwise there was total darkness, with the terrifying sound of the waves of jets screeching down for their attack runs, the explosion of anti-personnel bombs and ship-destroying shells, and the fearful yelling of the injured and frightened men in the sea.

At the same time scores of newly developed Green Bee coastal defence missiles were fired from batteries on Quemoy's west coast, all designed to home in on the now quiet emplacements of Brigadier Li's artillery force. The Green Bee had been perfected only two years before at Taiwan's Chungshan Institute of Science and Technology, and had been designed specifically to neutralise night-time artillery barrages.

That it took more than an hour to order the Green Bee platoons to retaliate was quite deliberate, a Taiwanese Defence Department spokesman was quoted as saying the next day. Their emplacements on Quemoy had been so wholly encased in concrete as to render them almost perfectly secure from the effects of mainland gunfire; and so long as they could survive the barrage it was regarded as "likely to be of much greater military effect" if the Communists could be lulled into sending their boat-borne infantrymen into deep and unfamiliar waters, before attacking them so brutally from the air.

It was a tactic that worked brilliantly. The shore batteries were knocked out in their entirety (though not the Krupp: a technical problem meant that it was never fired, and so did not offer an infra-red signature to the Green Bee spotters on Quemoy), and of the 2,000 men sent to invade the island, only sixty-three made it back.

For good measure the Taiwanese Air Force made a number of sorties over Xiamen itself, and one jet placed a smart bomb through an air vent in the radio transmitter main hall, and brought to an end an attempted fourth transmission of the so-called Victory Broadcast—which was probably as well, since the supposed victory had turned into a sudden, decisive and humiliating defeat.

Brigadier Li himself was killed in the onslaught, as were most of his planning officers. The political commissars attached to both the Brigadier's unit and to the 14th Tank Division both committed suicide the next day. Morale within the units remaining fell to a devastating low. There were mutinous mutterings over the coming weeks about the apparent inferiority of the mainland Chinese weapons, the lack of discipline and training, the fact, as many junior officers were wont to say, that "we don't know exactly what we are fighting for."

By the end of the autumn the situation within the entire 63rd Army based at Quanzhou had become untenable. An entire tank brigade had been lost. Morale in its most important tank division, the 14th, had fallen to the point where there was open talk of mutiny. The political commissars— replacements had been sent from Lazhou and Peking—were men of intolerably harsh political views, unwilling to yield even fractionally in their devotion to the "Lei Feng Way," despite the humiliating backwash from the most recent occasion when it had been put into practice. And so it was not a matter of total surprise when General Tang, while fighting hard on many fronts in Canton, heard through intermediaries that the operational commander of the 63rd Army Group, Major-General Chen Cong Da, had agreed to put all of his men and his equipment in with the Republican camp.

Not a shot was ever fired between the two armies. There was a last-minute attempt by General Nie in Nanjing to have Major-General Chen either arrested or shot before he sent the fatal message and announced the decision to his men—who came out in the barrack blocks by the thousands, cheering the decision and wishing "Long Life to Governor Yi Juan Ling and his Republican Party." But the attempt backfired badly: the assassination squad drawn from the 1st Army itself rebelled, and killed two of General Nie's staff officers, thereby indicating that the Republican infection had begun to spread even within the utterly loyal 1st Group Army.

By mid-autumn, therefore—and due in so no small part to the fervent lunacy of the Lei Feng Movement—the Republican rebellion had grown to sizeable proportions. China was beginning to spin rapidly, and horribly, out of control.

THE DZUNGARIAN GATE, NORTHERN XINJIANG

December

The winter cold of China's western Dzungarian Basin is almost unimaginable. The great Altai Mountain chain rises to the north, the jagged peaks of the Tien Shan to the south, and in between is a flat and featureless plain, dry as a bone, with howling winds in winter and weather that is equally inhospitable in the summer—the Dzungarian Basin.

There are a few lakes, and some marshy lowlands. There is scrubland and steppe. And there are patchy outcrops of sand that hint at the proximity of the great Taklamakan Desert lying over the Tien Shan to the south. Dzungaria is not a desert in the strict sense. There is some rainfall—1 foot a year. There are some rivers—the Bortala, the Ulungur, the Ili and the Ertix, which flows west into what once was Russia (but which by 1997 was independent Turkestan) and thence on up into the Arctic Ocean—thus becoming China's only riverine connection with the icefields of the North Pole. That it rises in Dzungaria seems only appropriate for so harsh and cheerless a place.

The main towns are as bleak and ugly as their setting. Ürümqi, all factories and pollution and blocks of workers' flats. Turfan, an oasis by the great depression of the same name, is far from being as splendid as its name suggests. And the other towns—Karamay, Kuytun, Shihezi—are as undistinguished and unattractive as only modern Chinese towns can be. Only the people—a vast mixture of Central Asian ethnic types, some blue-eyed, looking almost Nordic, others nomadic Kazakhs or Uighurs of Turkic stock with a smattering of Han Chinese—and the history give the place its due fascination.

Today the province of which Dzungaria is the northwestern part is that known as Xinjiang, or Sinkiang—the so-called Chinese New Territories, sharing the name with the northern portion of British Hong Kong. But here is no back garden of low hills and rice paddies, hastily annexed to protect a naval base. This is instead a massive and barely settled tract of country, three times the size of France, and yet with a total population not much larger than that of greater New York, and all wrested from the hands of the Russian and Ottoman Empires and made part of China instead of what it would otherwise have been, a country or a province named East Turkestan.

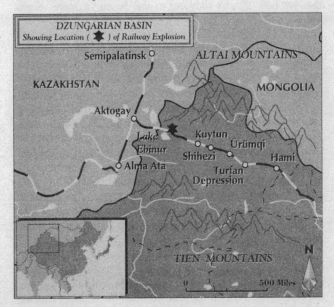

And Dzungaria has played its part in the world's politics before, just as it has begun to do once again. In particular there was the occasion when, for almost all of the 1870s,

Russia took control of a part of western Dzungaria, along the valley of the Ili River, and refused to hand it back until the Ching emperor paid a handsome bounty. That the Czar managed to do such a thing was indicative of the weakness of China in the wake of the Opium Wars and the Taiping Rebellion: another echo of the past in the events of today. For what happened by the Dzungarian Gate in the winter of 1997 and 1998 amply illustrates the weakened state of China in the wake of the 1997 Canton Rebellion. The tendency that China's neighbours have to gnaw away at her sickened carcass has been evident yet again.

There were specific triggers for both sets of troubles, too; and it is probably worth diverting briefly from the modern narrative to offer an outline of the Victorian problems, to indicate how similar they are to the events of more recent times.

In the last century, the beginnings of the particular afflictions of Xinjiang came about as a result of rebellions among the Muslims. Small outbreaks of trouble between Han Chinese self-defence groups and those Muslims who followed a peculiarly virulent form of imported Sufism known as the "New Faith" led, by the 1860s, to concerted mayhem throughout the province. The breakdown of order was exploited by a number of adventurers—and in particular by a memorable figure from Tashkent called Yakoob Beg. From his "capital" of Kashgar on the western edge of the Taklamakan Desert, Yakoob ruled a kingdom he came to call Kashgaria; and indeed the Ottoman Sultan declared Yakoob the Emir—the King of Kashgaria.

The Russians promptly took advantage of the disorder and seized parts of the Ili River valley, just to the south of the Dzungarian Gate and immediately (and to the outrage of the Manchu Emperor in far-away Peking) entered into a commercial treaty with Yakoob. The British, eager to see the emergence of a buffer state between the Russian Empire and their own territories in India, did the same, giving Kashgaria legitimate international recognition, and thus existence.

Kashgaria did not last long. The Chinese Emperor dispatched to the region his most seasoned military scholar-hero, Tso Tsung-tang. General Tso was a brilliant strategist. Within a year the rebels were either captured (and sentenced to death by the charmless Imperial means of slicing) or run to earth and (as in Yakoob's case) persuaded to commit suicide. By 1877 Xinjiang was clear of rebellion; it remained only for the Russians to be forced to leave Ili and sneak back through the Dzungarian Gate.

This they eventually did, but only after a briefly farcical interlude, a further humiliation for the Chinese Court. In 1879 an Imperial Chinese delegation, headed by one Chunghou, was sent to St. Petersburg to ask the Russians to vacate the Ili valley. The Russian court was on holiday in the seaside town of Livadia, and demanded the Chinese see them there. A treaty was eventually signed, whereby the Russians agreed to move out—but since Chung-hou had no idea of the geography of the disputed area, the Russians were able to dupe him into thinking they would move out completely, while the treaty specified their release of only a part of the region. In addition, they were able to establish seven consulates, and were promised a hugh indemnity.

When Chung-hou returned to Peking and the Court found out how he had been tricked there was an immense row, the hapless mandarin was sentenced to death and the two nations shaped up for war. In the end neither happened: a second treaty, this one properly drawn up in St. Petersburg in 1881, returned all of Ili to China—after which Xinjiang was in its entirety under Chinese control, and the embattled Manchus could once again say that they had suzerainty over all of historical China.

In 1997, too, the Muslims of western China were becoming restless. There has been no recent evidence of any outbreak of militant Sufism, as in the 1860s, nor have there been attacks by Islamic fundamentalists on any ordinary Han Chinese settlers. But throughout 1996 and 1997 there were numerous reported acts of petty vandalism—usually arson—on the smaller outposts of the Chinese Army and the Armed Police in western Xinjiang. Signs in Arabic script went up on walls and in handbills referring to an entity known as the Dzungarian Green Crescent Movement.

Some recent reports from Kashgar have also spoken of a growing enthusiasm among the local people for a "Return to Kashgaria"; but that movement is, at the time of writing, apparently only in its formative phase. By contrast that to the north, which spreads its influence throughout what official China refers to as the Ili Kazakh Autonomous Prefecture, is considerably more advanced.

The particular spur to local ambitions for a much greater degree of regional autonomy—indeed, for an independent Dzungaria—came in 1991 when independence was formally secured by the Republic of Kazahkstan. This was the third and last of the three eastern outposts of the old Governorate of Turkestan, which had its headquarters in Tashkent. Until 1917 Russian Central Asia had been divided politically into the Emirate of Bokhara, the Khanate of Khiva and the Governor-Generalship of Turkestan. The ethnic redistribution of the territories within these three units then began in 1924, and the three eastern parts—the Kazakh Autonomous SSR, the Kirgiz Autonomous SSR and the Tadjik SSR—were all formally established in 1936.

All three of these Republics were to become, with varying degrees of difficulty, President Yeltsin's attempted Commonwealth of Independent States. The Tadjiks and the Kirgiziyans won their independence in 1995 (with the latter renaming their capital Pishpek, after many years of being forced to name it Frunze, after a Red Army general). The Kazakhs, the most numerous and fractious of all, succeeded in electing a legislative assembly and both declaring and being granted full independence on 13 April 1996. They retained their capital's name as Alma Ata, since it actually was the city's ancient title; the "old" names of Virny and Zailiyskoye had been given by the Russians many years before, and were not wanted now.

(There has lately, and ominously, been some recent agitation among separatists in the tiny mountainous region of Gorno-Badakshan, near the Chinese Pamir mountains. The effects of this activity on China have so far been minimal.)

As has been mentioned, the appearance of an independent Kirgizia has caused some assertions of rights amongst inhabitants of the neighbouring China for a "Return to Kashgaria," which may yet spell danger for the Chinese authorities. But the more serious problems have been to the north, in the dry and windswept plains of Dzungaria. Here there has been real trouble; and not least the attack perpetrated on 27 December 1997, just inside the Chinese side of the Dzungarian Gate, on the much-vaunted "new lifeline of China"—the Alma Ata to Ürümqi link of the Great Transcontinental Railway.

This railway had been central to China's economic dreamings for a quarter of a century—a link, its planners had long said, "from Rotterdam to Lianyungang," that would ensure China's markets were fully opened both to east and west. For reasons financial, political, bureaucratic and of security, it took many years for the link to be established. The Russians had done as they had promised, and constructed an eastbound line from Aktogay Junction, on the Alma Ata to Novosibirsk main line; it halted at the western side of the Dzungarian Gate, at a station called Druzhba. But it was not until the mid-1980s that the Chinese began to build westwards from Ürümqi; their engineers succeeded in blasting and terracing their way through the Dzungarian Gate's narrow and windblown defiles by the spring of 1990. The line was formally pronounced complete in September of that year. The first freight trains passed through in March 1991, and the first passenger service began in 1993. Hitherto the journey from Alma Ata to Ürümqi was by bus, across the northern fringes of the Taklamakan, and would take a passenger two days. Now an express could in theory pass between the two cities in just eight hours.

However, a British diplomatic telegram written in 1991 on the subject of the railway and of the expected economic benefits it would bring to central and western China (as well as for the new port of Liangyungang, a strong competitor for Shanghai's business) was properly sceptical. A diplomat of some prescience, Philip Walden, wrote from

Peking that " . . . the 'new bridge' as the Chinese like to call it, will link the Pacific and the Atlantic coasts via the Soviet Union, and it could be successful—only if the Muslim republics that are crossed by the railway remain in the Union . . ."

As we now know, by the end of 1991 the Republic that was crossed by the Russian section of the line, Kazakhstan, chose to go its own way; and five years later that which was crossed by the Chinese section—the Ili Kazakh Autonomous Prefecture—was showing signs of wishing to secede from the People's Republic. A demonstration of the growing vigour of this sentiment came, as this narrative has been preparing to relate, on the afternoon of 27 December 1997.

Close to the border with Kazakhstan, on the Chinese side, is a shallow body of water, Lake Ebinur. From October to March it is frozen solid, as on this December afternoon: the temperature was some ten degrees below zero, and the northwesterly wind blowing down from the black ramparts of the Dzungarian Gate was gusting to hurricane force. The new railroad track passes along the northern shore of the lake for about ten miles, along a narrow terrace of rock cut into the cliffs. There are two tracks at this point which become a single track at the lowland station of Todog, and remain so all the way to Shihezi, across the bleakest part of the basin.

Shortly after 3:30 P.M. two express trains were passing along the lakeshore cliffs when there was a most fearful explosion. The outer train was hurled into the lake, and almost all of its fifteen carriages plunged eighty feet down the cliffside and through the ice—even though it was several feet thick—and sank instantly into the bitterly cold waters. The inner express, loaded with petroleum tank cars from the Central Siberian oil refineries, coiled up along the line and exploded in a massive series of fireballs. By the time Army helicopters from the forward border base at Bortala reached the spot there was not a living thing to be seen: just hundreds of yards of flame and red-hot metal, and a series of gaping holes in the lake ice, already beginning to freeze together to close the grave for the remainder of the winter.

The northbound train was a troop special, carrying two battalions of border troops from the 66th Division base at Ürümqi. They were due to take over from the 1,000 men who had been guarding the Dzungarian Gate section of the frontier—the Ili River to the Mongolian border—for the last three months. It was an unpopular posting: the frontier posts were bitterly cold, such local residents as the Chinese soldiers encountered were unfriendly, and now there was this new phenomenon of Islamic separatist sentiment, and terrorism. The Ebinur Lake explosion of 27 December 1997 was by far the most dramatic act of terror ever committed in the People's Republic—a terrifying indication of the powers that militant and disgruntled Islam was able to wield.

More than 1,000 soldiers—including two generals—died in the explosion. The train crews of forty died as well, and the entire two weeks' petrol supply for Ürümqi was destroyed. The line was put out of action for three months. A single bomb—containing about 500 lbs. of German explosive—was believed to have been used: it was detonated by remote control as the trains passed. The saboteurs clearly had knowledge of the timings of the trains—both of which were unscheduled specials—and of the fact that one held border troops. It was a brilliantly decisive act—and it fell as a hammer-blow on the effort that the Peking authorities were now frantically having to make to try to restore order in the fast-disintegrating south and centre of the nation.

For the next ten days transport plane after transport plane—all giant Antonov An-12s bought from Russia in the mid-1990s—ferried troops into the region. The Lanzhou headquarters, normally the administrative centre of a region that places most of its emphasis on its two high-prestige Second Artillery Corps Missile Groups, had just two Group armies—the 21st and the 65th. To cope with this emergency Peking ordered the immediate dispatch of units from Manchuria, Inner Mongolia and Yunnan, to the chagrin of commanders in Shenyang (who had already lost troops to Hong Kong, all of whom were still in custody there), Hohhot and Kunming respectively. Peking's calculation held that a rising absolutely had to be forestalled in Xianjiang: the situation in Manchuria was stable enough for the time being, and if either the Vietnamese or the Outer Mongolians provoked any trouble, then reinforcements could be sent in from Peking itself. The situation, Peking believed, was now so grave as to demand "extreme action," whatever the concomitant risk.

In a telegram from the British Embassy in London dated 30 January 1998, Sir Peter MacDuff essentially confirmed this judgement. He went on to say—despite the reputation that British diplomacy has for the writing of cool and disinterested analyses phrased in the serene tones of invitation penned in an Edwardian drawing-room—that there was now adequate reason to believe "that the morale of the Chinese leadership has fallen to its lowest-ever point, and that there is an increasing feeling that the Army in particular may not be able to hold the ring for too much longer. China is fast reaching boiling point, and the situation seems to be on the brink of uncontrollability."

THE BLACK DRAGON RIVER, NORTH MANCHURIA

Late January 1998

Although the small Chinese city of Heihe is not the most northerly settlement of China's dominions—that honour belongs to a small forest town called Mohe, another 100 miles up along the Black Dragon River—it is a place with the look and feel of a remote town on the far frontier. It is a rough and ready place, filled with itinerants and soldiers and members of strange and forgotten tribes. The voices of Manchuria can be heard too—guttural and harsh, so very different from the plaintive sing-song of *putonghua*.

Heihe's streets have a good deal of old, dark-stained wooden architecture, adorned with fretwork and, occasionally, with the slanted crosses and icons of the Russian Orthodox Church. Indeed, the proximity of Russia is visible everywhere—not least because Russian tourists, ferried over from Siberia on one-day passes, come to do their shopping in the town, and line up at the Chinese vodka shops, and get tight on pint bottles of the local version of *mao tai*,* which tastes like petrol and is called *alahai*.

Tourists used to come here too, particularly in winter, to see the aurora, the Northern Lights: on January nights back in the more peaceable days of the mid 1990s the parks would often be filled with people from Peking and Shanghai and Canton, wrapped up against the freezing cold, and gazing upward, open mouthed with wonder, at the pendulous fronds of red and green and yellow particles, ripping soundlessly across the immense backdrop of stars.

The town, which rises abruptly from the scrubby meadows of northern Heilongjiang Province—the most northerly of the three that make up what used to be called Manchuria, but which Peking insists is now to be referred to merely as *Dongbei*, the Northeast—ends just as abruptly on the banks of the Black Dragon River. There is a packed earth levee, to prevent any flooding during the spring melt, and the walkway along the top is filled with strollers and farmers returning from their fields. During the winter the stream is solid ice, and it is easy (though notionally forbidden) to walk the 500 yards across it, to the town on the northern shore.

The formal prohibition of such walking—or, in summer, the strict control on doing the same journey by skiff—stems from the fact that the river is the international frontier. The land on the far side is Russian Siberia, and the town that rises so close to Heihe on the other shore that it is possible for the citizens on each main street to shout back and forth at one another, is called Blagoveshchensk—the administrative centre of the Amur oblast of the old Russian SFSR, and now a county town in the Siberian Republic.

Blagoveshchensk (the name is painted on a great signboard by the ferry terminal, easily visible across the water,

*A clear spirit, served at the best banquets—a sort of Chinese vodka.

and thus comprehensible to any Chinese who can read Cyrillic script) is a town of increasing importance in the new Siberia. It has a railway station, from where trains go to Moscow and Vladivostok; it has a small airport; it has radio stations and a television station that receives CNN from Atlanta, and in to which Chinese could, in theory, tap.

The Chinese come in droves to stand on their levee and gape at its wonders. There is a shoreside fairground, with an American-built roller-coaster. There is a dock where small container ships load cargoes—Russian Far Eastern cargoes for the Sea of Okhotsk, and Japan. And there are fair-skinned peoples, girls in short skirts and men in well-cut suits, and some women with blonde or brown hair who, if they see the glint of the shoreside telescopes (ten *fen* for a two-minute look) will wave amiably at their curious neighbours. There are no telescopes on the Siberian shore, however. The people of Blagoveshchensk have little inclination to find out much about a people for whom they have no envy, and—given their own increasingly high standard of living—some very considerable disdain. They come and shop for the cheap wares on offer; but they scurry back at nightfall, eager for better food and better drink, and for a sense of joy that seems to be lacking on the Chinese side of the river.

There is, however, one small group of people whose lives and livelihoods are distributed equally across the two shores of the river, and who come from traditions where such modern devices as international frontiers represent no more than an inconvenience. This group is known inside China as the Oroqen; over in Siberia they are called the Amur people. There are perhaps 10,000 of them—6,000 on the Chinese side of the frontier—and they inhabit an area that stretches through the forests for about thirty miles on either side of the river and for about 100 miles upstream.

The Oroqen are of a kind of Caucasian stock—having no epicanthal fold to their upper eyelids, and with a significant portion of their population having fair skin and blond hair. They are nomadic, living in birch-bark tents in the forests and hunting for bears, wild boar and deer. They eat the animals' livers, raw; they like to drink the milk of mares, and they collect and make furiously strong drink from wild blueberries and leaves of a wild oak tree. They are excellent horsemen. They are possessed of native entrepreneurial instincts. They drink to perpetual excess, and they have the best voices of any minority groups in China. And they have a pathological loathing for the Han Chinese, who have tried to suppress and collectivise their energies, have tried to corral them to live in so-called "new towns" built of cinder block and corrugated tin, and who insert political commissars into their midst to instruct them in the ways of thinking correctly and following the Party line.

They were, in short, prime candidates for the practice of banditry—a feature that a politically active group in Siberia, known variously as the New Decembrists or the Pakbars, came to realise in late 1997. (The group, which had its headquarters near the old Decembrists' Museum in Irkutsk, were, like their namesakes of the previous century, middleclass and Masonic young men who were agitating—in today's case—for the return to power of one particular branch of the Tsarist family. "Pakbar," the signature on the handbills and the letters that the movement sent to newspapers, was an acronym of the initials of the five Decembrist martyrs executed after a famous nineteenth-century show-trial.)

It had become abundantly clear to many Siberian political scientists who studied China—as indeed to all analysts inside the Russian Commonwealth and its neighbours—that the country, for a variety of complicated reasons that had probably been triggered by the collapse of far-away Hong Kong, was now edging towards a very difficult, possibly fatal phase in its history. There was still little love lost among ordinary Siberians for a China who had caused her so many recent border problems—particularly downstream, on the Ussuri River. So it was desirable, the Decembrist leadership argued, that certain "cross-border activities" be generated with a view to making life unsettling for the local Chinese authorities. The more unsettling that life could be up on the Chinese peripheries, the Pakbar theorists believed, then the more quickly China could be reduced to a wholesale chaos that, in their peculiarly convoluted view, could only assist in the eventual return of the particular Romanov clan. A contribution to the decay of China could be made, in other words, even in these remote vastnesses of north Manchuria.

Accordingly, during the latter months of 1997, contacts were made by Pakbar groups with the Amur people who lived in and around the villages of Svobodnyi and Simanovsk, near a Black Dragon river tributary called the Zeja. It was suggested that the Siberian-based nomads might use the advantage of the winter freeze to cross into China, as they could do with consummate ease, and make contact with their opposite numbers—their country cousins—in Heilongjiang Province. The purpose of the contacts would be to encourage the Oroqen to form themselves into groups that, in the great traditions of Chinese banditry and warlordism, might then embark on careers of mayhem, to frustrate, frighten and destabilise the Chinese authorities.

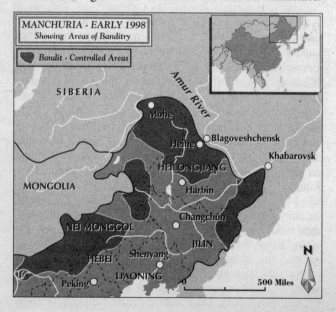

MANCHURIA - EARLY 1998
Showing Areas of Banditry

Bandit - Controlled Areas

It is now believed that all these contacts were duly made and the requirements and arrangements duly transmitted, and that the first meeting of the newly formed Oroqen bandit leadership occurred in or near the town of Heihe, some time in the last week of January 1998. The ceremony, which took place at night in a specially built tent in a thick forest a few miles west of town, was attended by two dozen elders of the tribe. The ritual was solemn: a freshly slaughtered wild pig was brought to the tent, its throat cut and the blood drunk and smeared on the foreheads of each of the participants. They swore an oath; to rid the northern lands of the immigrant Chinese who had no business there and to return them to their rightful owners, the Manchu and the other minorities who, like the Oroqen, had long been deprived of their property and their lands by the Chinese Communists.

Within days there were reports from all over northern Heilongjiang of small-scale acts of vandalism and banditry. A number of buses carrying forestry workers towards Mohe had their tyres slashed and earth poured into their petrol tanks. On one night in early February the flags flying from Communist Party offices in almost every town between Wudalianchi and Tsitsihar were set on fire. An oil pumping station working in the great Daqing oilfield was sabotaged, with chips of rock fed into the lubrication vent. And in an incident that was reported to the Reuters office in Peking and flashed around the world, making China a laughing-stock, a group of Oroqen horsemen succeeded in stopping an express passenger train between Beian and Harbin. They robbed the passengers (who included a Japanese tour group, some 100 veterans of the Kwantung Army who had fought in what was later to become the state of Manchukuo). More than $250,000 in cash and valuables was taken, and the bandits—flying yellow and blue banners—galloped away on their horses, and were never found again.

Manchuria, in short, has lately become a source of trouble and embarrassment for the Chinese authorities. There has at the time of writing been no major incident of actual terrorism—no splinter group in Manchuria has carried out any atrocity on the scale of the Ebinur Lake explosion. But the widespread nature of the agitation, and the evident support that its practitioners have been receiving from the local, non-Han population, must be a further indication of the steady decay of the nation's stability and self-confidence.

THE YALU RIVER, SOUTH MANCHURIA

Friday, 13 February 1998

EARLY MORNING

From their frontier watchtowers beside the railway bridge at Dandong the Chinese troops squinted into the early sun and over at their strange neighbour. At first blush the scene looked much as usual.

The four great red banners proclaiming *All Prosperity to the Great Democratic People's Republic of Korea; The Entire World Salutes the Magnificence of the Juche Idea, A Long and Happy Life to Our Great Leader Kim Jung Il and The Workers Give their Unyielding Salutation to the Memory of the Founder of Junche, Our Late Comrade Kim Il Sung* were still flying, as they had for the past three years. Over the loudspeakers the martial bands were endlessly playing versions of "Nay Nay Nay Nay, Kim Jong Il!"—and thereby wishing eternal glory to the pudgy-faced and ill-tempered youngster who had assumed power so smoothly (against all hopes and expectations) on his father's death in 1995. Steam trains were chuffing their way around the marshalling yards. The blue firefly flicker of a welding torch could be seen working on some rusty heaps of tubes by the water.

Down below, the sentries could see a small North Korean police boat picking its way around the piles of the old disused railway bridge, which had been destroyed by an American bombing raid a quarter of a century before. Chinese sentries were marching up and down the length of the other half of the same bridge. The North Koreans had long since destroyed their half of the wrecked structure, since it was an icon of their shame, and had left only the iron piles in the stream; but the Chinese, being either too poor or too lazy or having other priorities, had left their half of the bridge standing, reaching pointlessly midway into the stream. It was out on to that stubby iron peninsula that the guards marched to and fro, their breath clouding the crisp morning cold. The watchtowers, high concrete structures like airport control towers, lined the Chinese bank of the Yalu—one every half-mile, from here all the way to Changbai. After that the mountains, reaching up to the snowy summit of Paektu-san, made any crossing—like an escape from the insanities of North Korea into what by contrast seemed a Paradise, though it was only China—far less easy.

The unalloyed dullness of the place, the gloomy precision, the dourness, the mechanistic and unsmiling attitudes of the guards—all of those features that helped make North Korea strange even by the standards of a Manchurian border—were in place that icy February morning. Except that suddenly, as two of the sentries in the tower above the Lu Yao Matou pier looked through their binoculars, it became dramatically clear that something unexpected was happening.

North Korean soldiers by the thousand—perhaps even by the tens of thousands; neither sentry had seen so many uniformed men before—were streaming out of their border barrack-blocks, the ten-storey buff concrete "cockroach-cages" as the Chinese called them, that rose in long ranks—partly to obscure what was going on in the country just beyond—along the eastern shore of the river. But something could be seen now; under the proddings and goadings of men who appeared to be officers, the ranks, ill-clothed and armed with what at this distance looked to be antiquated weapons, were being loaded, and in a prodigious hurry, into what seemed to be hurriedly converted cattle cars. The sentries had all seen the cars—hundreds of them had been shunted into position in the marshalling yards during the night. They had assumed that some massing of winter livestock was about to be undertaken—the Kim regime did the most unpredictable of things, and moving thousands of cattle around the nation was well within the realms of the possible.

This, though, was no such trivial matter. There could be no doubt about what was happening—the scale and the speed of this move gave it away. Evidently the North Korean Army, or those units of it that had earlier been selected for frontier duty up near China, were now on the move. As the Chinese soldiers watched the trains chug away through the polluted haze, they peered hard to make sure which switches were being pulled. Within five minutes there could be no doubt: all the trains, with their tens of thousands of conscripts aboard, were heading south.

The senior sentry in Frontier Protection Tower 2319 accordingly called his unit command desk at Dandong barracks. Within minutes the news was in Peking. It only remained for China to pass it on to Washington and London, without the North Koreans realising it had done so.

DIPLOMATIC COMPOUND, PYONGYANG

Friday, 13 February 1998

MID-MORNING

Bengt Jacobsen, who had held the post of Swedish Ambassador to North Korea since early 1997, was sitting at his desk, drafting a telegram to his colleagues in Tokyo, when he heard the car draw up outside the Embassy. In the account that he later filed at his Ministry in Stockholm, and from which the following section of the narrative is drawn, he says that he recognised the sound of the car's engine—a Red Flag limousine. It was probably just a trusted driver bringing him that day's copy of the Foreign Ministry's newsletter. He didn't get up.

He was thus somewhat surprised and put out when Rong Chin-wen, the Chinese Ambassador, strode into the room with his finger pressed up against his lips. Jacobsen may have been irritated but he knew the drill. No conversation of any substance could take place inside the house—and certainly not on the telephone (which is presumably why the Chinese had not rung to make an appointment). There were microphones hidden everywhere; and both his Embassy's cleaning lady, and his own (who cleaned the flat in which he lived upstairs) were married to senior officials in Korean Broadcasting and the University of Pyongyang respectively, and certainly went through all his mail and his wastepaper baskets.

The only place in the Embassy that enjoyed even a moderate degree of security was down in the garden, under the grape arbour beside the empty swimming pool. Seeing Rong's sign Bengt Jacobsen nodded and walked briskly out into the garden. He said nothing until the two men were facing each other, sitting on plastic garden chairs in the cold, with dead leaves piled around their feet. The Embassy gardener, who was almost certainly spying on them, moved closer, raking leaves as he did so. The Ambassador could keep an eye on him by watching the low sun glinting on his one adornment—a small gold-coloured medal pinned to his left chest, and bearing the likeness of the Great Leader, Kim Jung Il.

"It will have been noted that I am here," Rong said quietly, by way of introduction. "And they will almost certainly suspect why. I have one brief message to pass on to you, and then I will go.

"Our frontier guards at Dandong have this morning seen very large numbers of Korean Army troops embarking on trains for the south. It is our belief from this and from other information we have gathered that the DPRK* is planning an assault on the Republic of Korea,† and probably very soon. We further believe that this move is being taken by Mr. Kim to consolidate his position which, as you will know, has been weakened of late by various changes within the Ministry of Defence.

"I have been instructed by my Ministry in Peking to report this to you and to you alone, and orally. It is our belief

*Democratic People's Republic of Korea: North Korea
†Republic of Korea: South Korea.

that Pyongyang is not yet aware of the extent of our knowledge of these moves. You may wish to communicate this matter to your Government speedily. I am aware that this is the second Friday in the month, which has some importance for you. You may wish to report this development by means that are perhaps more secure than those employed by embassies in Peking or by other embassies here. I am instructed to say nothing more. I am sorry. Perhaps we will meet again later."

And with that, and with what the Ambassador later described as "a nervous look"—the Swede knew something of the earlier dissension within the ranks of the Chinese Foreign Ministry, and knew also from a period of service in Peking that Mr. Rong had once been on more than passing familiar terms with the murdered Madame Zhang—he shook Jacobsen's hand, walked quickly up the garden path, got back into his Red Flag, and sped away.

Jacobsen, whose task as the sole Western diplomat in Pyongyang was to monitor the ever-present possibilities of such a development, admitted later to being "extremely excited" by the news. Ever since Kim Il Sung had died of throat cancer on 12 June 1995, the East had waited expectantly for some convulsion from within the secret fastnesses of North Korea. Kim Jung Il, the bloated and preternaturally angry, young, only son of the nation's founder had, as expected, assumed power—thereby becoming the first dynastic inheritor within the communist world (the hopes of the only other so-called Red Dynasty, that of the Ceaucescus in Romania, having come to an ugly end seven years before). But he had—and this ran counter to most Western expectations—survived.

It had been assumed, in Washington in particular (though not in London; papers released by the Policy Planning Department indicate an extraordinary prescience, considering the events that did take place) that President Kim's hold on the North Korean Army was precarious at best. The conventional wisdom held that he might last for one week after the death of his father. A *coup d'état* led by the Defence

Minister, O Jin U, conspiring with the Foreign Minister Yun Ki Chong, would result in his fall, after which the country would, with painful slowness, start to open up to Western ideas, and would go the way of Europe and all the Russias.

Precisely the reverse, however, seemed at first to have happened. Just ten days after the death of Kim Il Sung the Defence Minister disappeared, and was believed to have died in an unexplained plane crash. He was replaced by an Army general, Kim Jun Ki. The Foreign Minister was transferred to the Finance Ministry; the former Public Security chief, Paek Hak Rim, was given the Foreign Ministry. With two strokes Kim appeared to have consolidated his position, both within the country and with the allegedly disgruntled hierarchy in the armed forces.

And with these shifts in personnel, so the faint signs of a thaw in the relationship between North and South and between the North and the rest of the world—a thaw that had characterised the early 1990s—ended abruptly.

The flurry of cross-border exchanges at Panmunjom—of dance troupes, celadon-ware specialists, painters and marathon runners—was cancelled. Tourist visas to North Korea became suddenly extremely difficult to obtain, except for mainland Chinese and Party members. The amalgamated Korean football teams disbanded. The size of the famous "one-ton flag" which flew from a huge tower overlooking the border was doubled, and a tower half as high again was built for it: on very clear days the five-pointed red North Korean star, on a flag now 100 feet long and forty deep and flying from a steel tower that was a fifth of a mile high, could be seen from Seoul itself.

The Americans, who had maintained their mutual defence treaty with South Korea against mounting opposition in Congress, responded readily to what was perceived as the new and dangerous threat—and they were able to do so despite President Benson's 1996 budget cuts. All of the front-line troops who had been withdrawn from their guard duties in the Demilitarised Zone (DMZ) in 1992 were brought back after a number of threatening incidents of sabre-rattling had occurred at Panmunjom. Operation Team

Spirit, the country-wide US–Republic of Korea war games that had been held each springtime since the signing of the Korean armistice agreement in 1953, but which had been scaled down to a minimum after the 1992 North–South baseball matches had proved such a success, were started again in 1996. The USAF 8th Tactical Fighter Wing, the famous "Wolf Pack" which had been moved away from the Kunsan Air Base in the early 1990s was also brought back from California in 1996, with President Benson's spokesman referring to his decision as offering "the necessary support and sustenance to our friends in the Republic of Korea at a time when matters north of their international frontier give them legitimate and understandable cause for concern."

All of these moves took place against a domestic situation in North Korea that was chronically bad. Years of poor harvests and low industrial production, a total lack of foreign exchange, the loss of aid from and trading relations with the Russian Commonwealth, and a new instability within China that had diminished Peking's ability for neighbourliness—all of this conspired to reduce the standard of living of the average North Korean to dismal levels.

Propaganda, though, was skilfully applied as ever. The vast majority of the 25 million ordinary North Korean people still had no knowledge of anything other than the Kims' infamous "Juche" system based on the dual principles of proletariat power and self-sufficiency (one might describe it as an isolationist form of Stalinism). They had no conception of the economic or political situation anywhere else in the world—although a few very favoured cadres in the Potemkin city of Pyongyang had had some contact with visiting Koreans from Japan, and knew of the standards of life there. They had no knowledge of any God other than Kim Jung Il, no awareness of life proceeding to any other rhythm than their own. And so they were still, to the greatest extent that they themselves could imagine, quite content with their lot.

Their rice ration might go down—and maybe some of them did then wonder very briefly just why this had to be.

But when it was painstakingly explained to them by Workers' Party officials that this self-sacrificing move had been taken in the best interests of the nation, and would further serve to reinforce the nation's position in the world as the only Worker's Paradise, they cheerfully agreed, and they trooped in to work as usual the next day all wearing their little Kim Jung Il badges, assuming that this was how life was meant to be, and being not in the slightest aware that they might ever have the capacity or the imagination to do something other than accept their lot.

The North Korean economy thus staggered fitfully along—selling ill-made tractors to bankrupt African banana republics, or trading heavy artillery pieces to Middle Eastern despots who paid up in oil, or machine parts, or atomic secrets. The North Korean Army and police and the various intelligence services were well paid and remained quiescent.

The West—or at least the US State Department—had privately expressed its surprise and dismay at the survival of the man they had hoped and predicted would fall, and then, semi-publicly, had expressed chagrin at the naïvety of their earlier analysis. But these same analysts then went on to compound their earlier misjudgement by overcompensating, assuming in testimony before a variety of Senate and House Armed Services and Intelligence committees that Kim would probably now remain in power for all of his life, and would try to pass the line on to his son, Kim Jin Sung, who (though he had never been heard of until his father became President) was a rising star within the Army, now a brigadier based at the port of Wonsan.

The London analysts, in contrast, argued that President Kim would not long remain in office. He would, they said soon "overreach himself." The Foreign Office Policy Planning Staff's internal paper (later to become well-known by its bureaucratic number, 97/DPRK/RC/334) argued that by his doing so the nation would be "placed in grave peril" and there could be "a sudden and catastrophic change in the DPRK government under what might well be "highly unusual circumstances."

Bengt Jacobsen pondered on this last remark—which he had read after a transcript of the paper was handed to his Foreign Ministry—as he drove south from Pyongyang. He had hastily typed up a copy of the notes of his conversation with Ambassador Rong, making sure that he had printed only a single copy and then erased the file from his computer's memory. He was doing precisely as the Ambassador had suggested—he was meeting a colleague, as he did on the second Friday of each month, and handing him the news. This colleague, a Mr. Bauer, would then hand the paper personally to the Swedish and then the British and American Ambassadors in Seoul.

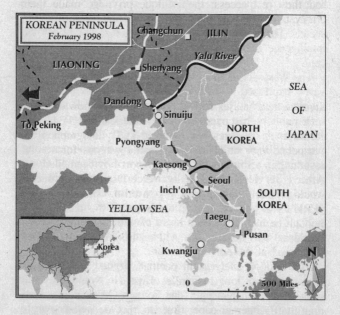

KOREAN PENINSULA
February 1998

Changchun   JILIN

LIAONING   Shenyang   Yalu River

Dandong   SEA

To Peking   Sinuiju   OF

Pyongyang   NORTH   JAPAN
KOREA

Kaesong

Seoul

Inch'on   SOUTH
KOREA

YELLOW SEA

Taegu

Pusan

Kwangju

Korea

0   500 Miles

N

Bauer had a unique and peculiar job, working for the Neutral Nations Supervisory Commission (NNSC) that had been set up in 1953 to monitor the cease-fire arrangements. A small team of Poles and Czechs did the monitoring on the Northern side of the Military Demarcation Line; an

identically sized team of Swiss and Swedes did from the
Southern side. Both teams had houses built precisely along
the line in a tiny compound just to the east of the
Panmunjom site, so that an Observer, like Mr. Bauer, would
look out of one of his living-room windows and see North
Korean artillery pieces pointing at him, and out of the other
and see American howitzers pointing at him from the opposite direction. The men, who served in the NNSC without
their families, were the only people permitted to travel between North and South Korea at will. Bauer would, from
time to time, drive up to Pyongyang for a lunch party, then
back to Seoul for dinner. None but he and his colleagues
had the same access; their unique privilege made them
highly useful for the passing of secret and sensitive messages between interested parties on the two sides of the
line. By handing the paper to Bauer, the Swedish Ambassador was ensuring security for the message: it would be in
Washington by mid-afternoon and the North Koreans would
have little idea that their troop movements from the Yalu
River rear-area bases had become common knowledge.

(It was later discovered that the American ERG-34 satellite scanning the area had detected and photographed the
unusual movement of scores of cattle wagons for several
days in early February; a routine report had been filed, together with a query to the Commerce Department's intelligence office, asking for information on the situation on the
DPRK's dairy farms. The information that was passed from
the Chinese Foreign Ministry via these two Swedish diplomats was the first credible data on troop movements that
Washington received.)

Jacobsen's Volvo would normally take less than two
hours to cover the fifty miles between Pyongyang and
Kaesong, where he was due to meet Bauer for their
monthly briefing session. But on this occasion it took
him more than three hours, as the four-lane Great Leader
Highway was stiff with traffic—petrol tankers, shipping
containers, and hundreds of other nondescript and tarpaulin-
shrouded goods vehicles.

None of the trucks had military markings, nor did they

have their headlights on—and so the movement did not have the appearance of (and would not have been detected by satellites as) a convoy. Most of the vehicles turned off to the east at Kumchon, however, and headed along a restricted road. A score of sentries stood at the turnoff, with searchlights and a sandbagged machine-gun emplacement. The road led towards the gap in the hills that marked the northern end of the so-called Uijongbu Corridor.

It was along this Corridor that three major North Korean units—the 3rd and 4th Infantry Divisions and the 105th Tank Division—had raced so destructively and impressively on that June Sunday, forty-eight years before. The 6th Division had gone west to secure the Ongin peninsula; the 1st had moved on Kaesong City; the 5th had been committed to the east of the Taebuk Mountains, to capture Kongnung and Samchok. And for four days and nights they raged ever southwards without meeting any serious resistance. They were well-equipped, they had the element of surprise, their foes were ill-trained and under-armed, and no match for the T-34 tanks and the 85 mm guns. Seoul fell after only three days—and it was only because the North Koreans stopped to rest and draw breath, and the West used the time to decide on its response (which of course involved the dispatch into the theatre of American ground forces), that the charge was halted, and battle was joined for the next three grinding years.

Much the same could now happen again. This time both the American forces, although only recently recalled to the border, and the South Koreans were well-disciplined and armed, and they behaved each day as though an attack might indeed be imminent. They would probably not be overrun even without having to resort to the tactical atomic weapons that were stored down at Kunsan. But at the same time, faced with nearly 2,000 of the Chinese T-69 Mark II battle tanks, all manner of other fearsome weapons and 1,000,000 men under arms, a surprise attack from North Korea would wreak terrible damage on the defending forces. Fighting of an intensity not seen since the Lunar

New Year offensive in Vietnam exactly thirty years before would be necessary to reverse the flow of battle.

All of this, and the single page of notes from the meeting with Ambassador Rong, was passed between the two diplomats as they drove around the Former Great Leader Park, up on the hill to the south of Kaesong. The park was dominated by a sixty-foot bronze statue of Kim Il Sung, bareheaded, wearing a long coat and with his hand pointing defiantly south, as if to urge on the process of unification. If you looked in the direction of the hand you could see, even on days that were not especially clear, the massive flag flying above Panmunjom. The South Korean equivalent, a mile or two beyond, was smaller and thus invisible.

The diplomats had discovered some weeks before that American Armed Forces Radio was quite audible in Kaesong, on their own radios (North Korean sets came with a coil that was pre-tuned to allow reception of the government station only). The two would amuse themselves by parking their cars beside Kim's statue, and letting American soul music boom out of their stereo speakers, the unfamiliar rock songs attracting small crowds of curious passers-by. But dour-faced men in coats as long as Kim's would invariably hurry over after a few moments, and they would quickly usher the townsfolk away. Once Jacobsen heard through his driver that a listener had been sent to a prison camp up near the Yalu River for having the audacity to try to mimic a Western song.

On this occasion Jacobsen and Bauer used the radio to hide any monitoring of their conversation—North Korean agents used boom microphones to hear the most distant talk—and they hid their lower faces with scarves, to frustrate the attentions of lip-readers. By 3 P.M. both men were on their way: Jacobsen back to the capital, Bauer down to the northern gate of the DMZ, to the Panmun-gak checkpoint, and then across the thin white line that marked the demarcation line itself. He called in briefly at the US Army's forward base at Camp Kitty Hawk to have a signal sent indicating that he was the bearer of "certain important intelligence" for immediate transmission to his Embassy. A helicopter was duly waiting for him at the Imjin-gak checkpoint, and he was in Seoul and with his Ambassador by 4 P.M. The Swede telephoned his opposite number in the American Embassy five minutes later and, in a brief conversation made between the two Embassies' debugged basement "coffin" rooms, formally told the representative of the United States government what he knew.

It was less than eight hours since the first Chinese sentry had telephoned the Dangdong PLA HQ from Frontier Protection Tower 2319, informing them of peculiar military movements on the North Korean side of the frontier. Now the State Department in Washington knew, and knew, moreover, that the southern half of North Korea was crawling with unexplained activity. The suggestion that the DPRK was about to launch an attack against the South was compelling indeed.

THE WHITE HOUSE, WASHINGTON, DC

Friday, 13 December 1998

7 A.M.

The soldiers and statesmen had deliberated in the very early hours of the morning, once the message had been flashed from the Seoul Embassy. The Intelligence Committee of the Joint Chiefs of Staff had reviewed the evidence—with later analysis that was provided by a closer examination of the previous day's satellite scans—and had concluded that an attack was imminent indeed.

The State Department, after consultations with the Foreign Office in London, had once again to admit that they had been caught flat-footed. The unpredictability of Kim Jung Il, as their analysts saw it, had led them to make incorrect assumptions; the likely train of events, they had ruefully to admit, would now probably follow the model that was outlined in the famous Foreign Office PPS Paper 97/DPRK/RC/334: Kim would attack, he would over-reach himself, the North Korean army would be routed and Kim would now in all probability fall.

State was also every bit as keenly interested in the role of the Chinese in the affair so far, and in the immediate future. Messages were not yet sent to the Peking Embassy because of the secrecy involved, which meant that extra layers of very complex cryptography would be needed on all messages relating to this subject which might reasonably engage the attention of Pyongyang's extensive spying networks; and such complicated cryptographic arrangements would take time. But a series of questions was framed for eventual transmission to Ambassador Burton.

Washington's parallel interest in the Chinese "angle" on these events should not suggest in any way that the United States was not urgently aware of the fast-developing military situation on the Korean DMZ. Rather, it indicates two things: that the planners inside the Pentagon had a reasonable degree of confidence that Kim Jung Il was acting out of desperation, and would be fairly swiftly defeated; and that geopolitical issues of far more profound consequences would derive from his defeat in which China's position was both central and crucial.

In order properly to design policy for the coming days and weeks, it was essential that Washington understood China's position in the most intimate detail. The country was now, after all, eight months into a debilitating civil war. Air wars and tank battles and infantry campaigns of mounting ferocity were raging intermittently and furiously in a great swath between Shanghai and Kunming. China's armies based in the frontier regions—particularly those in northern and western Xinjiang, in northern Manchuria, in Nei Monggol and Yunnan—were under dire pressure, both from externally assisted nationalist movements and internal dissensions. Bandit groups moved freely across much of rural northern China, their allegiance changing almost daily, their strikes increasing in ferocity as they captured more armouries and made off with more weapons and ammunition. Local warlords had gained power in Soochow and Hohhot, and were proving an additional trial to the hard-pressed security agencies. Most consuls had left the peripheral cities—only the Russians remained in Harbin, and the Americans and North Koreans in Shenyang.

North Korea and China, as the guards at Dandong knew only too well, shared another frontier—one which had so far been relatively quiescent. (In fact it was about the only Chinese frontier that had been quiet—except, oddly, for that with Pakistan, where the Karakoram Highway remained open, and bulldozed clear of winter snow. On the other hand, a wave of disturbances in Xizang–Tibet in December had led to the closure of the borders there, since Chinese intelligence believed the swiftly quelled rising almost certainly had been fomented by supporters of the Dalai Lama in India.)

What happened in the next few days within Korea would thus inevitably have serious consequences for China. Precisely how China reacted to these developments—indeed how she was able to act—depended on China's internal stability. The degree, nature and survival time of that stability could only be ascertained by constant diplomatic probing. Hence the deliberations in the State Department— ruminations that might otherwise appear irrelevant diplomatic niceties, in view of what now seemed an impending Korean border war. In fact the questions that the Foggy Bottom specialists were framing for transmission to Ambassador Burton in Peking were considered every bit as important for long-term American political strategy as were details of the numbers of tanks and artillery pieces at Kaesong for determining her short-term military strategy. For the considerations of history, they turned out to be of even greater significance.

The most important and immediate answer that Washington needed was whether the People's Republic of China's Ambassador to Pyongyang, Rong Chin-wen, had indeed enjoyed a professional and perhaps a political association with the late Madame Zhang, as was suspected? This question was designed to ascertain if Rong belonged to what was being called the "reformist" wing of the Foreign Ministry. For if he did, then there was good reason for wondering at his motives for disclosing the advance information about North Korean troop movements.

(It was by now assumed in America that Madame Zhang's motive for releasing the advance information about the appointment of Mao Ren-chin as Chief Executive in Hong Kong was to permit the speedy organisation of rebel groups in the territory, in the hope that these groups might spread their influence into South China and stimulate the embryonic rebel groups in Canton which were known to exist within the PLA. Madame Zhang paid dearly for her indiscretion—but the effect was precisely as the Ministry and PLA reformists had planned.)

If one assumed that Rong, like Madame Zhang, was a reformist, then was his decision to offer the information his own? Did he act unilaterally—or was he acting on behalf of, and at the behest of, an identifiable group of rebels within the Ministry? And if so, how large was this group, and how powerful was it? Further, could it be safely assumed that the same message about the Korean build-up was not passed more directly—straight to the Chinese Embassies in London or Washington, say—because the Ambassadors there, or their desk officers back in Peking, were not connected to this reformist group, and were probably hostile to its existence?

Then again—what was the motive in informing the Americans? The answer to that seemed clear: the Chinese who leaked the information were trying to make sure that Kim Jung Il was defeated. That much was apparent if one made a bold assumption about the reasoning behind the convoluted manner in which the information was passed—this elaborate backchannel that went via Mr. Rong to Mr. Jacobsen beside the Embassy swimming pool, then by hand to Mr. Bauer in a Kaesong car park, then by hand to the Swedish Ambassador, and finally to the US Ambassador in Seoul. Perhaps it was not just to ensure that Foreign Ministry conservatives did not discover that the information was being passed. It was to ensure that the North Koreans did not know either. And if the North Koreans did not know, and if the Americans were thus able to build up their

defences to ward off any attack, then surely Kim Jung Il
would be defeated.

But why, then, did the reformers within the Chinese Foreign Ministry want Kim to fall? For fall he most certainly
would, the analysts wrote: the Pyongyang generals would
never tolerate the first-ever defeat of their mighty and un-
vanquished armies. The answer was all too obvious. The
collapse of the regime in North Korea would, in time, lead
to its replacement by a non-Communist, non-totalitarian
government. There would be massive instability at first, of
course—the North Korean people had never known anything but the Kims, and the monstrosities of Juche—and to
wean them from so pervasive a system would trigger a psychological crisis of extraordinary proportions. In time,
though, a new government would emerge, and it would
almost certainly be one geared to capitalism, and—
unthinkable in the context of North Korea—perhaps even
democracy. And if this happened then *China, for the first
time since the creation of the People's Republic nearly half
a century before, would be surrounded in her entirety by
non-Communist nations*. Her last remaining ideological ally
would finally have gone the way of all the others. China
would be alone, ravaged by internal crisis, torn by frontier
wars, and now reduced to flailing around, without dignity,
in what would look like the agonising death throes of that
bizarre aberration that has come to be known as Maoism.

There were other, subsidiary questions of immediate
practical import. Would China (the conservative, official
China) now send men, the infamous People's Volunteers,
perhaps, and *matériel* to help the North Koreans? Would financial help be offered? And if either kind of assistance
was to be given, what would be the effect on China herself?
Could she afford to offer any assistance to try to protect her
single foreign friend? Or would her inability to do so assure
the fall of the North Korean regime—unless, that is, President Kim could spring so great a surprise on the Americans and the South Koreans that he could be so bold as to
bet on victory, in the end?

Such questions were sent down to the encoding computers in the basement of State late on the Friday morning: it would be some while before they went out, and some longer time before any answers came back to Washington, to help with the formulation of the next policy steps. In the meantime it was imperative to deal with the immediate threat—that of decisive military action about to begin across the Korean DMZ.

President Benson, who had been told of these fast-moving events and decisions just before breakfast, listened to his policymakers, his military analysts and his security chiefs. The Joint Chiefs of Staff met and put into place their well-oiled Crisis Action System, the six-tier progression by which American forces are prepared for war and then, at the proper moment, inserted into it. The President agreed readily to the simple plan that had been drawn up some months before, and which was designed to repel and defeat a sudden North Korean conventional-weapons attack.

The defending "trip-wire" forces in South Korea were to be put on immediate Defcon Three alert, and the heavy backup units that were stationed so close to the DMZ were ordered to be fully informed of the situation. It was crucial, the Pentagon insisted, that this alert was discreetly accomplished—to the extent that discretion was possible in the matter of putting almost an entire army on a war footing—so that the North Koreans would continue with whatever preparations they were making, and thereby allow the US intelligence agencies and the satellites to probe and analyse until there was near-total certainty about exactly what was about to happen.

Orders were thus transmitted to HQ 8th Army at Yongsan in Seoul, ordering—via a long pre-ordained code signal—a prudent and instant alert from the normal status of Defense Condition Four up to Defense Condition Three, then Two, for all United Nations forces in the northern tier of the Republic. The expected attack could now be met, contained and, in the view of all experienced field commanders, repulsed with relative ease and dispatch.

THE DMZ, KOREA

Sunday, 15 February 1999

Battle was joined, as expected, shortly after dawn on Sunday morning. It was brief, brutal and, from the perspective of the North Korean side, a lamentable and humiliating failure.

Heavy artillery opened up along almost the entire front at 6:35 A.M. A cannonade of extreme ferocity rained down on the American and South Korean forces dug into their bunkers, raking an area that ranged from the immediate southern side of the DMZ to a point about five miles beyond. The Imjin River bridge was hit; a UN forward headquarters building south of the river was damaged; there was severe shell and concussion damage to buildings at Camp Casey; and a radar dish at Camp Stanton was destroyed, temporarily "blinding" the commanders of this section of the battlefield who were preparing the operation from headquarters in Seoul.

The signal "DEFCON TWO"—signifying "Defense Condition Two, a conventional war in progress"—was immediately flashed from 8th Army Headquarters to all active units in Korea and the nearby Pacific island bases, as well as to the command ship USS *Blue Ridge* and the carrier USS *Independence*, based at Guam, and the huge landing ship USS *Peleliu*, lately based at Mactan on the central Philippine island of Cebu. This powerful mini-armada was waiting, men and planes already well-prepared under DefCon Three, to the east of the island of Ullung-do, 100 miles off South Korea's east coast. They had slipped into position after being summoned from the Western Pacific late on Friday evening. Messages were also sent to CINCPAC at Camp H. M. Smith in Hawaii, and from there to the White House and the Pentagon. A prepared statement from the White House press office, issued at 6 P.M. Eastern Standard Time on Saturday, was baldly uninformative:

Following several days of preparations that have been closely monitored by United States Forces in the Western

Pacific, the army of the Democratic People's Republic of Korea—North Korea—launched an unprovoked attack at 6:35 A.M., Korean time, Sunday morning, against United Nations and South Korean ground forces to the south of the Demilitarised Zone. The attack had been fully expected, and is now being met with a well-prepared defensive operation codenamed Operation Eastern Union. The United States, under the terms of its Joint Defence Treaty with the Republic of Korea, has already committed a considerable number of ground troops, aircraft and warships in the theater, and is prepared if necessary to augment these forces. Units of the 82nd Airborne Division at Fort Bragg have already been placed on alert and will fly out to Korea if conditions justify.

The United States Government, which has undertaken Operation Eastern Union after consultation with our allies and with the full foreknowledge of the Russian Commonwealth, and after formally notifying the UN Secretary-General of our intention to defend the Republic of Korea under the terms of the Treaty, hereby demands that the government of the Democratic People's Republic of Korea immediately ceases its belligerent operations and withdraws any advancing troops to the positions they held at noon local time yesterday. Failing to meet this demand will result in exacting and punitive military retaliation with the full use of United States and Republic of Korea military power.

The North Korean artillery barrage had been under way for less than three minutes when the first of the F-111 bombers, the low-radar-profile bombing-support aircraft, and F-16 fighters, moved secretly from Guam to the Suwon forward air base, were scrambled. High-altitude surveillance aircraft and targeted satellite reconnaissance that had been conducted during Saturday had indicated with precision the position of the main armoured and infantry units of the Korean People's Army. Now they were being struck with accuracy and absolute ferocity by laser-guided ordnance. The Americans used huge bombs, like the BLU-109A concrete-piercing weapon that had been specially designed to destroy North Korean armoured artillery positions; and they used them with extraordinary effect. The blitzkrieg that rained down on the North Korean forces throughout that Sunday morning—before they had even been given orders to advance—was terrifying, debilitating and ruinous. A-10 Warthog tank-killing aircraft raced above the long lines of North Korean T-62s, pumping tens of thousands of rounds of heavy depleted-uranium shells into their flanks, disabling them by the score. Heavy artillery operating from well south of the DMZ then opened up, causing further demoralisation and disintegration of the command structure, and foiling attempts to get a squadron of MiG-29 fighters into the air in an attempt to deal with the withering onslaught.

And though the North Koreans seemed to have lost the power and the will to put up a fight, still the Americans would not end their bombardment. By late Sunday, all through the night and into Monday, the ceaseless pounding had begun to take on a merciless appearance. Newspapers in the West, despite having no affection at all for the barbarisms of the North Korean polity, started to question the need for such a ceaseless onslaught. Both the *Guardian* and the *Washington Post* ran editorials on Monday headlined "Stop the Bloodletting Now." But it had no effect.

Squadron after squadron of heavy bombers roared in from Guam (the closer and tactically more useful Clark Field had been closed down by the effects of a Philippine volcano in 1991, and the Subic Bay naval facility had finally been abandoned in 1994 following Philippine political pressure that had started during the volcano year). Meeting no resistance at all—either from planes, missiles or anti-aircraft weapons—the bombers systematically attacked prestige targets in and around Pyongyang. By the late afternoon of Tuesday all the great landmarks of the city had been demolished.

The 600-foot-tall Tower of the Juche Idea was but a mass of wrecked concrete and marble, its illuminated crown crushed and half submerged in the Taedong River. The

Revolutionary Museum was on fire, the great bronze statues of Kim Il Sung and Kim Jung Il that had stood together outside were broken and toppled into the plaza. The Koryo Hotel was in ruins, and the 1,000-foot windowless pinnacles of the Ryugyong Hotel was peppered with jagged holes, gobbets of flame licking from its flanks.

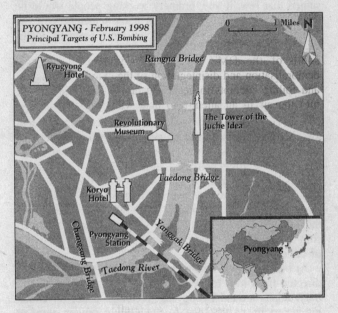

PYONGYANG · February 1998
Principal Targets of U.S. Bombing

0   1 Miles

N

Ryugyong Hotel

Rungna Bridge

The Tower of the Juche Idea

Revolutionary Museum

Taedong Bridge

Koryo Hotel

Pyongyang Station

Yanggak Bridge

Pyongyang

Chungsong Bridge

Taedong River

Four of the main Taedong River bridges—the Rungna, the Yanggak, the Chungsong and the all-important Taedong railway bridge—were wrecked. Demolition bombs had devastated the main Pyongyang International Airport terminal building, and had put both of its runways out of action. And smoke and flames pouring from the ground near Pyongyang main railway station suggested that special laser-guided ordnance had also managed to penetrate the city's legendary Metro system, with its ice-cream-castle architecture, and its scores of marble renderings of members of the heroic Kim dynasty. All of that now appeared to have been wrecked as well, with possible—and the Americans later said, regrettable—loss of civilian life.

"It is our belief that only senior members of the Korean Workers' Party would have been permitted entry to those shelters," a Pentagon spokesman said on Tuesday after word of the attack on the Metro system spread. "We assumed that few, if any, ordinary working people would be given access. In that the tunnels housed members of the country's ruling élite we considered them perfectly legitimate targets."

The Swedish Ambassador to North Korea, Bengt Jacobsen, later reportedly confirmed this American assumption. When the air raids began he saw scores of burgundy-coloured Lexus sedans—the current favourite of the North Korean political hierarchy—ferrying families from the senior cadres' apartment blocks on Changgwang Street and Haebangsan Street, across to the main Metro entrances. At the same time helmeted policemen were preventing passers-by entering these same stations, Jacobsen said. Instead they were forced to run and take cover in parking garages and basements of nearby office buildings. In the event they were the lucky ones: the privileges of senior membership of the Korean Workers' Party proved in the end to be of dubious benefit.

At the same time heat-seeking surface-to-surface missiles directed from mobile rocket launchers hit a variety of military targets around Pyongyang: a storage depot for strategic weapons parts close to the atomic power plant at Yongbyon, sixty miles north of the capital; a terrorism school and explosives store near Wonsan; the Wonsan naval base itself; and the early stages of the construction of a large "offensive dam" on the Upper Han River that Kim had started building for the sole purpose of creating a Damoclean lake that would threaten the very existence of Seoul, which lay further down the river. All the launch sites for the so-called "Super-Scud" that North Korea was said to have been developing were located and destroyed, a Pentagon spokesman said.

All of these targets, and more, were hit and damaged or

destroyed within seventy-two hours of the first North Korean artillery salvoes. Not a single North Korean soldier had penetrated the northern wire of the DMZ. There were just three casualties on the Allied side—an American observer in a forward radar base was killed by shrapnel on Sunday morning, and two Koreans assigned to an American obstacle-clearing unit were killed when their M728 Combat Engineering Vehicle overturned into a shell crater, crushing them.

There was, at first, total silence on the diplomatic front. The Chinese apparently made an abortive attempt to move elements of the 39th Group Army towards the border, and their defensive radar sites in Central Manchuria were turned around to detect any possible overflying of their territory by enemy warplanes scouting the Yalu Valley (although American pilots were under strict orders to keep at least ten miles south of the Chinese border at all times). The local commanders appeared, however, to have problems of their own: satellite photographs of the Shenyang region showed a series of apparent explosions in a barracks that were believed to house the 77th Mechanised Infantry Division, and an anti-aircraft missile site south of Tonghua was reportedly sabotaged. The US Consulate in Shenyang spoke later of unconfirmed rumours of intense bandit activity in the border area in the immediate aftermath of the first skirmishes.

The Chinese media made no reference to the fighting in its domestic broadcasts. The Voice of America and Radio Japan transmitters both, as was the usual case, increased their regional broadcasting hours to provide coverage of the conflict; the BBC, which had abandoned its Korean language service in the 1980s, found itself unable to compete for listeners among Korean speakers, though it commanded its traditionally faithful audiences within China itself. (The BBC had in any case a considerably enlarged following among educated Chinese, since it had reported the shifting events in the Chinese civil disturbances very comprehensively. Its listenership had benefited considerably from the rebel-inspired destruction of a Chinese Broadcasting Ministry jamming transmitter in southern Fujian that had been interrupting BBC broadcasting throughout southern China. The Chinese had shut down the Hong Kong transmitter as soon as they took over the territory in July 1997; but once the rebel forces had taken control they were able to restart broadcasts, with the full co-operation of Bush House in London. The Communists responded by trying to jam the signal, but with only limited effect.)

Listeners to the international coverage of the Korean conflict noted with keen interest the tone of reporting from NHK, the Japanese government radio system. Although the English-speaking reporting was eminently even-handed, in line with traditional NHK policies, the Japanese and Korean language versions presented a rather different picture.

References were made to the unstable situation that now obtained both in the Korean peninsula and, more ominously, in China; comparisons were offered between the situation of today, and the "very much more agreeable and assured situation that obtained in the 1930s," in the words of the announcer. Foreign diplomats and analysts at the Caversham Listening Service in England wrote later that the tone of these broadcasts from Tokyo was the first of a series of indications—usually subtle—that Japan was beginning to take an alarmed interest in developments among the countries on her western flank.

An internal PPU document circulated six months later within the Foreign Office in London concluded, with an uncharacteristic literary flourish, that "there will be those who wonder whether, in some extremist and perhaps even not-so-extremist circles within Japan, there are men who even now are looking back fondly to the times when their own Empire was able to embrace and envelop those nearby countries that seemed to be suffering in such a dire manner. Echoes of the Japanese *Manchukuo*,* and of the Japanese

---

*The name given by Japan to Manchuria after 1931 once she had conquered it and was running it as her own, with the last Emperor of China, Henry Pu Yi, as its puppet ruler. Only two countries ever recognised Manchukuo: El Salvador and the Vatican.

Chosun,* are being heard and felt ever more strongly in certain circles in Tokyo today. That the noble and august NHK, so closely and intimately linked to the Japanese establishment, has chosen also to broadcast a political tune that will find so many distant harmonies from within these groups, is both understandable and, to those who have had to deal with Nipponese expansion and tyranny before, both regrettable and alarming. Japan should perhaps be prevailed upon by the international community to insist that she harbours no designs on her much weakened and long-suffering neighbours."

But neither the Japanese nor the Chinese governments said anything, publicly, about the conflict. There was a long and worrying silence, but one that was interrupted finally when the Pentagon announced a two-hour bombing pause at 5 P.M., local time, on Tuesday 17 February. They had been told, via another complicated backchannel once again involving the Swedish government, that the Democratic People's Republic of Korea was about to make a brief but important statement to the nation and, through the International Service of Radio Korea, to the world.

The statement was exceptionally difficult to hear. The radio transmitters had clearly taken a pounding, and the electricity supplies, even to central government offices in Pyongyang, were fitful. The National Security Agency, using enhancement techniques, managed to have the text translated and broadcast on US and British radio networks by 6:15 P.M. (9:15 A.M. GMT). The statement was read by a hitherto unknown Mr. Kim Hyun Hwee, who described himself as "an official with the Information Department of the Provisional North Korean Government, speaking on behalf of the North Korean Armed Forces' and Citizens' Committees"—significance already being attached by Western analysts to the phrase "North Korean," which had never

---

*The old name for Korea and, in this context, the name given to Korea by Japan when she ran it as a colony from 1910–1945.

been in use in the country before. The brief text was as follows:

Fellow Koreans! You will all be aware that many tragic events have befallen our beloved country in the last three days. Foreign soldiers and airmen, mainly from the United States of America, but with the assistance of our brothers from the Republic of South Korea, have mounted a series of cruel attacks on our people and our cities. Much of our nation has been destroyed and devastated, and many of our people have died. This is indeed a sad, sad day for all Koreans, everywhere.

But there are those among us who feel that our leadership has not been wholly without blame in these matters. The brutal attacks made against us have come about in response to a wholly unauthorised series of attacks which our armed forces were ordered to make on our brother Koreans living south of the 38th parallel on Sunday morning last. There was no need whatsoever for this military action; and whilst the ferocity of the response is, in our view, quite unjustified, the former leadership of this nation has to bear much responsibility for the events of the past days.

Accordingly, some ten hours ago, senior members of the Korean Armed Forces, on whose behalf and with whose authority I have the honour and privilege to address you this evening, took control of this nation's government. The fate of former members of the leadership will be made known in due course, after a fair and public examination of their conduct while in office.

The first decision that has been taken by the North Korean Armed Forces' and Citizens' Committee is that the fighting must come to an immediate stop. I therefore announce that our Armed Forces will agree without reservation to meet all conditions announced by the Government of the United States and the United Nations Command on Sunday, 15 February 1998. A cease-fire has been ordered among all members of the North Korean Armed Forces. Senior members of our armed forces are prepared to meet members of the United Nations Command in the Joint Security Area at Panmunjom, under the auspices of the Neutral Nations Supervisory Committee, at any time after 1000 GMT today. Following the signing of certain documents, members of the United Nations Command are at liberty to make inspection tours within our nation, and to station personnel to ensure compliance with the demands of these agreements.

Dear Korean people. You have suffered much in recent days—and in recent years. Your suffering is now at an end. Much will be happening in the days and months to come. There will be trials ahead. But the interests of our beloved country will come first once again, after many years when that has not, regrettably, been true.

I leave you now with the music that unites all of our country, in the hope that the events of these last days may hasten the time when the Korean peninsula is, at long last, a whole nation once again.

The strains of the love-song "Arirang" could then be heard, faintly, before the broadcast ended. Solemn Western classical music followed. There was no further mention made of any member of the Kim family.

All American hostile operations were halted forthwith. The Panmunjom meeting took place at 1030 GMT, with the Eighth Army Commander, General Hotchkiss, signing a brief document headed "Cessation of Hostilities," on behalf of the United Nations. General O Sik Yong, Commander-in-Chief, North Korean Land Forces, signed on behalf of the Forces' and Citizens' Committee of North Korea. After which the two generals got into an American Humvee and sped off, with escorts, to dinner at a hastily reopened restaurant in Kaesong. Both men returned to their barracks in high good humour: it was evident that the situation on the Korean peninsula was changed for ever.

It was later reported by the North Korean News Agency that Kim Jung Il had been sentenced to death by a "People's Court" on Thursday, 19 February, and that the sentence had been carried out immediately. Other members of his family were said to have died in an unexplained traffic accident on the outskirts of Pyongyang a day later. All statues of Kim Jung Il were removed from public view within a week after his death. The massive statue of Kim Il Sung that stood on the hill at Kaesong was left standing, however, "as a memorial"; the huge flag on its 1,000-foot tower just to the north of the DMZ was taken down within a further week; and work started on clearing the minefields of the DMZ, and cutting down the wire fences, in April.

This latter task—which was being undertaken by the Samsung Construction Company—was not expected to be completed until the end of the year, at least. There was a lone protest entered by the World Wildlife Fund, which argued that the half-century of total inactivity within the DMZ had allowed thousands of specimens of the previously rare Manchurian Crane to breed between the two wire barricades. A professor from Wisconsin was brought over to supervise the demolition in those parts of the DMZ where the cranes lived. All were said to have been saved.

CHAPTER TEN

Daydreams of Samurai

TOKYO AND WASHINGTON, DC

Early 1999

The situation within China, watched intently by diplomats and military planners across the world, became ever more confused and desperate during the ensuing weeks and months.

The traumatic, mercifully brief, events on the Korean peninsula in the early part of the year took some time to wreak their inevitable direct effort on the Manchurian border regions. A significant proportion of the hundreds of thousands of ethnic Koreans living in Jilin and Liaoning Provinces, close to the Korean frontier, took part in anti-Chinese demonstrations. There was a steady increase, probably linked to this phenomenon, in the audacity and the scale of banditry in the region.

The detonation of a large bomb outside a PLA munitions dump south of Harbin in June, and the derailing of no fewer than nineteen goods and passenger trains travelling on Manchurian routes between Dalian, Shenyang, Harbin and at the Shanhaiguan Gap—where the Great Wall nears the sea—continued to cause major headaches for the administration of north-east China. It was some small comfort to the central government, however, that the region's three Group Armies—which were all headed by politically conservative generals—remained loyal to Peking during the year. But then again, there had been losses, and there were still acute military problems.

The total strength of loyal forces in the Chinese northeast had been attenuated since June 1997 by the dispatch of the soldiers of the 37th Division to Hong Kong, and by their subsequent rout and imprisonment following the recapture of the territory by Republican forces. (Most of these former Shenyang-based soldiers were reportedly still penned by Republican troops—though now under Red Cross supervision—on the island that had been reclaimed as a site for the former colony's proposed new airport). In addition, the military commanders were plagued by trouble in a variety of guises that was initiated by Oroqen and other Manchu bandit groups along the length of the Amur River valley. There were almost daily reports of assassinations, kidnappings, bank robberies and arson (huge forest fires were being regularly set, many of them as large and destructive and as difficult to handle as the immense accidental blazes of the mid-Eighties). The remaining Armies might be loyal, but it was a loyalty that was now, the commanders agreed, somewhat less of an asset, and more of an absolute necessity. If it faltered, then the control of the entire north-east of China would be put in jeopardy.

If the practical effects of the Korean situation on China were inconvenient, the symbolic consequence of the fall of the Kim dynasty was devastating. There could be no doubt, all Western embassies reported throughout the year, that the loss to China of her sole remaining political ally in Asia— even so perverse and erratic an ally as Kim Jung Il and his father had been—was distressing in the extreme. Those few Peking-based diplomats still in contact with the Chinese leadership—and it has to be recalled that the political divisions within the Foreign Ministry made it exceptionally difficult for these envoys to know who was speaking for whom—reported that the defeat of the North Korean regime had a grave psychological impact on the battered and demoralised leadership in Peking.

The debilitating effect it had on morale further exacerbated the apparently pathological inability of the Chinese leaders to deal decisively with the deteriorating situation in the nation. Rebel leaders in the south, bandit groups on the peripheries, and a variety of foes both actual and potential seemed at this stage to take an almost perverse delight in exploiting the tragic situation of this wounded giant. An analyst for a leading American brokerage house, writing an almost sympathetic-sounding internal end-of-year memorandum in December 1998, compared (if in somewhat purple phrases) China's appalling present situation with that of a victim of that most awful of Imperial punishments—slicing.

First the executioners start with the hands and the feet. Their tiny razors are wielded with menacing precision, taking away millimetre-thin layers of flesh each time. They make almost imperceptible lesions, but wounds that suddenly, when an artery is nicked or a nerve is cut, gush blood or trigger some massive muscular crisis. Before the victim knows, an entire arm is unusable, or a leg is utterly gone—and the brain suddenly and chillingly comes to the realisation that before long the heart is just not going to be able to cope. The brain, itself quite undamaged, begins to suffer from the perception that it, too, is ultimately doomed—that it will receive the final cuts, and that having lost control of those areas of the body that might have been able to put up some resistance, it can do little to halt the terrible progress of the little flashing knives. And so it is at this moment that the organs of the head, which has been deliberately left untouched so that it can observe the whole slow process of dying, begin to howl with dismay and pain. China is just now beginning to howl—because she knows that nothing can be done any longer to save her from extinction. She can only hope that in the way of the Oriental soul, the rebirth of this wretched ancient will bring forth a stronger and more determined China, a nation and a people who will never let such punishment befall her again.

The razors were at their devilish work throughout the year. Huge tank and infantry battles raged at places whose names will soon pass into the convoluted history of the region, once again sounding echoes from earlier fights at the very same places. The Battle of Wuhan was fought out as expected in March: the long-awaited showdown between the two bitterly opposed armies, between the Republican General Tang and the loyalist General Yang, resulted in the eventual defeat of the 15th Army. Wuhan was secured for the Republicans, and sufficient of the hinterland was captured and a sufficient protective barrier of anti-aircraft positions was established for the city to house the administrative and military headquarters for the entire rebel-held region.

Central to the undoing of General Yang's battle plan for Wuhan was in any case the wholesale defection of the leadership of the Air Force's crack MiG-29 squadron, which had been expected to protect the loyalist tank formations from Republican bombers. In the event the bombers managed time and again to penetrate all air defences and pummel Yang's forces, leaving the way open for heavy artillery to slug it out across the Yangtze and then, after the northern banks had been stormed, for the Republican infantry to take and secure Wuhan City. The battle took three weeks from start to finish: it is estimated that 56,000 men died in the fighting.

The Wuhan victory was hard won, with the loyalist forces putting up a remarkable fight. In psychological terms the result was crushing for the morale of the northern leaders—who then had to look on in dismay and horror as a formally constituted Provisional Mainland Chinese Republican government was established in the city on 10 October, 1998. Taiwan immediately recognised this new government—though it has been, at the time of writing, still the only major country to do so. It set up a small Embassy in Wuhan, and the PMCR Government set up an office in Taipei.

The British and Americans, who had briefly closed their Consulates in Canton and Hong Kong in the spring, reopened them in mid-summer, once the threat of air raids had diminished in both cities, and once the remaining Communist cells had been rooted out and eliminated.

The reestablishment of these missions necessitated some complicated diplomatic manoeuvres, since neither government wanted a total breach in relations with the People's Republic, however serious her situation might be. Thus both governments stated publicly in late October that they would not, for the time being, establish diplomatic relations with the PMCRG—it was, they explained, only "provisional"—and that they would not, for the time being, open missions in Wuhan City. Their diplomats in Hong Kong and Canton were, Washington and London insisted, still officially accredited to the People's Republic government in Peking.

But since there was now no physical contact or communication between Canton and Hong Kong on the one side, and Peking and other "loyal" cities on the other, and since it was known that the Consuls saw and privately entertained members of the Republican government, it was generally agreed that the accreditation was a diplomatic fiction, and one that cannot be sustained indefinitely.

Peking did not, however, object publicly to the slight. A Western spokesman commented in November that the Chinese side, in preferring not to create a diplomatic incident over the matter of the southern Consulates, was reacting with "considerable grace" under the pressure of the times.

But if China restrained itself in its dealings with the West, it took a wholly different approach in dealing with its most important and most deeply feared neighbour, Japan.

For although only Taiwan actually recognised the PMCRG, a small number of other nations, including the Japanese, did invite the rebel leaders to secret talks; and a number of medium-level Japanese and Korean diplomats flew to Hong Kong in mid-November to discuss "matters of mutual interest." These matters were believed to include the present and future status and protection of the Nissan and Hyundai car-assembly factories that had been built in the mid-1990s in Changsha and Fuzhou—cities that were now both firmly in Republican hands—as well as those of the Mitsubishi Heavy Industries plants in Baoshan, north of Shanghai—a city that was still, for the most part, held by forces loyal to the Peking government.

In the aftermath of these Hong Kong talks it was reported, though it has still not been confirmed, that during the meeting the Japanese government had requested permission of the Republican leadership to be allowed to send a small detachment of its lightly armed Self-Defence Force troops to protect their plant and personnel in Changsha "during this period of difficulty."

This was a request that was, of course, heavy with symbolism. The Chinese, of whatever temporary stripe, would never allow themselves to forget the enmity that had dogged relations between the two countries for centuries past, and which flared at regular intervals into real and terrible conflict. This past century alone has seen the two ancient empires clash repeatedly, and with a violence and a vehemence unknown between other neighbours anywhere on the planet (though the venom displayed within the Indian subcontinent since Partition may develop in a similar way—a depressing thought indeed). The Sino-Japanese war at the turn of the century, the Japanese occupation of Manchuria in the 1930s, and the full-scale war between the two countries that raged after the Marco Polo Bridge incident of 1937 until the defeat of Japan in 1945—all of these were vicious conflicts, peppered with unforgettably horrific episodes.

The eight years of the last Sino-Japanese war took an estimated 40 million dead—3 million in the actual fighting, and more than twelve times that number who perished from starvation and in flooding that might have been avoided in conditions of peace. Lin Yutang, a novelist of the period, said the war was "the most terrible, the most unhuman, the most brutal, the most devastating" in all of Asia's history.

The powers that were pitted against one another—those led by Peking (its characters representing Northern Capital) and Tokyo (or Dongjing, its characters meaning Eastern Capital)—represented in that war, and in the conflicts before, the colliding ambitions of tradition and development, the confrontation between popular power and technological power, a contest that was rooted in national pride, the pride of being Asian and the pride that would be gained by the inheritance of Asian leadership.

Which Empire, which people were truly emblematic of the region that the Assyrians had long since named Asia, *the place in the world that sees the rising of the sun?* Was it China: the country that first gave the region its linguistic and cultural underpinnings, the nation that was immeasurably more vast and populous than any other on the face of the earth and had enjoyed or suffered or patiently endured 5,000 years of what was once the most advanced of civilisations?

Or was it Japan, the small and fog-bound group of islands to the east of the Chinese landmass that could trace two millennia of unbroken imperial lineage from the Sun Goddess? The islands whose people are, unlike their neighbours on all sides, ethnically and linguistically and culturally fused into one seamless whole? A people whose economic and mercantile success has been unparalleled in world history, whose triumphs have always been accomplished with unprecedented speed and in a manner that the rest of civilisation has long envied, and attempted to emulate? A nation that has never caved in to white imperialism, and which, according to its own reckoning, had fought a world war with America in an effort to bring pride back to an Asia ruined by the despoliation and humiliation of centuries of Western colonial dominion?

The impertinence of the Japanese request to station soldiers inside Republican China, seen in such a context, is all the more grotesque. The earlier conflicts between the two countries had been accompanied by the most frightful atrocities, committed largely by the Japanese side. While the Japanese have managed, conveniently, almost to erase them from popular memory, they have never been forgotten by the Chinese, where they remain peculiarly and intensely painful. It was thus not surprising that the Republican Chinese refused the request—or this "offer for limited military assistance" as it was reported by two Western correspondents based in the Japanese capital—point blank.

But though there was a predictably cool response from the Republican camp, a far more hostile reaction was to come from the Communists, leading to regional and global consequences that have become all too familiar.

The first suggestion of Japanese proposals for sending troops into China had appeared simultaneously in the Friday 13 November editions of the Baltimore *Sun* and the London *Daily Telegraph*, both of which papers had experienced and well-connected correspondents in Tokyo. The Japanese Prime Minister, Mr. Tanaka, under extreme pressure from the vocal right wing of the ruling Liberal Democratic Party, reportedly sent an envoy to Hong Kong to consult Governor Yi about stationing troops at the threatened factories. The Governor, using the excuse that the factories and such Japanese supervisors as had remained were well-protected by Republican troops, declined the offer politely. It was reportedly his courtesy, as much as anything, that made the North blow its top.

Radio Peking, which immediately seized on the story of the Changsha troops demand, was almost hysterical in its hostility. The language of its commentary, which was repeated several times on all the domestic and foreign services, was filled with the rhetoric of the Cultural Revolution, and was highly inflammatory, to say the very least:

It is beyond belief that these running-dogs and scabs who have temporarily seized a small number of our southern cities would even contemplate talking to the swinish Japanese. It was only sixty years ago that those wretched dregs of humanity, the Japanese invading army, behaved with fearful, unforgivable and unforgettable depravity in our country, committing barbarisms which, though possibly allowable under the bankrupt moral codes of Nippon, are unacceptable in all civilised nations throughout the rest of the world.

Have the foul traitors in Wuhan forgotten what terror the Japanese wrought in Nanjing? Have they conveniently overlooked how the vile incursionists stole vast tracts of our country, how they bombed our cities, raped our women, machine-gunned our peasants, and committed the most terrible barbaric acts against millions of our people?

Even to think of inviting more soldiers, the heirs of such inhuman behaviour, back on to China's hallowed ground—just who are the filth who imagine doing such a thing? What rights have they to even dream of issuing such invitations, or to bow before such typically revolting Japanese demands? Does this not show, to all the rest of the people of China and to the world, that these traitorous swine are mere animals, greedy for their own benefit, while at the same time peddling the birthright of our nation to the beasts who tried so viciously to ruin and ravage it only so very short a time ago?

This broadcast, read in a number of languages (including Japanese), will probably be remembered as one of the more incautious and unwise examples of megaphone diplomacy ever to have been conducted. And once Japanese analysts had concluded that the text was indeed genuine, and that it did in fact represent the official thinking of at least the loyalist wing of the Chinese Foreign Ministry, it triggered a result that could well have been predicted.

Within hours, the Chinese Ambassador to Tokyo was summoned by the Ministry of Foreign Affairs and was told in no uncertain terms that Japan was "insulted" and "absolutely outraged" by the Chinese government's sentiments and by the choice of words it had chosen to authorise for use on its radio stations. The Japanese Foreign Minister, Mr. Abe, was angry and upset, and upbraided the Ambassador for more than thirty minutes—an unprecedented length of time. But the Chinese Ambassador had evidently been told to stand his ground. Indeed, he repeated his government's assertion that it would be "criminal" (as the Tokyo press statement said the next day) to permit the stationing of Japanese soldiers on Chinese soil again—"now, tomorrow, or ever again." And according to the same press briefing, having delivered that terse message, he then stormed angrily out of the meeting.

The Japanese Ambassador to Peking was promptly summoned back to Tokyo for "discussions," and at the time of writing he has not returned. His functions were from that moment on performed by a First Secretary.

Meanwhile, within Japan itself there was a nationwide outpouring of anger expressed at the Radio Peking broadcast—anger which, significantly, was not on this occasion confined to the right-wing extremist groups who had first urged the Prime Minister to send troops to the PMCRG-controlled region. These groups had, until now, been in the vanguard, fomenting anti-Chinese sentiment inside Japan. In the wake of the Radio Peking broadcast, the reaction of the mainstream Japanese was precisely as they had hoped. Indeed, the scale of the reaction provided persuasive evidence that their campaign to achieve such a result had been planned with thought, foresight and much sophistication.

The first indications of the campaign's success had come some nine months before when, it will be recalled, eyebrows had been raised around the world at the tone of the Japanese radio and television coverage of the brief Korean conflict.

The NHK commentators had on several occasions (and with the presumed sanction of the Japanese government), remarked on the uneasy state of the Korean peninsula and on the similarly unstable and unpredictable nature of contemporary China. Remarks about the relative tranquillity of this part of the world in the 1930s were made in several broadcasts. Remarks that were widely regarded as suggesting ominously that the world situation had somehow been rather better sixty years before, when both Korea and Manchuria were controlled by Japan—and when Japan also had obvious and increasing designs on China as a whole.

Perhaps, foreign relations specialists around the world wondered out loud, Japan did once again have designs on China—now that the latter was so weakened and exhausted, and overrun with refractory and disloyal soldiers, administrators and warlords. In Washington the HK7 Committee, which was still meeting regularly under the chairmanship of Assistant Secretary of State Hugh Charlesworth, made a particular point of voicing its concerns during the months following the Korean liberation, and of ensuring that these concerns were heard in the most senior levels of the Administration.

The White House later acknowledged that four times, in March and October 1998, in the immediate aftermath of the Baltimore *Sun* story in November, and once again in March 1999, the potential for some degree of active Japanese involvement in the situation was discussed by the full National Security Committee. Meetings during the spring, summer and autumn of 1999 were then held regularly as the momentum of the crisis gathered. In June 1999 the Joint Chiefs, working under the terms of their Joint Operations Planning System, drew up a series of options for President Benson to consider—options which were designed to prevent any Japanese involvement in the deteriorating situation.

The crisis should be seen in the context of severe strains in US-Japanese relations which had begun in the mid-1990s. President Benson had little doubt for example that his stunning election victory in November 1996 over his Democratic Party challenger, Tom Harkin, was due in no small measure to his ceaseless rhetorical attacks on Japan and all things Japanese. President Bush had bowed to the necessity of abrogating the Mutual Security Treaty two years before; and the early stages of the 1996 Presidential campaign coincided with the final withdrawal of American forces from their bases in Japan, with the emotional impact of the ending of an occupation that had been in place for more than half a century.

On Okinawa, in particular, the impact of the US Forces'

departure was enormous, for both sides. Kadena Air Base was vacated, to be reoccupied by Japanese Air Self-Defence Force. Camps Courtney, Hansen and Schwab were closed. The Marine Artillery Regiment was withdrawn from Zukeran, the airborne special forces group left Torii for Korea. The island of Okinawa had been all but an American protectorate—traffic drove on the right until the mid-Seventies, to satisfy American, not Japanese, motoring habits. Every other restaurant in Naha seemed to be a Burger King or a Pizza Hut. The Stars and Stripes flew from almost every building in town. There was a formidable number of mixed marriages, and in the wake of the treaty abrogation a similarly formidable number of divorces and broken homes. And now, at a stroke, it was all ended, with the marines and the soldiers and airmen pulling out amidst a torrent of anti-American rhetoric and ill-feeling.

The situation was far worse on the mainland, with noisy demonstrations and angry protests at the alleged tardiness of the US withdrawal. The US Army headquarters at Zama was firebombed, and demonstrators fouled the screws of the carrier USS *Independence* in mid-summer, preventing her from leaving her home port of Yokosuka bound for her new base near Guam. An American child was kidnapped on his way to school north of Yokohama, with a right-wing group demanding a ransom payment which the Tokyo Metropolitan Government agreed to pay—to the official fury of Washington.

By the time the last detachment of Army clerks and senior officers left the country in early October 1996 after a hastily organised flag-lowering ceremony at Yokota Air Base, relations between the two countries were at a post-war low point—making it all the easier for Mr. Benson to trounce his opponent a month later for being, allegedly, "soft on Japan."

Benson took forty-nine of the states, and the government of the United States which assembled in mid-January 1997 had a complexion that commentators described as more obviously right-wing in its views—particularly in its international views—than any since President Nixon's second administration of the early Seventies. And the new Secretary of State, Richard Crowther, made an early point of letting the *Washington Post* know that his grandfather had died at the hands of the Japanese, at Guadalcanal.

It therefore came as no surprise to learn that the official policy line devised by the Benson administration was wholly opposed to any interference by Japan in the China crisis. Diplomatic niceties were observed, however: in the immediate wake of the Baltimore *Sun* story the on-the-record State Department briefings were restrained, and simply offered the view that any such interference would be manifestly "unhealthy" and inimical to regional stability. But the background briefings went rather further. The growing apprehension in Washington and in Europe was that the competition between American and Japanese economic and political interests in the Pacific was now coming to a head, and Washington would regard with "great disfavour" any attempt on the part of Tokyo to adopt a hegemonic approach to the current regional disorder.

"The Japanese should be persuaded to remember," said a Department of State memorandum that was considered by the NSC, and a précis of which was leaked to the *New York Times*, "that their exploitation of the weakened state of China in the 1930s led them on to pursue an escalating series of ambitions that resulted, eventually, in the attack on Pearl Harbor. To permit such ambitions to be pursued again would have serious implications, and the United States should look to its responsibilities to see that such a massively destabilising situation *is not permitted* to come to pass [author's italics]."

The Joint Chiefs also considered one further aspect of this possible development: whether, if the Japanese did decide to send troops into China, they would meet any significant resistance from the Chinese. The conclusion was exceptionally alarming. It was estimated that the weakened state of the Chinese military machine was such that the Japanese could, in fact, and without meeting resistance, land soldiers in certain areas—Manchuria, in particular—in which they had commercial and industrial installations that they needed "to protect." But the Chinese would eventually retaliate: and when they did so, all intelligence reports indicated, they would do so *with atomic weapons*.

"It has been noted with some admiration," a study carried out for the Joint Chiefs remarked, "that the Chinese Communists have so far restrained any temptation to make use of their Second Artillery strategic assets or of any of their tactical atomic weapons to deal with the various troubling military situations that beset them. Precisely why they have been so restrained remains unclear—and the threat that some elements within the People's Liberation Army may in desperation resort to the use of these weapons in a domestic scenario is ongoing. However, diplomatic contacts in Peking suggest that it is most unlikely that nuclear weapons will be used in the conflict.

"The same cannot be said, however, in the event of any kind of unwarranted interference by an outside Power. In particular, the tone and tenor of Chinese antipathy to the possibility of Japanese involvement in their internal crisis suggest that theatre atomic weapons might well be deployed against Japanese forces.

"The United States, which has privately stated its opposition to any Japanese interference in China's internal troubles, thus has an additional reason to be concerned with Japan's current alleged intentions."

But these "alleged intentions" were in fact quite firmly rooted, and not simply "current." During the months that followed the Korean conflict, during which, as has been noted, the situation inside China progressively deteriorated, there had been a disturbing number of rallies, marches and protests inside Japan, all suggesting precisely what had been feared. The old, moribund and until lately little-regarded right-wing groups—the Cherry Blossom Society, the Black Dragon Society and the ludicrous *Ketsumeidan*, the Blood Brotherhood, prominent among them—were in the forefront, lobbying politicians, staging demonstrations, placing advertisements in the popular press.

All chanted the same essential message: the collapse of Communism in Europe and Russia, and its now inevitable collapse in China, was about to bring a period of utter chaos to the Far East—chaos that would be similar in scale and extent to, but far greater in perilous consequence than, the instability of seventy years ago. The only nation that was capable of restoring order to the region, of acting as regional policeman and disciplinarian, was the nation that had acted in this role once before, albeit in an effort that was misguidedly thwarted and attenuated by the white colonial powers: Japan.

Japan, these groups all chorused, should therefore intervene at once in China, both to protect her own considerable investments in the country, and also to prevent further bloodshed and to assist in stabilising the neighbour-nation. "It is our duty as patriots," a spokesman for the Cherry Blossom Society said in an interview on NHK. "We are deeply disappointed at China's weakness, his seeming inability to deal with his internal problems. China is our own nation's dearest brother, and we have an obligation to go to his assistance in this, his hour of need. We go to his side not out of anger at his actions, but with sorrow at his lack of fortitude and decisiveness, and with deep fraternal sadness for his prodigal ways."

China protested angrily at the increasing frequency of such remarks and demonstrations, and few were the weeks during the spring and summer of 1998 when the Chinese Ambassador to Tokyo did not have cause and occasion to interview Japanese ministers to complain.

He was especially furious at his own treatment. Beginning in March, convoys of huge sound-trucks had been constantly circling his residence, blasting humiliating insults at him in *putonghua*, reminding him of the Sino-Japanese War, the Twenty-One Demands, the Mukden Incident, the Marco Polo Bridge Incident, the bombing of Shanghai and the Rape of Nanjing and a hundred and one other waystations in Japan's half-century of infamous behaviour within the bounds of the Middle Kingdom.

The laws relating to free speech in Japan generally permitted such noisy demonstrations, although the city police had in the past usually prevented any disturbance to foreign ambassadors, citing some special but unspecified provisions of Japanese Diplomatic Regulations. In the particular case of the PRC Embassy in the summer of 1998, however, the city police took no action, and the Ambassador spent several sleepless nights before being forced to move to a hotel.

Even so it was not long before he was run to ground—first at his penthouse suite at the Imperial, then at the Okura, then the Shinjuku Hilton, from each of which he was obliged to leave in turn when the management complained that other "innocent" guests were being deprived of their rest by the blasting and screeching from the soundtrucks. In the end the hapless diplomat had no course other than to return to his Embassy, and, while continuing his daily and duly ignored protests at the Ministry, to take liberal quantities each evening of a well-known Chinese herbal sleeping-draught.

The tone of the broadcast on Radio Peking in November provided a heaven-sent opportunity for those right-wingers to intensify their demands for some form of Japanese intervention in China. But on this occasion it was not simply the old reactionaries of tradition who led the assault, but the underworld gangs—the infamous *yakuza* and their violent motorcycling cousins, the *bosozuka*. The leaders of these tightly disciplined groups of hoodlums and swindlers announced they had formed themselves into the vanguard of a wholly new organisation, to be called the Young Officers' Association. The name itself was significant—a throwback to the more "romantic" age of the Japanese right wing, when patriotic swells in the Imperial army tried to instigate a coup to overthrow what they contemptuously regarded as the weak-willed and complaisant government of the day.

The involvement of the *yakuza*, whose network of influence reached right into the heart of the nation—or at least, if not into the Imperial Palace, then with certainty directly into the National Police and, most importantly, into the Army—suddenly triggered a large-scale outpouring of national frustration. Young people in particular were known to have expressed themselves as feeling exceptionally jaded and disillusioned by the affluence and flabbiness, as their leaders put it, of the Japanese middle class. "The nation must return to its traditional posture of disciplined asceticism," said one poster that became popular on Japanese university bulletin-boards. "Only by this means can we achieve the respect that is necessary for resuming the leadership of Asia, of the Pacific and, as is our due, of the entire world."

In contrast to the situation in President Benson's United States, where everything Japanese was reviled, Japan's virulent anti-American rhetoric which had been such a hallmark of the mid-1990s, and which had become the rallying-cry of most Japanese right-wing groups, had cooled. Once it had achieved its results—the abrogation of the Mutual Security Treaty and the withdrawal of all of the remaining US military personnel—that particular aspect of the movement had essentially quietened. A year later and there was actually some nostalgic yearning—and not only, as cynics suggested, in the brothels of Yokohama—for the Americans to return. Such antipathy as had precipitated the crisis was confined now to the American side.

But if anti-American sentiment no longer drove the Japanese right, other forces did. Their other dominant anxiety in the late Nineties seemed to centre on what they saw as the laxity and informality of the present Imperial Court. The Emperor Showa (or Hirohito as he had been known in life) was their chosen hero, and there was much private disquiet expressed at the attempts of his son and successor Akihito to demystify the whole Imperial system, and make it accessible to the Japanese public. The moves, these strident students declared, were just further indications that Japan, under foreign influence, had abandoned her sacred responsibility to exert her cultural and moral influence on her people and her region. The much-vaunted "demystification" of the sacred and unbroken chain of two millennia of Japanese emperors was an "unnecessary and insulting intrusion, forced on Japan by her foreign conquerors of half a century before." It should have been resisted then; it should and it could be resisted now.

Talk like that went down well among the young members of the Japanese élite of the late 1990s. Once the *yakuza*, who were given discreet support by such right-wing politicians as realised the jingoistic possibilities that could be stimulated by the Radio Peking broadcast, had taken up the call, so the message began to penetrate the ranks of the ordinary Japanese with extraordinary and alarming rapidity. By the end of 1998 the nation was in ferment: the leadership of the Liberal Democratic Party, still in power in Tokyo as it had been since the end of the Second World War, was now forced to accept that in order to continue to remain in office, it had to move swiftly to accommodate the fast-developing national mood. In a sense, developments forced on the nation by events helped to foster such changes.

The most profound change was perhaps related to Japan's attitude to her own post-war constitution. The Japanese Navy's peripheral involvement in the Gulf War of 1991 was the harbinger of this change. There was initial resistance to the sending of ships, but it was a resistance that was soon and quite painlessly overcome. And once it was overcome so it was felt, both inside and beyond Japan, that the most critical element of Japan's modern psyche—the principle enshrined in Article Nine of the Constitution, which essentially held that war was outlawed as an instrument of Japanese policy, and that Japanese forces should never be used for any purpose than the defence of the realm, strictly construed—had been fatally damaged.

It was not too much longer before the Article's effectiveness as a self-disciplinary check on the hallowed spirit of *bushido** vanished completely in 1993, when Japanese ground forces were sent to Cambodia to try to restore peace there, and were drawn into a shooting war with the Khmer Rouge—in which, as it happens, they performed with tremendous efficiency and courage.

The principle is still written into the Constitution— Article Nine still exists—but it is generally agreed that it is no longer regarded as binding upon the activities of the mil-

---

*Bushido is the Japanese code of chivalry, practised by the *samurai*.

itary. The regional situation has long since changed, Japan argues. In any case, as an editorial in January 1999 in the influential conservative American journal the *National Review* was to point out, Japan "has a lengthy history of disregarding what were once seen as the most hallowed of international treaties and conventions and protocols. Tokyo's current expressed disdain for even so sacred a document as an article of their nation's very own constitution should hardly cause a ripple of moral concern, nor even a momentary stab of conscience . . ."

It was in this context that, during the first three months of 1999, there were significant changes in the siting of the Japanese armed forces throughout the islands of the nation. The troop movements caused immediate concern in Washington, and resulted in Secretary of State Crowther summoning the Japanese Ambassador for an explanation—which essentially went as follows. The Director-General of the Japanese Defence Agency had explained, the Ambassador told Crowther, that: "the changing conditions that have followed the Russian Republic's decision to hand over the Southern Kurile Islands in 1995 have altered the priorities for the siting of our self-defence forces. There is no more sinister interpretation that needs to be placed upon what is, in any case, the internal affair of a sovereign nation. That an explanation is being demanded at all appears to the Japanese people to be a serious discourtesy on the part of the United States. That the Director-General has deigned to offer this explanation indicates the sincerity of the Japanese nation, which is at variance with the current posture of the United States Government—a posture which we trust will soon be reversed."

Russia's decision to give back the four groups of contested islands in 1995 ended more than half a century of argument between Tokyo and Moscow. It also meant that, for the first time since the end of the Second World War, Japan could afford to lower its guard on the northern island of Hokkaido, off the coast of which the Russian-held islands lay. Until then the Army—which had been at least 15 per cent under-strength, but which by 1997 was, given the prevailing mood, winning recruits at a record rate—had concentrated its strength in the north, as well as in the far south (the latter to cope with any threat from North Korea).

From March 1999, the Japanese indicated, matters would be reversed. The build-up on Hokkaido would be ended, and the forces on Kyushu would be augmented further, and quickly. It was this latter aspect, the speed of the redeployment of so much of the Northern Army, and of its precipitate relocation in Kyushu—which has two naval ports, Kagoshima and Sasebo, that were *less than a full day's steaming from Shanghai*—that led promptly to Washington's questions about the real intent behind the move.

The shifts that were announced in January 1999 placed a formidable amount of Japanese manpower and firepower conveniently close to the coast of China, leading to a series of interpretations that Tokyo was not, despite its initial "explanation," over-eager to deny. Under the new arrangements the existing 4th and 8th Infantry Divisions, the 1st Combined Brigade and the 3rd Artillery Group, all on the island of Kyushu, were joined by the 2nd, 5th and 7th Infantry Divisions and the 1st Artillery Brigade—meaning that within a matter of months the numerical strength in the Japanese Army bases closest to China had risen from 16,000 to 45,000, and included 600 of the new high-performance T-90 tanks.

Two entire Fleet Escort Flotillas, including three of the four 7,200-ton brand-new AEGIS super-fast destroyers—ships that since the early Nineties had been regarded as having far greater power than was necessary for the simple "self-defence" of the country—were at the same time moved to Kyushu, to be home-based at Sasebo near Nagasaki, and at Kagoshima. The 4th and 5th Fleet Air Wings were also moved to a new base outside Sasebo.

The 83rd Air Wing and 5th Air Defence Missile Groups at Naha in Okinawa were to be strengthened, and an additional Wing—the 2nd, previously based at Chitose, near Sapporo—was to be moved south to augment the 5th and 8th, near the city of Fukuoka.

 All told, by the early spring of 1999, more than a quarter of Japan's land forces, nearly half of her navy and a third of her air force were stationed on or near Kyushu—in easy striking distance of China. The specific purpose was not to be stated for several more months, but by late August the Washington planners had little doubt. Contingency orders were thus set in place to implement one of the three principal plans that had been drawn up: in particular, an operation, all details of which were Top Secret and which were passed to no other foreign government, that was to be named Operation Typhoon Warning.

As part of the plan, a series of urgent but discreet messages were passed by friendly third-country diplomats, as well as by the usual more direct diplomatic channels, warning Tokyo against precipitate and unilateral action. The United States, together with the overwhelming majority of its allies, was implacably opposed to any Japanese intervention in the China crisis. Suggestions that had been voiced in some sections of the Tokyo press in recent months, to the effect that Japanese troops should be airlifted into those parts of China in which vital Japanese-owned industrial plants were situated, were now being taken seriously in Washington. Such moves would not, the messages all said in unison, be tolerated.

The United States would not permit the landing of troops or of men or *matériel* by Japan on any part of China for any pretext; any attempt by the government of Japan to follow such a course of action would be met with resistance of the greatest magnitude.

There was no indication that Japan paid any heed to these warnings. In early November a flotilla of troop ships was reported to have left Kagoshima port for Naha, Okinawa, with elements of two infantry divisions embarked. The men would reportedly spend the next two weeks on Okinawa "in training." At the same time the 1st and 3rd Tactical Airlift Divisions of the Air Self-Defence Force's Support Command were dispatched to Kadena for their existing bases at Komaki and Miho respectively.

The United States took a steadily more aggressive tone as November wore on, demanding that the Japanese premier make a statement "clarifying" the reasons for the unusual troop movements. But there was no statement from Tokyo, and the White House recalled its Ambassador to Tokyo for consultations, and to offer a further sign of its displeasure.

In China, meanwhile, the fighting continued without respite, although without major advances or retreats on either side. There was a lengthy battle for control of a bridge across the Huang He—the Yellow River—at Jinan, which was eventually repulsed by well-reinforced Communist troops; and Wuhan was again seriously bombed and shelled by loyalist forces, suggesting to Governor Yi that it might be prudent to move the seat of his provisional government back to the relative safety of Canton. But otherwise, central and southern China was simply beset by the ebb and flow of inconclusive fighting, with a mounting toll of casualties and refugees and ruined cities providing graphic testimony to the utter futility and tragedy of yet another Chinese civil war.

And then, late on the night of Sunday, 21 November, there was an incident in Harbin, a northern Manchurian industrial city that had so far been little scarred by the fighting. It was an incident that suddenly and decisively changed the course of history.

A mysterious—and still unexplained—dynamite explosion severely damaged the administrative office building of the Sumitomo Metals Company's chromium smelter. An entire corner of the building was destroyed, collapsing all of the seven floors of the structure. Normally the building would, at that time on a Sunday, have been deserted; but on this occasion there was one employee on duty. He was Mr. Shimizu Tokuya, a Sumitomo accountant who had been asked to work late on a special and urgent financial project. His office was sited directly above the bomb's blast core, and he was killed instantly. His wife and three small children were on home leave at the time in the northern Japanese city of Niigata: they were informed of his death by an emissary from the Foreign Ministry in Tokyo, after news of the incident had been passed from the Chinese.

Angry crowds—whose anger Western diplomats later agreed appeared to have been somewhat orchestrated—promptly gathered both outside Mrs. Shimizu's house in Niigata, and next morning outside the Japanese Diet and other public buildings in Tokyo. They protested loudly at the continuing "instability" of China, they pointed to the evident danger of leaving unprotected the many Japanese industrial installations that were still functioning there, and they condemned the prudence of permitting Japanese workers to continue to do business in China without "proper security measures."

The Tokyo demonstrations continued throughout Monday well into the evening. Hundreds of National Riot Police were brought in to try to calm the crowds, but in fact only succeeded in exacerbating the situation, which then erupted into a number of running battles fought along Showa-dori

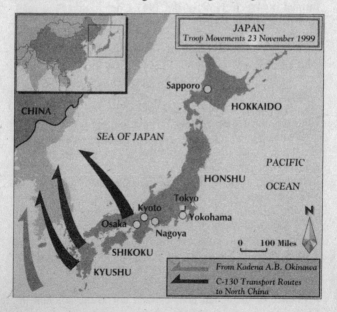

JAPAN
Troop Movements 23 November 1999

Sapporo

HOKKAIDO

CHINA

SEA OF JAPAN

PACIFIC

HONSHU

OCEAN

Kyoto   Tokyo

Osaka   Yokohama

Nagoya

N

0   100 Miles

SHIKOKU

From Kadena A.B. Okinawa

KYUSHU

*C-130 Transport Routes
to North China*

and in the back streets of Ginza, with some casualties sustained by both sides, and a great deal of fires and property damage.

The Japanese Prime Minister went on national television the next day in an additional effort to calm the people. Towards the end of his short speech he made his long-awaited, long-feared announcement.

In accordance with the urgent need for security, Tanaka said, that was now being felt by the owners and operators of some 26 major and 145 standard-sized Japanese industrial installations inside China, and in order to protect the lives and livelihoods of some tens of thousands of Japanese workers inside the country, he had authorised the immediate dispatch to China of some 6,000 lightly armed Japanese troops.

These troops would, the premier insisted, "and as a reassurance to our foreign friends," operate only as defensive forces, and would uphold to the letter the principles enshrined in Article Nine of the 1947 Constitution. The relevant passage continues:

> Our men are travelling today in the name of the Emperor to be deployed to a number of places within China in an effort to guard and to protect our nation's property. That is the sole reason they are going to China. There is no state of war. There will not be a state of war. We have no argument with any nation and any people—and least of all with our ancient friends, the people of China. We only wish for the stability of our assets, and for the protection of our people.
>
> We are, in short, simply trying to do today what we attempted but failed nearly seven decades ago—and that is to bring calm and stability to a region that is still beset by historical feuds and ancient enmities. We all have to realise that the troubles that afflict the region today came as a direct consequence of foreign imperialism and adventurism in south China. Our role in this limited action, and in possible future actions, is to return Asia to the influence of the Asian peoples, and not to the colonial in-

fluences of the whites. Our cause is therefore just, and noble, and we ask the entire world to support us in our endeavour.

A seemingly endless procession of fully laden Japanese Lockheed C-130H troop transport planes, with fighter escorts, took off during the early morning of Tuesday, 23 November from the former US Air Force Base at Kadena and from other tactical bases in western Kyushu and northern Honshu. Most of the planes were making for airfields in Manchuria—to Harbin, where the explosion had taken place, to Changchun and Shenyang; but other aircraft were later discovered to have landed at Jinan, Xian, Shanghai and Chengdu, where there were Japanese-owned car factories, computer-chip assembly plants, steel mills and coal processing plants.

By late afternoon, China time—early Tuesday morning in Washington—all of Japan's troops were in place. There had been no resistance from the Chinese: no anti-aircraft fire, no interference on the ground. The aircraft had landed at the destination airfields, the troops had deployed to their target installations and set themselves up inside the buildings or in tented encampments, and had begun immediate high-visibility patrolling to ensure, as a press statement had it, "that there are no further incidents that might affect the smooth running of our commercial operations in China."

A grim-faced President Benson addressed the American nation later that afternoon.

What he said was short, and to the point. He said that for the past nine months there had been growing indications that Japan wished to become involved in the steadily deteriorating situation in China, so as to be able to "exploit" the country's disarray "for Japan's own territorial ambitions." The rest of the world, which had once before this century experienced the effects of such action on the part of Japan, could not and would not tolerate such a step. Diplomatic pressure was applied to dissuade Japan from doing so, but to no avail. All approaches had been ignored or rebuffed.

"Last Sunday night," the President continued, "there was an incident in Harbin, a remote town in the cold waste of northern Manchuria, in which a Japanese factory was damaged, and an employee of the plant, a Japanese national, was killed. It is not known whose hand was behind this fatal explosion. But one should learn from history. One should remember the infamous incident in 1931 that prompted Japan to send troops to Manchuria in almost precisely similar circumstances to these: it has always been assumed that agents working for Japan staged that earlier incident to provide Japan with an excuse to deploy her army. It is not too far-fetched to suppose that this incident too may have been staged, so as to offer Tokyo an excuse to send in her soldiers.

"Whatever the precise origins of this deployment, only history will be able to judge. But as the United States and its allies have made repeatedly clear, this deployment, this interference in the affairs of the world's most populous nation, will not be permitted. The United States is resolved to use all and any means at its disposal to ensure that Japan's troops are removed from the People's Republic of China.

"Accordingly I hereby announce that the United States has set a deadline of 5 P.M. Eastern Standard Time on Thursday—just over two days from now—by which we must have firm evidence that the troops are withdrawing to their home bases. Failing satisfactory and unambiguous evidence that such return movement is taking place, the United States will take extreme measures to ensure compliance. There will be no further warning, no further announcement.

"It is as simple as I have stated. All of Japan's troops must be on their way out of China by 5 P.M. on Thursday, 25 November—Thanksgiving Day. The time is equivalent to 6 A.M. on Friday in China, and 7 A.M. on Friday in Tokyo. If the troops are not out, or on their way out, then I have to say, as calmly and as firmly as I am able, that there will be no holds barred in the actions of this nation to enforce the wishes of the rational world.

"At this exceptionally difficult time I ask for your prayers, that all may be accomplished in peace and with wisdom and good will. God bless the United States of America."

CHAPTER ELEVEN

Nightmare

Wednesday, 24 November 1999

2159 ZULU

The three aircraft reached the assembly point precisely on schedule, at one minute before seven in the morning, local time. The flight commanders verified their status with the Global Positioning System computers, and immediately slowed, as ordered, to cruising speed. There was, to the relief of all six crewmen, no indication that their arrival had been noticed. Despite the excellence of Japan's air defences—all on full alert since President Benson's television address—the B-2s were all but invisible to any of the detection technology that was available to the Japanese pilots and ground radar sites.

The skies were to all intents and purposes empty. Radio traffic indicated just a couple of early-morning freighters inbound from Europe, and a single passenger plane taking off from Haneda, heading for Osaka. Otherwise, nothing.

To the west—to the left of the aircraft—it was still quite dark. Ahead and to the right, barely visible on the horizon in the early dawn glimmer, was Cape Nojima, the southern tip of the Boso-hanto peninsula. Directly ahead, and only visible on the radar, was the small island of Miyake, with its 2,400-foot volcano, Mt. Oyama. Beyond that were the cliffs of Cape Iro, and the Izu Peninsula.

In daylight it would have been a breathtaking sight. Irozaki and Nojima-zaki were the twin gateways to Tokyo Bay, and between their gaunt cliffs, each day and night, scores of mighty ships would be sailing, bringing in the raw materials, taking out cars and televisions and lawnmowers and steel bars. Even now Bill Pringle could look down six miles from his lead aircraft and see the tiny firefly sparkles of a couple of ships heading southwards, out into the Pacific Ocean. Another tiny streak of light near Nojima-zaki indicated early morning traffic on the coast freeway, Route 16: the cars and trucks were heading north towards the junction with the new Kanto Skybridge—the world's longest, it was said—where they would cross the entire sweep of Tokyo Bay to the factories at Kawasaki and Yokohama.

But the pilots had little time to consider the view, nor the implications of what might lie ahead. The only question was whether the orders—any orders—would be transmitted. Operation Typhoon Warning indicated with absolute precision that an Execute Order would be transmitted at 2200 Zulu. If it was not transmitted within sixty seconds of that time, the planes would all return to Refuelling Position "R," and then return to Hawaii and home.

The clocks snapped up to 2200 and instantly the screen of the satellite data link terminal lit up. A message was indeed being transmitted. The President in Washington had decided to give the Execute Order. The planes were now going to attack. The pilots felt the sudden rush of adrenaline, and then, equally suddenly, the awful calm that years of relentless training can bring—a calm that has the effect of turning each man into an emotionless, dedicated, intelligent machine for the critical moments of the bombing mission.

The message was brief. It ordered a single aircraft, designated Chase Bravo, to descend immediately to 5,000 feet and to fly directly at full speed towards the target position at 35° 23′N, 139° 47′E and to release on target a single B-61 nuclear weapon.

Technicians in Hawaii had already preset the bomb to burst at sea level—in part to reduce very slightly the effects on surrounding population centres and structures, but principally to maximise the demonstratory nature of a medium-range atomic blast. The Operation was not called Typhoon Warning for nothing: the purpose of this most dreadful of detonations was to warn, not to destroy—although a weapon of this size and type would bring an immense amount of destruction in its wake, no matter what cosmetic precautions might be taken.

Major Pringle wiggled his plane's massive single wing as a message to his colleagues—who turned away into a holding position—and then began his dive towards Sagami Bay, to the west of the main Tokyo Bay. As the altimeter started to spiral downwards he punched the target coordinates into the weapons delivery computer, and added figures relating to the windspeed, atmospheric pressure and other crucial data about the target.

He reached his designated flight level at six minutes after seven, local time, and swept northwards towards his target. The computer beeped softly. To ensure that he was nowhere near the blast effect when the weapon exploded he would execute a "toss-and-loft" manoeuvre some five miles short of the target: he would begin a steep climb, release a single bomb as he was doing so and then, as soon as it was indicated to him that he was clear of the weapon, he would extend his turn into a backward loop and clear the area as rapidly as possible.

At eleven minutes after seven, having levelled out and completed his targeting procedures, he had a few seconds to notice where he was, and where his bomb would land. The Global Positioning System computer was now linked into his automatic pilot, and it was steering him relentlessly towards his goal. He glanced at his map: the target was at the mouth of Tokyo Bay itself, at about its widest point, midway between Yokohama on the west and the reclaimed land by Kisarazu airfield in Chiba prefecture on the east.

He began to climb rapidly as he passed beside Yokosuka, the former headquarters of the US Naval Forces, Japan. A few seconds later, having checked the datalink for any indication of a countermand order, Major Pringle assumed his place in history by lifting the plexiglass flap and punching the bright red Execute button.

The weapons-delivery computer then took control of the system, and at precisely 7:15 A.M. the Major heard the distinct clicks of the bomb-bay latches snap open, and a few seconds later felt the small but perceptible relief from the plane's four engines as a third of a ton of steel and high explosive and uranium and electronic weaponry tumbled from the belly of his aircraft, first up, then along and then finally free-falling down towards the designated Ground Zero in the centre of the Bay.

The confirmation that the weapon had been released came within a further second. Major Pringle immediately gunned his engines, climbed vertically for two miles—little caring if at this point the Japanese fighters spotted his heat trails and found reflections from his turbine blades, though the infra-red suppressors and RAM baffles fitted to the engines should confuse them for several more minutes, at least.

Once at 20,000 feet he set in motion a long, fast overhead loop and roll, and then climbed steadily back up to the rendezvous point. He was just in sight of his two colleagues when he felt the distant detonation of the bomb.

All three planes had switched on their light-sensitive cockpit shield protectors, which had the effect of enclosing the aircraft in enormous non-reflective polarising sunglasses. Even so, the flash of pure white light was impressive—a searing, scorching dazzle that was followed seconds later by an upward-roaring fireball and a cigar-shaped plume of water and steam and—if the dark adornments to its sides could be said to have solidity—the vaporised carcasses of half a dozen cargo ships that had been caught in the blast.

The electromagnetic pulse, the high energy radio waves that can wreak such havoc on electronics, hit briefly. It caused, as planned, just a momentary flicker in the instruments—a flicker that was easily compensated for by the lightweight surge suppressors and the Faraday-caged backup computer. And then, as expected, came the blast—manifesting itself as a huge and sudden shove in the back, a lurch that hurled the planes forward briefly, and set them rocking in the sky—alarmingly, but not dangerously.

The training had covered all of this, and none of the pilots expressed any concern. The small squadron flew on, resuming its flight level of 45,000 feet, until the giant tankers from Hickam came into view. They broke radio silence at this point, connected their drogues, refilled their tanks with aviation spirit and continued down normally towards Hawaii.

In Tokyo, however, nothing continued, and nothing was normal any more. The relatively small bomb which Major Pringle had dropped had been specifically designed to inflict some damage to the industrial structures that lined Tokyo Bay, and to knock out some of the high-prestige constructions that had been built in the Bay during the con-

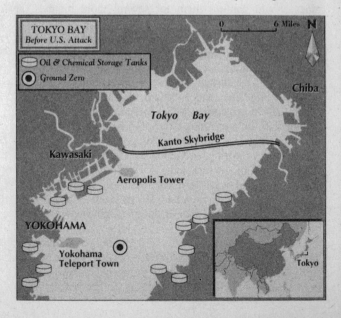

TOKYO BAY
Before U.S. Attack

⬭ Oil & Chemical Storage Tanks
◉ Ground Zero

0   6 Miles N

Chiba

Tokyo   Bay

Kanto Skybridge

Kawasaki

Aeropolis Tower

YOKOHAMA

Yokohama
Teleport Town ◉

Tokyo

struction frenzy of the early Nineties. But the people of Tokyo itself, which was some 18 miles from Ground Zero, were, as had also been planned, essentially safe from a 50-kiloton explosion—and though the shock wave blew out some few thousand windows and blinded a few score of people unlucky enough to have been looking out of their windows towards the Bay entrance, there were few enough casualties, and no disruption of the government and rescue services.

The real damage was done to ships in the Bay, to the Chiba-Kawasaki Sky Bridge (one third of a mile of which vanished into the sea), and to the two ultra-high-prestige constructions that had been started in early 1998— Yokohama Teleport Town, a 50,000-unit apartment complex that was being built on an artificial island near Sarushima, and the 500-storey Aeropolis Tower, a mile and a quarter high, which had been started on a tiny island seven miles from Ground Zero.

The tower, which had been designed by the Ohbayashi Corporation and was expected to be the most spectacular and "intelligent" building on the planet—the Emperor had laid the foundation stone in 1997—had already reached 180 storeys when Major Pringle dropped the bomb. When the fire and smoke had cleared the stunned residents of Yokohama could see the Aeropolis, which had become a familiar landmark, had been almost completely demolished.

Much damage was done to a number of vital electronic components factories in Kawasaki. In addition there was severe destruction around the so-called "poison necklace" of inflammable and noxious chemical storage depots near the various city docks, and which, when on fire and mixed into one another, form a cocktail of the most lethal pollution. The fires that raged in plants belonging to Sumitomo Chemicals, Nippon Oil, Tokyo Gas, Mitsui Petrochemicals and Mobil Oil raged for days. A southerly winter wind brought the clouds over the city, and blanketed Tokyo with a fine rain of filthy black chemicals that lingered for weeks. Radiation from the bomb was, however, light: the Department of Defense had called for a "clean" weapon, and it was not their concern that the subsequent fires caused the air over Tokyo to be chokingly filthy for weeks to come.

The final casualty figures were relatively light: 810 dead, 12,604 suffering from a variety of injuries—though very few of the injuries were flash burns, as had been experienced in Hiroshima and Nagasaki fifty years before. The city hospitals found themselves generally well able to cope with the emergency. Aside from the Sky Bridge, all of the city's major infrastructural links had remained intact; and although the population was stunned and demoralised by what had happened, all of the affected areas—even Yokohama and Kawasaki, which were the closest to the explosion—were functioning more or less normally within two weeks.

The psychological effect was incalculable, however, and profound. The Civil Defence authorities quickly established that the destruction caused by the bomb was manageable, but warned that the Americans could well send in their planes once again and engage in far more devastating attacks. The politicians and senior members of the military assimilated this message with equal rapidity, and by mid-morning a message of conciliation was ordered sent by diplomatic cable to the American government. President Benson made mention of the receipt of such a message when he broadcast to the American people at 9 P.M. Washington time, informing them of Operation Typhoon Warning, and of the fact that an atomic weapon had been dropped, once again, on Japan.

Emperor Akihito then broadcast to his nation on radio and television an hour later, at 11 A.M., Tokyo Time. Wearing a dark suit and a black tie, and with his Empress sitting by his side, he spoke firmly and softly for ten minutes about the tragedy that now afflicted both Japan and China, and which, he admitted "might to some degree have been of our own making."

He continued: "It may be that the decision to send members of our Land Self-Defence Forces into Chinese territory has not worked wholly to our nation's advantage. Accordingly I am announcing the agreement of my government to comply with the request made three days ago by President Benson. I have instructed force commanders in this matter, moves are already under way, and I am assured that the request will have been fully complied with by midnight tonight, Japan Standard Time . . ."

News of the beginning of the Japanese withdrawal from China was broadcast to the American people shortly before midnight on Thursday. President Benson made the formal announcement, and was not slow to point out that he was able to do so, just, on what on the East coast was at the very close of Thanksgiving Day. It was not the end of the day in the rest of America, he went on: perhaps some appropriate gratitude might be expressed.

Reports from police traffic departments across the United States soon confirmed that many in the nation took their President's advice. Soon after the broadcast scores of roads were clogged with a rush of late-night churchgoers, all of them apparently wishing to offer their thanks in person for the satisfactory ending of this chapter in the crisis—and, the pastors later said, to pray for all of the victims, so far away, whose leaders had so very nearly brought their conflict to engulf the entire world.

The commonly held view all across the United States that night was that since the spectre of so terrible a war had, at the very last moment, been averted, so it seemed right and proper to consider the implications in the quiet and private world of Church, at the close of the very last Thanksgiving of the American century.

EPILOGUE

The world was stunned by the enormity of events, horrified at the seemingly uncontrollable speed of developments in the Far East and, almost universally, appalled by what President Benson had ordered done. That the United States had decided, in secrecy and without any apparent prior consultation, to unleash an atomic bomb against a country with whom it was not itself at war and which had made no threatening gesture towards the United States or any of its possessions or interests, was condemned on all sides. The UN Security Council was called into emergency session, and a resolution of the General Assembly excoriating the United States for its unilateral use of nuclear weaponry was passed by an overwhelming vote.

Four days later, with what seemed a somewhat weary and condescending calm, the United States commenced a campaign to explain the rationale behind its action. Robert Upshaw, the Under-Secretary for the US Air Force, held a news conference at the Pentagon on Monday afternoon, an event timed to coincide with the main BBC World Service television news for Europe, the Americas and West Asia. He announced, to widespread astonishment, that he was staging the conference in his capacity as Director of the National Reconnaissance Office, and that he would produce evidence to indicate just how close the world had come to total catastrophe.

The National Reconnaissance Office was an organisation

whose very existence had only rarely been confirmed. The first indication that there was such an intelligence-gathering bureau buried deep inside the Pentagon came, mistakenly, in a 1973 Congressional budget report. For years following that error—and even during the early post–Cold War period, when the need for obsessive secrecy seemed to have declined in proportion to the strength of the perceived threat from Moscow—the NRO remained a "black" programme, rarely discussed, never publicly acknowledged, its funding and staff kept wholly classified.

Its basic function, however, was known to be the management of satellite reconnaissance and intelligence-gathering programmes. Mr Upshaw's news conference was called to give details of what were code-named "Ruff" images—ultra high definition three-dimensional photographs—that had been transmitted during the previous week from the NRO's new synthetic aperture radar-imaging satellite, a four-ton high-performance monster that had been launched from the Cape York Satellite Centre the previous July under the number Keyhole-16, and to which the Pentagon had given the Byeman designation Lacrosse V. The Lacrosse satellites were in low Earth orbits—about 300 miles up—and took photographs of any one portion of the planet at 90-minute intervals. Lacrosse V had been specifically tasked to cover northern China.

The Lacrosse Ruff images, which Upshaw showed on a series of wall-to-ceiling screens, were in full colour and were of incredible clarity—far more impressive than even the best of the high-definition televisions that had been in use in the US for the past two years. They depicted an area of northern China to the northeast of the Manchurian city of Harbin and were shown in rapid sequence, the series beginning on Monday morning, 22 November. The pictures, despite being taken in five-minute bursts by a variety of cameras and lenses trained down during each of the passes at 90-minute intervals, were shown in such a way as to take on the appearance of a moving film. They were also accompanied by a commentary—a translation of the so-called "Zarf" signals intelligence intercepts from a geostationary satellite code-named Magnum 9, which had been ordered to listen to (and if possible to decode) all signals emanating from the Chinese military forces in the areas under surveillance.

The satellite operators working on Lacrosse V could use wide-angle shots, or close-ups. In the latter the imaging systems could show parked vehicles and their number plates, Chinese Army personnel and their shoulder-badges, the rescuers working in the damaged Sumitomo Metals building in Harbin City, the expressions on the faces of the bystanders—whether Harbin was in darkness, or bathed in the light of the late autumn sun. The technological triumph of the system was evident (something of which the Hughes Aircraft Company, the Lacrosse V's manufacturers, were later to make much). But it was the wide-angle pictures that were much more dramatic, in terms of illustrating just how close the world had come to the brink: it was on those—some fifty separate images—that Secretary Upshaw spent most of the news conference.

Twelve Japanese transport aircraft were shown landing on the Tuesday morning at an airfield five miles north of Harbin. Men and vehicles—mostly Japanese, though with some commandeered PLA troop-carriers in the convoys—were then to be seen securing the Sumitomo plant, established in a tented encampment beside the frozen Sungari River, constructing defences. Orders from the operational headquarters in Hakata were decoded and translated: the Japanese, it seemed, were bent on remaining in Harbin for an indefinite period, and reinforcements were due within the week.

The Lacrosse cameras were then switched to a Chinese air base at Suihua, fifty miles further north. It was here, Secretary Upshaw insisted, that direct and critical evidence first emerged of what would have happened next.

The pictures showed bleak hillsides, their northern flanks covered with snow. At the centre of the screen was the Suihua base, close to a small town of the same name. There was evidently extreme security around the base: a sanitised area two miles wide completely surrounded the airfield and the pod-shaped structures that were ranged beside the runway. Triple fences ringed both the cordon and the base itself; there were watchtowers and, visible even from 300 miles, scores of guard dogs.

The Suihua base was home to the 453rd Strategic Rocket Unit of China's Second Artillery, Upshaw explained. The twelve pods beside the main runway each housed a single

CSS-7 medium-range ballistic missile, each with a cone-shaped warhead, a copy of a Russian design of the late 1980s, that held ten individual targeted nuclear-fission bombs. Each one of these weapons had a yield of 500 kilotons-equivalent: they were in short powerful, dirty and extremely dangerous nuclear missiles.

When the Suihua base was first opened in the mid-1970s the weapons were kept in first-rate condition and the teams who were trained to fire them were kept under constant training. The weapons themselves were programmed to be fired either at targets in Alaska or Siberia, since both the United States and the then USSR were regarded in Peking as presenting apparent dangers to China. But with the lessening of global tension two decades later the base—like most of the Second Artillery's bases and weapons—had become of rather less potential use. There had been reported talk in Peking of standing the missile crews down and of removing the active warheads. But the turmoil within China halted that debate, and at the time when the NRO's Lacrosse V satellite was ordered to take an active interest in the Suihua base, all the missiles' firing stations were secured and manned ready for immediate action.

While the camera steadied on a series of pictures of the base, journalists in the Pentagon briefing room—and, via the BBC and CNN cameras, scores of hundreds of millions of viewers around the world—listened to the decoded transcripts of the signals proceeding to and from, and conversations proceeding within the headquarters buildings at the centre of the screen.

This signal traffic began with routine reports of the arrival of the Japanese troops in Harbin, and of their deployment. (Alert messages concerning the Japanese intrusion on Chinese airspace had already come in from the Chinese Air Force's defensive tracking station in Taiyuan in Shanxi Province; the more useful station, considering the direction of the planes' approach, would have been that at Changle in Fujian Province but this had fallen into Republican hands some months before, and its reports were presumably being given only to the Republican force commanders down in

Wuhan, Canton and Hong Kong. This, the Pentagon said, was the essential reason for the lack of Communist Chinese air defence activity during the Japanese incursion.)

Later in the morning and in the early afternoon signals were sent from the base to the Commander, Heilongjiang Military District, in Harbin, to the Commander, Shenyang Military Region, and to the Commander, Second Artillery, asking—with some asperity—what response, if any, should come from the missiles of the 453rd. But there was no reply for the following seven hours.

Just before midnight another flurry of messages was intercepted, going up the line from the Suihua commander. One reply came on this occasion, from the Shenyang commander, who insisted on his belief that the Japanese would probably leave Harbin within a matter of days, and that there was probably no need for "any kind" of military response from China. However, at about this time it became evident that Suihua was also given the stark news that the Japanese had not just landed their troops near by, in Harbin, but that their men were also now present in strength at Jinan, Xian, Chengdu and, most ominously of all, outside Shanghai itself. All China, it seemed, was under threat.

It was at this point—identified both on the Lacrosse images and through the transcripts collected by the Magnum 9—that the Suihua base commander (who was since identified as a Brigadier Deng, a veteran of the Vietnam border war) decided he had had enough of the battle-weary indecision which, he must have judged, was now infecting his senior colleagues in Peking and Shenyang. The Magnum intercepts report the Brigadier taking over the camp's public address system and announcing to all his personnel on the base that, in view of what he called the "brutal invasion of our nation by the vile armies of Japan," the 453rd Strategic Rocket Unit would now take "an appropriate and unilateral response."

All twelve of the missiles under his command would now be targeted on military, industrial and communications centres in Japan, he said. The re-assigning of targets would take the base technicians three days to complete. "If there is no clear undertaking from Japan that they will remove their troops and aircraft from our soil by midday, Friday," Brigadier Deng continued, "then the Suihua base will launch a full nuclear strike against Japan, one that will have the most dreadful consequences."

The next sequence of satellite pictures, all taken during the night, showed dozens of special vehicles moving out to the various pods, the lids of these pods being opened, the orange warheads of the weapons poking up through the snow, scores of men swarming over the weapons, or beginning complex fuel-replacement and countdown operations in the bunkers dotted along the northern edge of the airstrip.

One of the Lacrosse pictures that Upshaw displayed was taken with a zoom lens: it showed one of the open nosecones and, poking through, ten bulbous objects arrayed in splayed cluster, as though in some monstrous piece of botany. Each of the bulbs, four feet long and two wide, contained enough nuclear material to destroy the centre of Tokyo, or turn every wooden temple within a ten-mile radius of Kyoto into a pile of ashes.

Secretary Upshaw turned off the screens, and ordered the transcript tape halted. The lights came up in the briefing room. The audience was quite silent.

"The last series of intercepts came in to the NRO action room at 3 P.M. last Tuesday afternoon, our time. There was no doubt in our minds that Base Commander Deng had both the intention and the ability to release his weapons at targets in Japan, and that he would do so without compunction or concern for the consequences. The implications for the Japanese people would have been incalculable, of course. The implications to the world economy of the destruction or decimation of Japan's manufacturing ability would have been equally profound. It was thus imperative that we acted to halt the Japanese before a freelance Chinese commander such as Brigadier Deng or other like-minded commanders with whom we know he was planning to make contact acted unilaterally to do the same thing—but with much more frightening consequences.

"The United States naturally regrets having to take the action it did, in dropping a single nuclear gravity weapon over Tokyo Bay. It naturally regrets the loss of life and the destruction of property. But I trust, however, that you will find credible the evidence that we have presented here today—evidence that indicates beyond any reasonable doubt that, had we not taken the action that we did, Japan would be in far worse shape than she is today, and the entire world economy would have been put at risk. It is true that our relations with Japan are currently very poor, and our strike this week will inevitably have made them much poorer. It is not for a military man to become engaged in diplomatic matters. It is my hope, however, that the government of Japan, too, will one day come to realise that the attack by the United States, while achieving its short-term objective, succeeded also in averting a situation that was immeasurably more terrible than that which befell the people of Tokyo and Yokohama."

Diplomatic relations between the United States and Japan were restored early in 2000—an indication that the Ministry of Foreign Affairs in Tokyo, probably under pressure from the Imperial Palace, was persuaded to see the sense in the argument that was initially advanced so bluntly by Air Force Secretary Upshaw. There was, in addition, a good deal of American domestic sympathy for the Japanese victims of the Yokohama bomb—sympathy which went some long way to reverse the tide of anti-Japanism that had marked President Benson's first term. At the time of writing the US President was expected to visit Tokyo, to inspect repairs and to see if the United States could offer any assistance.

There was talk also of a joint US-Japanese-Russian mission to calm the civil war that was continuing to disrupt life inside China herself. But virtually all the countries on China's immense periphery had taken the attack on Tokyo as a warning that they, too, should keep aloof from their neighbour's internal problems. The cross-border skirmishing and terrorism in the far north and west was thus soon largely stilled, and the incidence of banditry grew steadily less disruptive.

Elsewhere in the region a sense of cautious optimism began to return. In Korea—the newly united Korea—democratic elections were held in February 2000. The residents of what had been North Korea took to the idea of voting with alacrity—voter turnout in Pyongyang was far greater than in Seoul, for example—with the result that a left-leaning slate of candidates, the Social Democratic Union, was elected into office. The new Korean premier, Lee Chun-ok—in a remark that underscored the notion that the newly united nation would rapidly become a formidable economic and political power—immediately offered his good offices as well, to help bring about an end to the Chinese conflict. There was no immediate reply, however, from either Canton or Peking.

The Hong Kong provisional government, which had occupied itself repairing the city in the wake of the fighting, also announced elections—the first in which all citizens on the rolls would have the opportunity to vote for their local leadership. Foreign investment, which had drained away to nothing in the months leading up to June 1997, began to seep back into the city: the first notable infusion of foreign money was a two-billion-dollar reclamation scheme in western Lantau that was financed entirely by Korean banks and which was due to be constructed by a subsidiary of Daewoo corporation, based in the former North Korean port city of Nampo. Hong Kong, in summary, appeared to be recovering with characteristic swiftness from its two years of travails.

In November 1999 the world's great powers clashed suddenly, briefly, violently, horribly. It could all, however, have been so very much worse. Millions could have died, where only thousands fell. The dull background roar to which China's internal battling has now faded could have continued at full pace for decades yet to come, with still many more dead, and the attendant possibility of the rest of the world—neighbours, allies, friends, foes, or those with ill-defined "interests"—becoming embroiled again and again and again.

But a single bombing mission, performed in secret by three mysterious aircraft based in the icy hills of western Missouri, appears to have changed all that. Instant history, like that contained in this account, can only offer an instant judgement, with all the attendant imperfections. More sober and serious documents will soon be written, no doubt, and the benefit of perspective will permit others to analyse and debate and draw more considered conclusions on the tide of events. And there will be no shortage of material: for there can be little doubt that the implications of Operation Typhoon Warning, like the sound of the explosion itself, will reverberate for decades around the nations of the world, and will echo down the years for as long as history continues to be written.

INDEX